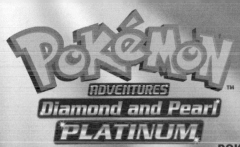

POKÉMON ADVENTURES: DIAMOND AND PEARL/PLATINUM

Volume 6
VIZ Media Edition

Story by **HIDENORI KUSAKA**
Art by **SATOSHI YAMAMOTO**

© 2012 Pokémon.
© 1995–2010 Nintendo / Creatures Inc. / GAME FREAK inc.
TM, ®, and character names are trademarks of Nintendo.
POCKET MONSTERS SPECIAL Vol. 6 (35)
by Hidenori KUSAKA, Satoshi YAMAMOTO
© 1997 Hidenori KUSAKA, Satoshi YAMAMOTO
All rights reserved.
Original Japanese edition published by SHOGAKUKAN.
English translation rights in the United States of America, Canada, the United Kingdom,
Ireland, Australia, New Zealand and India arranged with SHOGAKUKAN.

Translation/Katherine Schilling
English Adaptation/Bryant Turnage
Touch-up & Lettering/Annaliese Christman
Design/Yukiko Whitley
Editor/Annette Roman

Published by VIZ Media, LLC
P.O. Box 77010
San Francisco, CA 94107

10 9 8 7 6
First printing, October 2012
Sixth printing, June 2020

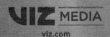

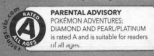

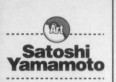
Art
Satoshi Yamamoto

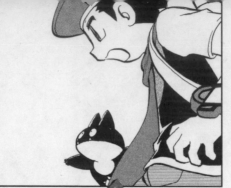

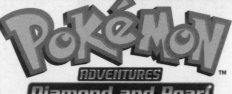

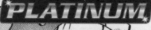

POKÉMON
ADVENTURES
Diamond and Pearl
PLATINUM

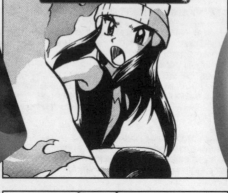

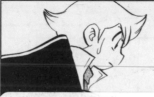

Story
Hidenori Kusaka

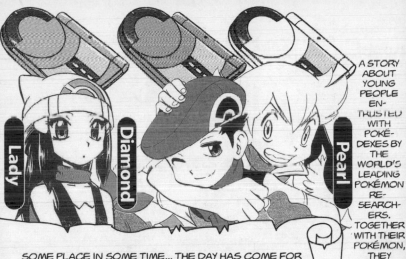

Lady

Diamond

Pearl

Our Story So Far...

A STORY ABOUT YOUNG PEOPLE EN-TRUSTED WITH POKÉ-DEXES BY THE WORLD'S LEADING POKÉMON RE-SEARCH-ERS. TOGETHER WITH THEIR POKÉMON, THEY TRAVEL, BATTLE, AND EVOLVE!

SOME PLACE IN SOME TIME... THE DAY HAS COME FOR A YOUNG LADY, THE ONLY DAUGHTER OF THE BERLITZ FAMILY, THE WEALTHIEST IN THE SINNOH REGION, TO EMBARK ON A JOURNEY. IN ORDER TO MAKE A SPECIAL EMBLEM BEARING HER FAMILY CREST, SHE MUST PERSONALLY FIND AND GATHER THE MATERIALS AT THE PEAK OF MT. CORONET. SHE SETS OUT ON HER JOURNEY WITH THE INTENTION OF MEETING UP WITH TWO BODYGUARDS ASSIGNED TO ESCORT HER.

MEANWHILE, POKÉMON TRAINERS PEARL AND DIAMOND, WHO DREAM OF BECOMING STAND-UP COMEDIANS, ENTER A COMEDY CONTEST IN JUBILIFE AND WIN THE SPECIAL MERIT AWARD. BUT THEIR PRIZE OF AN ALL-EXPENSES PAID TRIP GETS SWITCHED WITH THE CONTRACT FOR LADY'S BODYGUARDS!

THUS PEARL AND DIAMOND THINK LADY IS THEIR TOUR GUIDE, AND LADY THINKS THEY ARE HER BODYGUARDS! DESPITE THE CASES OF MISTAKEN IDENTITY, THE TRIO TRAVEL TOGETHER QUITE HAPPILY THROUGH THE VAST COUNTRYSIDE.

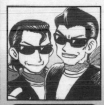

Paka & Uji

THE REAL BODYGUARDS HIRED TO ESCORT LADY.

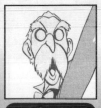

Sebastian

THE BERLITZ FAMILY BUTLER, WHO IS ALWAYS WORRYING ABOUT LADY.

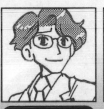

Mr. Berlitz

LADY'S FATHER, WHO ASSISTS PROFESSOR ROWAN.

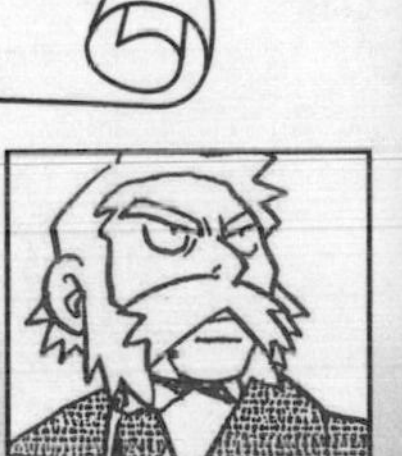

Professor Rowan

A LEADING RESEARCHER OF POKÉMON EVOLUTION. HE CAN BE QUITE INTIMIDATING!

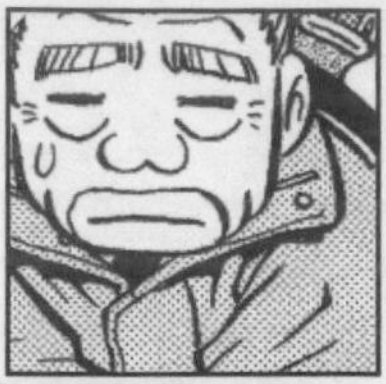

Mr. Fuego

OWNER OF THE FUEGO IRONWORKS. TRICKED BY TEAM GALACTIC INTO FORGING PARTS FOR THEIR GALACTIC BOMB.

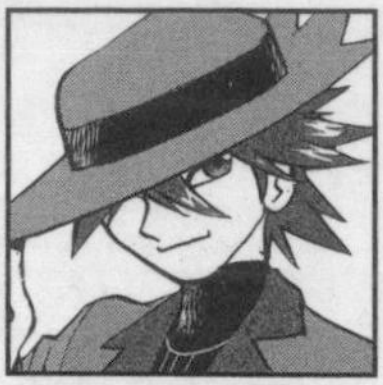

Riley

A POWERFUL TRAINER BASED ON IRON ISLAND WHO TRAINED DIA.

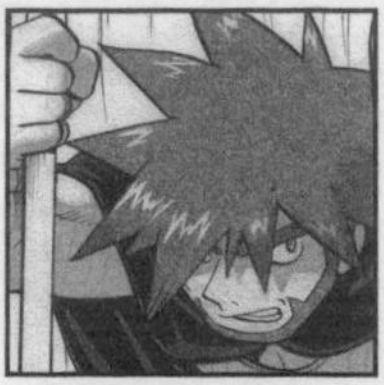

Byron

CANALAVE CITY'S GYM LEADER AND FATHER OF OREBURGH CITY'S GYM LEADER, ROARK.

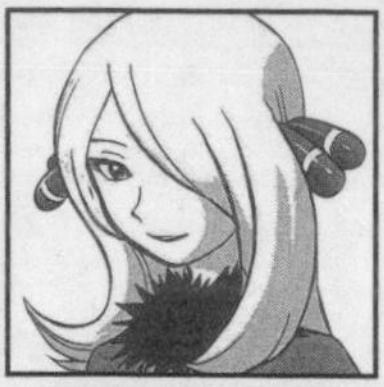

Cynthia

A MYSTERIOUS WOMAN WHO SEEMS TO BE INVESTIGATING A MYSTERY.

THE TWO BODYGUARDS ENTRUSTED WITH ESCORTING LADY ARE AWARE OF THE MIX-UP AND SET OUT TO CATCH UP WITH DIA, PEARL, AND LADY. BUT THEN THEY GET MIXED UP WITH MYSTERIOUS TEAM GALACTIC, WHO ARE BUSY CREATING TROUBLE IN THE SINNOH REGION. THEIR DEVIOUS PLAN IS TO CREATE A GALACTIC BOMB. WHAT WILL THIS STRANGE DEVICE DO?

THEN, TO RAISE MONEY FOR THEIR NEFARIOUS PROJECT, TEAM GALACTIC EXTORTS MONEY FROM LADY'S WEALTHY FATHER, MR. BERLITZ. WHILE RESCUING LADY'S FATHER, DIA AND PEARL FINALLY REVEAL THAT THEY ARE NOT LADY'S REAL BODYGUARDS, AND THOUGH IT SHAKES HER UP FOR A MOMENT, LADY (WHOSE REAL NAME "PLATINUM" HAS NOW BEEN REVEALED) RESOLVES TO STICK BY HER FRIENDS AND TRUST THEM AGAIN. BUT THEN THE TRIO SEPARATE AND EACH SETS OUT ALONE FOR ONE OF THE THREE SINNOH LAKES WHERE THREE POKÉMON OF LEGEND—UXIE, MESPRIT, AND AZELF—SLUMBER.

FOR THE FIRST TIME SINCE THEIR JOURNEY BEGAN, OUR HEROES ARE ALONE. WILL THEY BE ABLE TO PROTECT THESE LEGENDARY POKÉMON IN TIME?!

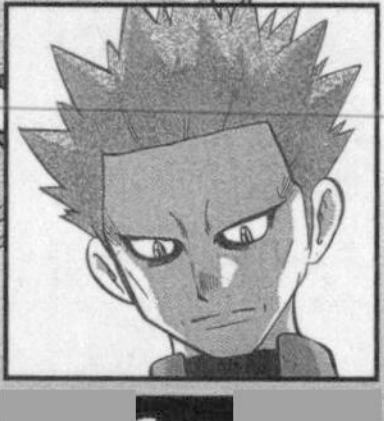

Cyrus

TEAM GALACTIC'S BOSS. AN OVERBEARING, INTENSE MAN.

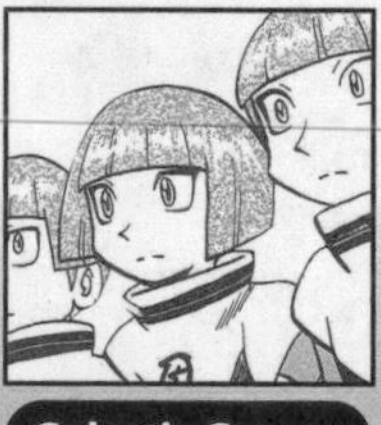

Galactic Grunts

THE TEAM GALACTIC TROOPS, WHO CARRY OUT THEIR LEADER'S BIDDING WITHOUT QUESTION. CREEPY!

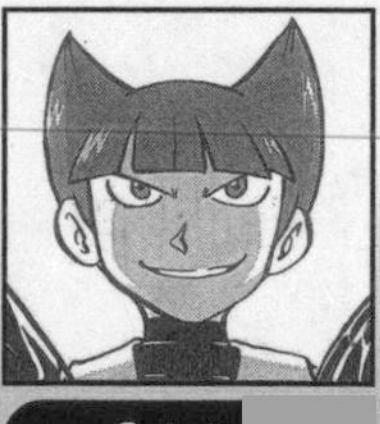

Saturn

HE IS IN CHARGE OF THE BOMB AND RARELY STEPS ONTO THE BATTLEFIELD HIMSELF.

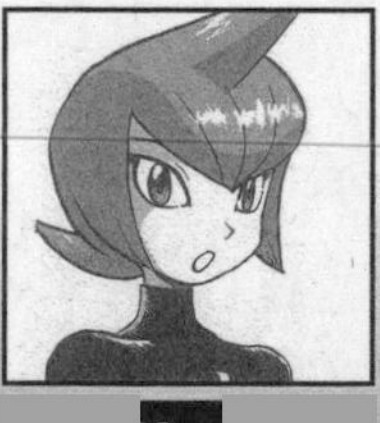

Mars

A TEAM GALACTIC LEADER. HER PERSONALITY IS HARD TO PIN DOWN.

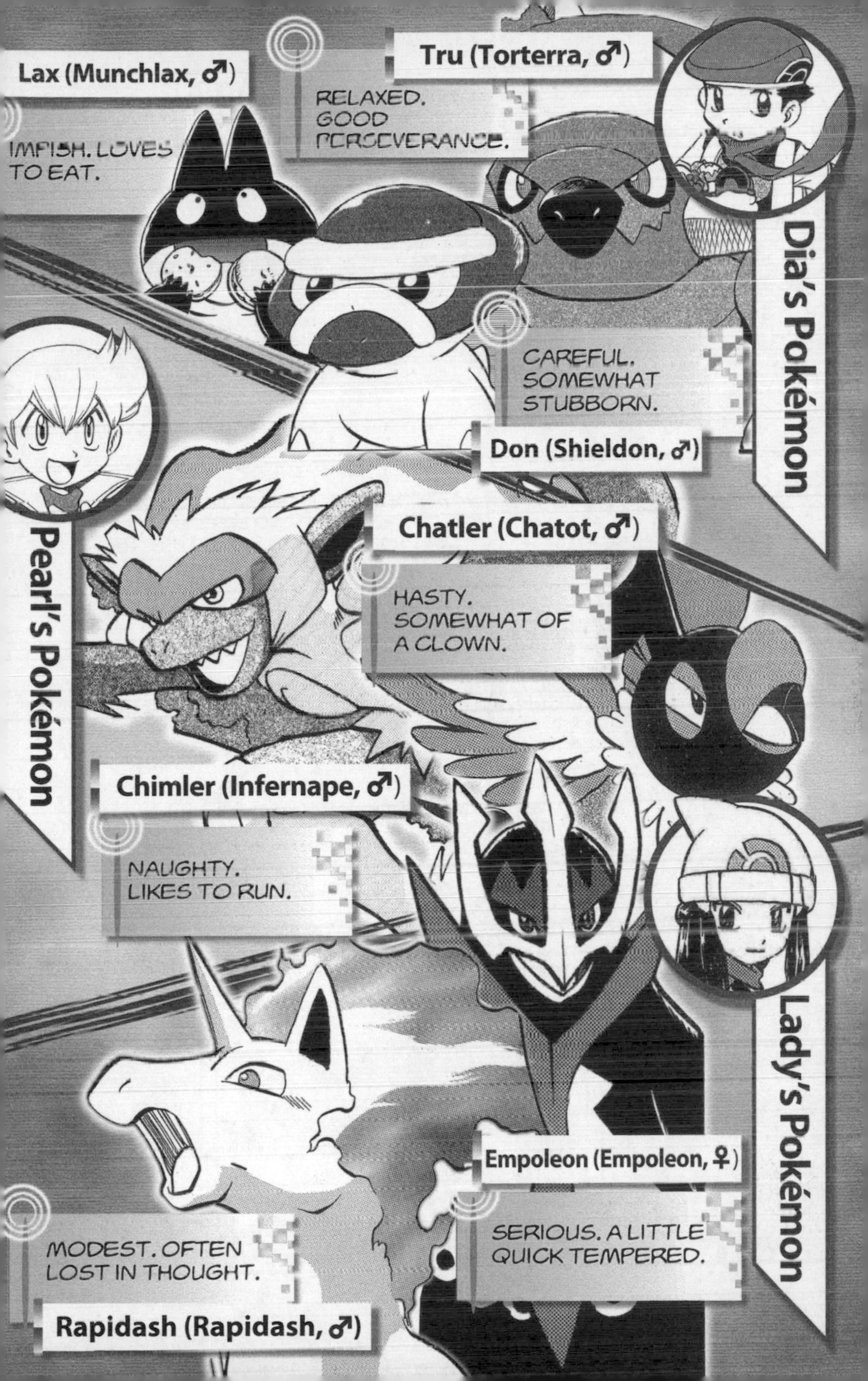
Dia's Pokémon
Tru (Torterra, ♂)
RELAXED. GOOD PERSEVERANCE.
Lax (Munchlax, ♂)
IMPISH. LOVES TO EAT.
Don (Shieldon, ♂)
CAREFUL. SOMEWHAT STUBBORN.
Pearl's Pokémon
Chatler (Chatot, ♂)
HASTY. SOMEWHAT OF A CLOWN.
Chimler (Infernape, ♂)
NAUGHTY. LIKES TO RUN.
Lady's Pokémon
Empoleon (Empoleon, ♀)
SERIOUS. A LITTLE QUICK TEMPERED.
Rapidash (Rapidash, ♂)
MODEST. OFTEN LOST IN THOUGHT.

POKÉMON

ADVENTURES
Diamond and Pearl
PLATINUM

6

CONTENTS

48

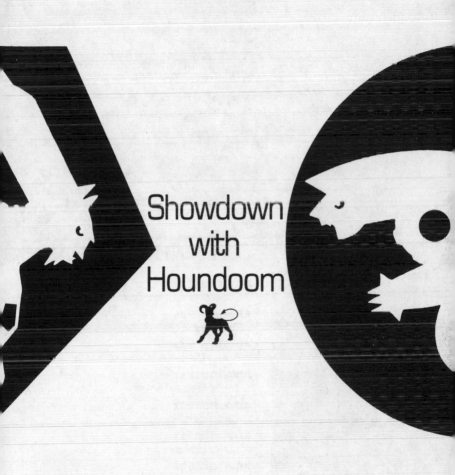

Showdown
with
Houndoom

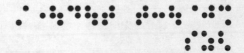

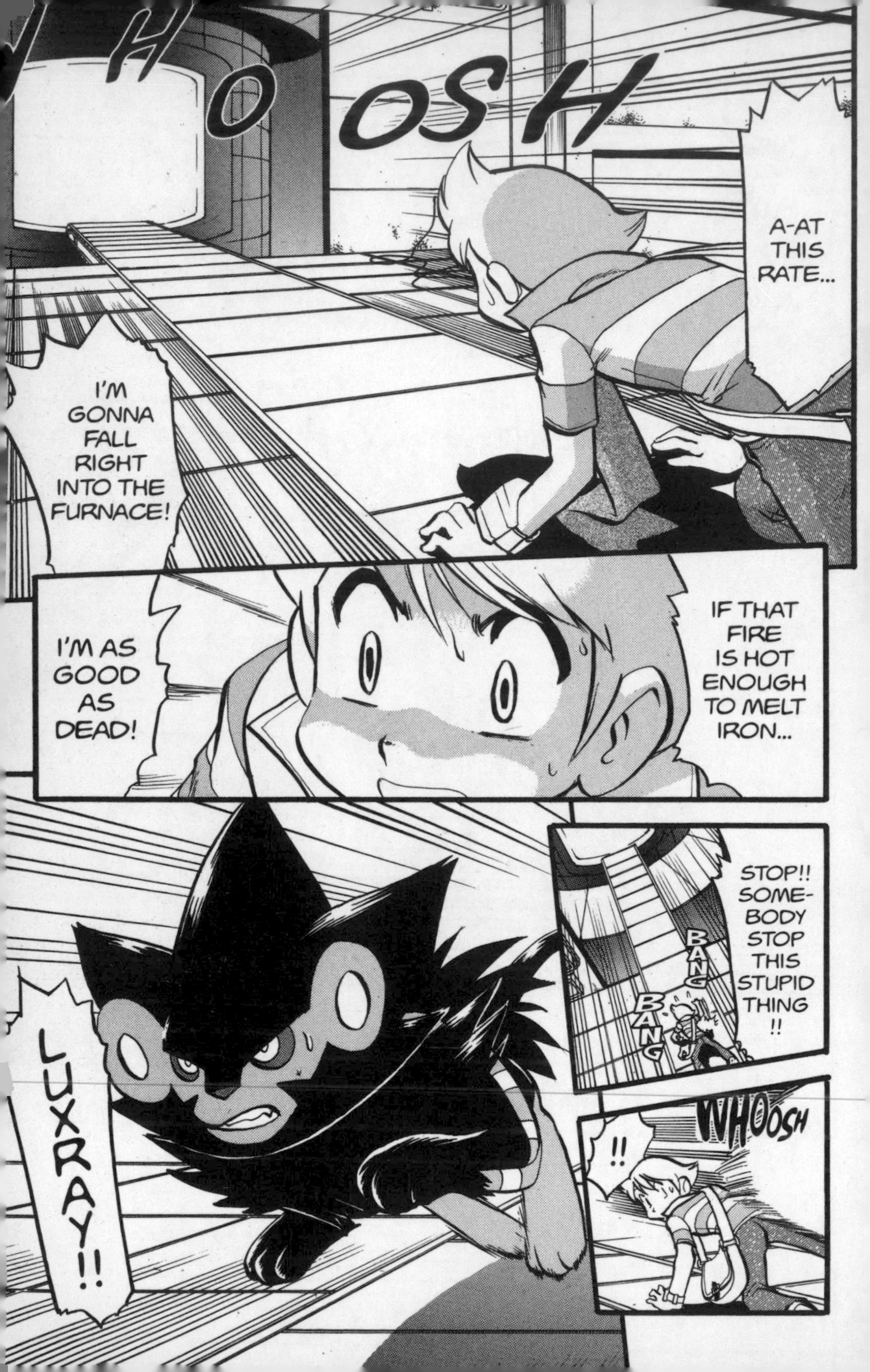
WHOOSH
A-AT THIS RATE...
I'M GONNA FALL RIGHT INTO THE FURNACE!
IF THAT FIRE IS HOT ENOUGH TO MELT IRON...
I'M AS GOOD AS DEAD!
STOP!! SOME-BODY STOP THIS STUPID THING!!
BANG
BANG
BANG
WHOOSH
!!
LUXRAY!!

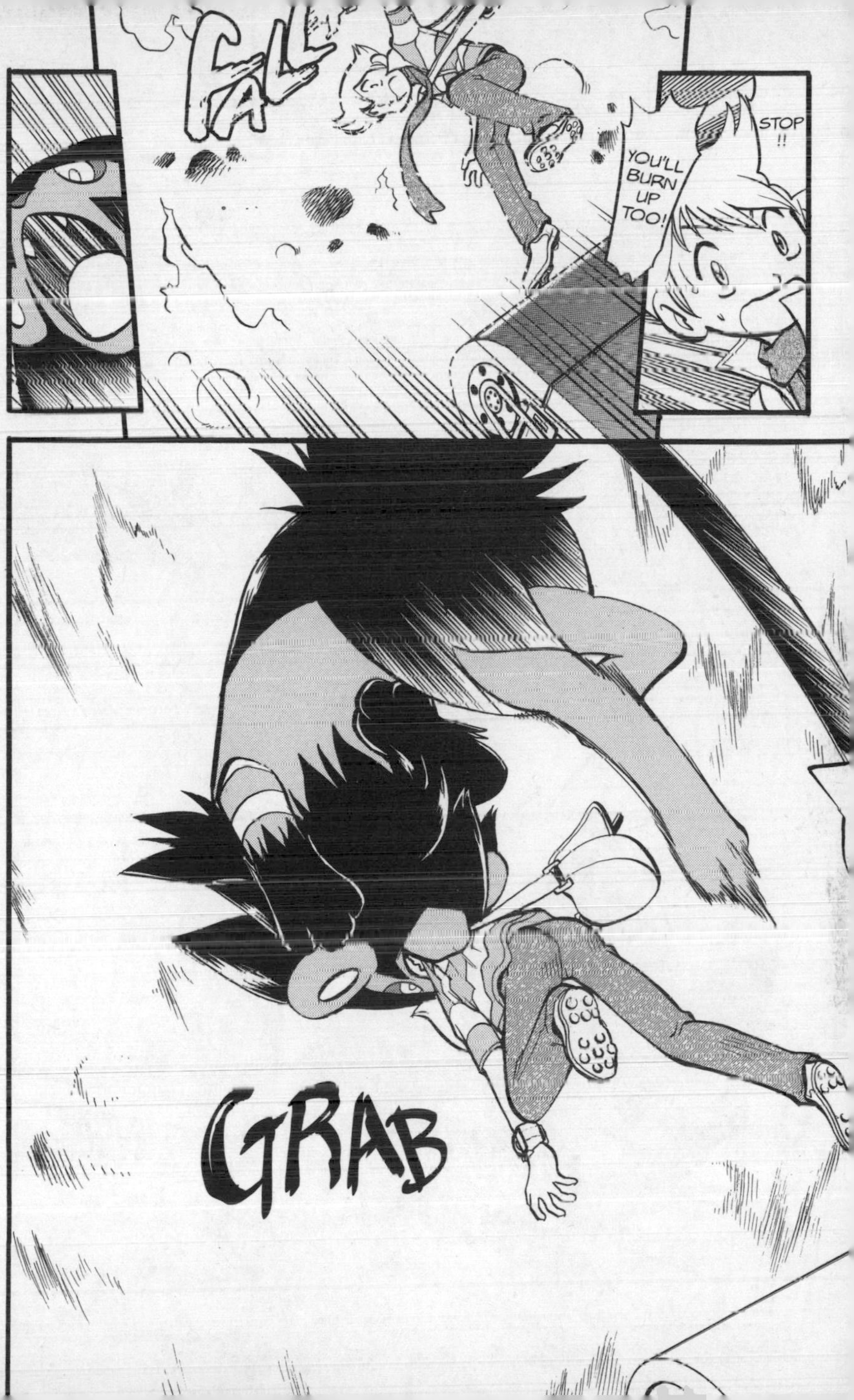
STOP !!
YOU'LL BURN UP TOO!
FALL
GRAB

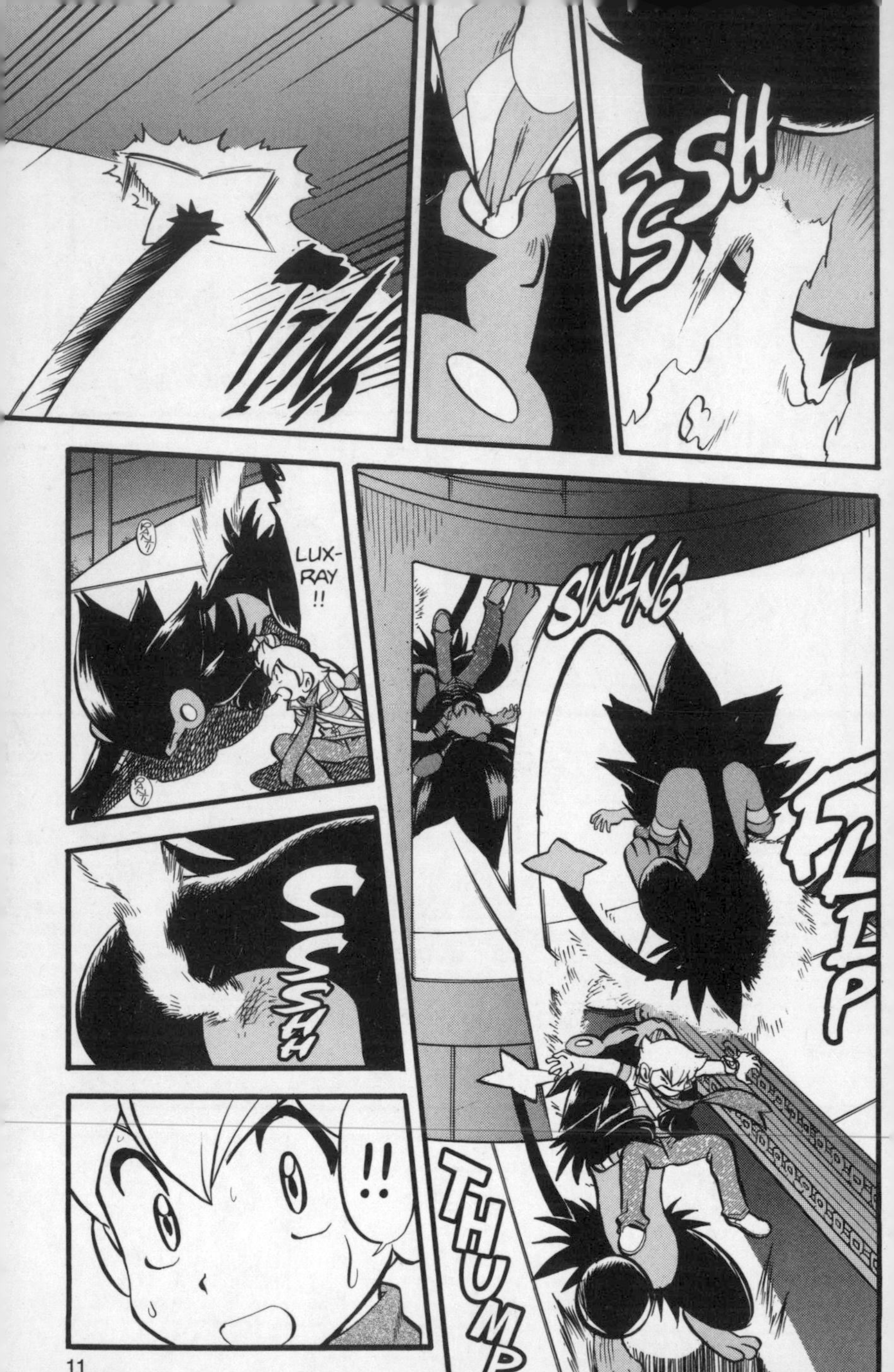
FSSH
TINK
SWING
FLIP
THUMP
LUX-
RAY
!!
SSSSHH
!!

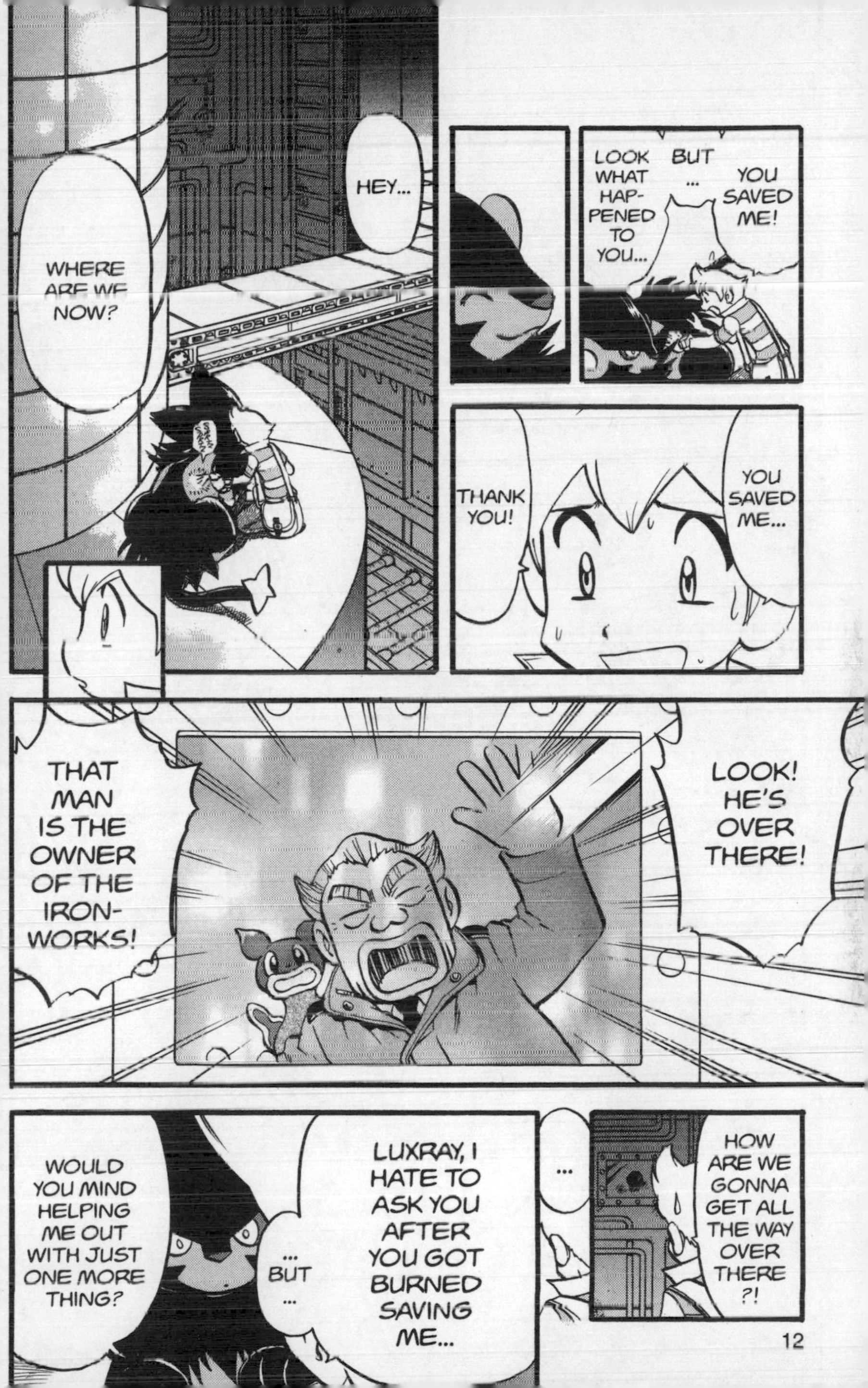
YOU SAVED ME!
BUT ...
LOOK WHAT HAP-PENED TO YOU...
YOU SAVED ME...
THANK YOU!
HEY...
WHERE ARE WE NOW?
LOOK! HE'S OVER THERE!
THAT MAN IS THE OWNER OF THE IRON-WORKS!
HOW ARE WE GONNA GET ALL THE WAY OVER THERE?!
...
LUXRAY, I HATE TO ASK YOU AFTER YOU GOT BURNED SAVING ME...
... BUT ...
WOULD YOU MIND HELPING ME OUT WITH JUST ONE MORE THING?

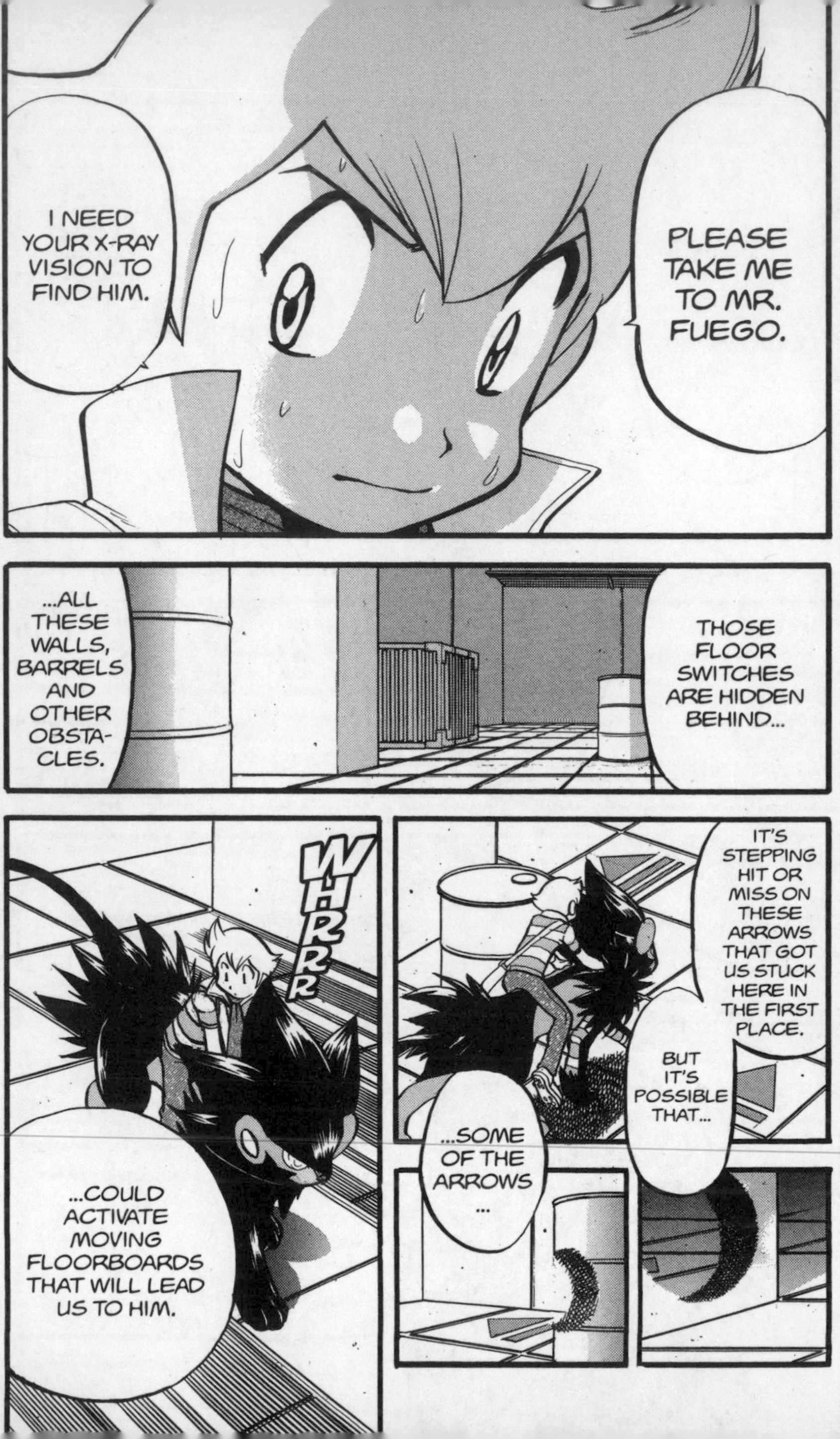
PLEASE TAKE ME TO MR. FUEGO.
I NEED YOUR X-RAY VISION TO FIND HIM.
THOSE FLOOR SWITCHES ARE HIDDEN BEHIND...
...ALL THESE WALLS, BARRELS AND OTHER OBSTA-CLES.
IT'S STEPPING HIT OR MISS ON THESE ARROWS THAT GOT US STUCK HERE IN THE FIRST PLACE.
BUT IT'S POSSIBLE THAT...
...SOME OF THE ARROWS ...
WHRRR
...COULD ACTIVATE MOVING FLOORBOARDS THAT WILL LEAD US TO HIM.

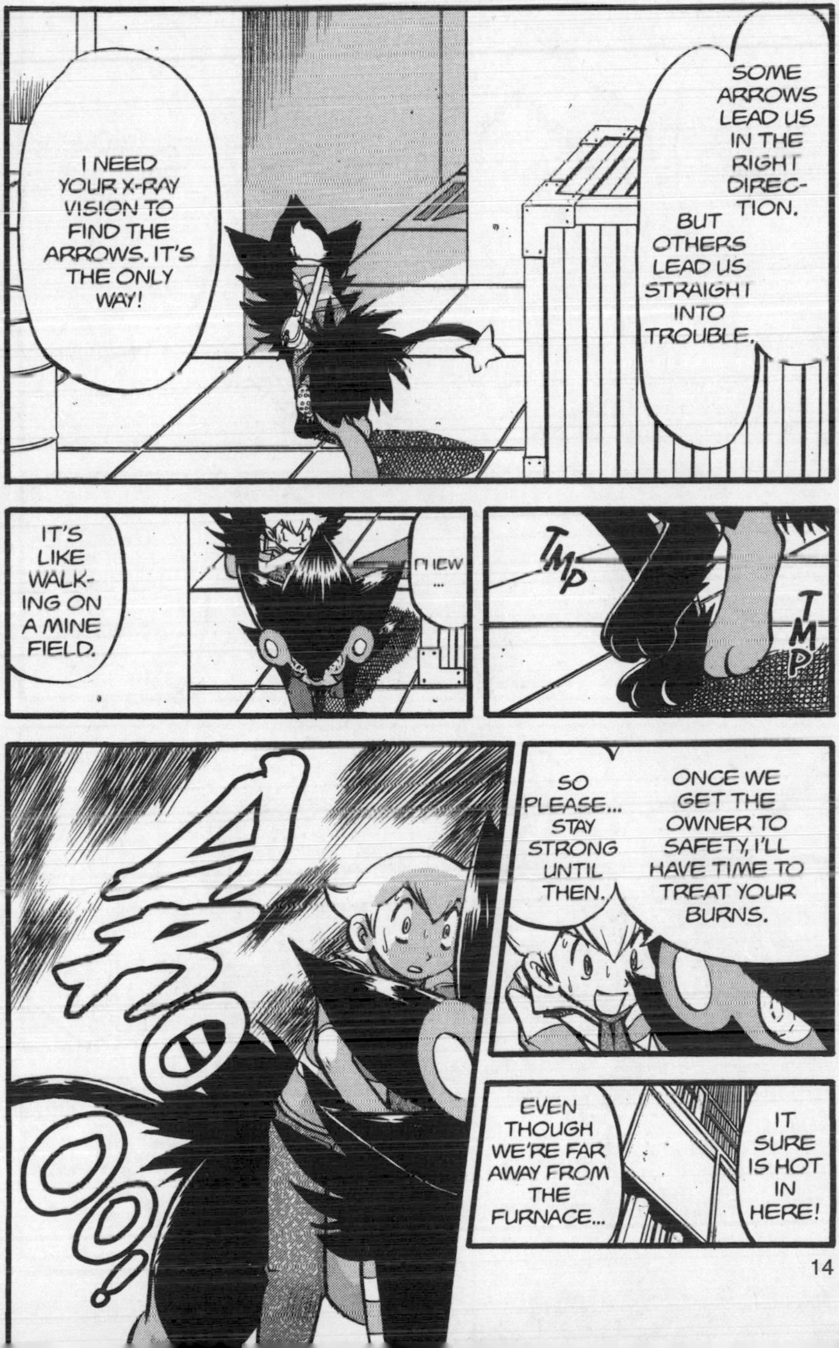

SOME ARROWS LEAD US IN THE RIGHT DIREC- TION.
BUT OTHERS LEAD US STRAIGHT INTO TROUBLE.
I NEED YOUR X-RAY VISION TO FIND THE ARROWS. IT'S THE ONLY WAY!
TMP
TMP
MEW ...
IT'S LIKE WALK- ING ON A MINE FIELD.
ONCE WE GET THE OWNER TO SAFETY, I'LL HAVE TIME TO TREAT YOUR BURNS.
SO PLEASE... STAY STRONG UNTIL THEN.
IT SURE IS HOT IN HERE!
EVEN THOUGH WE'RE FAR AWAY FROM THE FURNACE...
AROOO!

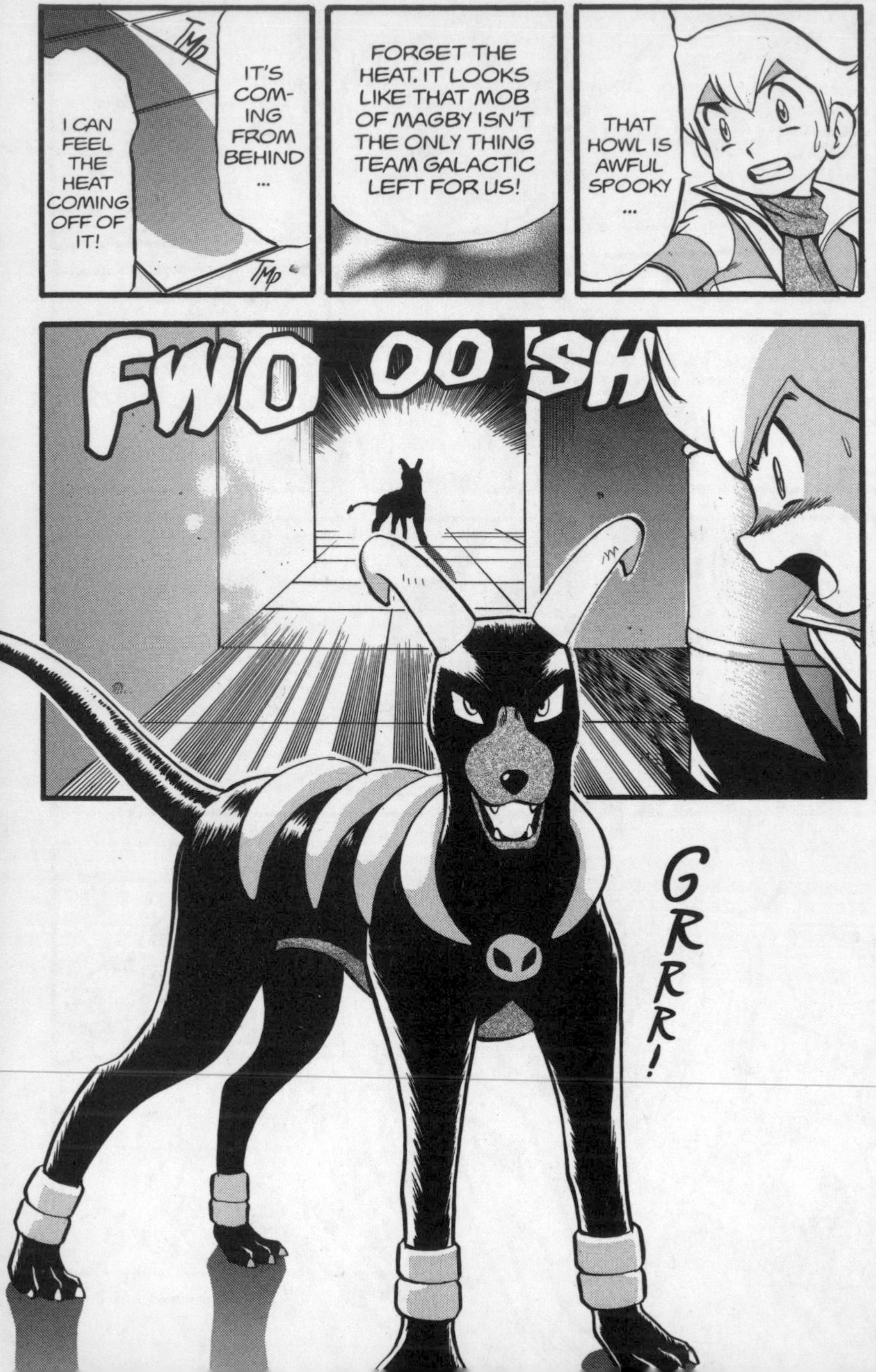
THAT HOWL IS AWFUL SPOOKY ...
FORGET THE HEAT. IT LOOKS LIKE THAT MOB OF MAGBY ISN'T THE ONLY THING TEAM GALACTIC LEFT FOR US!
IT'S COM-ING FROM BEHIND ...
TMP
I CAN FEEL THE HEAT COMING OFF OF IT!
TMP
FWOOOSH
GRRR!

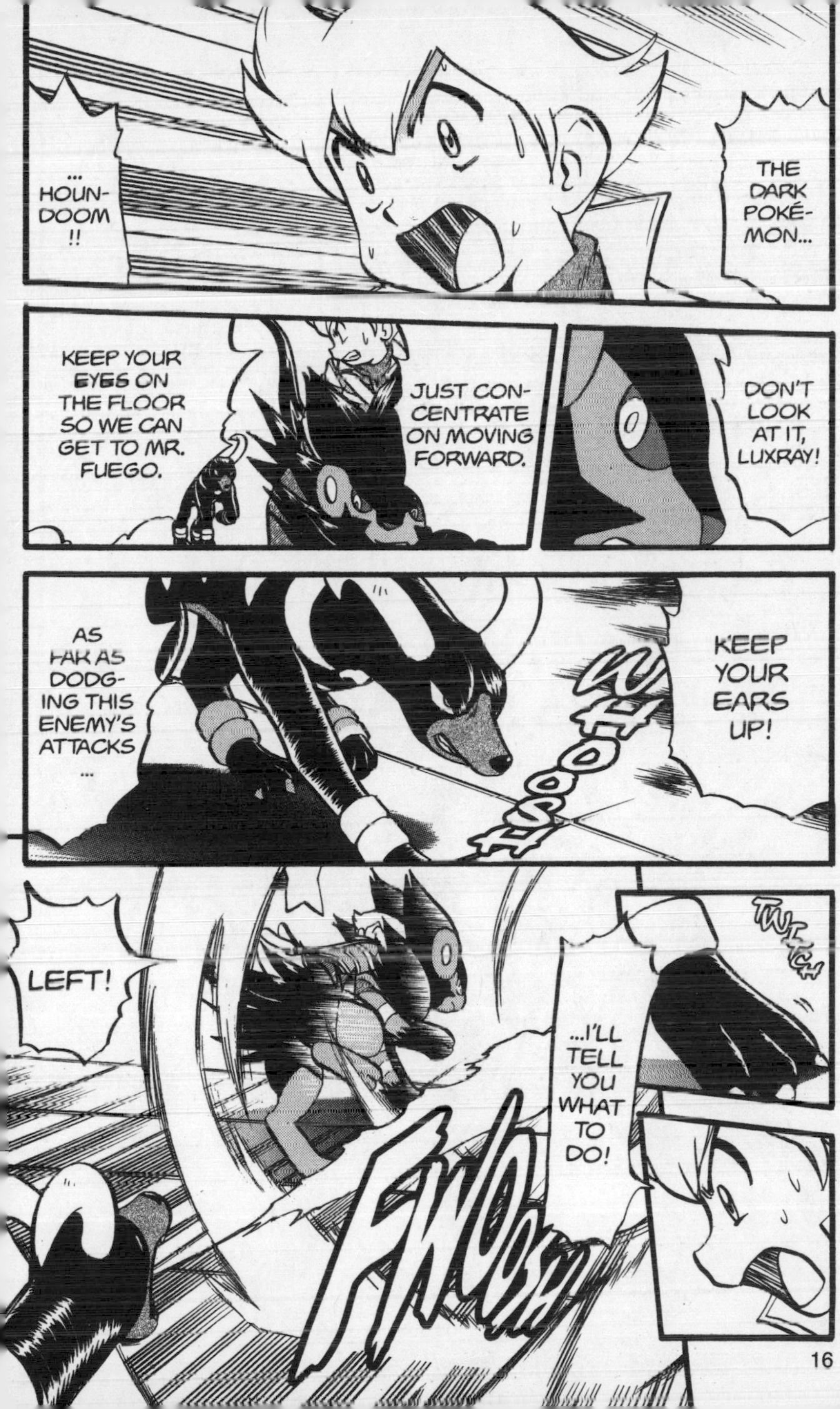
THE DARK POKÉMON...
... HOUN-DOOM !!
DON'T LOOK AT IT, LUXRAY!
JUST CON-CENTRATE ON MOVING FORWARD.
KEEP YOUR EYES ON THE FLOOR SO WE CAN GET TO MR. FUEGO.
KEEP YOUR EARS UP!
WHOOSH
AS FAR AS DODG-ING THIS ENEMY'S ATTACKS ...
TWITCH
...I'LL TELL YOU WHAT TO DO!
LEFT!

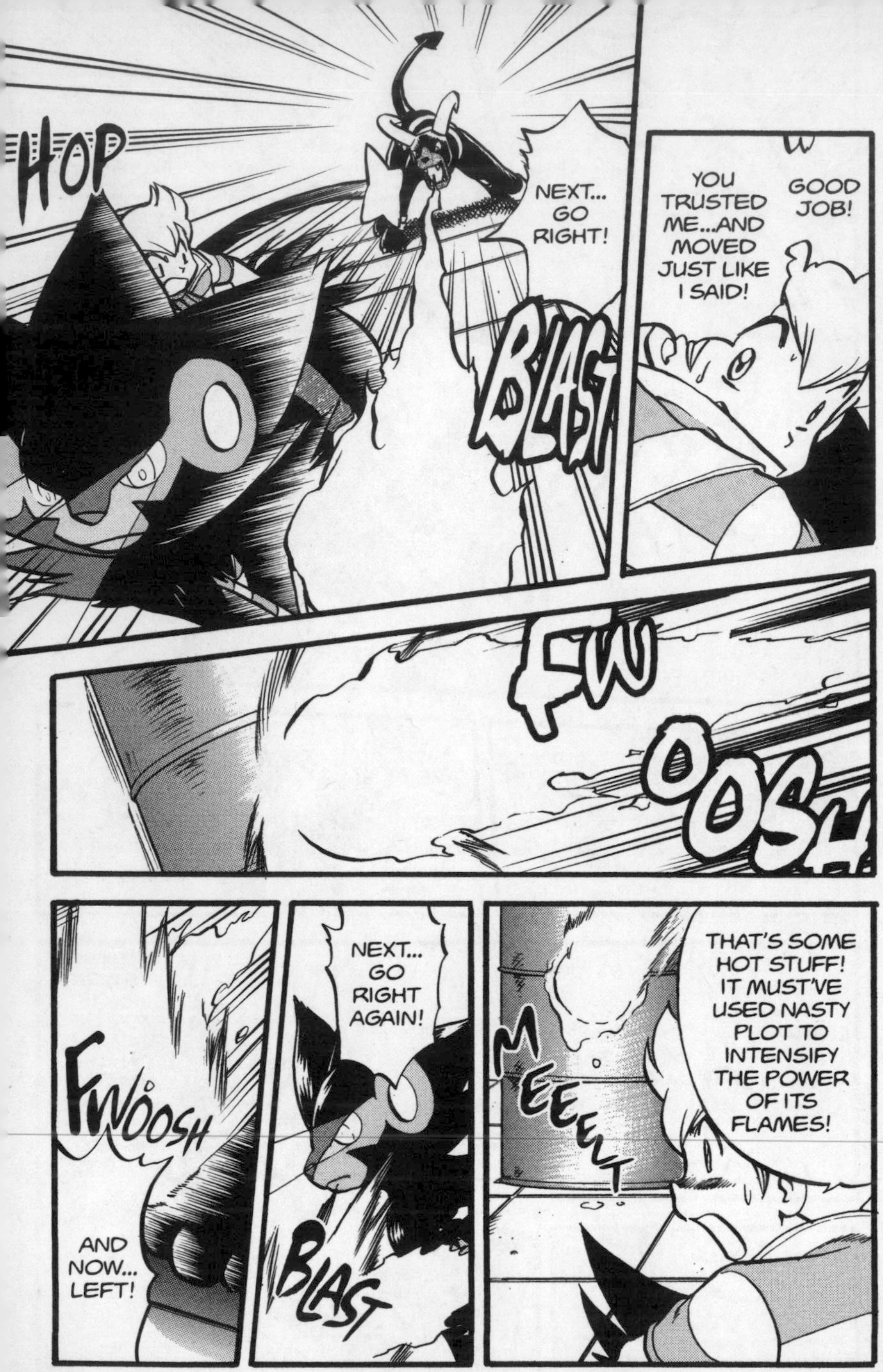

GOOD JOB!
YOU TRUSTED ME...AND MOVED JUST LIKE I SAID!
NEXT... GO RIGHT!
HOP
BLAST
FWOOSH
THAT'S SOME HOT STUFF! IT MUST'VE USED NASTY PLOT TO INTENSIFY THE POWER OF ITS FLAMES!
MEEELT
NEXT... GO RIGHT AGAIN!
BLAST
FWOOSH
AND NOW... LEFT!

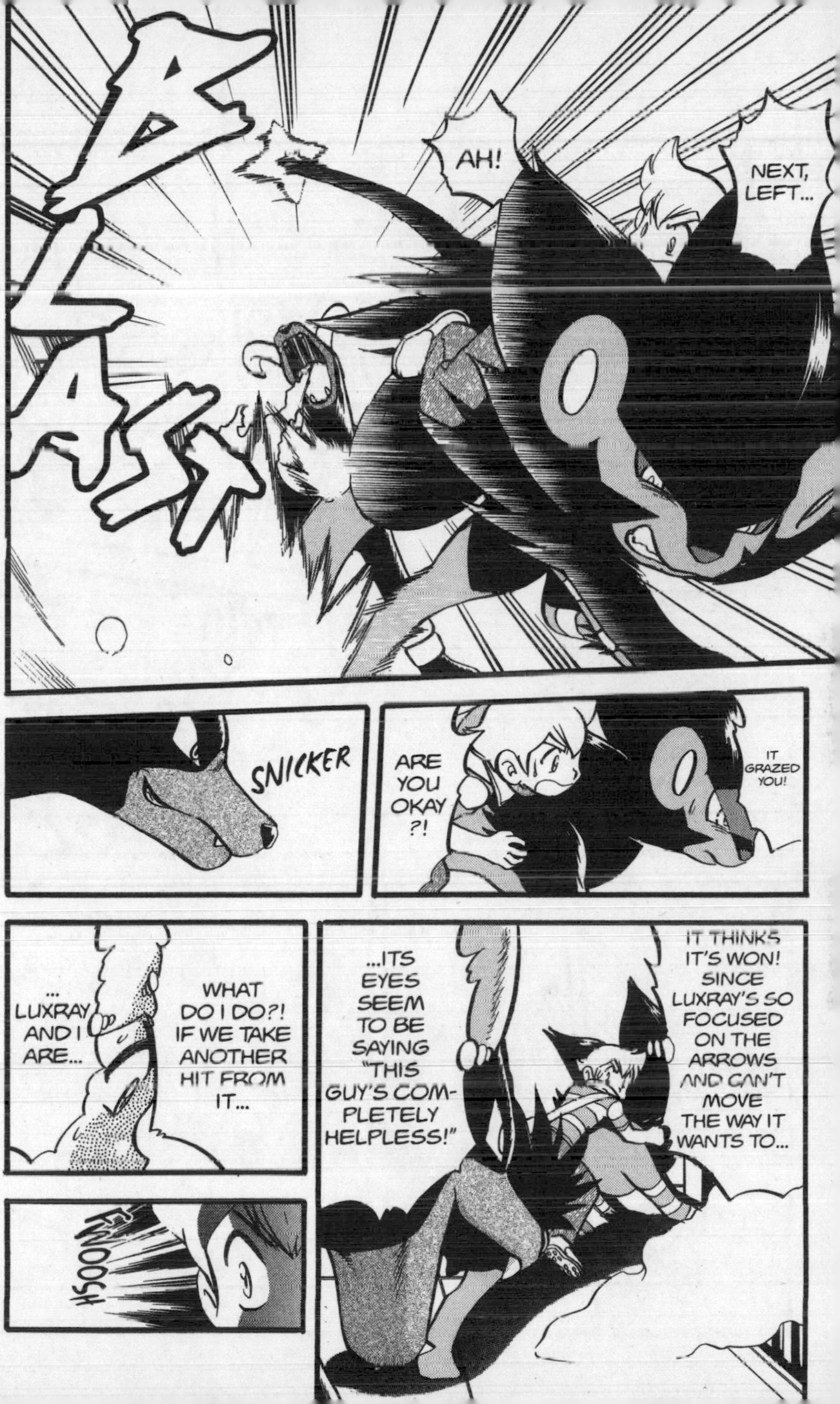
NEXT, LEFT...
AH!
BLAST
IT GRAZED YOU!
ARE YOU OKAY?!
SNICKER
IT THINKS IT'S WON! SINCE LUXRAY'S SO FOCUSED ON THE ARROWS AND CAN'T MOVE THE WAY IT WANTS TO...
...ITS EYES SEEM TO BE SAYING "THIS GUY'S COMPLETELY HELPLESS!"
WHAT DO I DO?! IF WE TAKE ANOTHER HIT FROM IT...
...LUXRAY AND I ARE...
FWOOSH

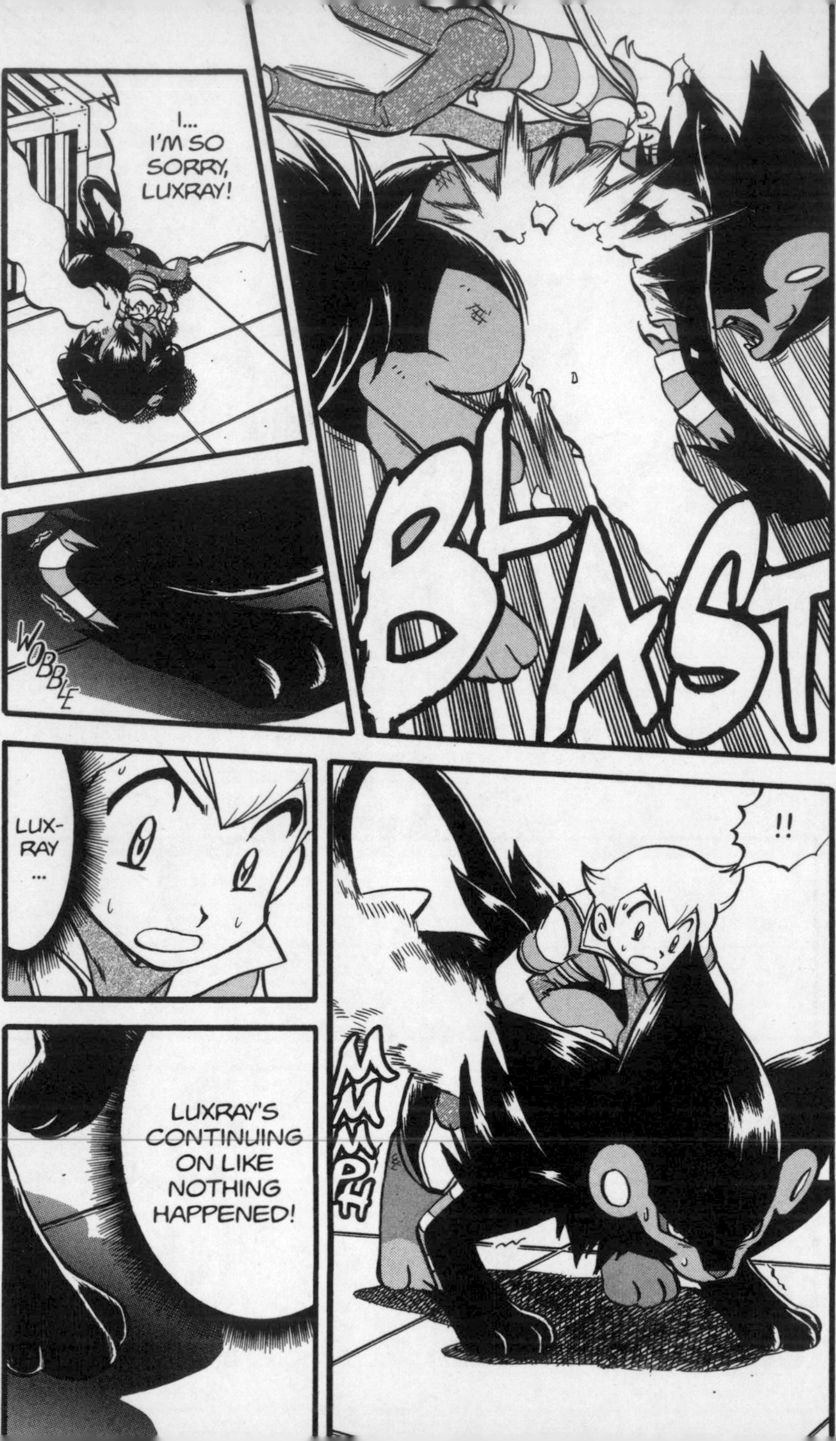
BLAST
I... I'M SO SORRY, LUXRAY!
WOBBLE
!!
MMMPH
LUX-RAY ...
LUXRAY'S CONTINUING ON LIKE NOTHING HAPPENED!

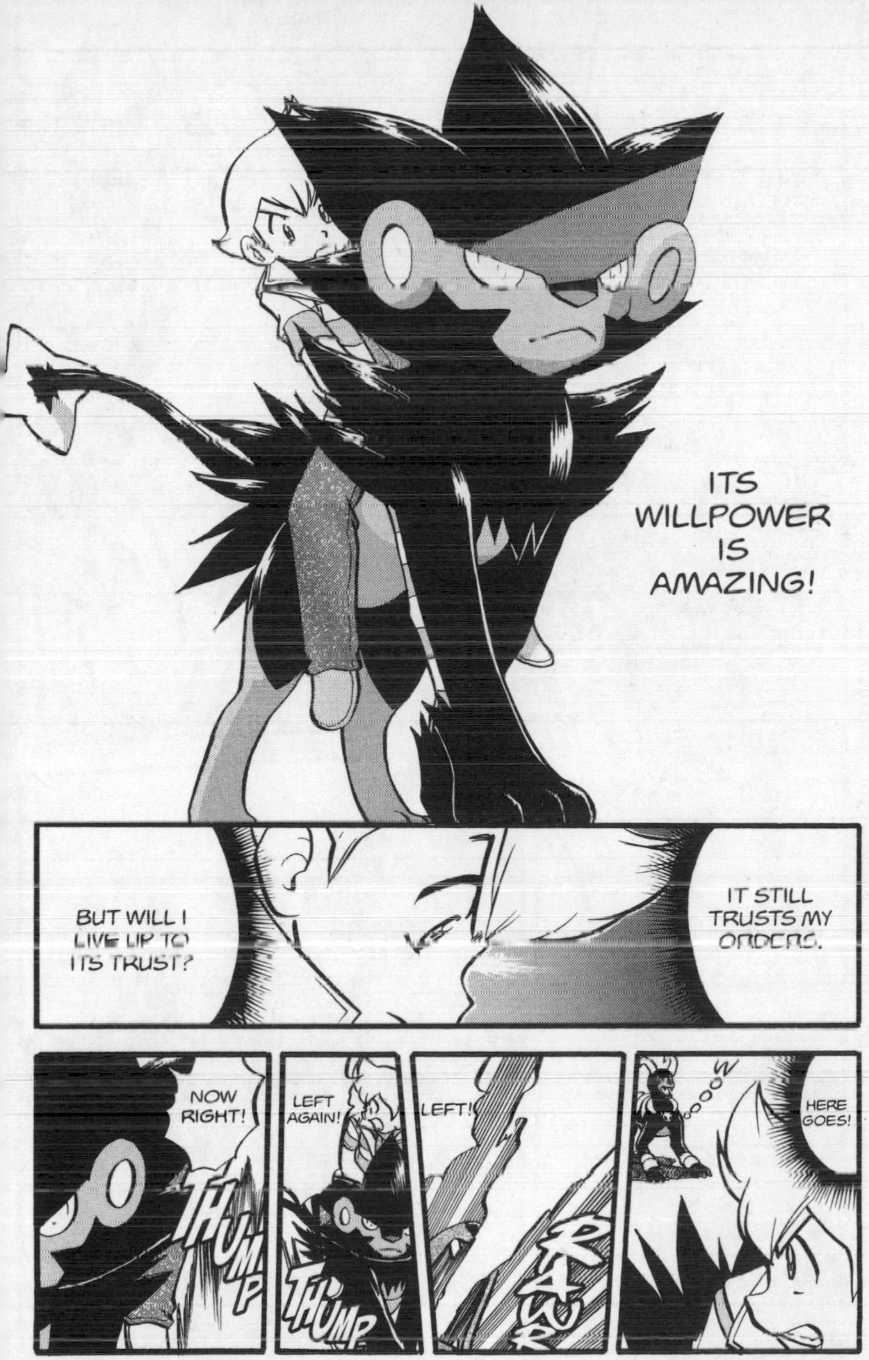
ITS WILLPOWER IS AMAZING!
IT STILL TRUSTS MY ORDERS.
BUT WILL I LIVE UP TO ITS TRUST?
HERE GOES!
WOOOW
LEFT!
RAWR
LEFT AGAIN!
THUMP
NOW RIGHT!
THUMP

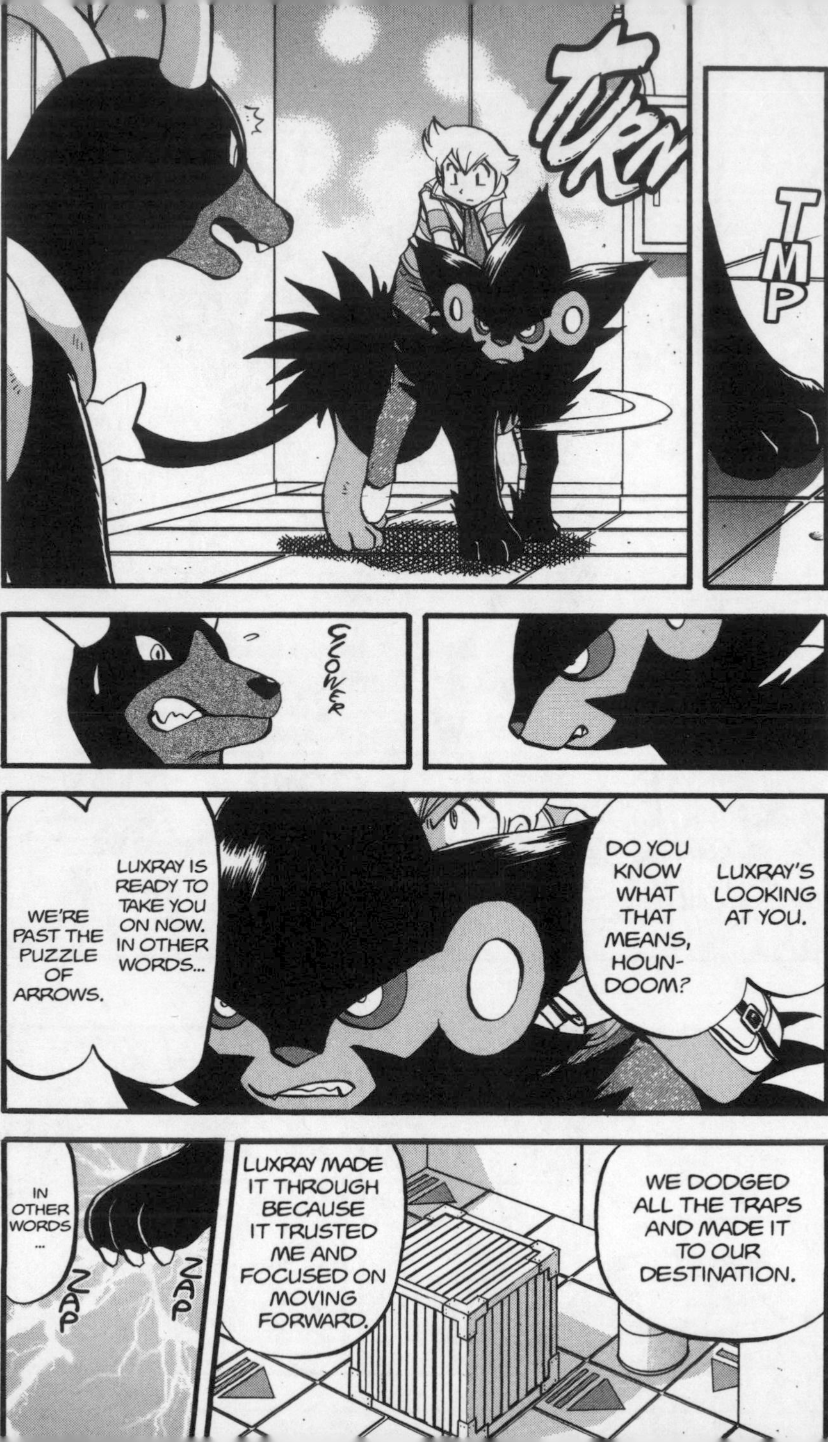
TMP
TURN
GLOWER
LUXRAY'S LOOKING AT YOU.
DO YOU KNOW WHAT THAT MEANS, HOUN-DOOM?
LUXRAY IS READY TO TAKE YOU ON NOW. IN OTHER WORDS...
WE'RE PAST THE PUZZLE OF ARROWS.
WE DODGED ALL THE TRAPS AND MADE IT TO OUR DESTINATION.
LUXRAY MADE IT THROUGH BECAUSE IT TRUSTED ME AND FOCUSED ON MOVING FORWARD.
IN OTHER WORDS...
ZAP
ZAP

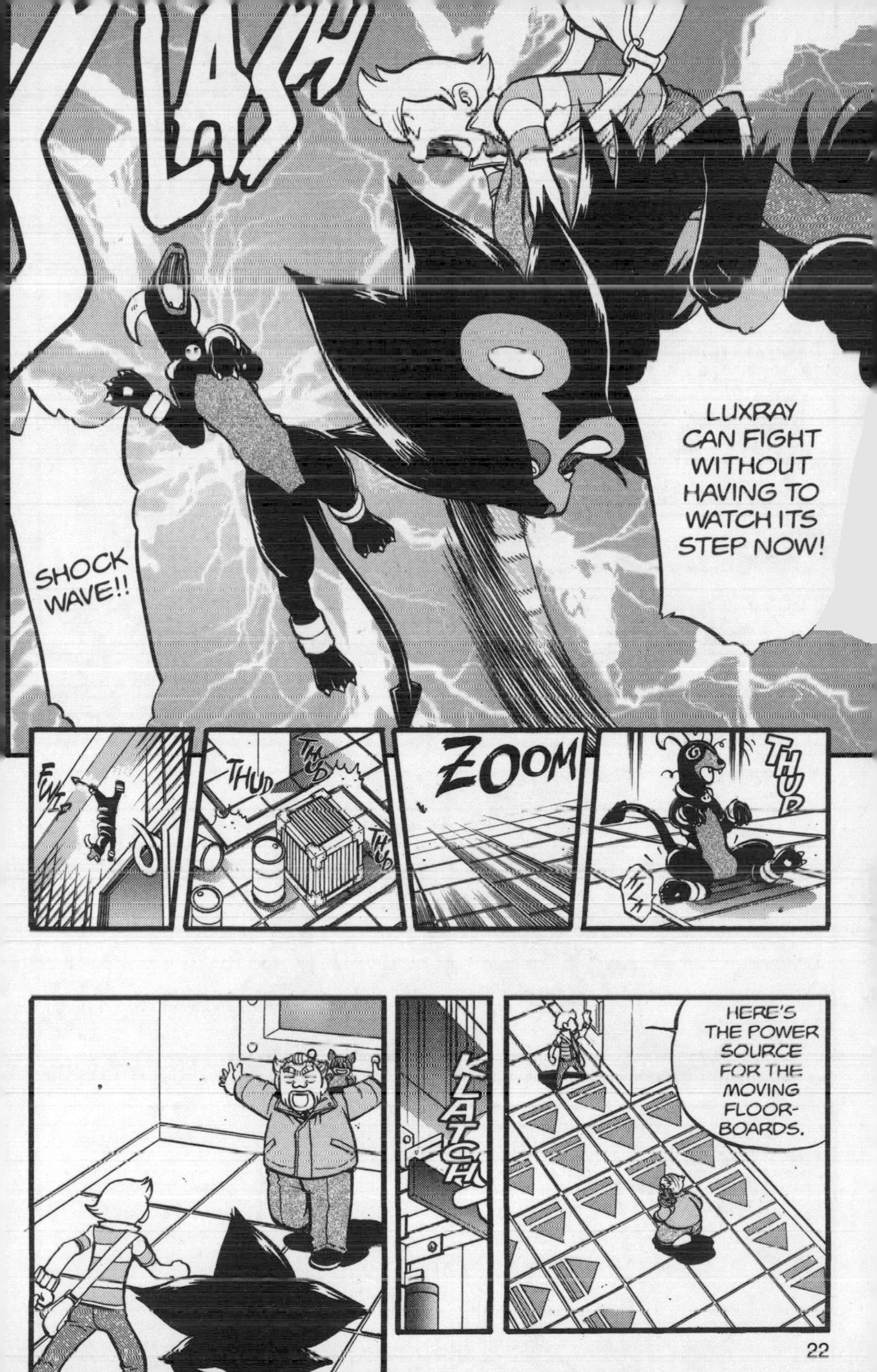
KLASH
LUXRAY CAN FIGHT WITHOUT HAVING TO WATCH ITS STEP NOW!
SHOCK WAVE!!
THUD
KLIK
ZOOM
THUD
THUD
THUD
HERE'S THE POWER SOURCE FOR THE MOVING FLOOR-BOARDS.
KLATCH

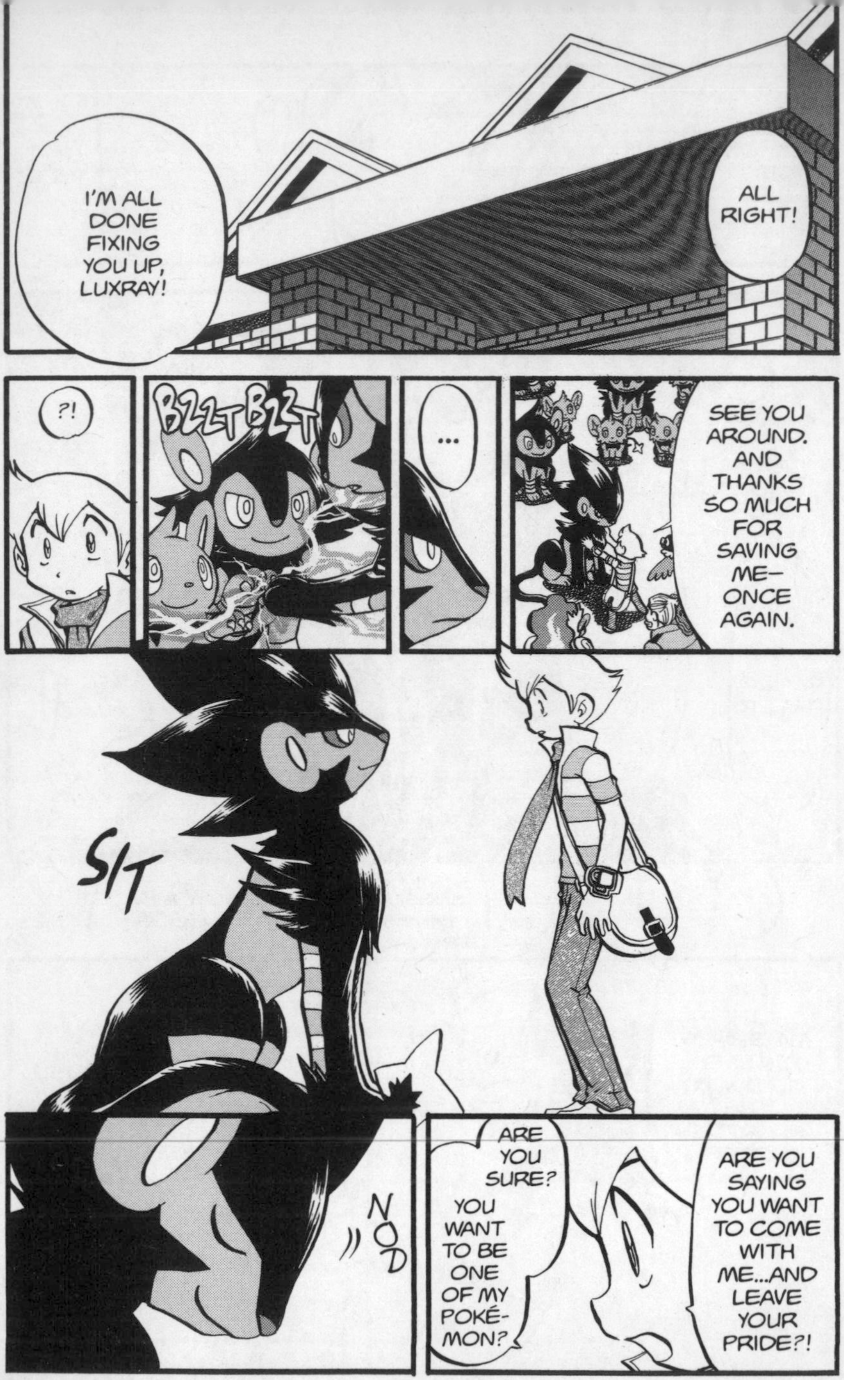
ALL RIGHT!
I'M ALL DONE FIXING YOU UP, LUXRAY!
SEE YOU AROUND. AND THANKS SO MUCH FOR SAVING ME—ONCE AGAIN.
...
BZZT BZZT
?!
SIT
ARE YOU SAYING YOU WANT TO COME WITH ME...AND LEAVE YOUR PRIDE?!
ARE YOU SURE?
YOU WANT TO BE ONE OF MY POKÉMON?
NOD

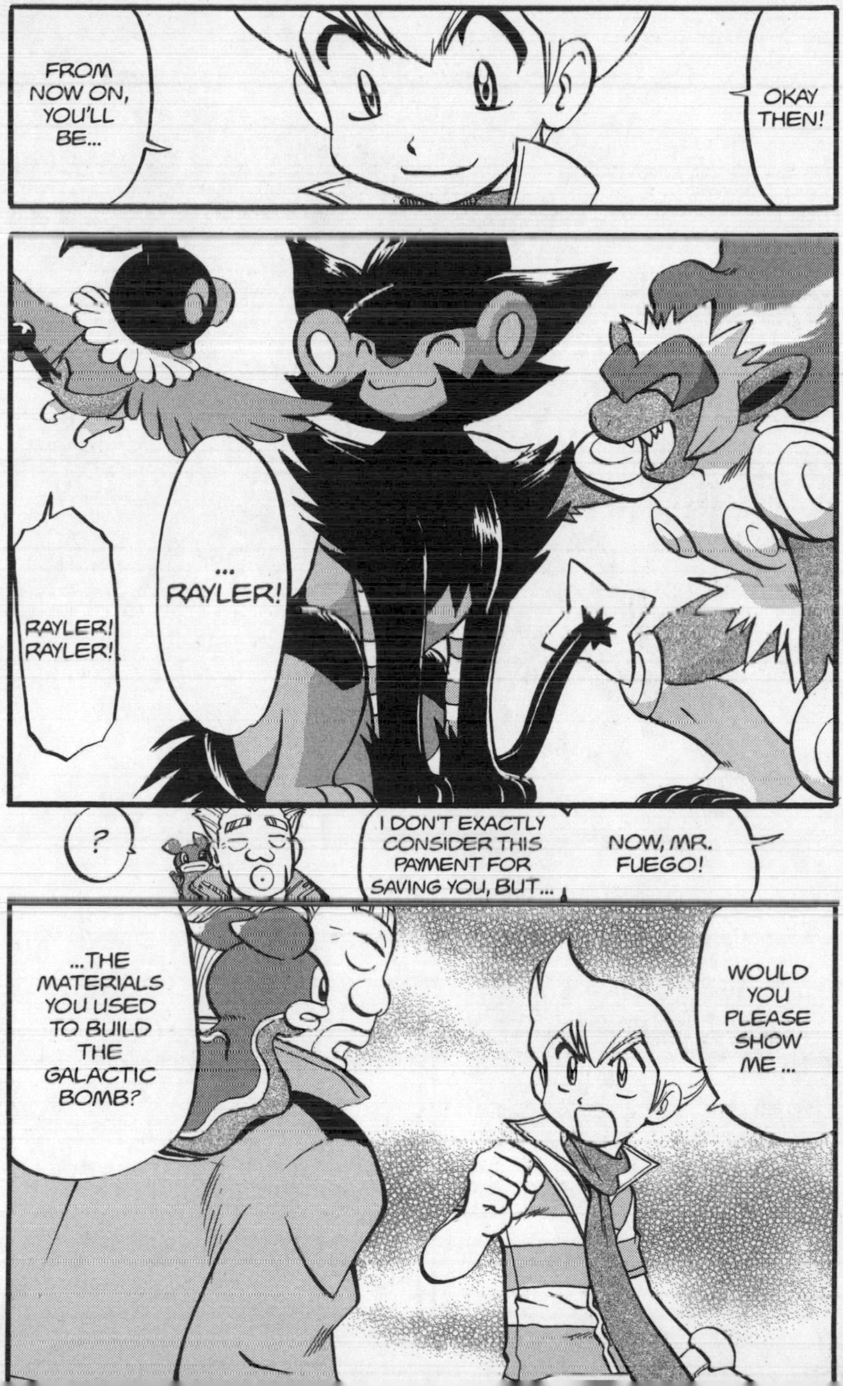
OKAY THEN!
FROM NOW ON, YOU'LL BE...
...RAYLER!
RAYLER! RAYLER!
NOW, MR. FUEGO!
I DON'T EXACTLY CONSIDER THIS PAYMENT FOR SAVING YOU, BUT...
?
WOULD YOU PLEASE SHOW ME ...
...THE MATERIALS YOU USED TO BUILD THE GALACTIC BOMB?

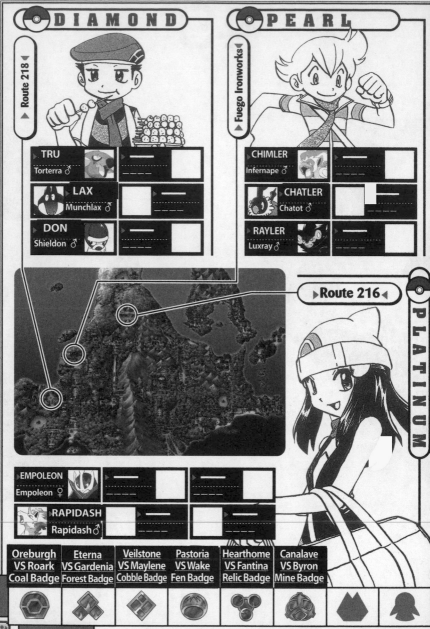

ADVENTURE MAP

DIAMOND

◄ Route 218

TRU
Torterra ♂

LAX
Munchlax ♂

DON
Shieldon ♂

PEARL

◄ Fuego Ironworks

CHIMLER
Infernape ♂

CHATLER
Chatot ♂

RAYLER
Luxray ♂

►Route 216◄

PLATINUM

▶EMPOLEON
Empoleon ♀

RAPIDASH
Rapidash ♂

Oreburgh	Eterna	Veilstone	Pastoria	Hearthome	Canalave
VS Roark	VS Gardenia	VS Maylene	VS Wake	VS Fantina	VS Byron
Coal Badge	Forest Badge	Cobble Badge	Fen Badge	Relic Badge	Mine Badge

49

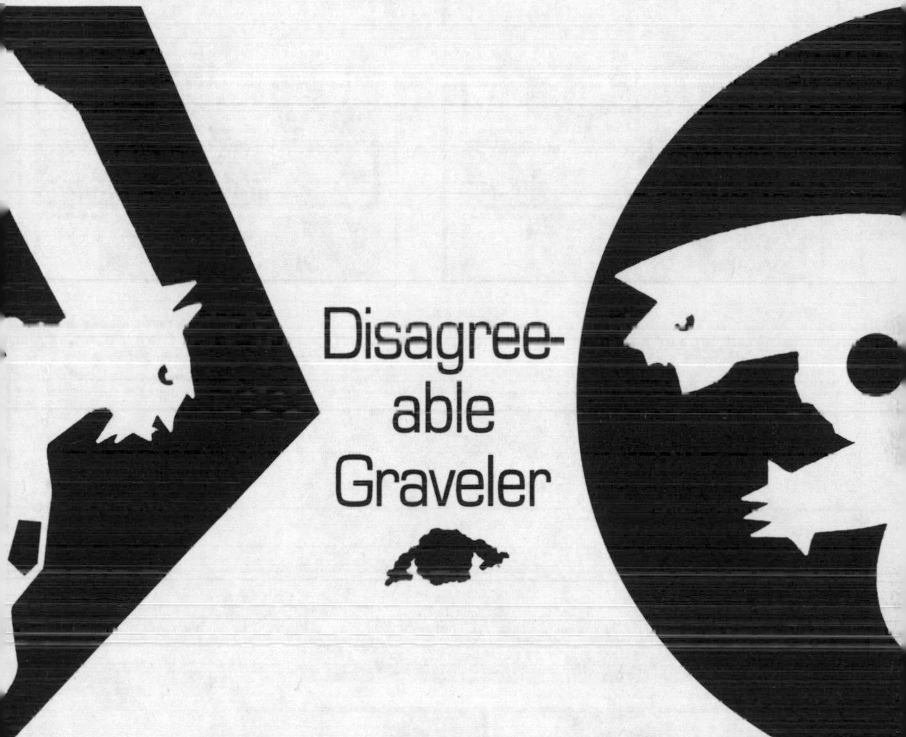

Disagreeable Graveler

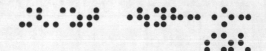

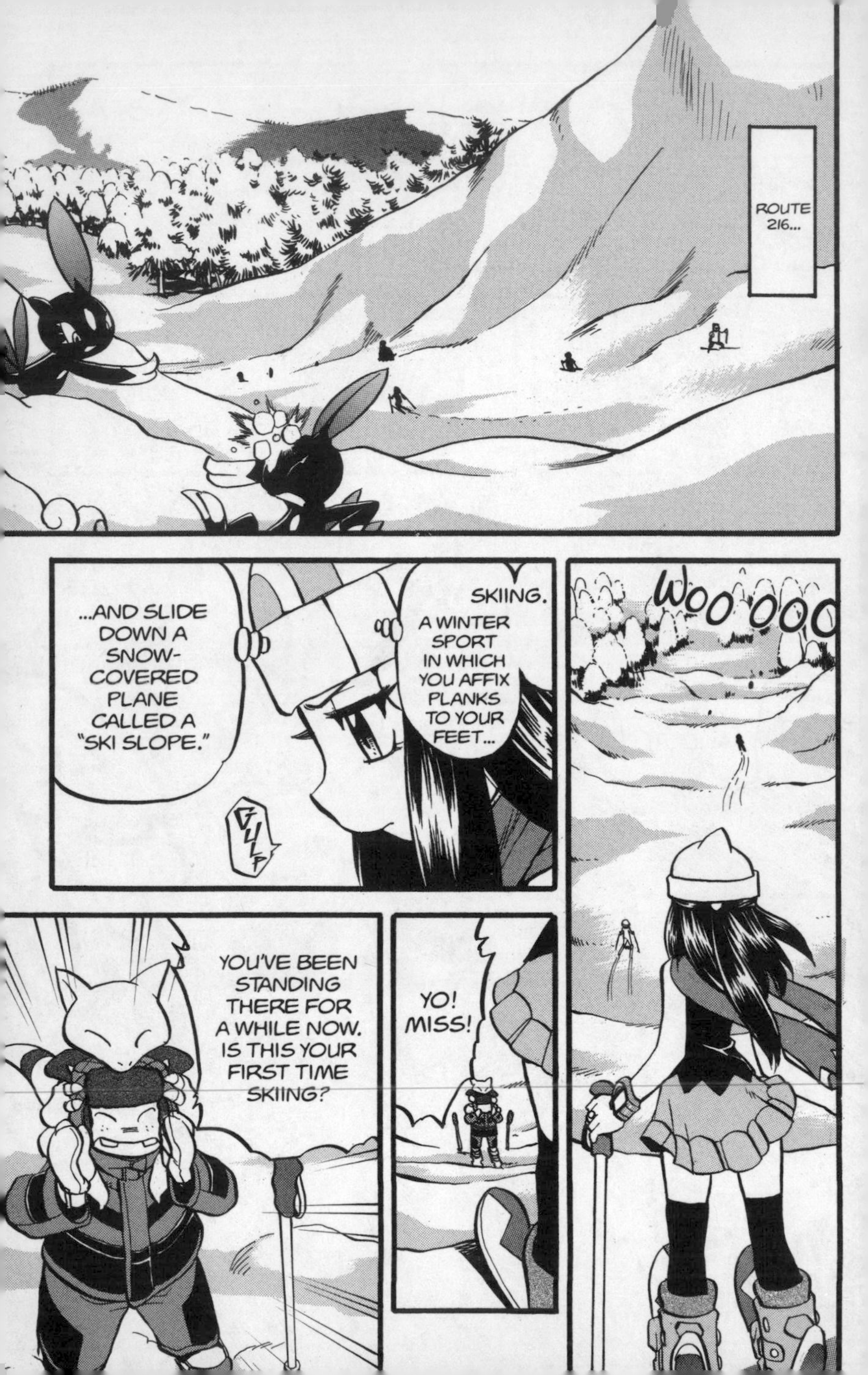
ROUTE 216...
WOO OOO
SKIING. A WINTER SPORT IN WHICH YOU AFFIX PLANKS TO YOUR FEET...
...AND SLIDE DOWN A SNOW-COVERED PLANE CALLED A "SKI SLOPE."
GULP
YO! MISS!
YOU'VE BEEN STANDING THERE FOR A WHILE NOW. IS THIS YOUR FIRST TIME SKIING?

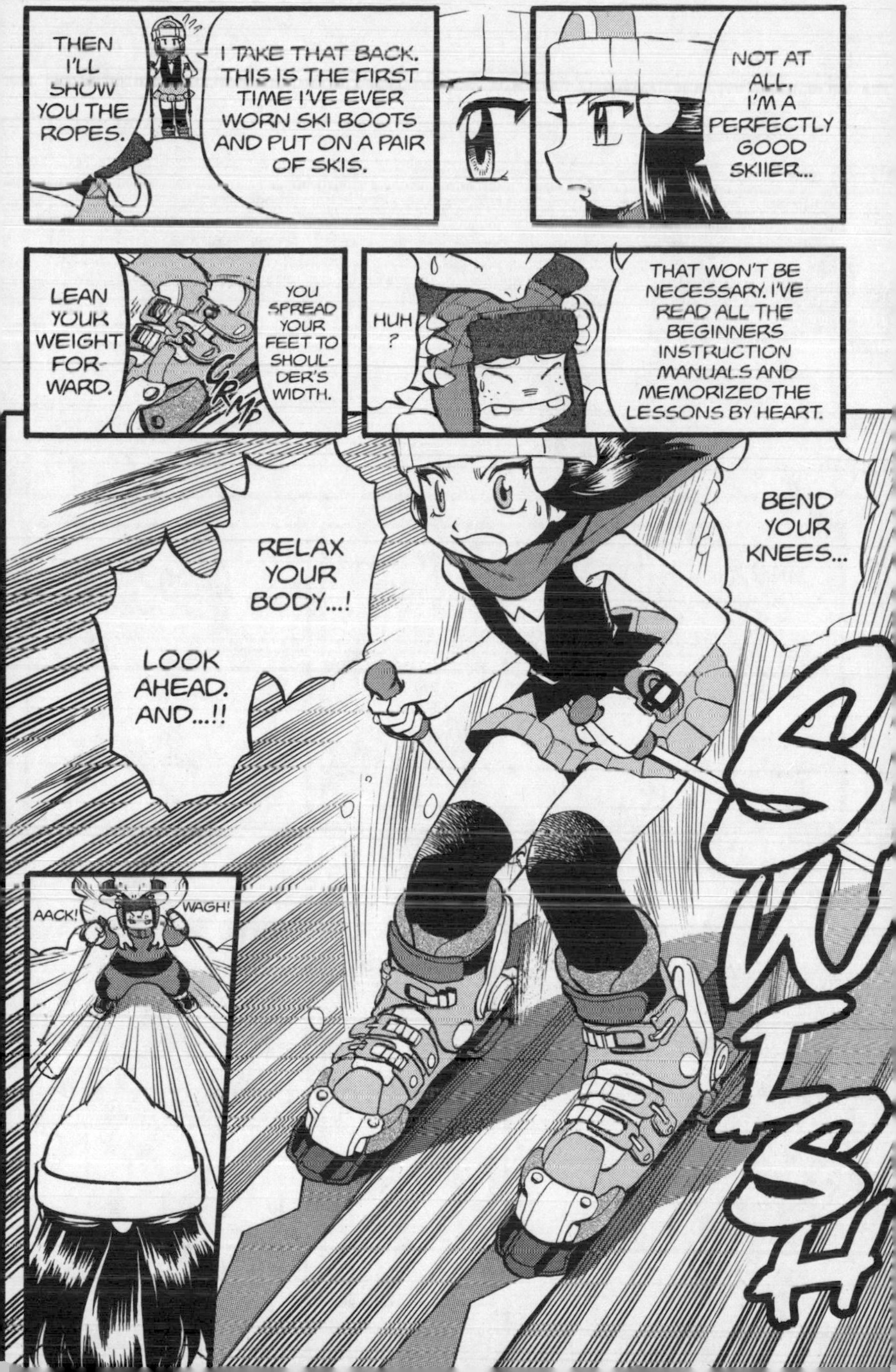
NOT AT ALL. I'M A PERFECTLY GOOD SKIIER...
I TAKE THAT BACK. THIS IS THE FIRST TIME I'VE EVER WORN SKI BOOTS AND PUT ON A PAIR OF SKIS.
THEN I'LL SHOW YOU THE ROPES.
THAT WON'T BE NECESSARY. I'VE READ ALL THE BEGINNERS INSTRUCTION MANUALS AND MEMORIZED THE LESSONS BY HEART.
HUH?
YOU SPREAD YOUR FEET TO SHOUL-DER'S WIDTH.
CRMP
LEAN YOUR WEIGHT FOR-WARD.
BEND YOUR KNEES...
RELAX YOUR BODY...!
LOOK AHEAD. AND...!!
SWISH
WAGH!
AACK!

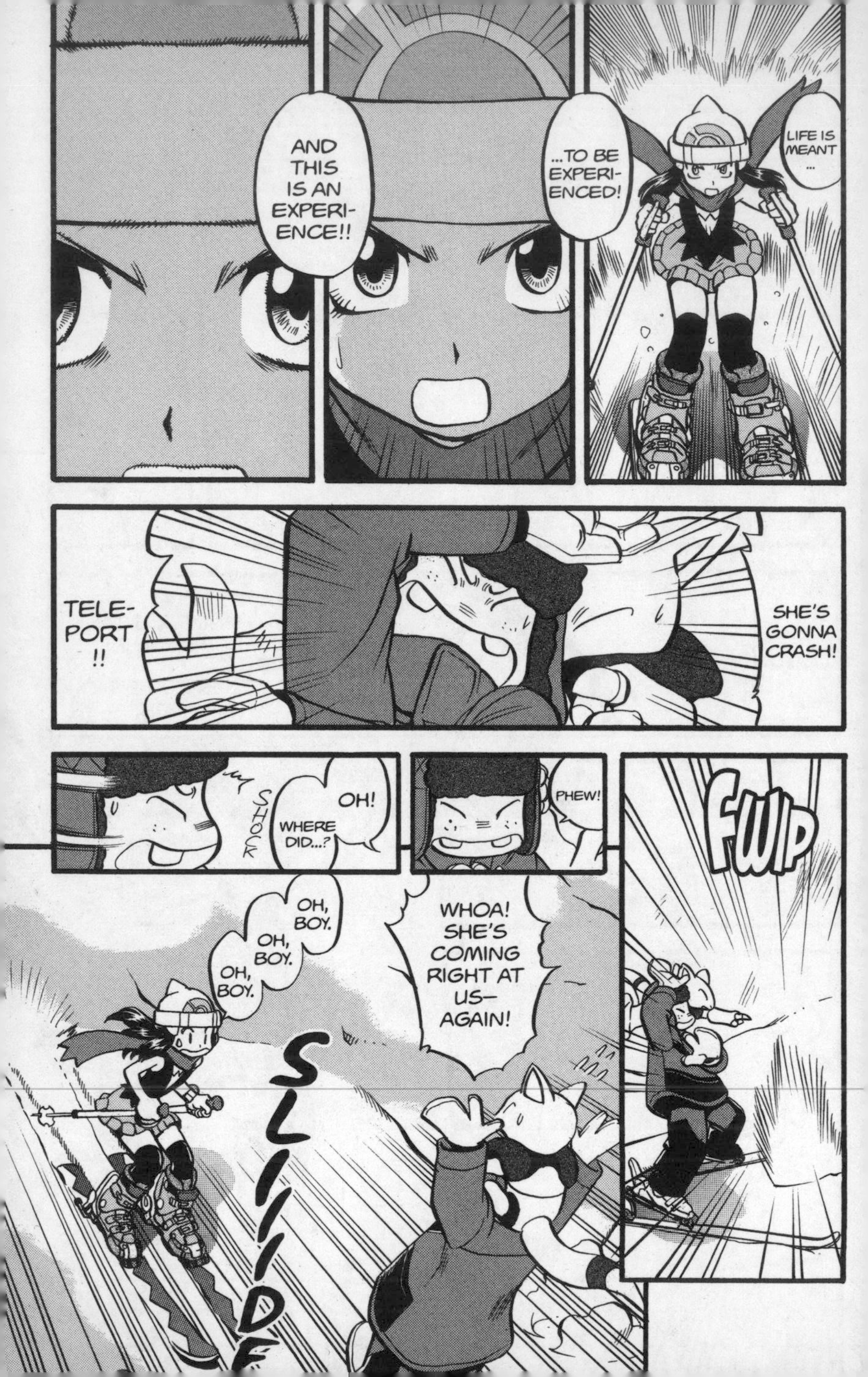

LIFE IS MEANT ...
...TO BE EXPERI-ENCED!
AND THIS IS AN EXPERI-ENCE!!
SHE'S GONNA CRASH!
TELE-PORT !!
FWIP
PHEW!
OH! WHERE DID...?
SHOCK
WHOA! SHE'S COMING RIGHT AT US— AGAIN!
OH, BOY.
OH, BOY.
OH, BOY.
SLIIIDE

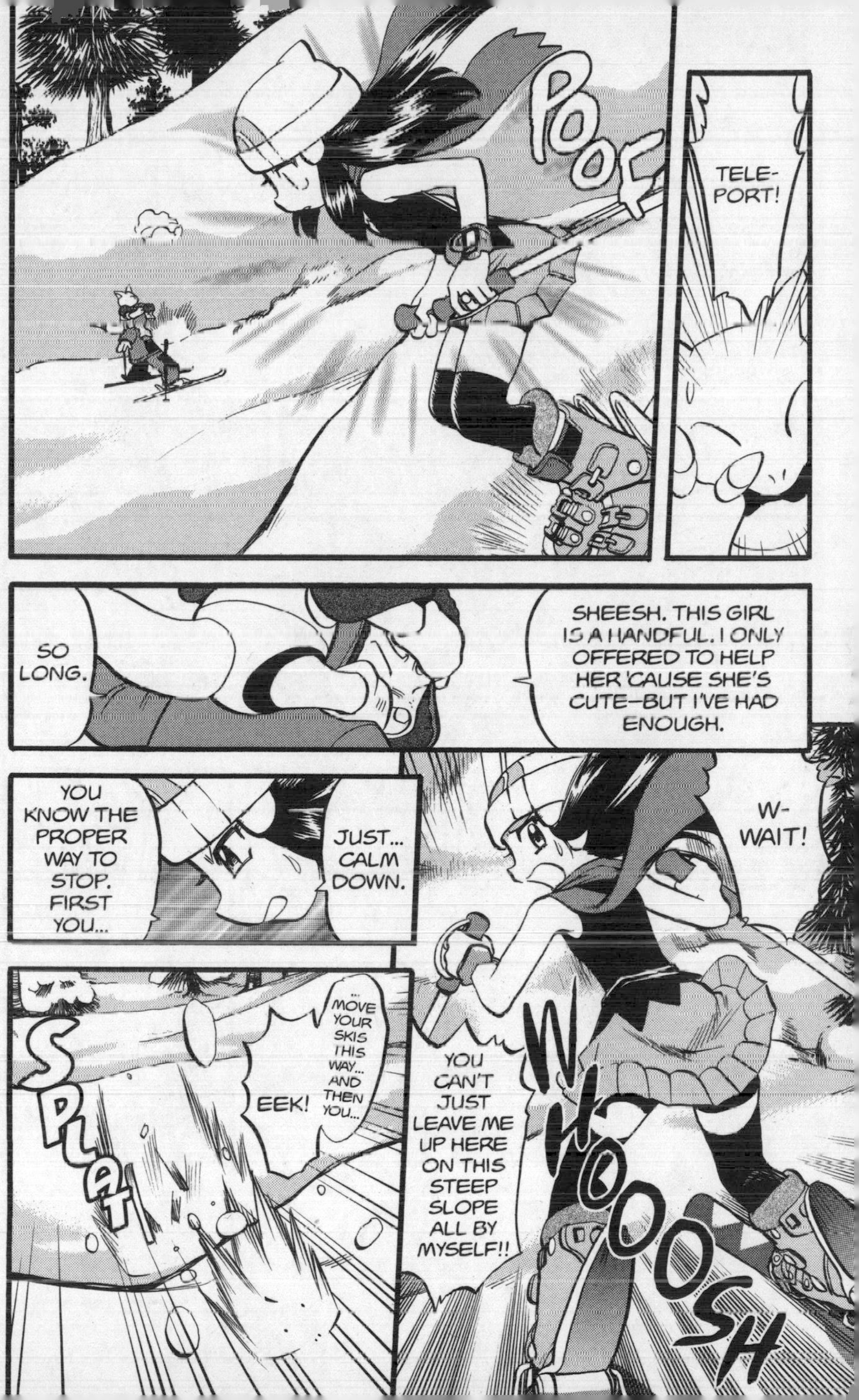
TELE-PORT!
POOF
SHEESH. THIS GIRL IS A HANDFUL. I ONLY OFFERED TO HELP HER 'CAUSE SHE'S CUTE—BUT I'VE HAD ENOUGH.
SO LONG.
W-WAIT!
YOU CAN'T JUST LEAVE ME UP HERE ON THIS STEEP SLOPE ALL BY MYSELF!!
WHOOOSH
JUST... CALM DOWN.
YOU KNOW THE PROPER WAY TO STOP. FIRST YOU...
...MOVE YOUR SKIS THIS WAY... AND THEN YOU...
EEK!
SPLAT

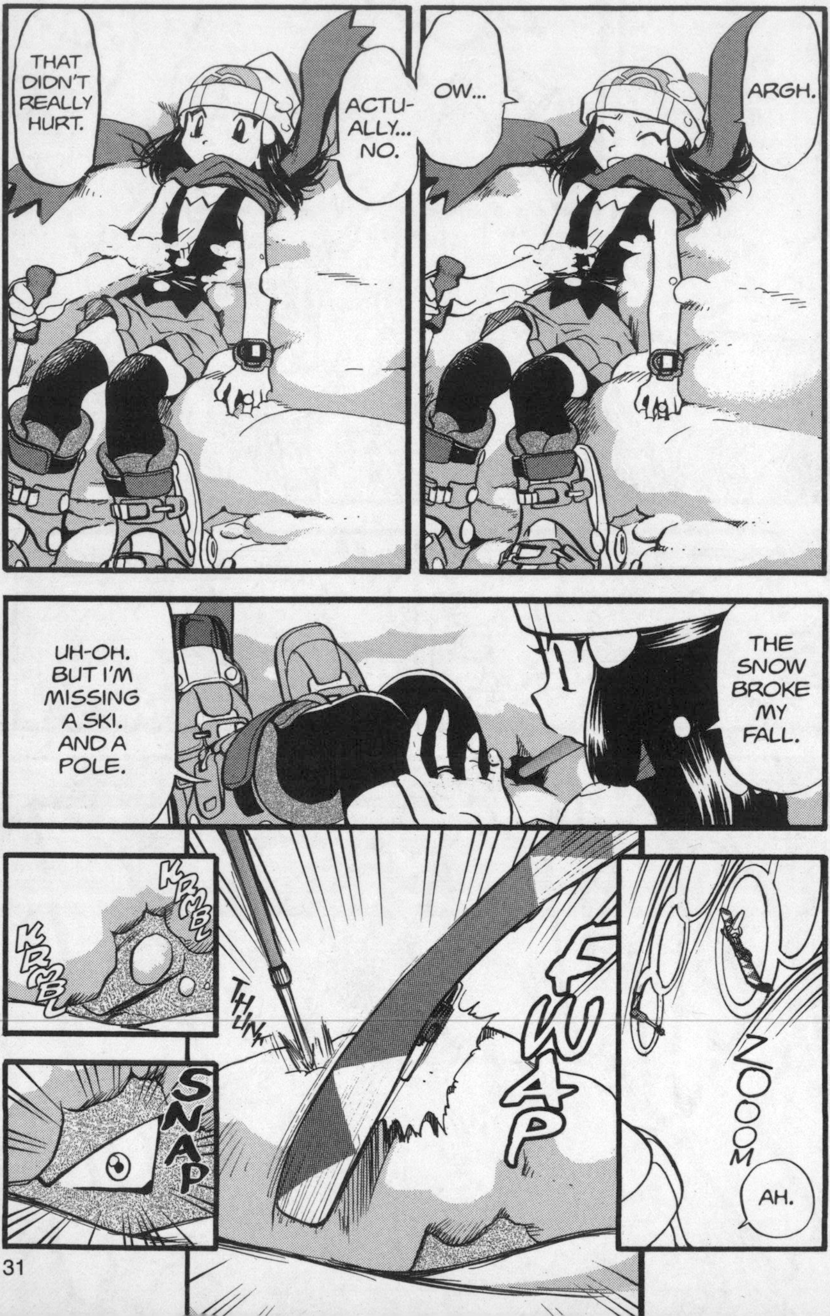
ARGH.
OW...
ACTU-ALLY... NO.
THAT DIDN'T REALLY HURT.
THE SNOW BROKE MY FALL.
UH-OH. BUT I'M MISSING A SKI. AND A POLE.
ZOOOOM
AH.
FWAP
THUNK
KRMBL
KRMBL
SNAP

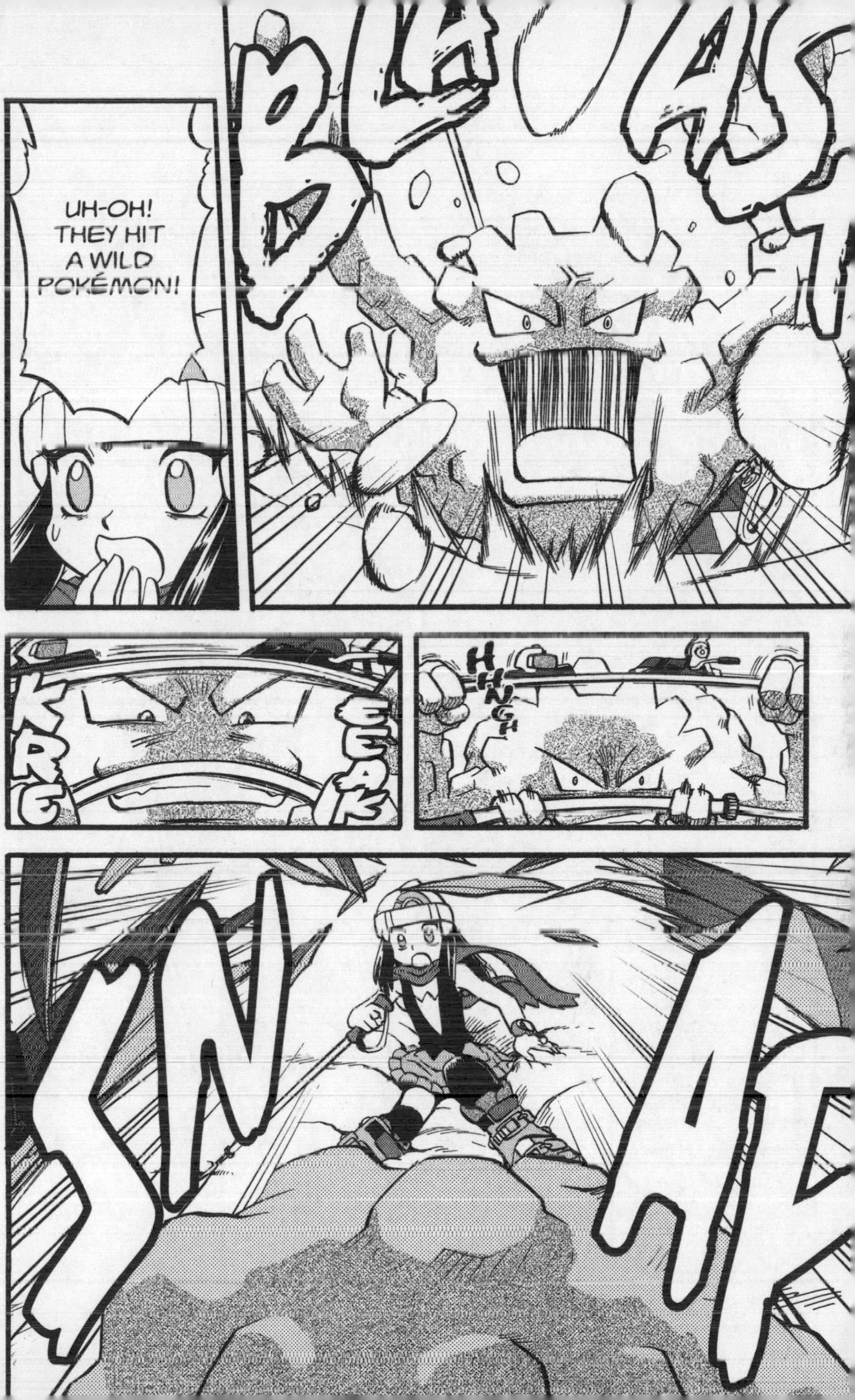
BLAST
UH-OH! THEY HIT A WILD POKÉMON!
HHNGH
KREEAK
SNAP

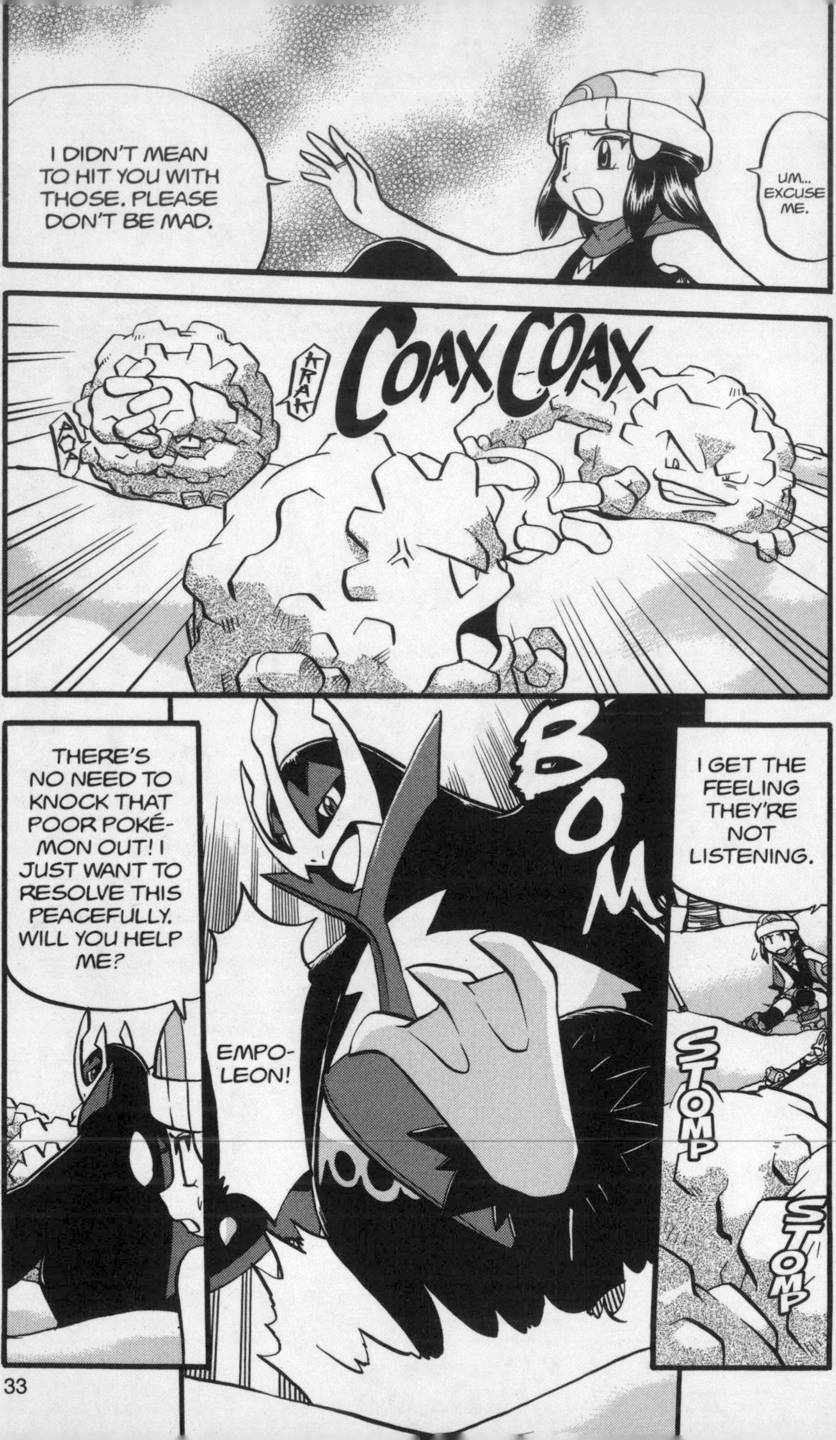
UM... EXCUSE ME.
I DIDN'T MEAN TO HIT YOU WITH THOSE. PLEASE DON'T BE MAD.
KRAK
COAX COAX
I GET THE FEELING THEY'RE NOT LISTENING.
STOMP
STOMP
BOOM
THERE'S NO NEED TO KNOCK THAT POOR POKÉMON OUT! I JUST WANT TO RESOLVE THIS PEACEFULLY. WILL YOU HELP ME?
EMPOLEON!

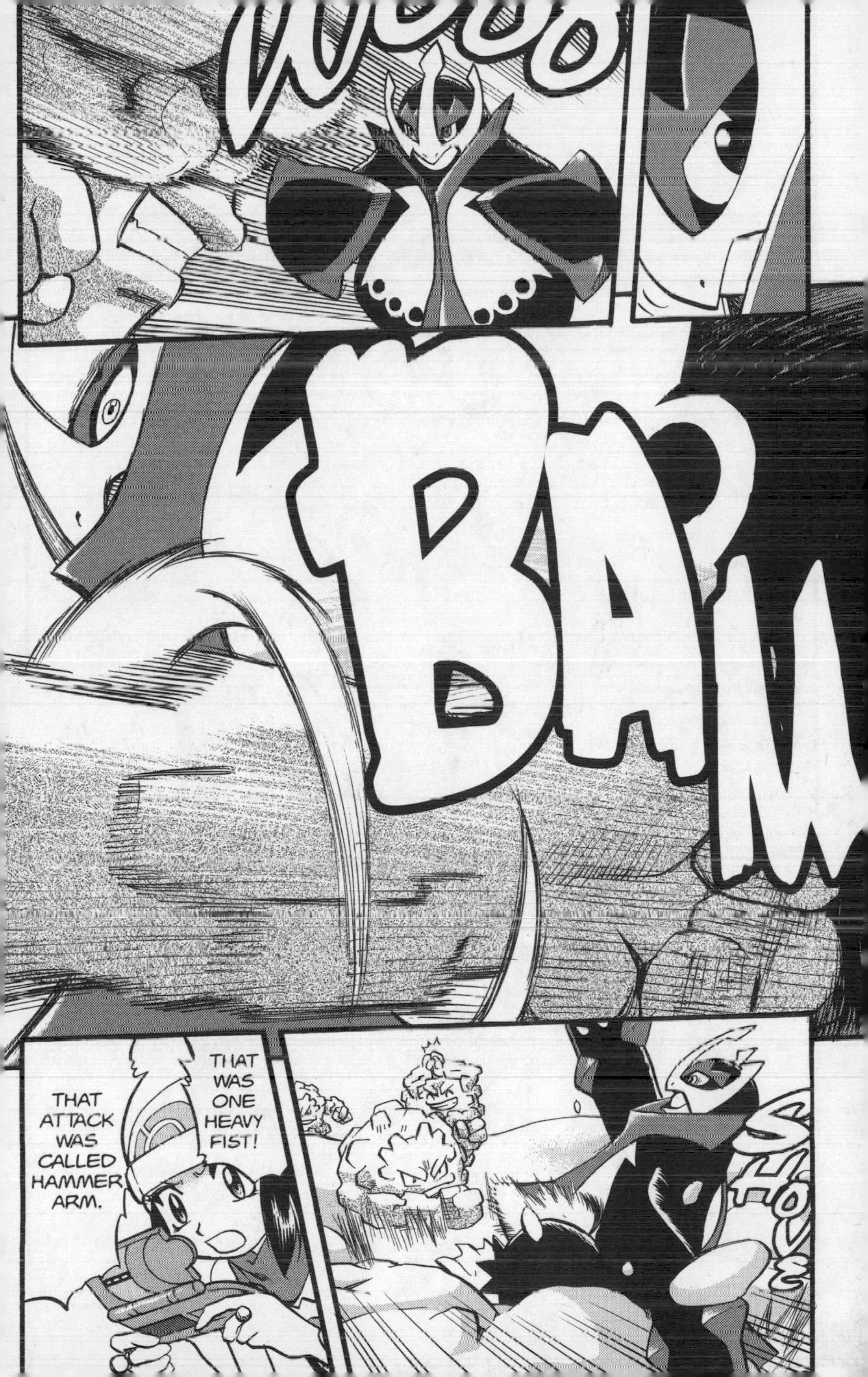
BAM
SHOVE
THAT WAS ONE HEAVY FIST!
THAT ATTACK WAS CALLED HAMMER ARM.

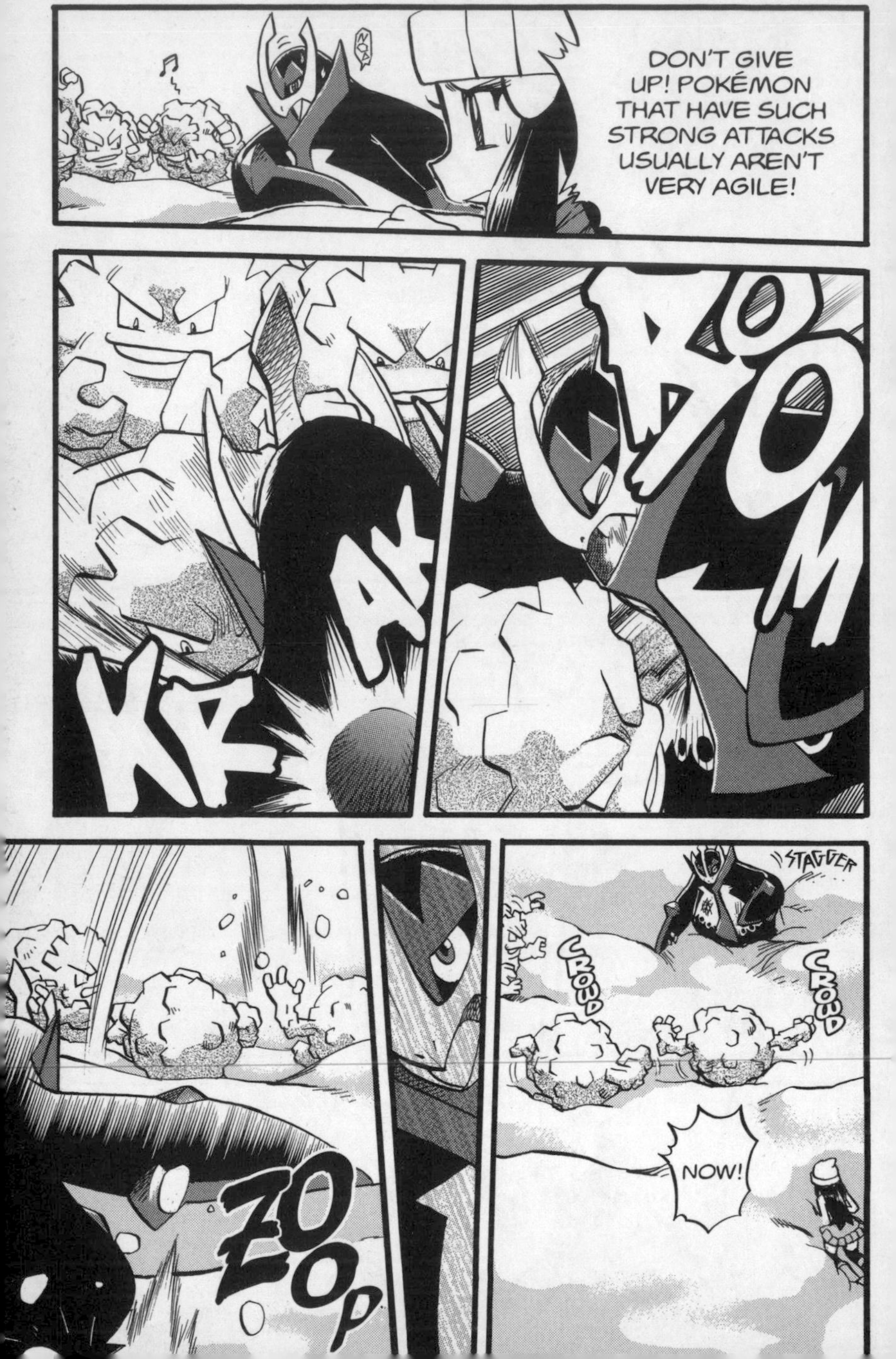
DON'T GIVE UP! POKÉMON THAT HAVE SUCH STRONG ATTACKS USUALLY AREN'T VERY AGILE!
BOOM
KRAK
STAGGER
CROUD
CROUD
NOW!
ZOOP

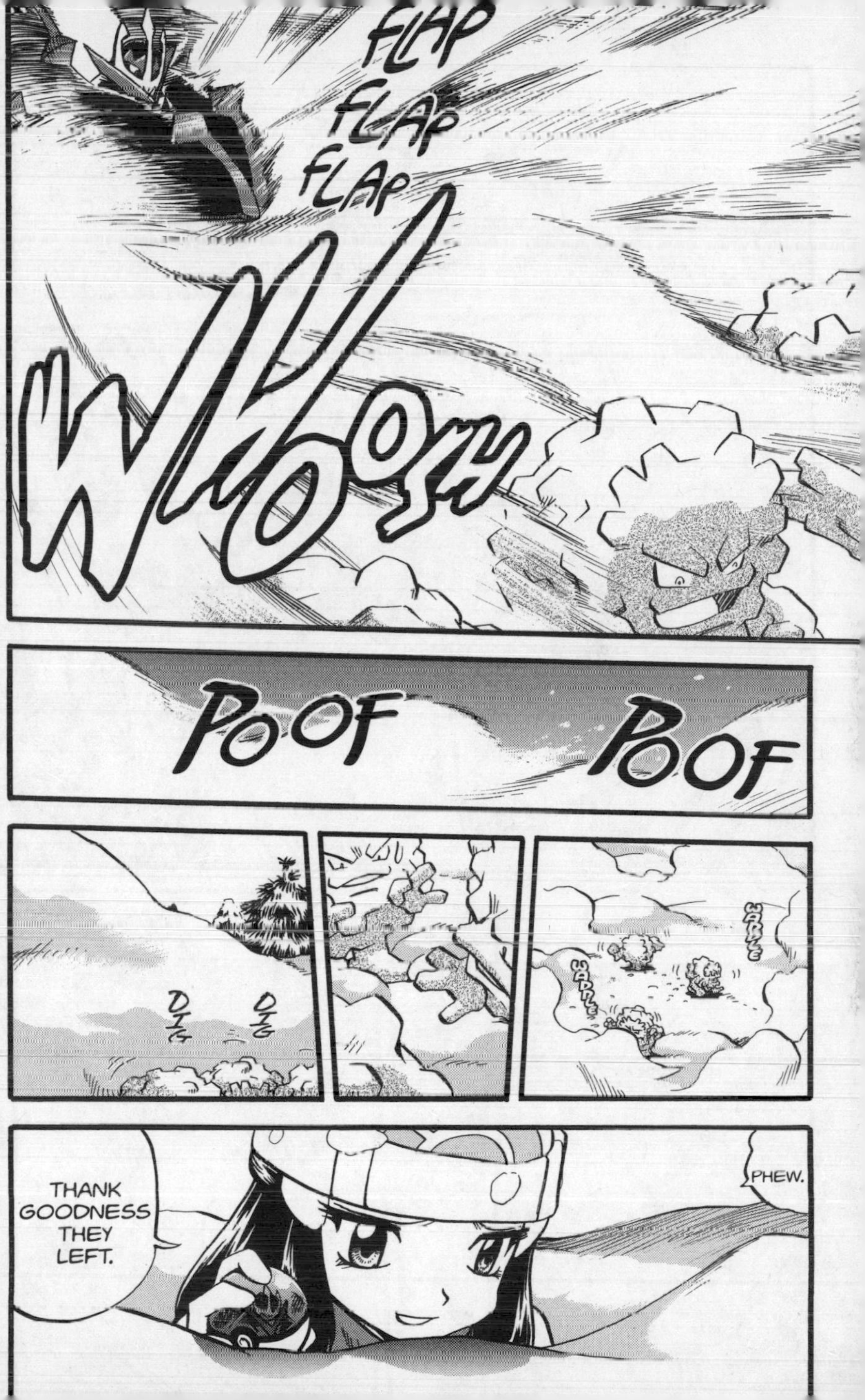
FLAP
FLAP
FLAP
WHOOSH
POOF
POOF
WADDLE
WADDLE
DIG
DIG
PHEW.
THANK GOODNESS THEY LEFT.

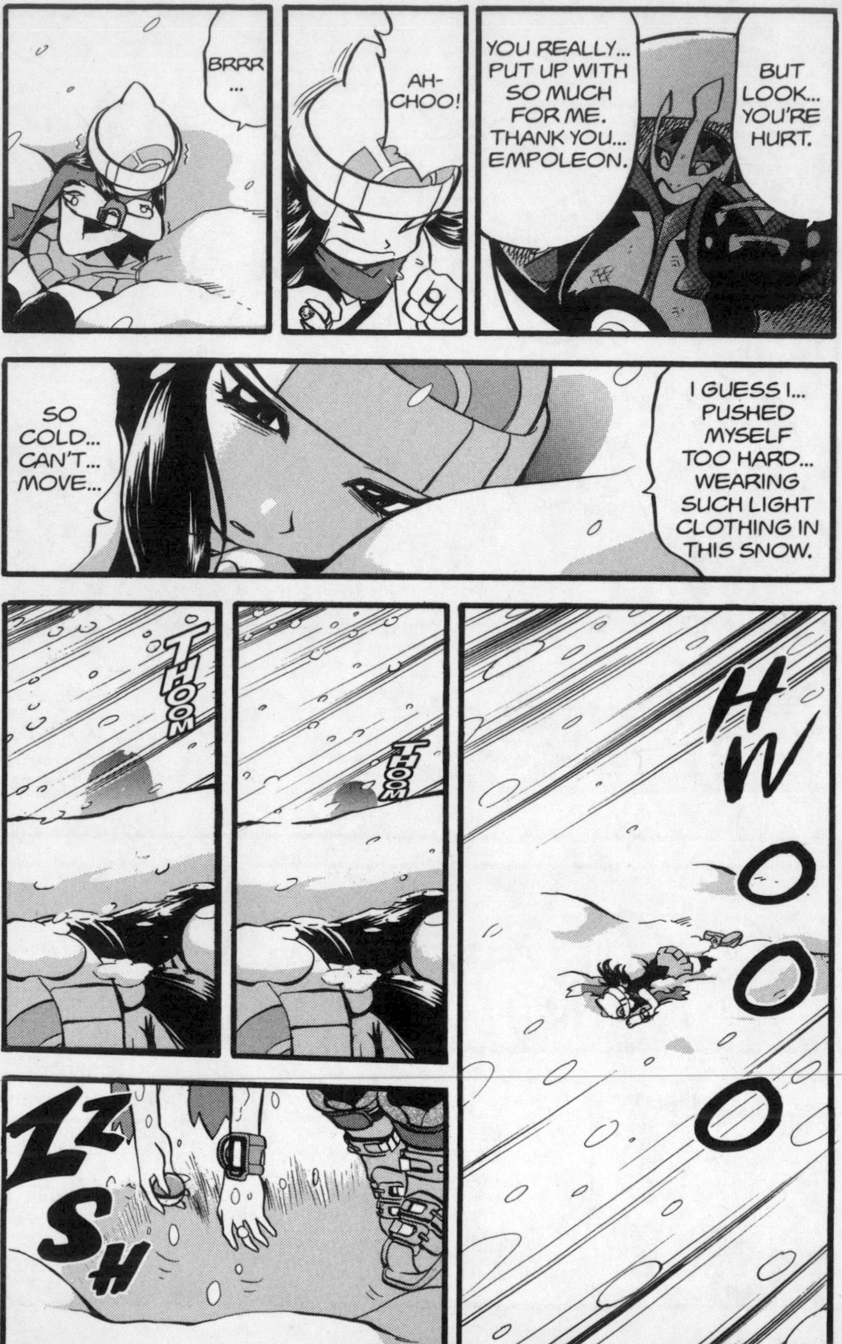
BUT LOOK... YOU'RE HURT.
YOU REALLY... PUT UP WITH SO MUCH FOR ME. THANK YOU... EMPOLEON.
AH-CHOO!
BRRR ...
I GUESS I... PUSHED MYSELF TOO HARD... WEARING SUCH LIGHT CLOTHING IN THIS SNOW.
SO COLD... CAN'T... MOVE...
HWOOOO
THOOM
THOOM
ZZSH

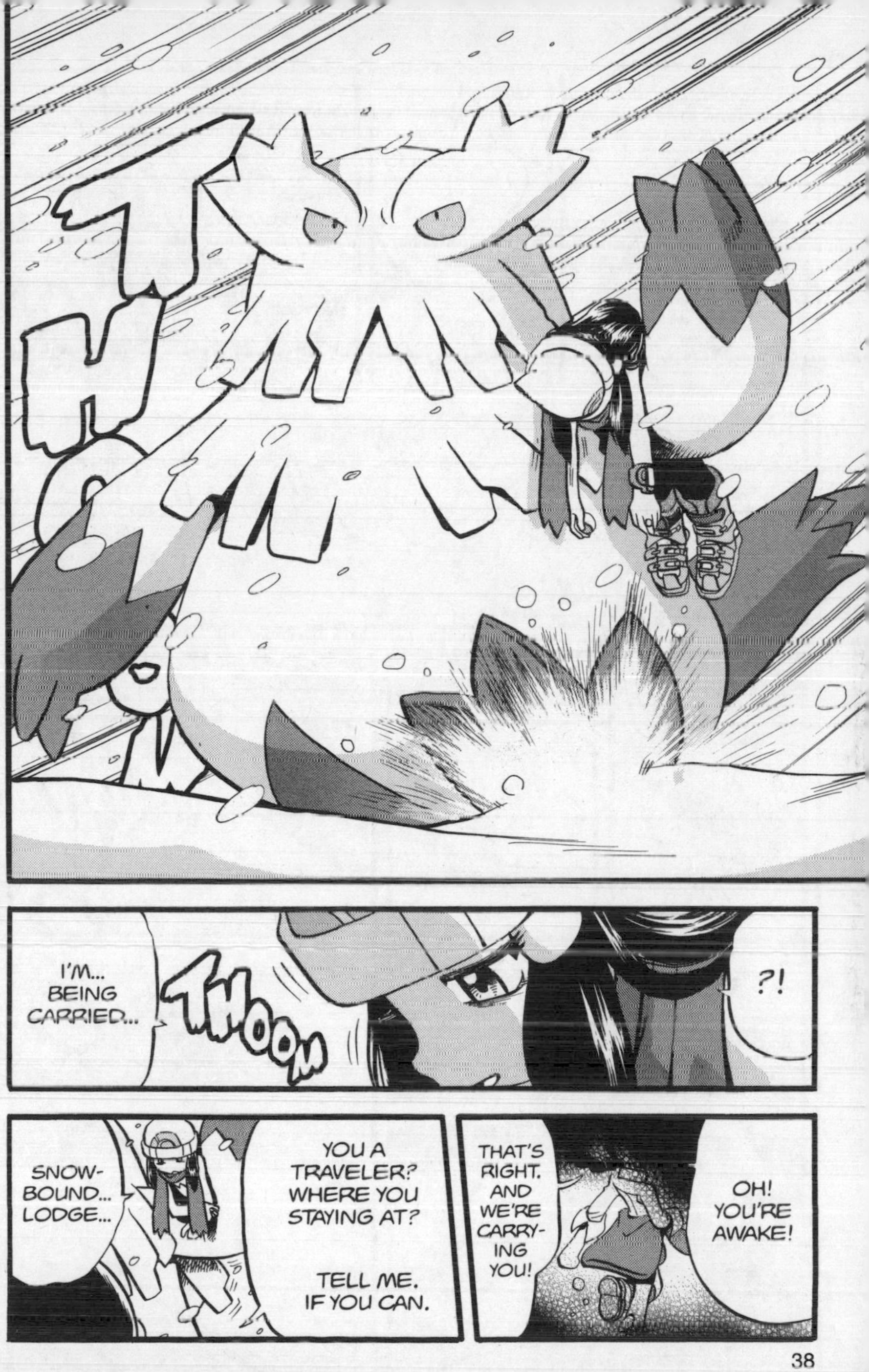
?!
THOOM
I'M... BEING CARRIED...
OH! YOU'RE AWAKE!
THAT'S RIGHT. AND WE'RE CARRY-ING YOU!
YOU A TRAVELER? WHERE YOU STAYING AT?
TELL ME. IF YOU CAN.
SNOW-BOUND... LODGE...

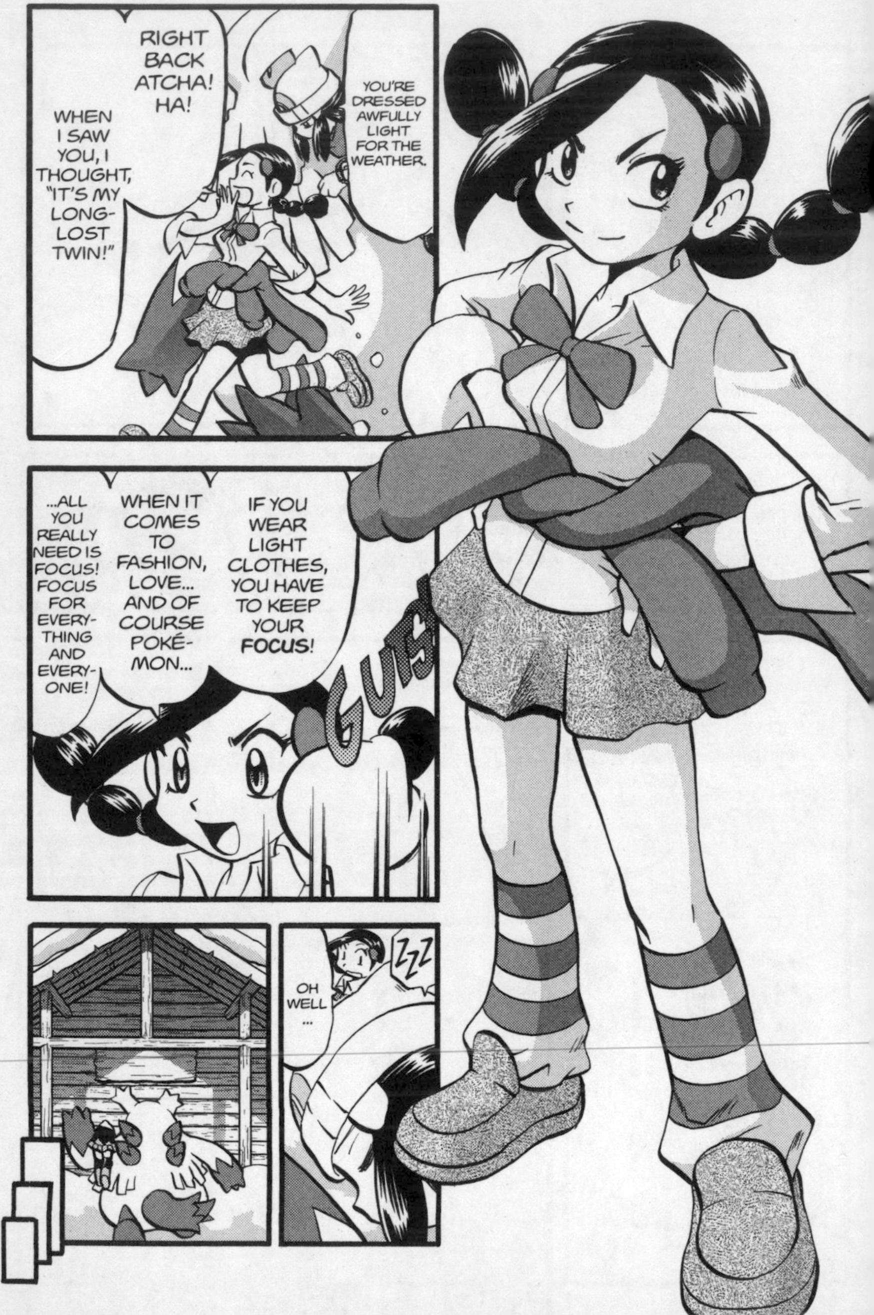

YOU'RE DRESSED AWFULLY LIGHT FOR THE WEATHER.
RIGHT BACK ATCHA! HA!
WHEN I SAW YOU, I THOUGHT, "IT'S MY LONG-LOST TWIN!"
IF YOU WEAR LIGHT CLOTHES, YOU HAVE TO KEEP YOUR **FOCUS**!
WHEN IT COMES TO FASHION, LOVE... AND OF COURSE POKÉMON...
...ALL YOU REALLY NEED IS FOCUS! FOCUS FOR EVERYTHING AND EVERYONE!
GUTS!
ZZZ
OH WELL ...

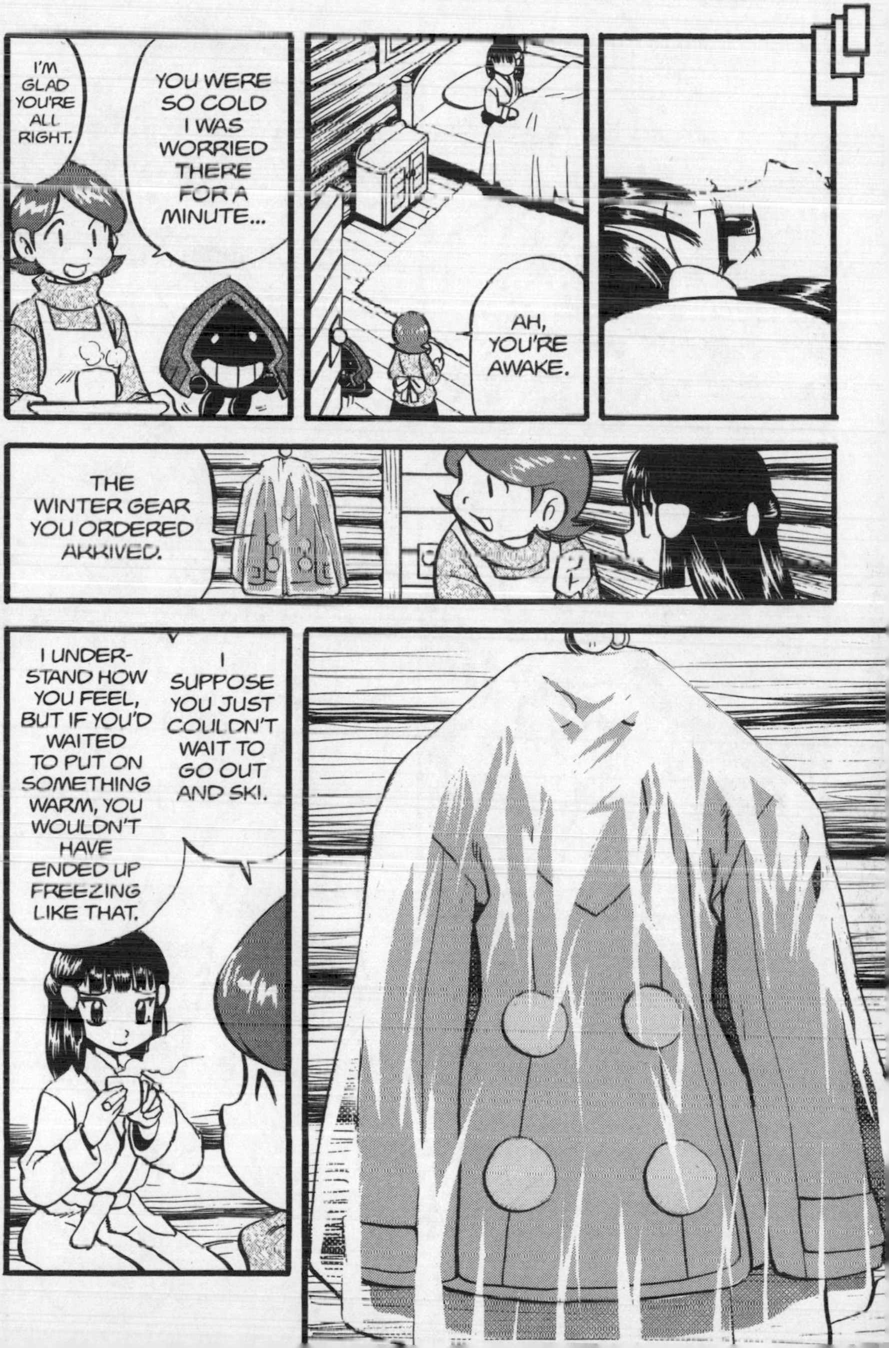
AH, YOU'RE AWAKE.
YOU WERE SO COLD I WAS WORRIED THERE FOR A MINUTE...
I'M GLAD YOU'RE ALL RIGHT.
THE WINTER GEAR YOU ORDERED ARRIVED.
I SUPPOSE YOU JUST COULDN'T WAIT TO GO OUT AND SKI.
I UNDER-STAND HOW YOU FEEL, BUT IF YOU'D WAITED TO PUT ON SOMETHING WARM, YOU WOULDN'T HAVE ENDED UP FREEZING LIKE THAT.

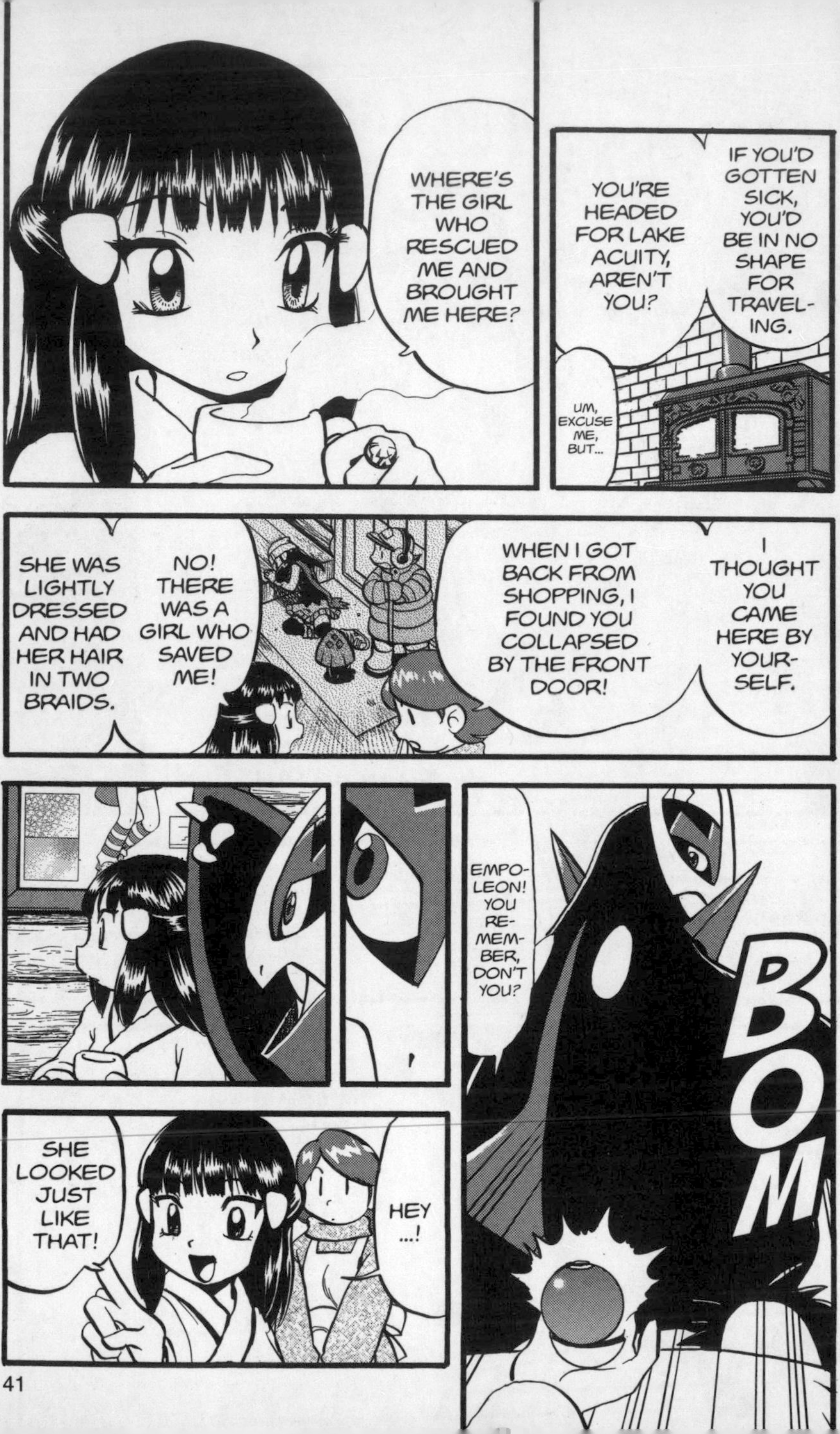
IF YOU'D GOTTEN SICK, YOU'D BE IN NO SHAPE FOR TRAVEL- ING.
YOU'RE HEADED FOR LAKE ACUITY, AREN'T YOU?
UM, EXCUSE ME, BUT...
WHERE'S THE GIRL WHO RESCUED ME AND BROUGHT ME HERE?
I THOUGHT YOU CAME HERE BY YOUR- SELF.
WHEN I GOT BACK FROM SHOPPING, I FOUND YOU COLLAPSED BY THE FRONT DOOR!
NO! THERE WAS A GIRL WHO SAVED ME!
SHE WAS LIGHTLY DRESSED AND HAD HER HAIR IN TWO BRAIDS.
EMPO- LEON! YOU RE- MEM- BER, DON'T YOU?
BOM
HEY ...!
SHE LOOKED JUST LIKE THAT!

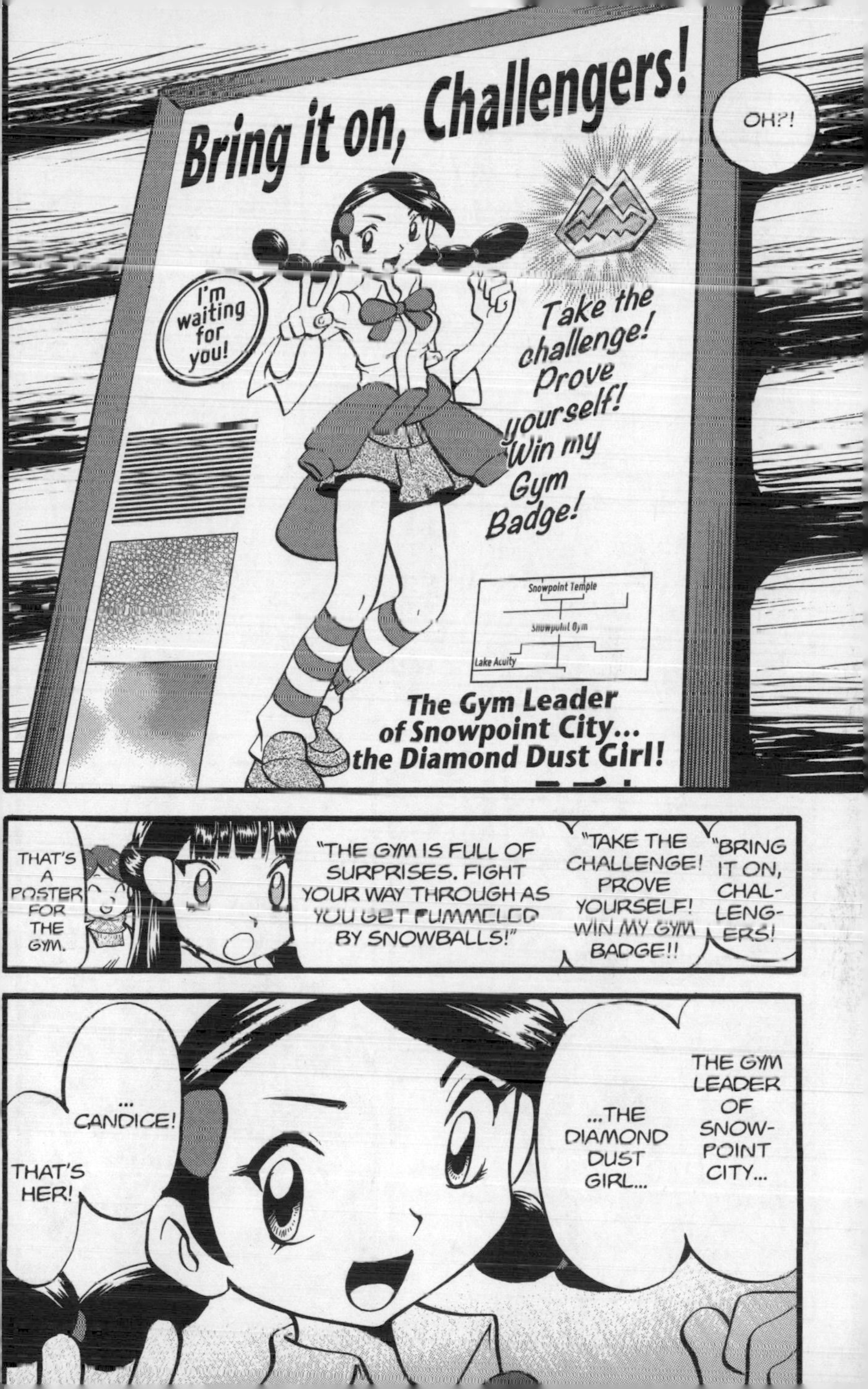
OH?!
Bring it on, Challengers!
I'm waiting for you!
Take the challenge! Prove yourself! Win my Gym Badge!
Snowpoint Temple
Snowpoint Gym
Lake Acuity
The Gym Leader of Snowpoint City... the Diamond Dust Girl!
"BRING IT ON, CHAL-LENG-ERS!
"TAKE THE CHALLENGE! PROVE YOURSELF! WIN MY GYM BADGE!!
"THE GYM IS FULL OF SURPRISES. FIGHT YOUR WAY THROUGH AS YOU GET PUMMELED BY SNOWBALLS!"
THAT'S A POSTER FOR THE GYM.
THE GYM LEADER OF SNOW-POINT CITY...
...THE DIAMOND DUST GIRL...
...CANDICE!
THAT'S HER!

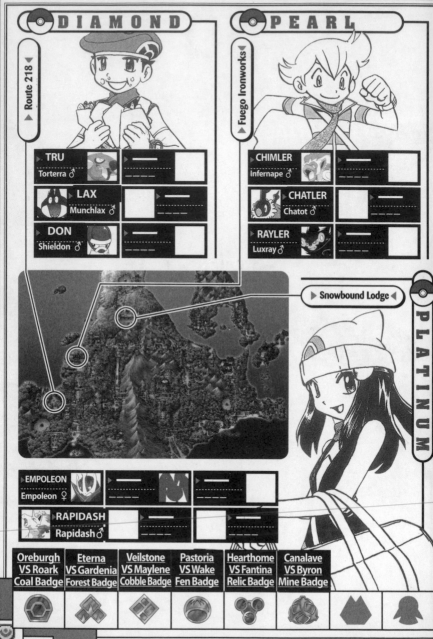

DIAMOND

◄ Route 218 ▼

TRU
Torterra ♂

LAX
Munchlax ♂

DON
Shieldon ♂

PEARL

◄ Fuego Ironworks ▼

CHIMLER
Infernape ♂

CHATLER
Chatot ♂

RAYLER
Luxray ♂

▶ Snowbound Lodge ◀

PLATINUM

▶ **EMPOLEON**
Empoleon ♀

▶ **RAPIDASH**
Rapidash ♂

| Oreburgh VS Roark Coal Badge | Eterna VS Gardenia Forest Badge | Veilstone VS Maylene Cobble Badge | Pastoria VS Wake Fen Badge | Hearthome VS Fantina Relic Badge | Canalave VS Byron Mine Badge | | |

50

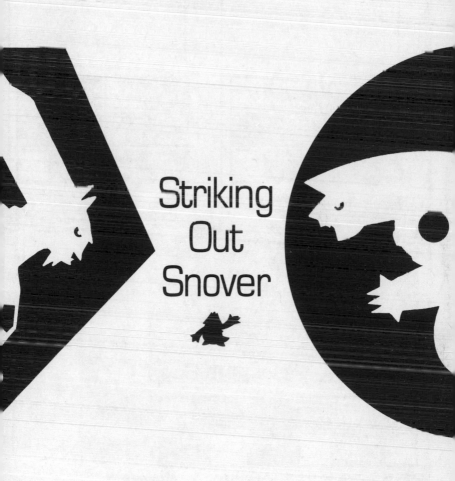

Striking
Out
Snover

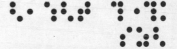

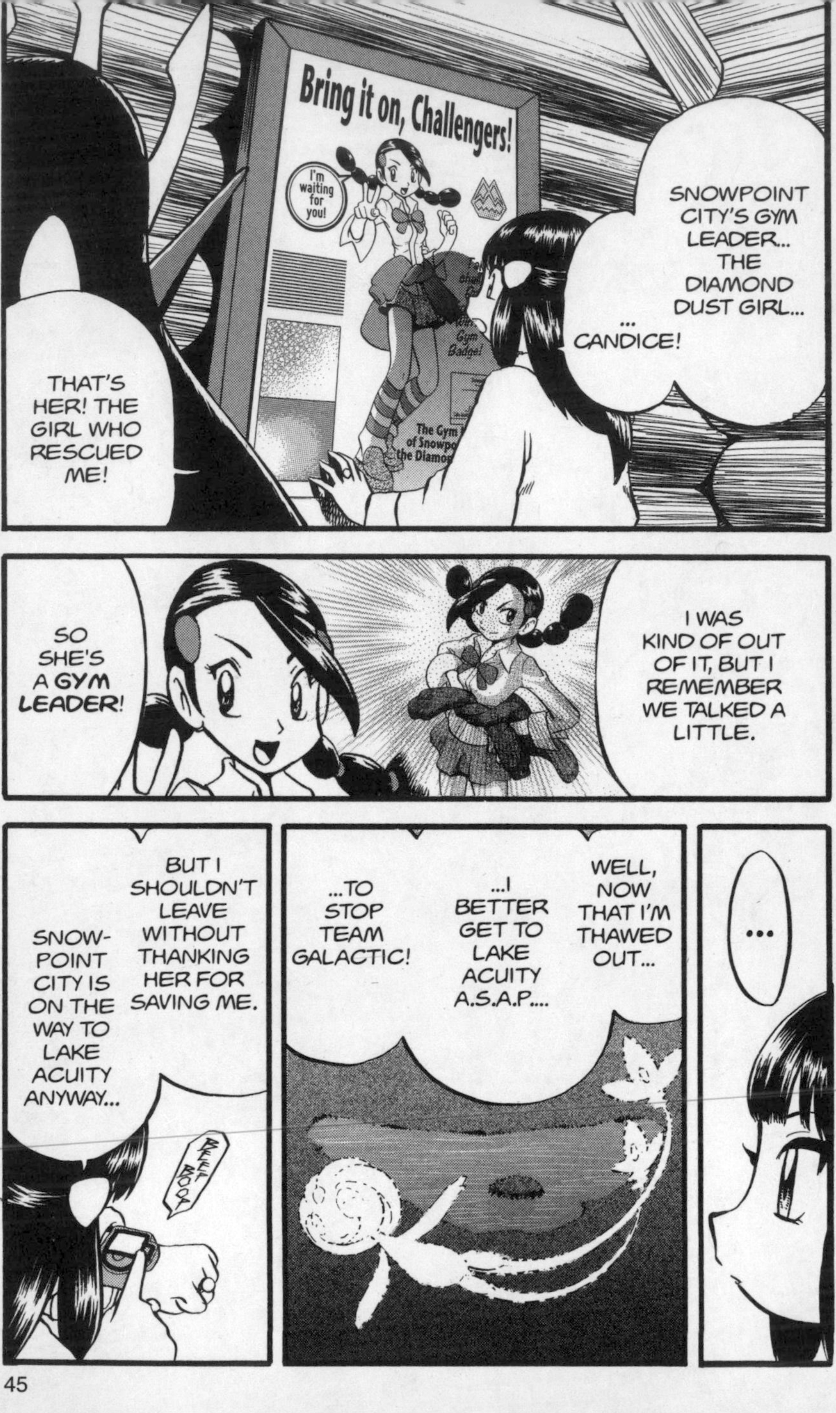
Bring it on, Challengers!
I'm waiting for you!
SNOWPOINT CITY'S GYM LEADER... THE DIAMOND DUST GIRL... ...CANDICE!
THAT'S HER! THE GIRL WHO RESCUED ME!
I WAS KIND OF OUT OF IT, BUT I REMEMBER WE TALKED A LITTLE.
SO SHE'S A GYM LEADER!
...
WELL, NOW THAT I'M THAWED OUT...
...I BETTER GET TO LAKE ACUITY A.S.A.P....
...TO STOP TEAM GALACTIC!
BUT I SHOULDN'T LEAVE WITHOUT THANKING HER FOR SAVING ME.
SNOW-POINT CITY IS ON THE WAY TO LAKE ACUITY ANYWAY...

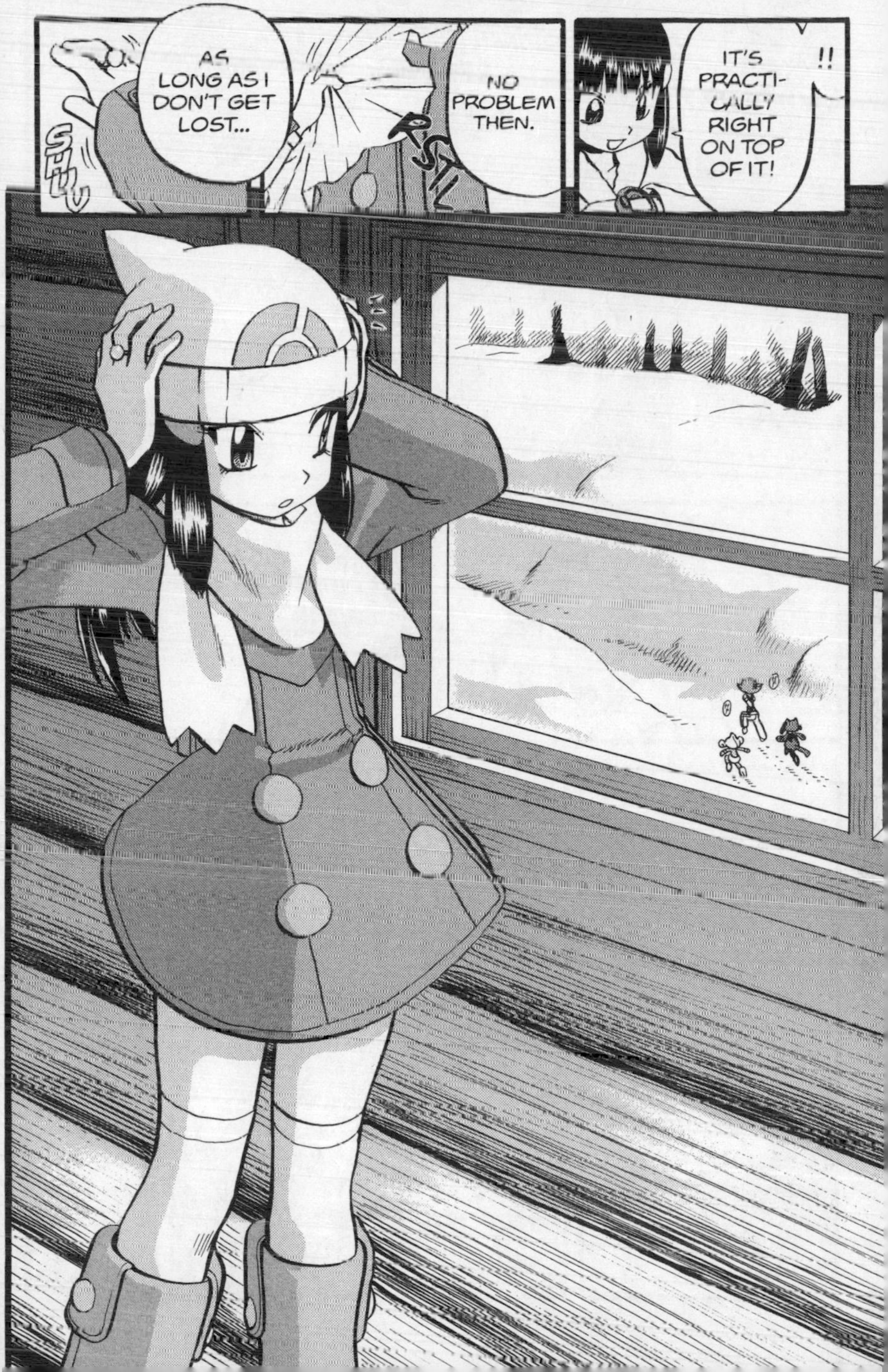
!!
IT'S PRACTI-CALLY RIGHT ON TOP OF IT!
NO PROBLEM THEN.
AS LONG AS I DON'T GET LOST...

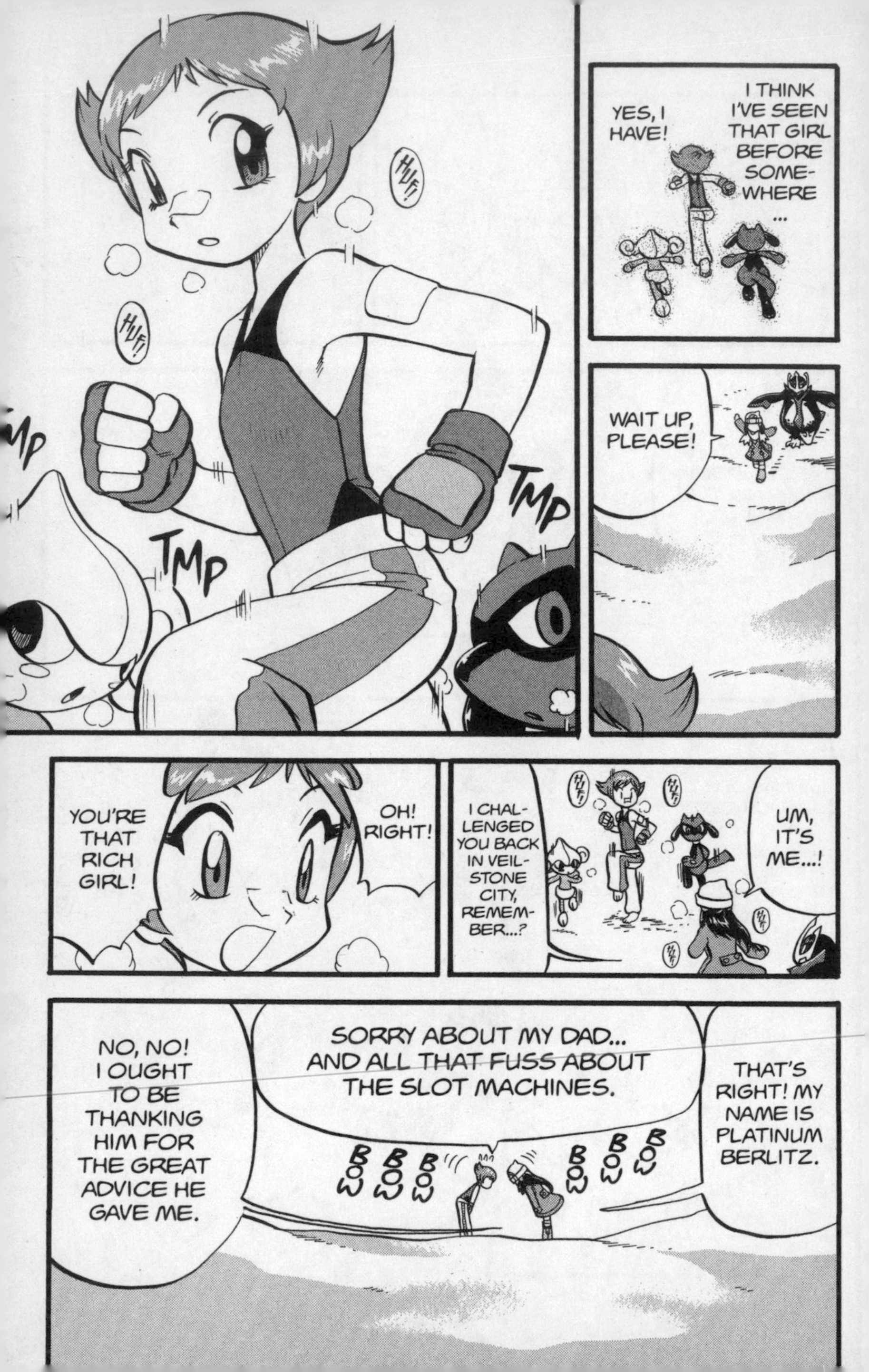
I THINK I'VE SEEN THAT GIRL BEFORE SOME-WHERE ...
YES, I HAVE!
WAIT UP, PLEASE!
HUF!
HUF!
TMP
TMP
TMP
UM, IT'S ME...!
I CHAL-LENGED YOU BACK IN VEIL-STONE CITY, REMEM-BER...?
HUF!
HUF!
OH! RIGHT!
YOU'RE THAT RICH GIRL!
THAT'S RIGHT! MY NAME IS PLATINUM BERLITZ.
SORRY ABOUT MY DAD... AND ALL THAT FUSS ABOUT THE SLOT MACHINES.
BOW BOW BOW
BOW BOW BOW
NO, NO! I OUGHT TO BE THANKING HIM FOR THE GREAT ADVICE HE GAVE ME.

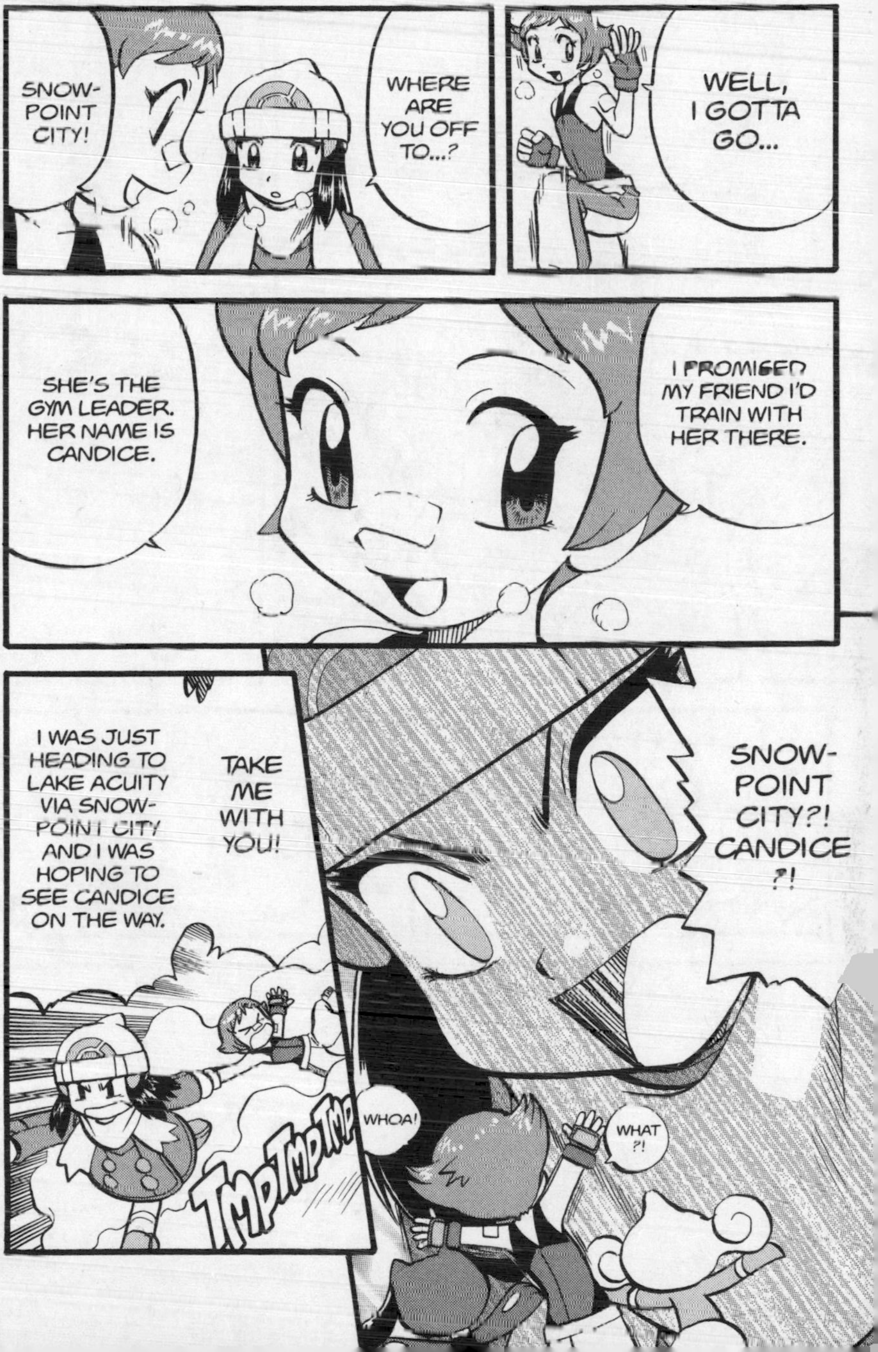
WELL, I GOTTA GO...
WHERE ARE YOU OFF TO...?
SNOW-POINT CITY!
I PROMISED MY FRIEND I'D TRAIN WITH HER THERE.
SHE'S THE GYM LEADER. HER NAME IS CANDICE.
SNOW-POINT CITY?! CANDICE?!
TAKE ME WITH YOU!
I WAS JUST HEADING TO LAKE ACUITY VIA SNOW-POINT CITY AND I WAS HOPING TO SEE CANDICE ON THE WAY.
WHAT?!
WHOA!
TMPTMPTMP

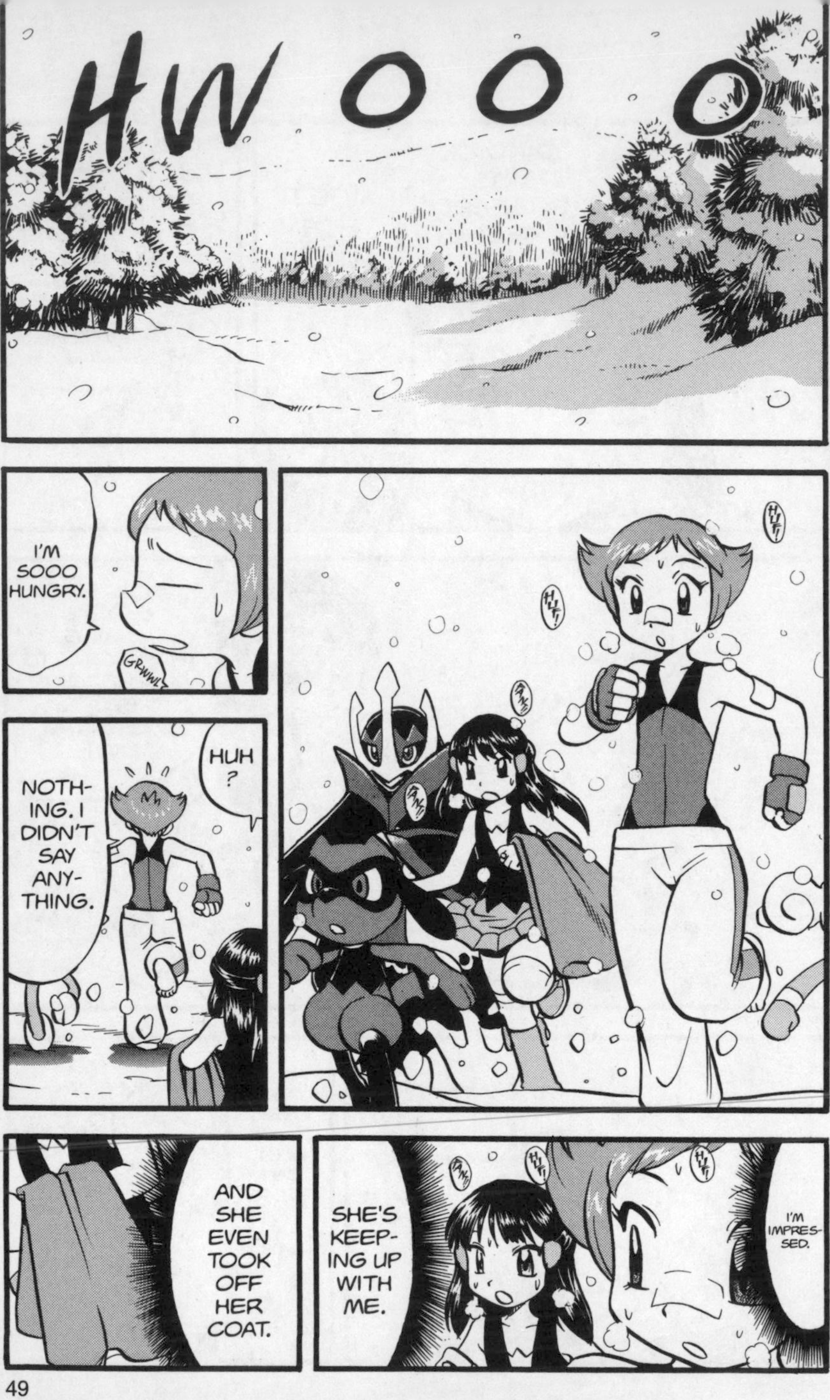
HWOOO
I'M SOOO HUNGRY.
GRWWL
HUH?
NOTHING. I DIDN'T SAY ANYTHING.
I'M IMPRESSED.
SHE'S KEEPING UP WITH ME.
AND SHE EVEN TOOK OFF HER COAT.

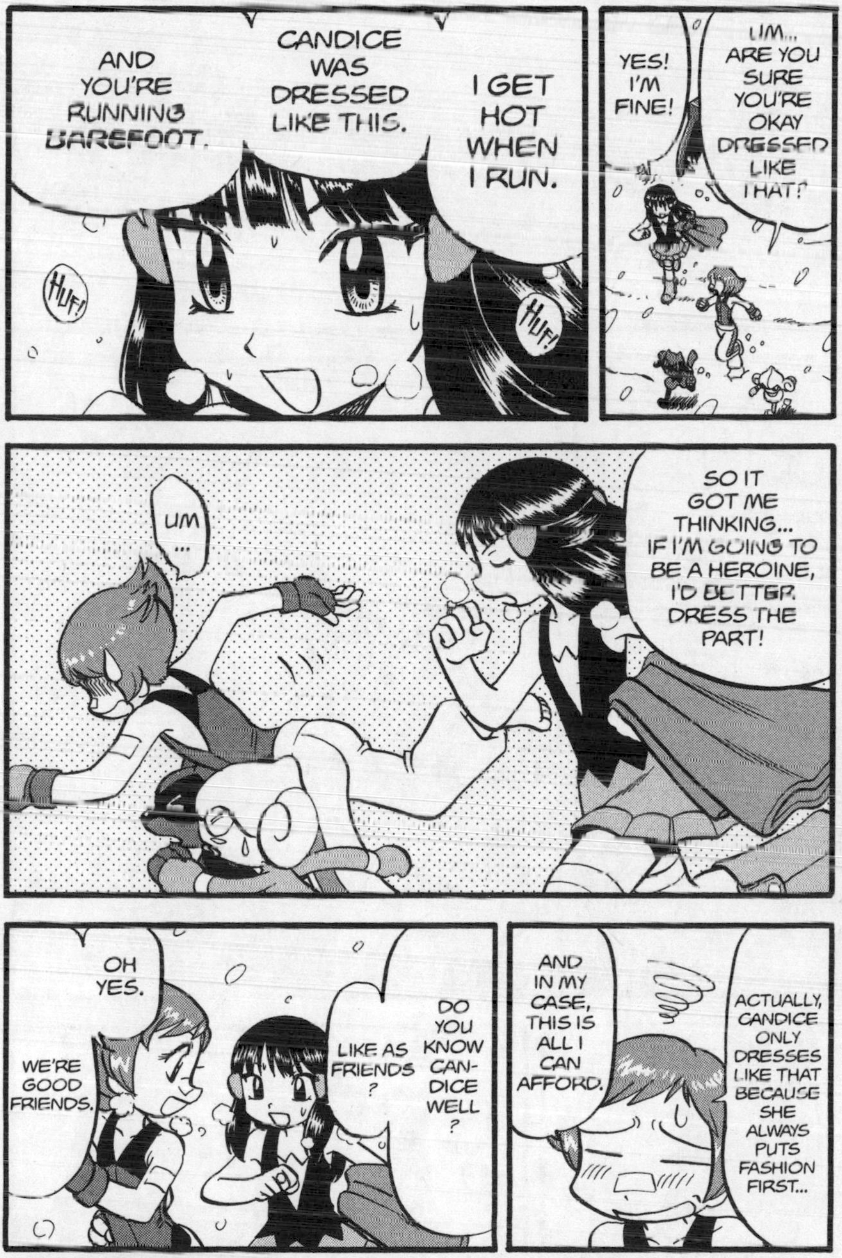
UM... ARE YOU SURE YOU'RE OKAY DRESSED LIKE THAT?
YES! I'M FINE!
I GET HOT WHEN I RUN.
CANDICE WAS DRESSED LIKE THIS.
AND YOU'RE RUNNING BAREFOOT.
HUF!
HUF!
SO IT GOT ME THINKING... IF I'M GOING TO BE A HEROINE, I'D BETTER DRESS THE PART!
UM ...
ACTUALLY, CANDICE ONLY DRESSES LIKE THAT BECAUSE SHE ALWAYS PUTS FASHION FIRST...
AND IN MY CASE, THIS IS ALL I CAN AFFORD.
DO YOU KNOW CAN-DICE WELL?
LIKE AS FRIENDS?
OH YES.
WE'RE GOOD FRIENDS.

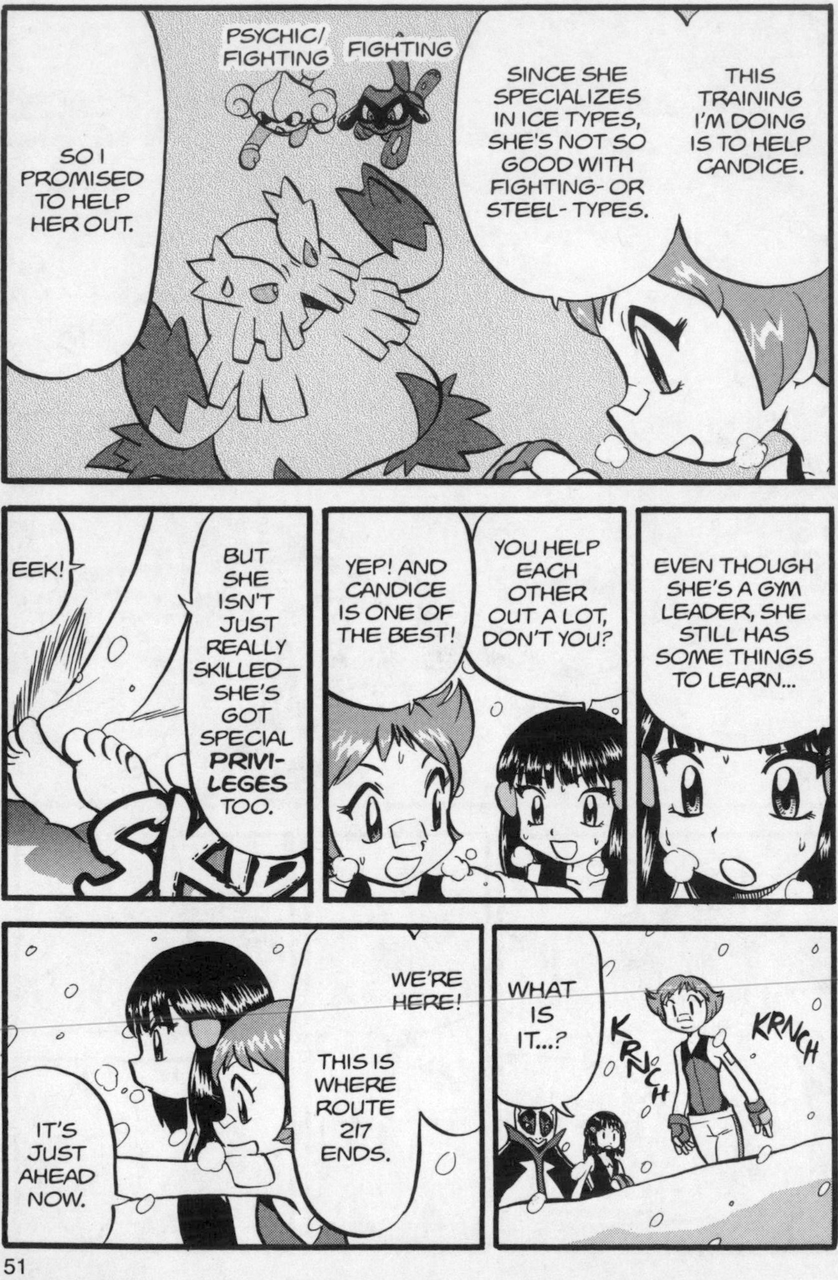
THIS TRAINING I'M DOING IS TO HELP CANDICE.
SINCE SHE SPECIALIZES IN ICE TYPES, SHE'S NOT SO GOOD WITH FIGHTING- OR STEEL- TYPES.
FIGHTING
PSYCHIC/ FIGHTING
SO I PROMISED TO HELP HER OUT.
EVEN THOUGH SHE'S A GYM LEADER, SHE STILL HAS SOME THINGS TO LEARN...
YOU HELP EACH OTHER OUT A LOT, DON'T YOU?
YEP! AND CANDICE IS ONE OF THE BEST!
BUT SHE ISN'T JUST REALLY SKILLED— SHE'S GOT SPECIAL PRIVI- LEGES TOO.
EEK!
SKID
WHAT IS IT...?
KRNCH
KRNCH
WE'RE HERE!
THIS IS WHERE ROUTE 217 ENDS.
IT'S JUST AHEAD NOW.

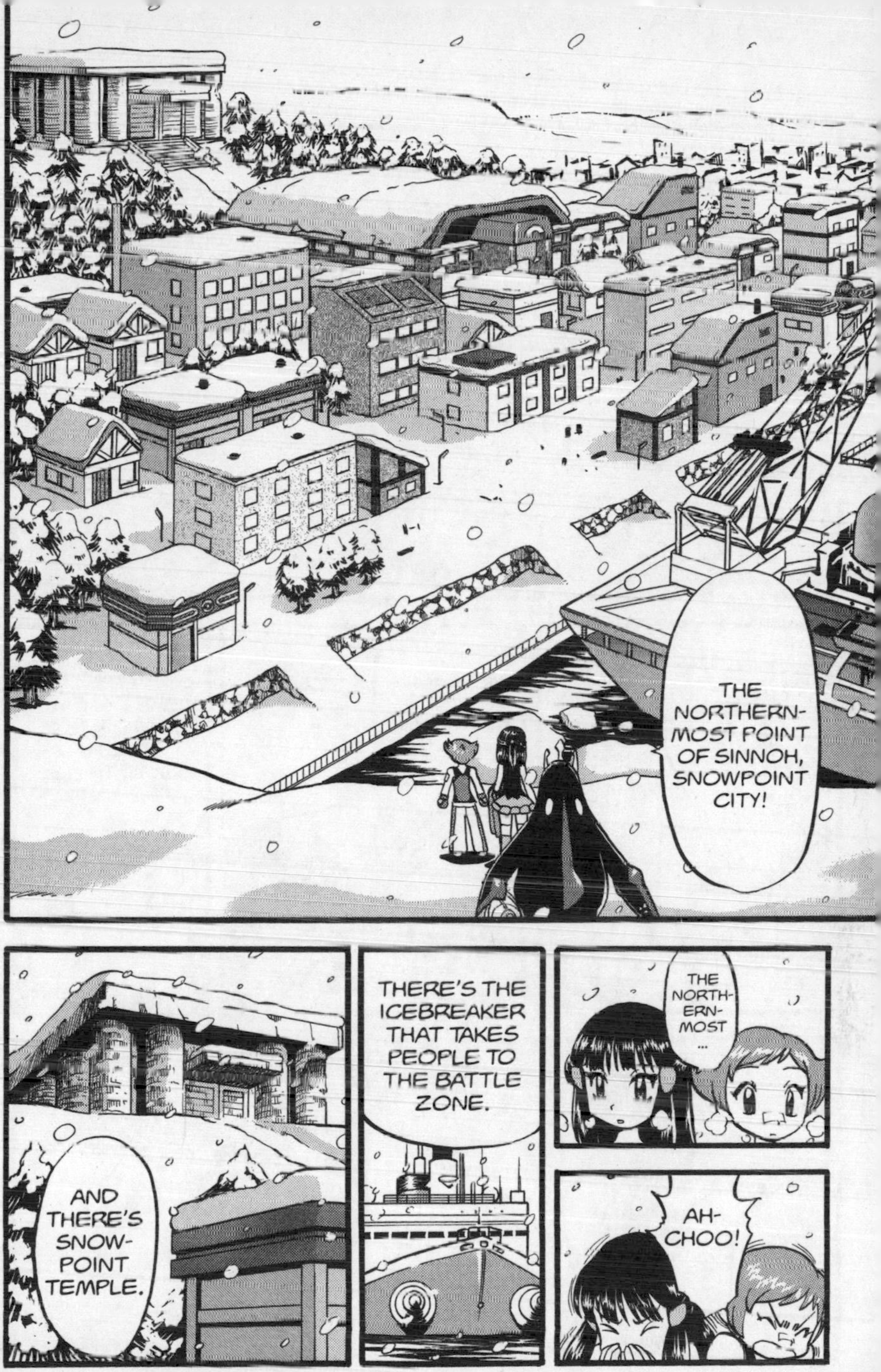
THE NORTHERN-MOST POINT OF SINNOH, SNOWPOINT CITY!
THE NORTH-ERN-MOST ...
AH-CHOO!
THERE'S THE ICEBREAKER THAT TAKES PEOPLE TO THE BATTLE ZONE.
AND THERE'S SNOW-POINT TEMPLE.

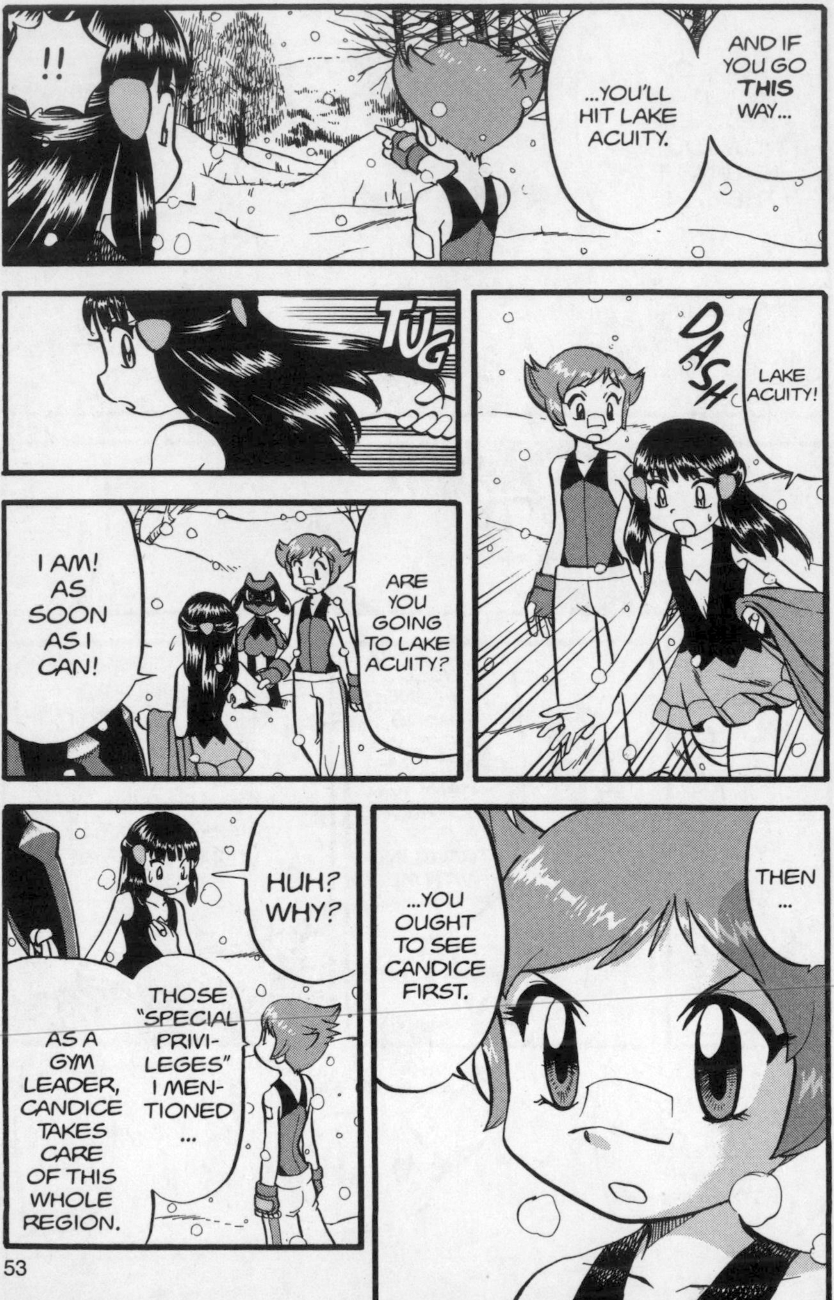
AND IF YOU GO THIS WAY...
...YOU'LL HIT LAKE ACUITY.
!!
DASH
LAKE ACUITY!
TUG
ARE YOU GOING TO LAKE ACUITY?
I AM! AS SOON AS I CAN!
THEN ...
...YOU OUGHT TO SEE CANDICE FIRST.
HUH? WHY?
THOSE "SPECIAL PRIVI-LEGES" I MEN-TIONED ...
AS A GYM LEADER, CANDICE TAKES CARE OF THIS WHOLE REGION.

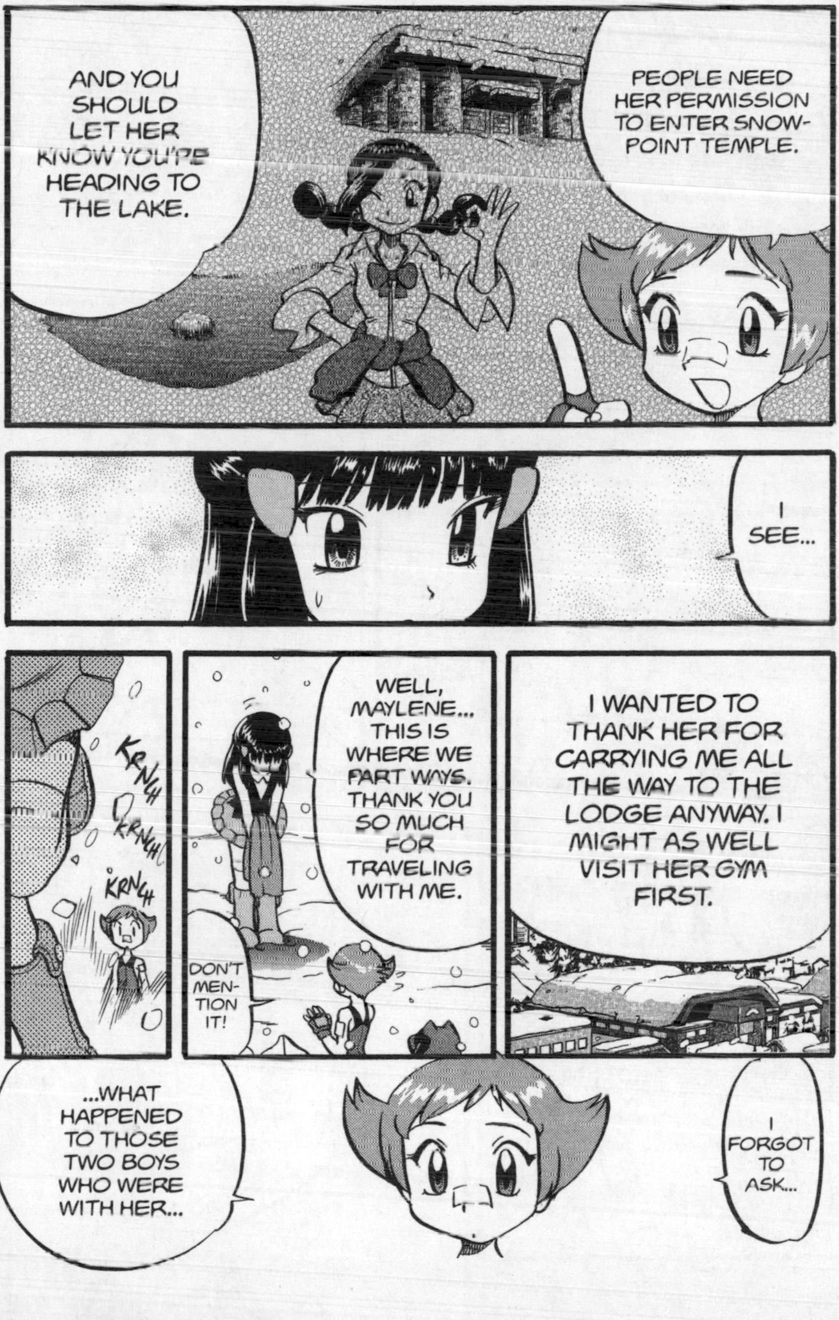
PEOPLE NEED HER PERMISSION TO ENTER SNOW-POINT TEMPLE.
AND YOU SHOULD LET HER KNOW YOU'RE HEADING TO THE LAKE.
I SEE...
I WANTED TO THANK HER FOR CARRYING ME ALL THE WAY TO THE LODGE ANYWAY. I MIGHT AS WELL VISIT HER GYM FIRST.
WELL, MAYLENE... THIS IS WHERE WE PART WAYS. THANK YOU SO MUCH FOR TRAVELING WITH ME.
DON'T MEN-TION IT!
KRNCH
KRNCH
KRNCH
I FORGOT TO ASK...
...WHAT HAPPENED TO THOSE TWO BOYS WHO WERE WITH HER...

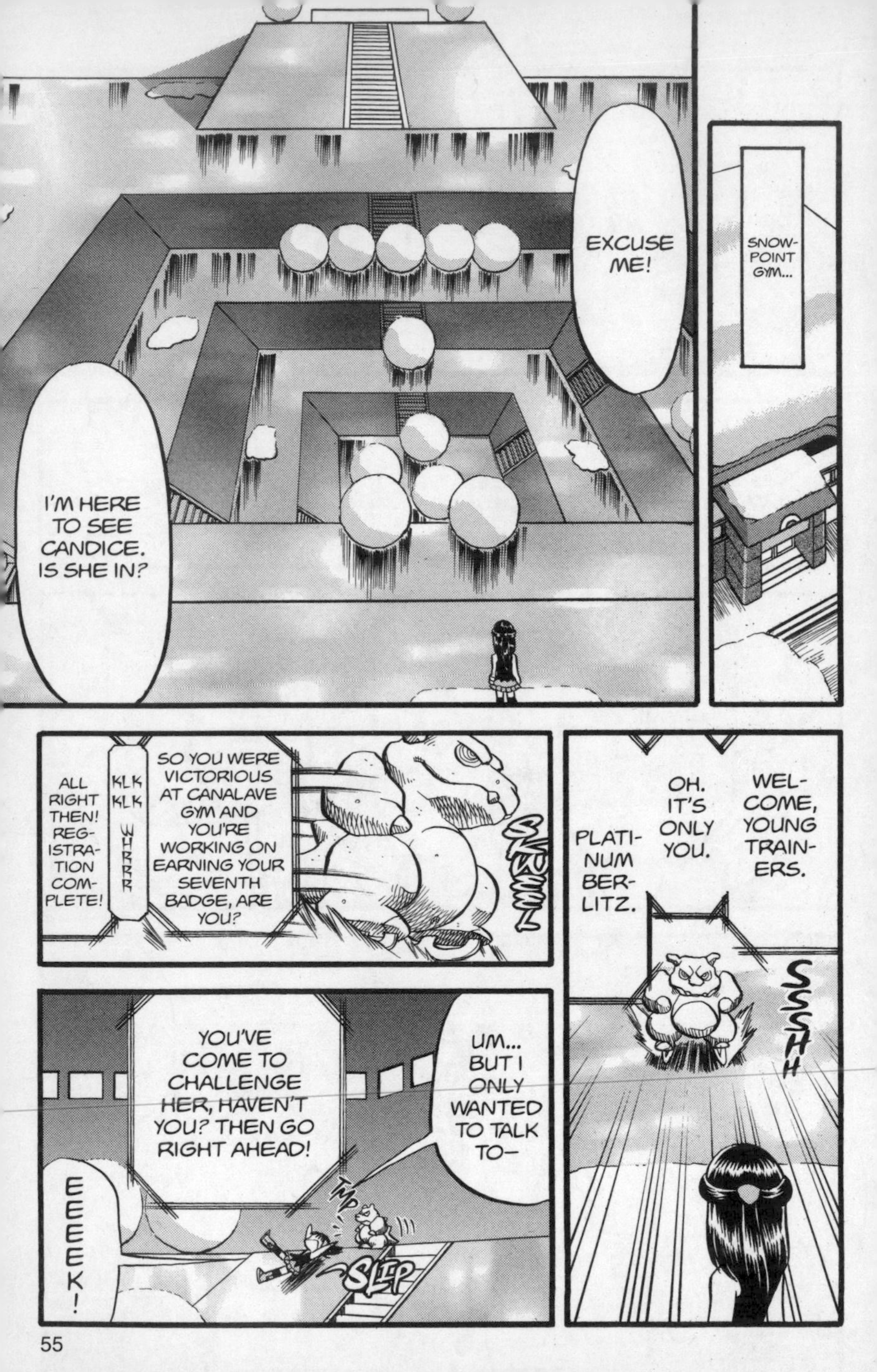
SNOWPOINT GYM...
EXCUSE ME!
I'M HERE TO SEE CANDICE. IS SHE IN?
WELCOME, YOUNG TRAINERS.
OH. IT'S ONLY YOU.
PLATINUM BERLITZ.
SSSHH
SO YOU WERE VICTORIOUS AT CANALAVE GYM AND YOU'RE WORKING ON EARNING YOUR SEVENTH BADGE, ARE YOU?
KLK KLK WHRRR
ALL RIGHT THEN! REGISTRATION COMPLETE!
UM... BUT I ONLY WANTED TO TALK TO—
YOU'VE COME TO CHALLENGE HER, HAVEN'T YOU? THEN GO RIGHT AHEAD!
TMP
SLIP
EEEEEK!

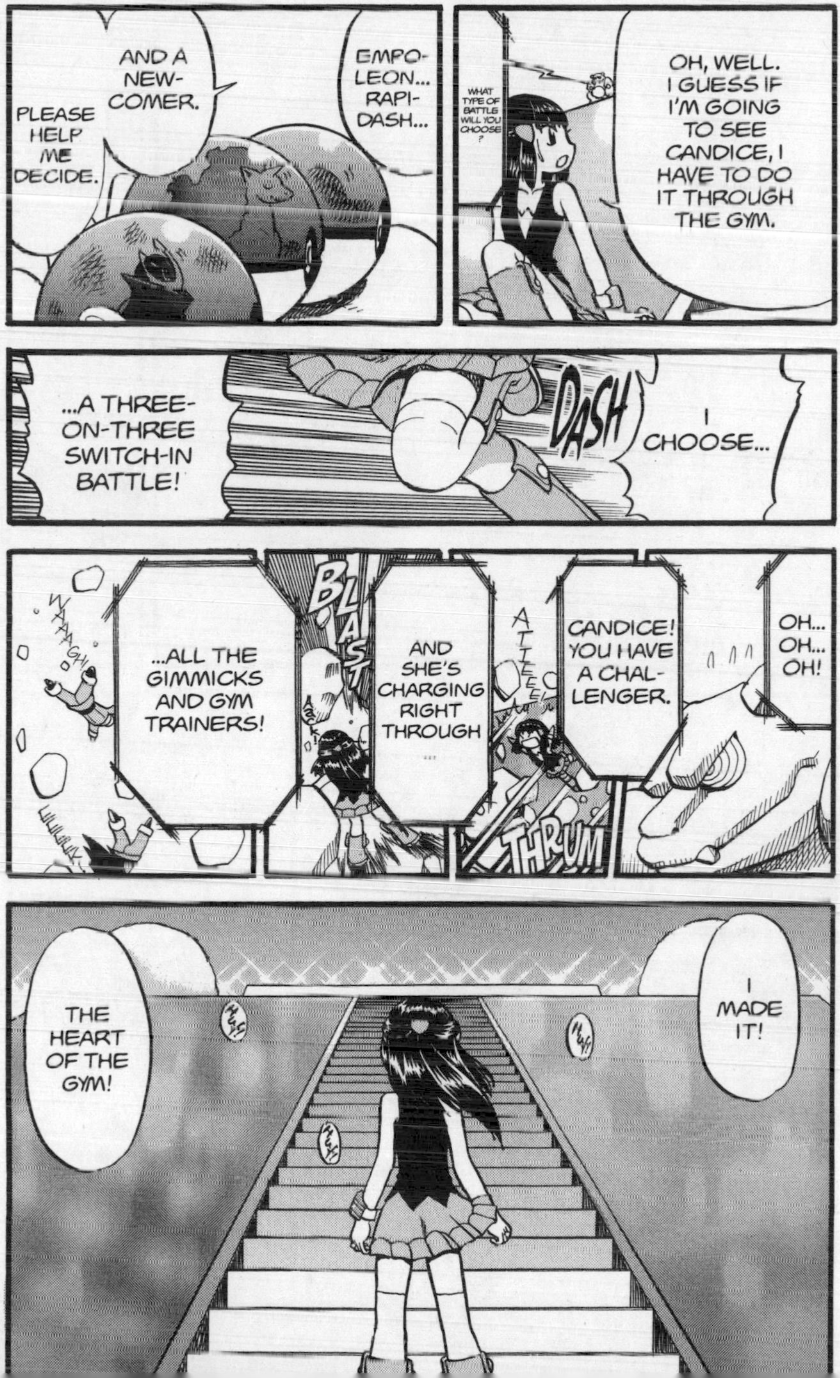
OH, WELL. I GUESS IF I'M GOING TO SEE CANDICE, I HAVE TO DO IT THROUGH THE GYM.
WHAT TYPE OF BATTLE WILL YOU CHOOSE?
EMPO-LEON... RAPI-DASH...
AND A NEW-COMER.
PLEASE HELP ME DECIDE.
I CHOOSE...
DASH
...A THREE-ON-THREE SWITCH-IN BATTLE!
OH... OH... OH!
CANDICE! YOU HAVE A CHAL-LENGER.
AIEEEE!
THRUM
AND SHE'S CHARGING RIGHT THROUGH
BLAST
ACK!
...ALL THE GIMMICKS AND GYM TRAINERS!
WAAAGH!
I MADE IT!
THE HEART OF THE GYM!

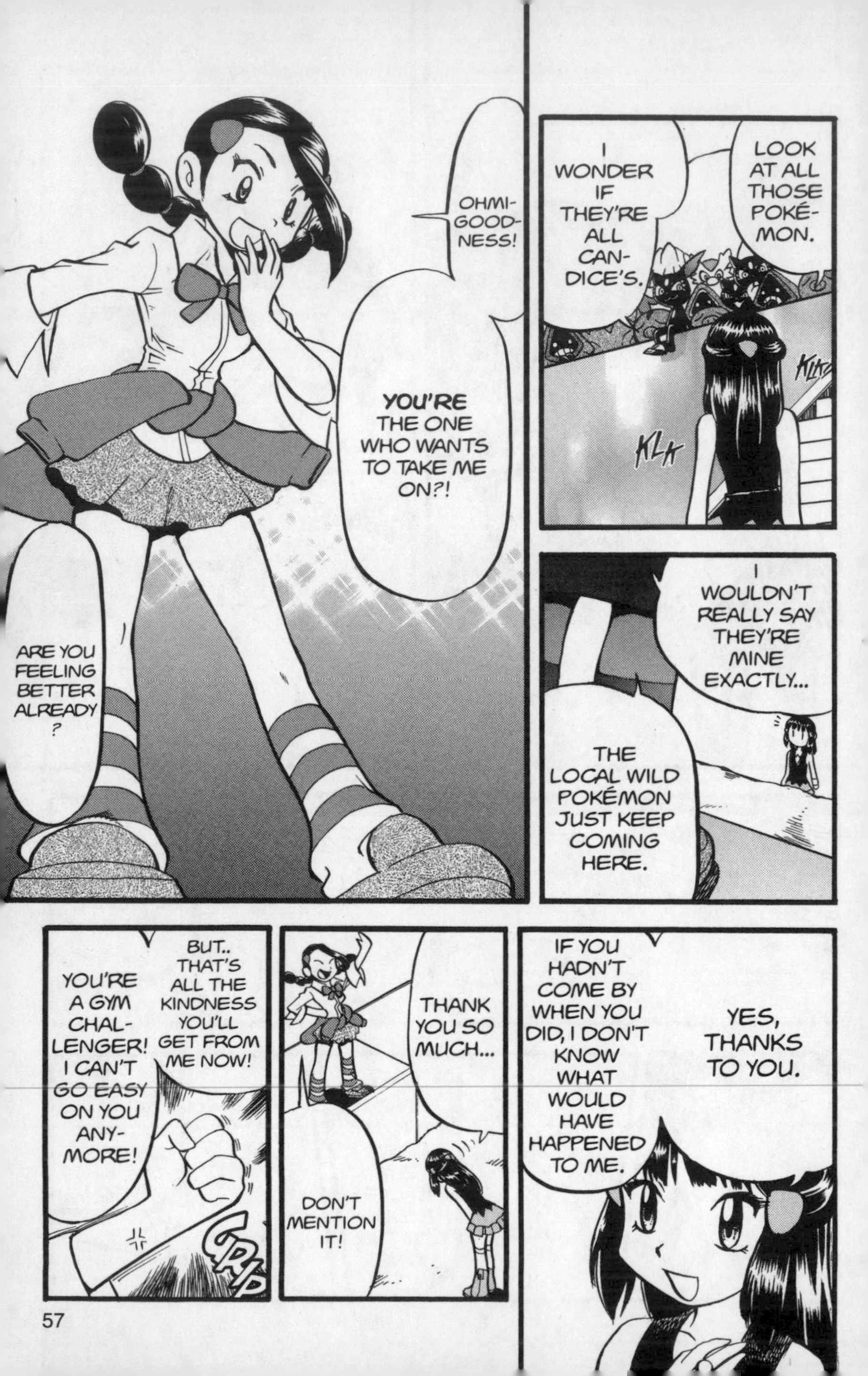
LOOK AT ALL THOSE POKÉ-MON.
I WONDER IF THEY'RE ALL CAN-DICE'S.
KLK
KLK
I WOULDN'T REALLY SAY THEY'RE MINE EXACTLY...
THE LOCAL WILD POKÉMON JUST KEEP COMING HERE.
OHMI-GOOD-NESS!
YOU'RE THE ONE WHO WANTS TO TAKE ME ON?!
ARE YOU FEELING BETTER ALREADY ?
YES, THANKS TO YOU.
IF YOU HADN'T COME BY WHEN YOU DID, I DON'T KNOW WHAT WOULD HAVE HAPPENED TO ME.
THANK YOU SO MUCH...
DON'T MENTION IT!
BUT.. THAT'S ALL THE KINDNESS YOU'LL GET FROM ME NOW!
YOU'RE A GYM CHAL-LENGER! I CAN'T GO EASY ON YOU ANY-MORE!
GRIP

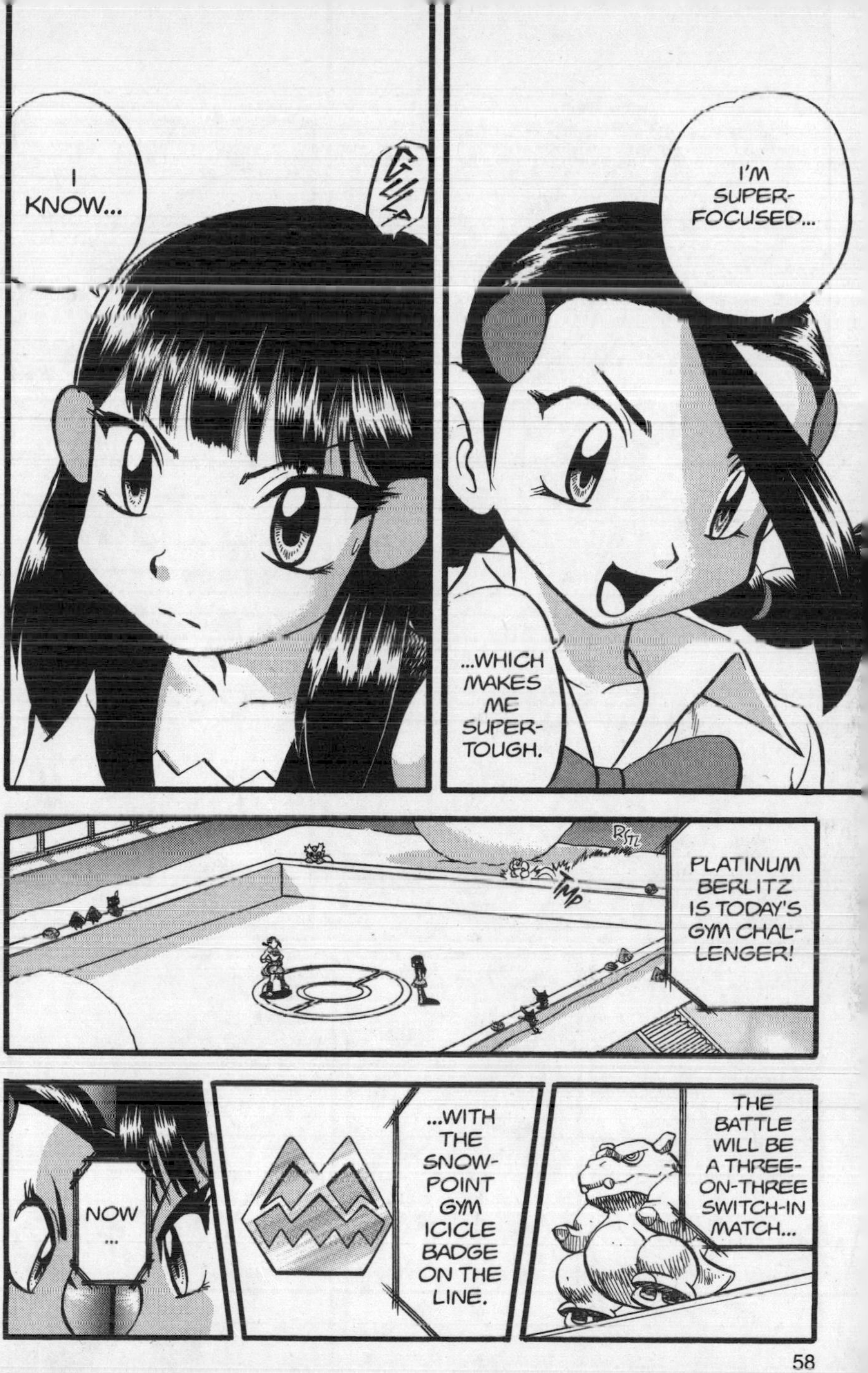
I'M SUPER-FOCUSED...
...WHICH MAKES ME SUPER-TOUGH.
I KNOW...
PLATINUM BERLITZ IS TODAY'S GYM CHALLENGER!
THE BATTLE WILL BE A THREE-ON-THREE SWITCH-IN MATCH...
...WITH THE SNOWPOINT GYM ICICLE BADGE ON THE LINE.
NOW ...

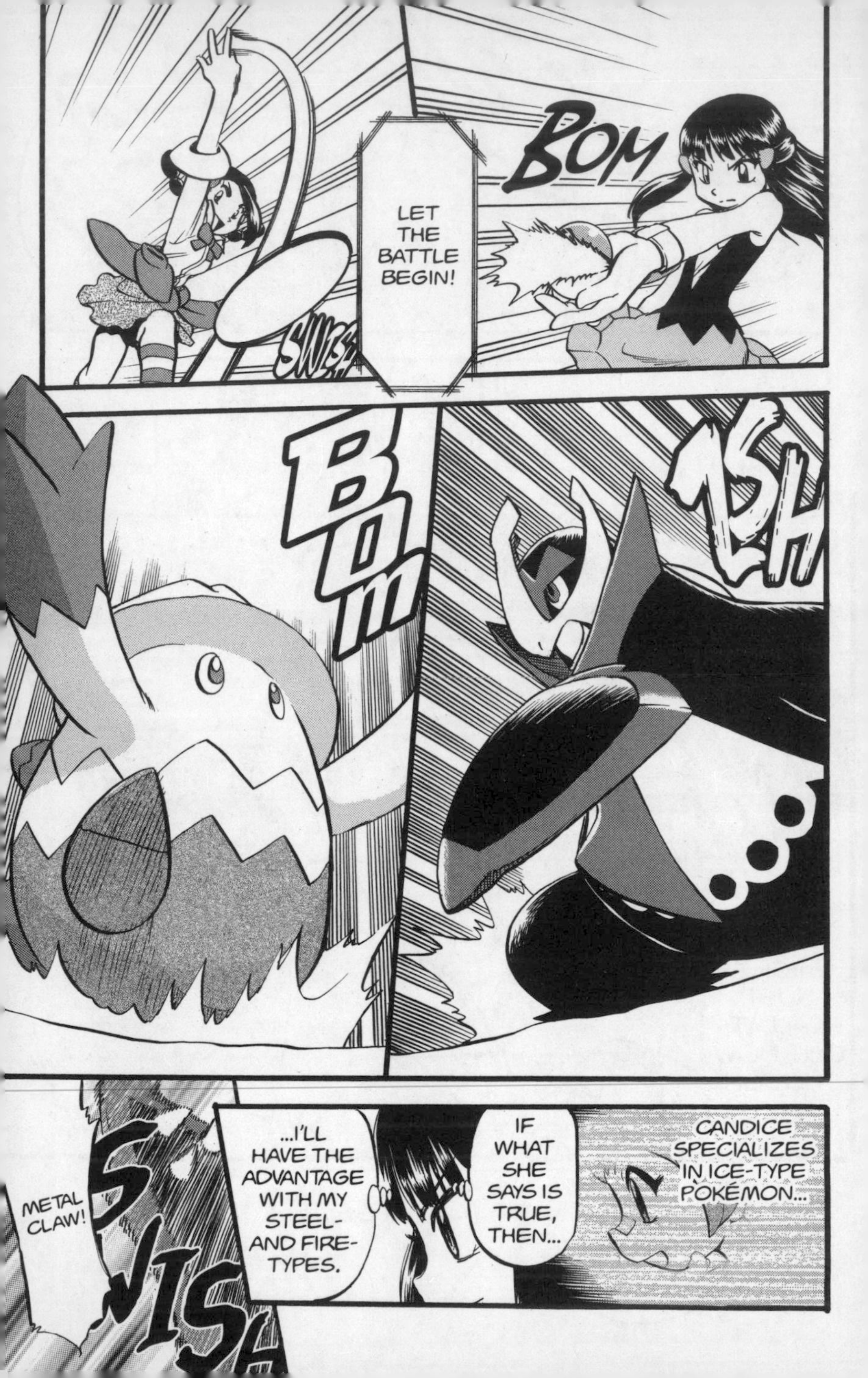
BOM
LET THE BATTLE BEGIN!
SWISH
SH
BOM
CANDICE SPECIALIZES IN ICE-TYPE POKÉMON...
IF WHAT SHE SAYS IS TRUE, THEN...
...I'LL HAVE THE ADVANTAGE WITH MY STEEL- AND FIRE-TYPES.
METAL CLAW!
SWISH

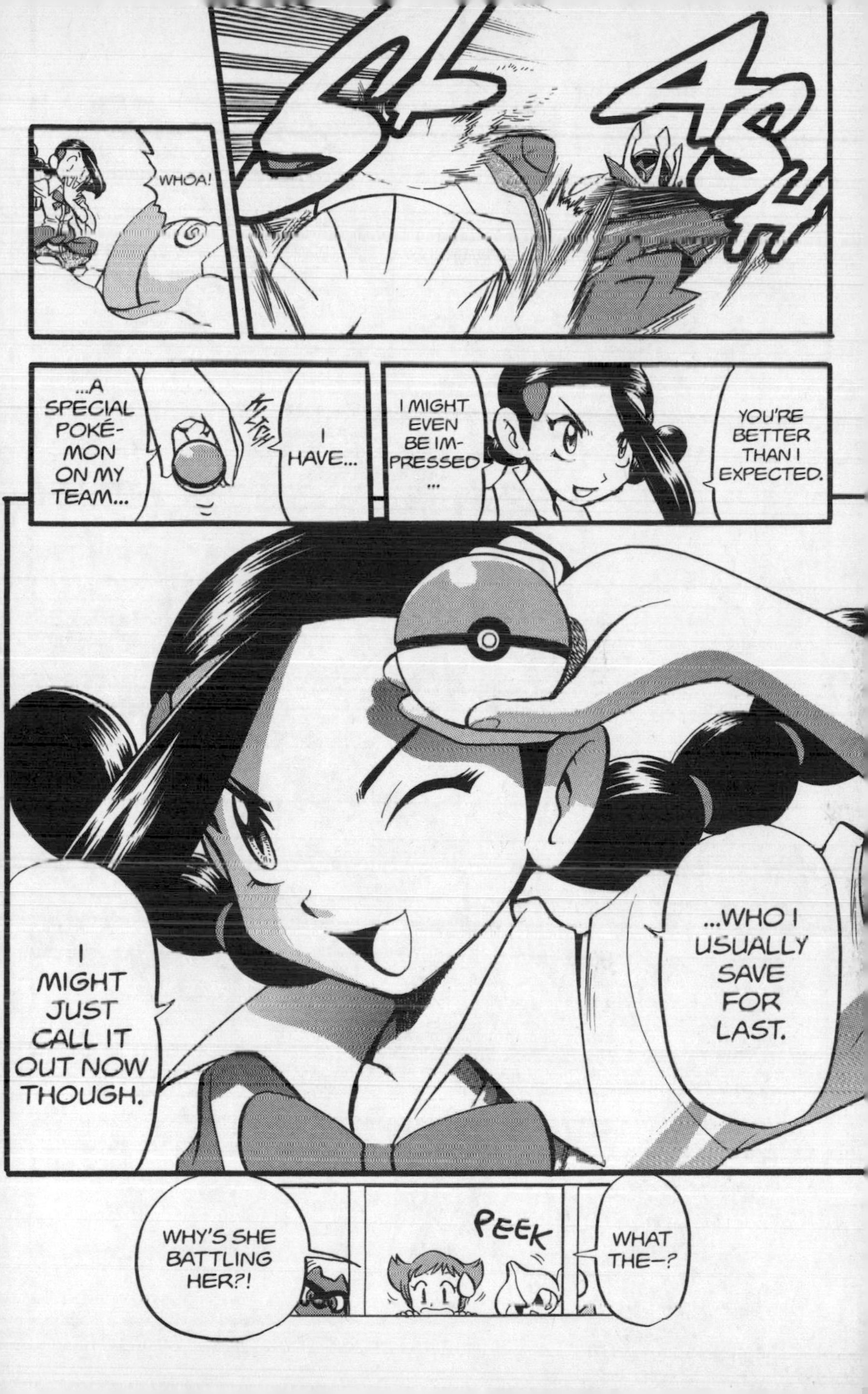
SLASH
WHOA!
YOU'RE BETTER THAN I EXPECTED.
I MIGHT EVEN BE IMPRESSED...
I HAVE...
...A SPECIAL POKÉMON ON MY TEAM...
...WHO I USUALLY SAVE FOR LAST.
I MIGHT JUST CALL IT OUT NOW THOUGH.
WHAT THE–?
PEEK
WHY'S SHE BATTLING HER?!

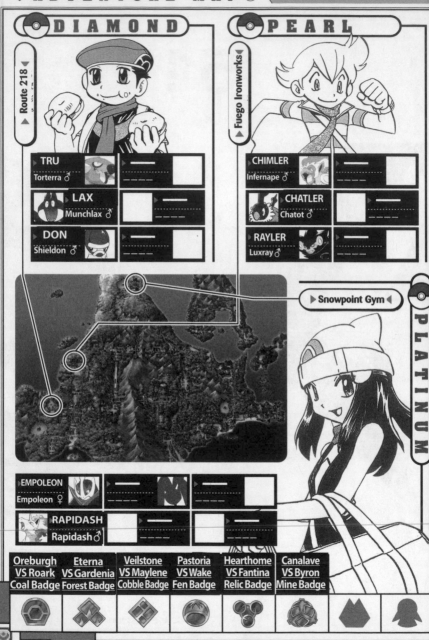

ADVENTURE MAP

DIAMOND

◀ Route 218 ▼

TRU
Torterra ♂

LAX
Munchlax ♂

DON
Shieldon ♂

PEARL

◀ Fuego Ironworks ▼

CHIMLER
Infernape ♂

CHATLER
Chatot ♂

RAYLER
Luxray ♂

▶ Snowpoint Gym ◀

PLATINUM

EMPOLEON
Empoleon ♀

RAPIDASH
Rapidash ♂

Oreburgh	Eterna	Veilstone	Pastoria	Hearthome	Canalave
VS Roark	VS Gardenia	VS Maylene	VS Wake	VS Fantina	VS Byron
Coal Badge	Forest Badge	Cobble Badge	Fen Badge	Relic Badge	Mine Badge

51

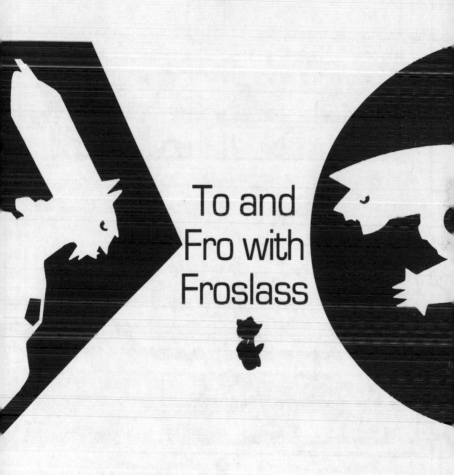

To and
Fro with
Froslass

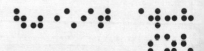

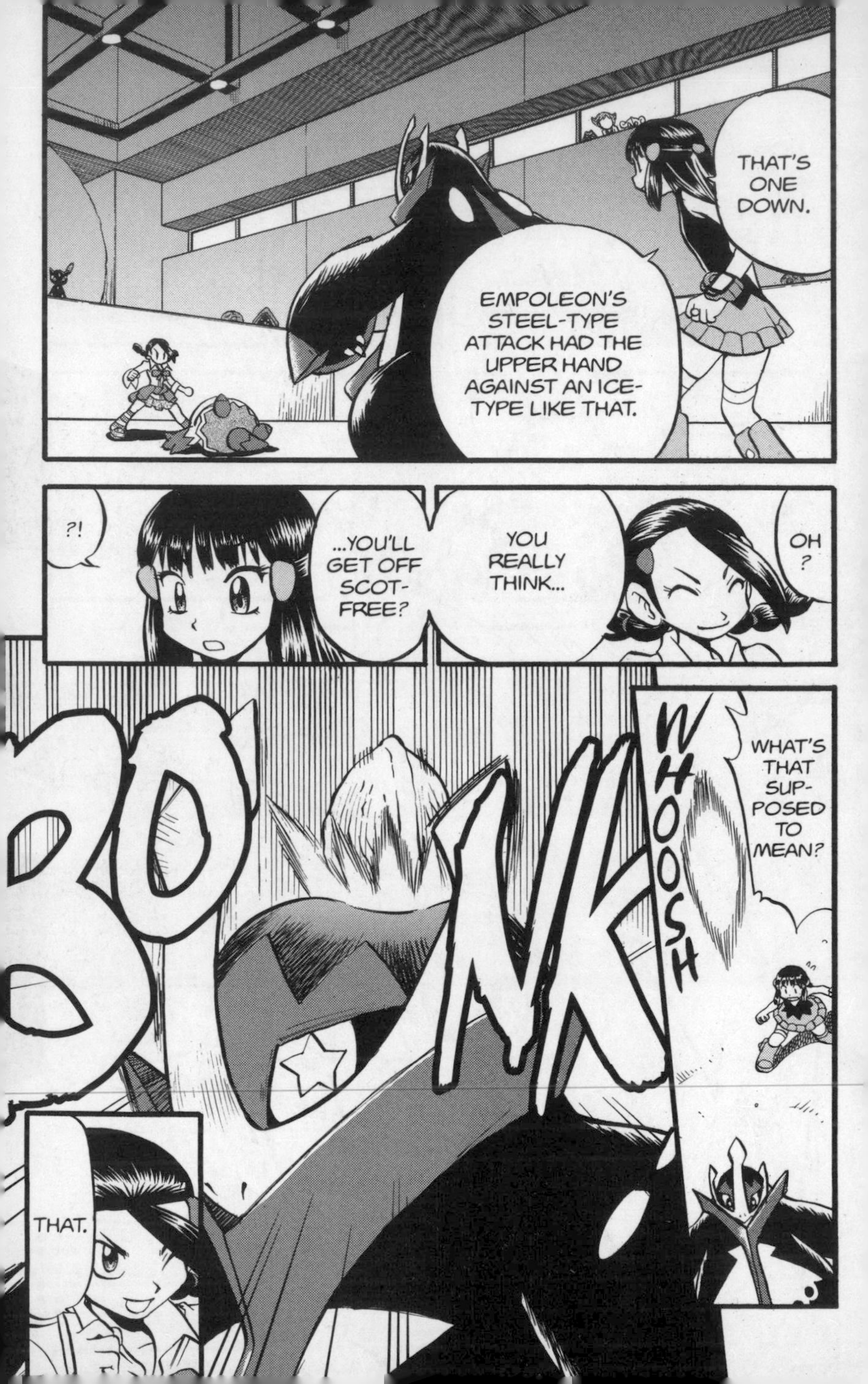
THAT'S ONE DOWN.
EMPOLEON'S STEEL-TYPE ATTACK HAD THE UPPER HAND AGAINST AN ICE-TYPE LIKE THAT.
OH?
YOU REALLY THINK...
...YOU'LL GET OFF SCOT-FREE?
?!
WHAT'S THAT SUP-POSED TO MEAN?
WHOOOSH
BONK
THAT.

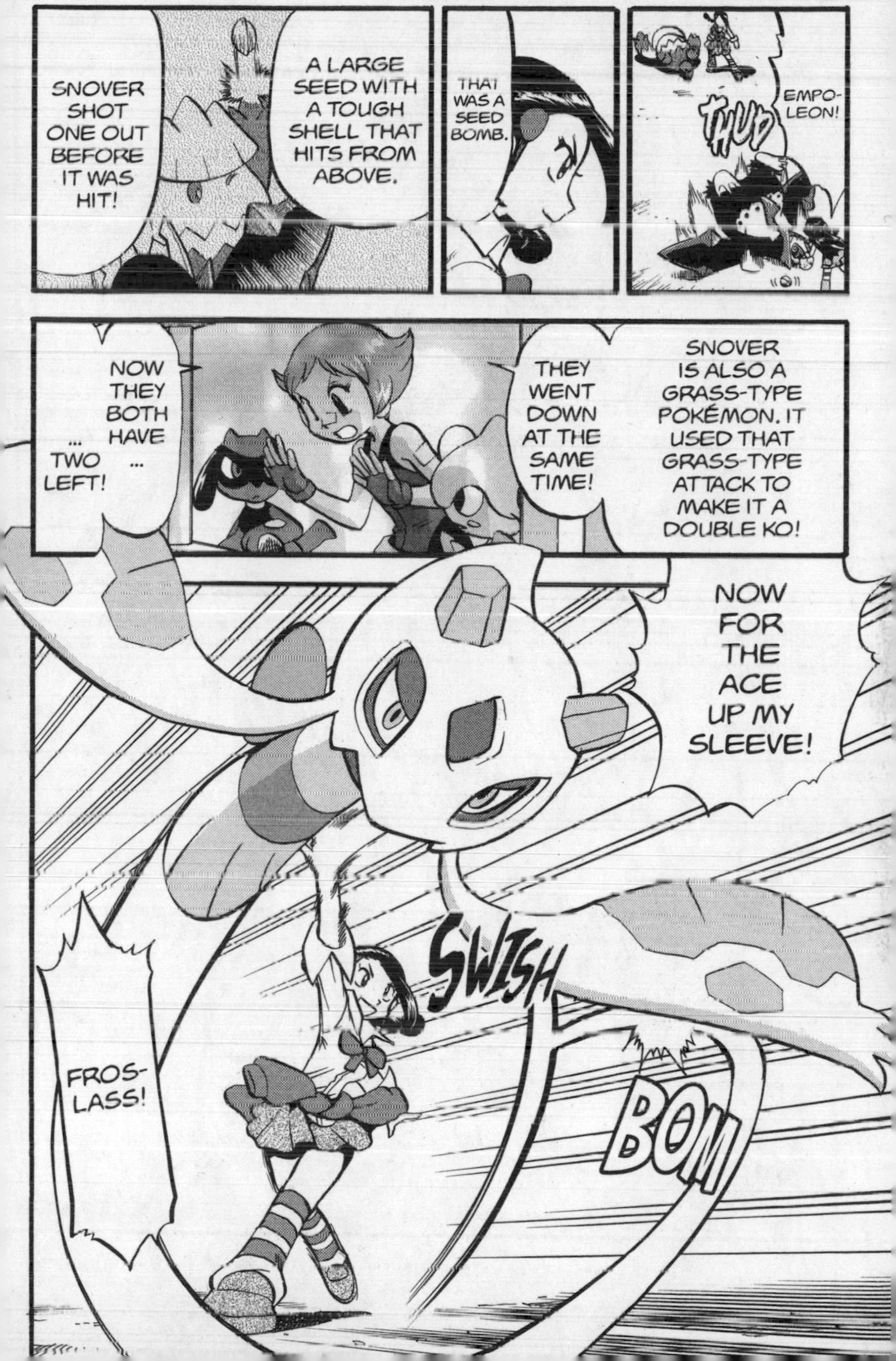
EMPO-LEON!
THUD
THAT WAS A SEED BOMB.
A LARGE SEED WITH A TOUGH SHELL THAT HITS FROM ABOVE.
SNOVER SHOT ONE OUT BEFORE IT WAS HIT!
SNOVER IS ALSO A GRASS-TYPE POKÉMON. IT USED THAT GRASS-TYPE ATTACK TO MAKE IT A DOUBLE KO!
THEY WENT DOWN AT THE SAME TIME!
... ...
NOW THEY BOTH HAVE TWO LEFT!
NOW FOR THE ACE UP MY SLEEVE!
SWISH
BOM
FROS-LASS!

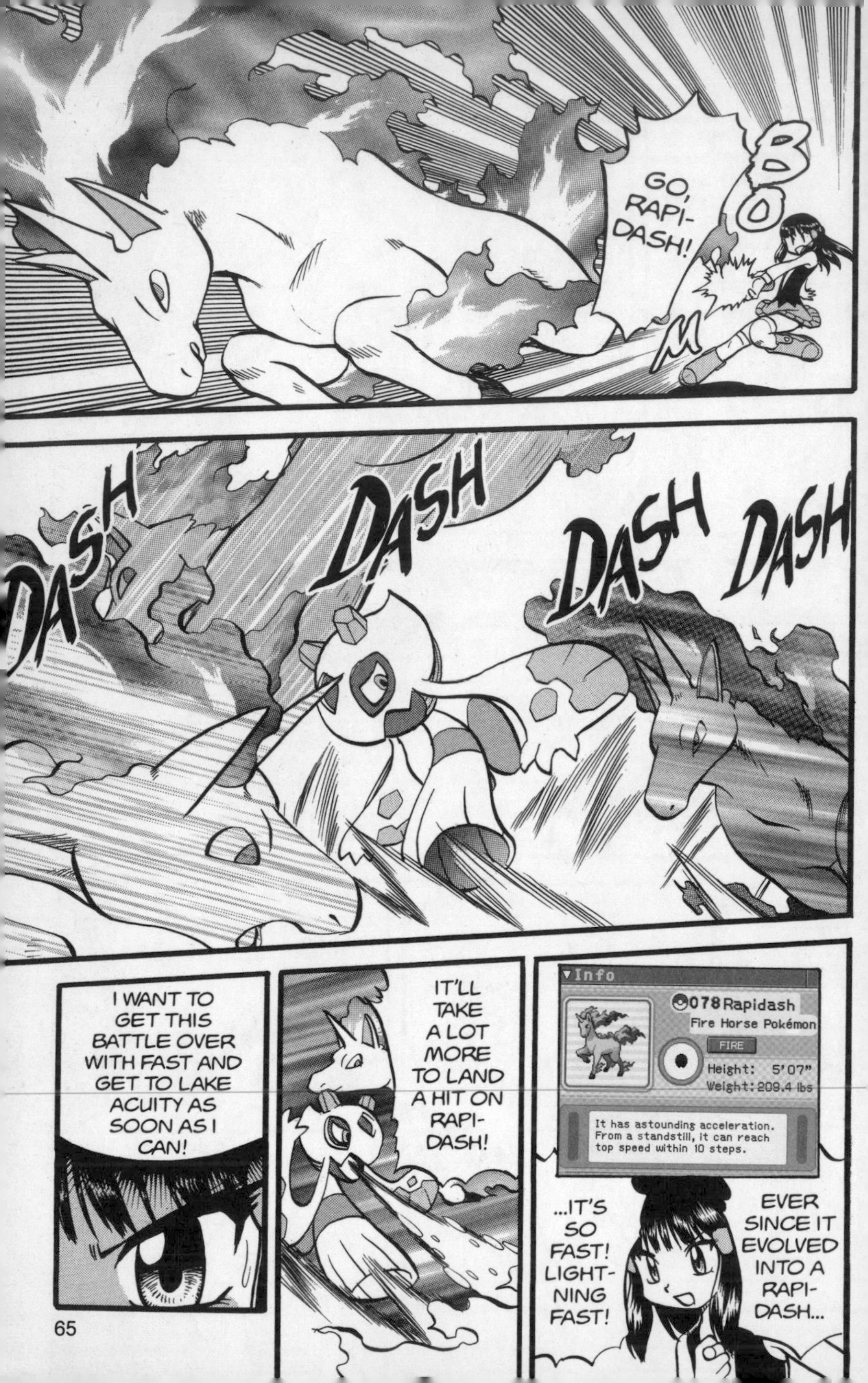
BOOM
GO, RAPIDASH!
DASH DASH DASH DASH
▼Info
078 Rapidash
Fire Horse Pokémon
FIRE
Height: 5'07"
Weight: 209.4 lbs
It has astounding acceleration. From a standstill, it can reach top speed within 10 steps.
EVER SINCE IT EVOLVED INTO A RAPIDASH...
...IT'S SO FAST! LIGHTNING FAST!
IT'LL TAKE A LOT MORE TO LAND A HIT ON RAPIDASH!
I WANT TO GET THIS BATTLE OVER WITH FAST AND GET TO LAKE ACUITY AS SOON AS I CAN!

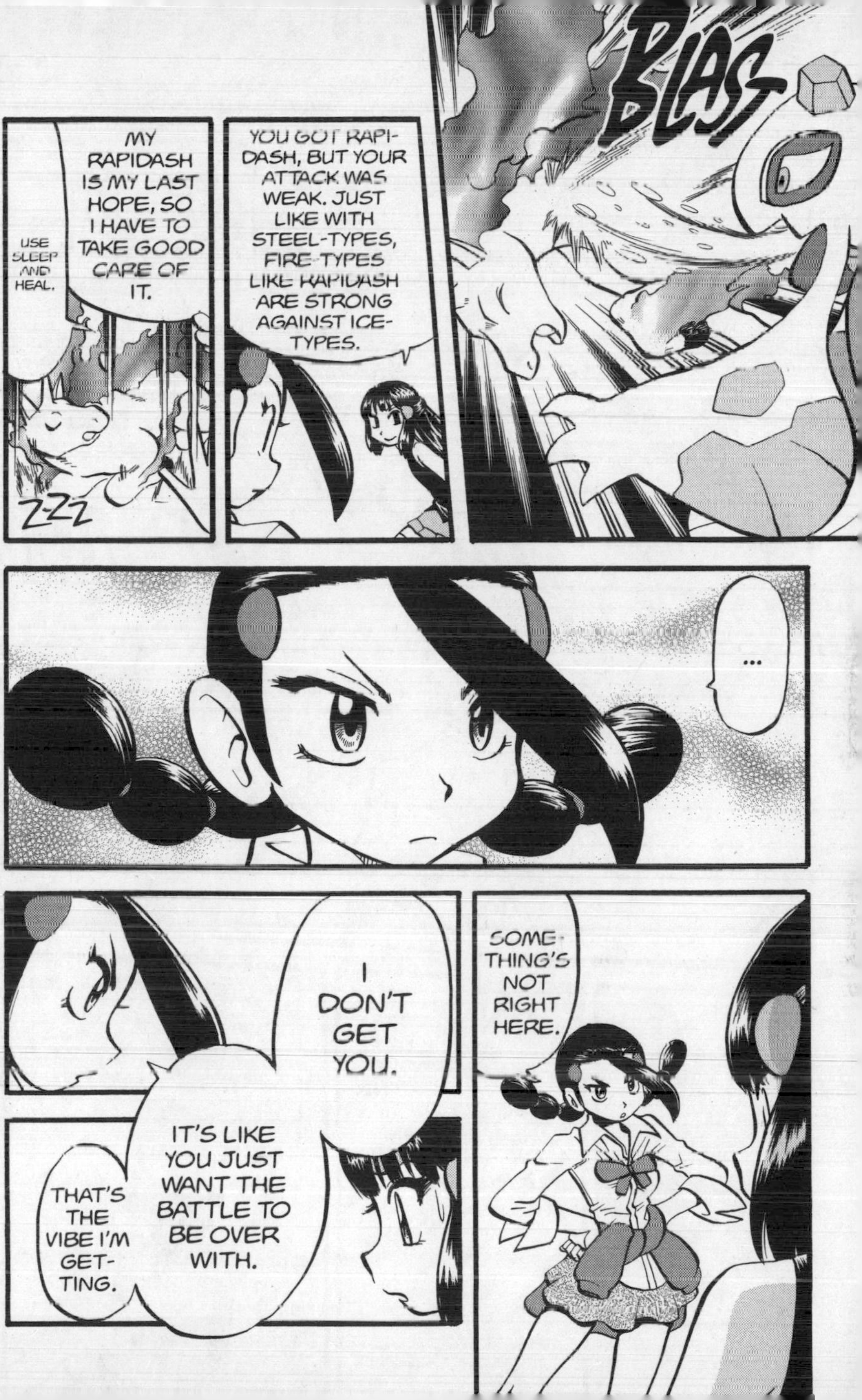
BLAS
YOU GOT RAPI-DASH, BUT YOUR ATTACK WAS WEAK. JUST LIKE WITH STEEL-TYPES, FIRE-TYPES LIKE RAPIDASH ARE STRONG AGAINST ICE-TYPES.
MY RAPIDASH IS MY LAST HOPE, SO I HAVE TO TAKE GOOD CARE OF IT.
USE SLEEP AND HEAL.
Z-Z-Z
...
SOME-THING'S NOT RIGHT HERE.
I DON'T GET YOU.
IT'S LIKE YOU JUST WANT THE BATTLE TO BE OVER WITH.
THAT'S THE VIBE I'M GET-TING.

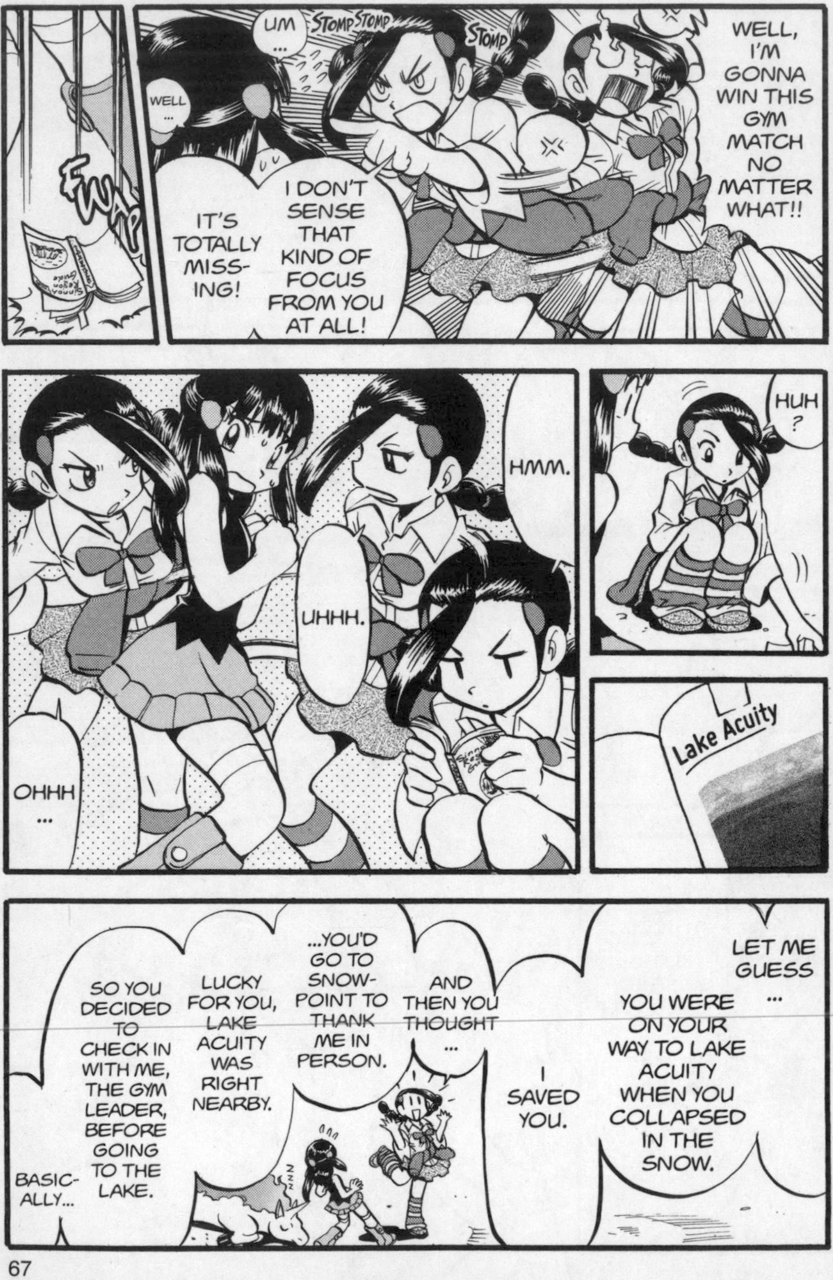
WELL, I'M GONNA WIN THIS GYM MATCH NO MATTER WHAT!!
STOMP
STOMP STOMP
UM ...
WELL ...
I DON'T SENSE THAT KIND OF FOCUS FROM YOU AT ALL!
IT'S TOTALLY MISS-ING!
FWAP
HUH ?
Lake Acuity
HMM.
UHHH.
OHHH ...
LET ME GUESS ...
YOU WERE ON YOUR WAY TO LAKE ACUITY WHEN YOU COLLAPSED IN THE SNOW.
I SAVED YOU.
AND THEN YOU THOUGHT ...
...YOU'D GO TO SNOW-POINT TO THANK ME IN PERSON.
LUCKY FOR YOU, LAKE ACUITY WAS RIGHT NEARBY.
SO YOU DECIDED TO CHECK IN WITH ME, THE GYM LEADER, BEFORE GOING TO THE LAKE.
BASIC-ALLY...

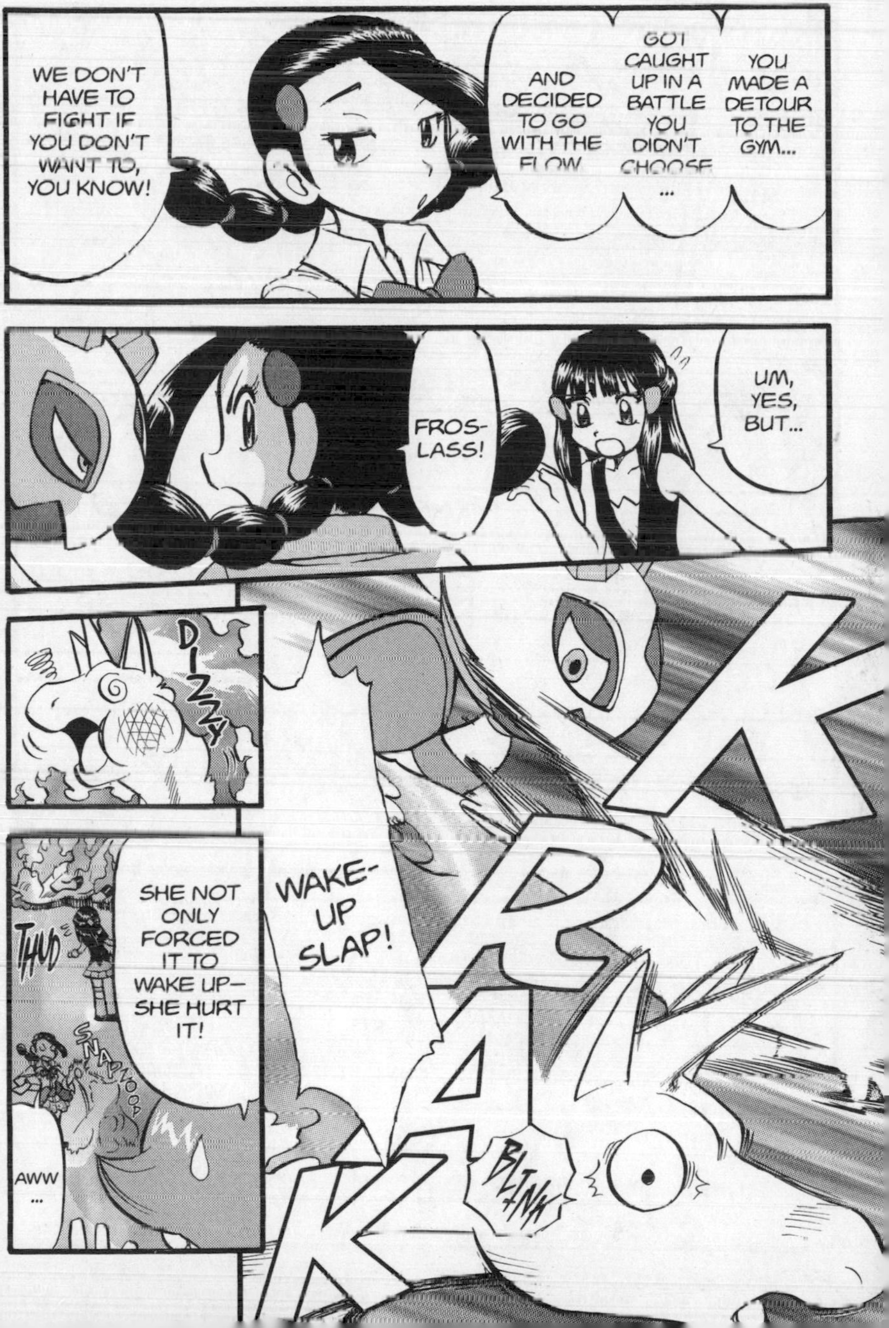
YOU MADE A DETOUR TO THE GYM...
GOT CAUGHT UP IN A BATTLE YOU DIDN'T CHOOSE...
AND DECIDED TO GO WITH THE FLOW.
WE DON'T HAVE TO FIGHT IF YOU DON'T WANT TO, YOU KNOW!
UM, YES, BUT...
FROS-LASS!
KRAK
WAKE-UP SLAP!
BLINK
DIZZY
THUD
SNAP
SHE NOT ONLY FORCED IT TO WAKE UP—SHE HURT IT!
AWW...

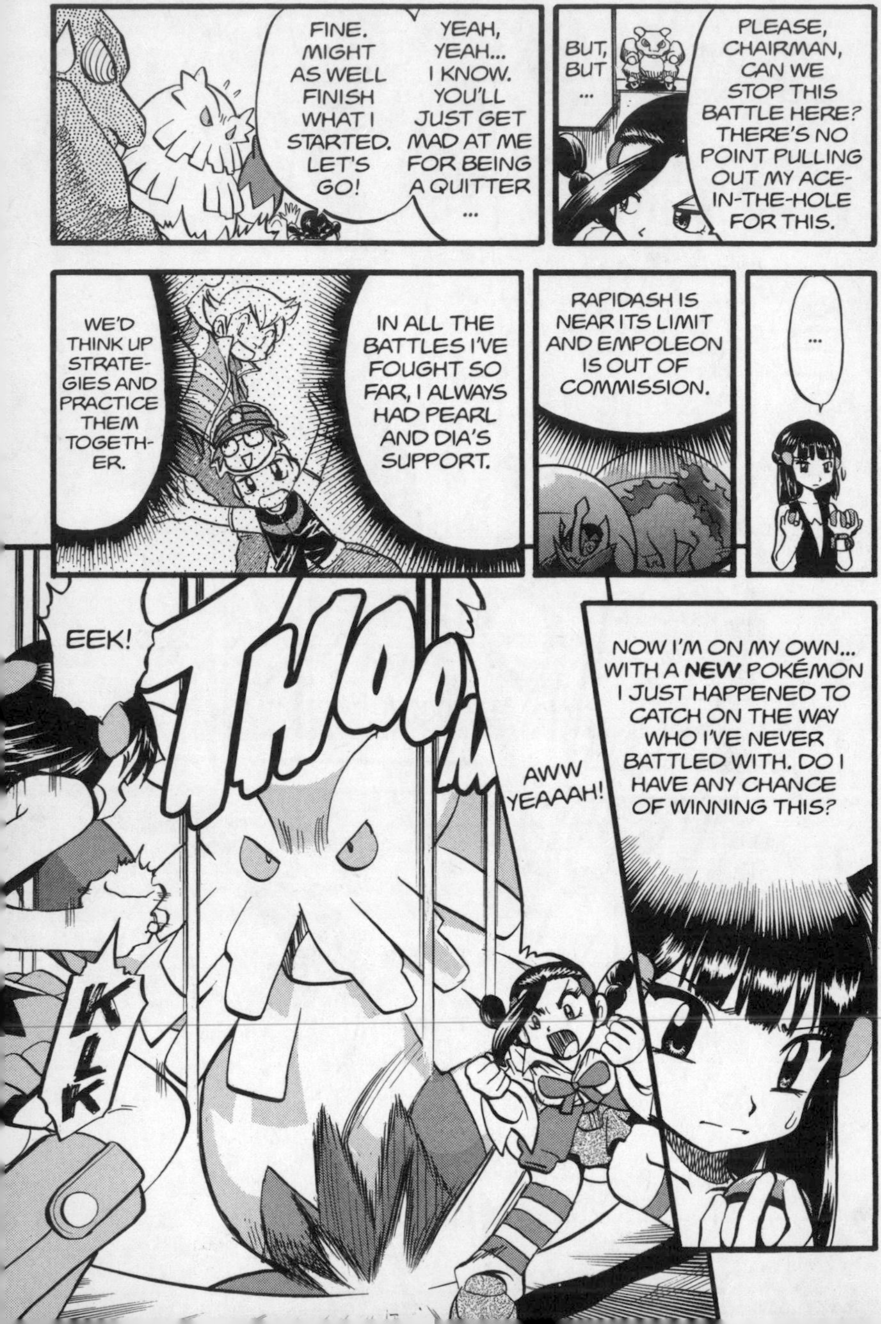
PLEASE, CHAIRMAN, CAN WE STOP THIS BATTLE HERE? THERE'S NO POINT PULLING OUT MY ACE-IN-THE-HOLE FOR THIS.
BUT, BUT ...
YEAH, YEAH... I KNOW. YOU'LL JUST GET MAD AT ME FOR BEING A QUITTER ...
FINE. MIGHT AS WELL FINISH WHAT I STARTED. LET'S GO!
...
RAPIDASH IS NEAR ITS LIMIT AND EMPOLEON IS OUT OF COMMISSION.
IN ALL THE BATTLES I'VE FOUGHT SO FAR, I ALWAYS HAD PEARL AND DIA'S SUPPORT.
WE'D THINK UP STRATEGIES AND PRACTICE THEM TOGETHER.
NOW I'M ON MY OWN... WITH A **NEW** POKéMON I JUST HAPPENED TO CATCH ON THE WAY WHO I'VE NEVER BATTLED WITH. DO I HAVE ANY CHANCE OF WINNING THIS?
AWW YEAAAH!
THOO
EEK!
KLIK

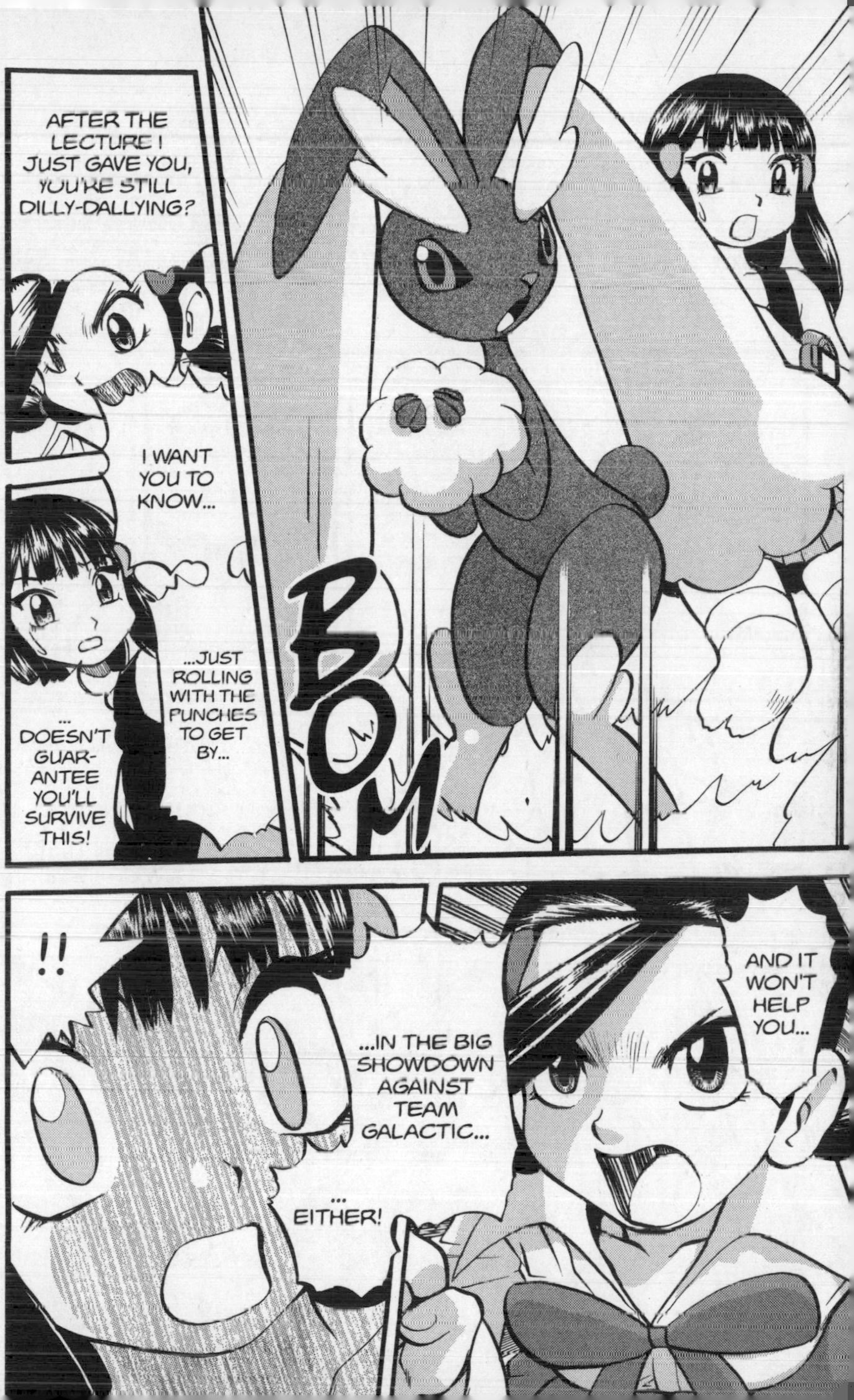
BOM
AFTER THE LECTURE I JUST GAVE YOU, YOU'RE STILL DILLY-DALLYING?
I WANT YOU TO KNOW...
...JUST ROLLING WITH THE PUNCHES TO GET BY...
...DOESN'T GUAR-ANTEE YOU'LL SURVIVE THIS!
AND IT WON'T HELP YOU...
...IN THE BIG SHOWDOWN AGAINST TEAM GALACTIC...
...EITHER!
!!

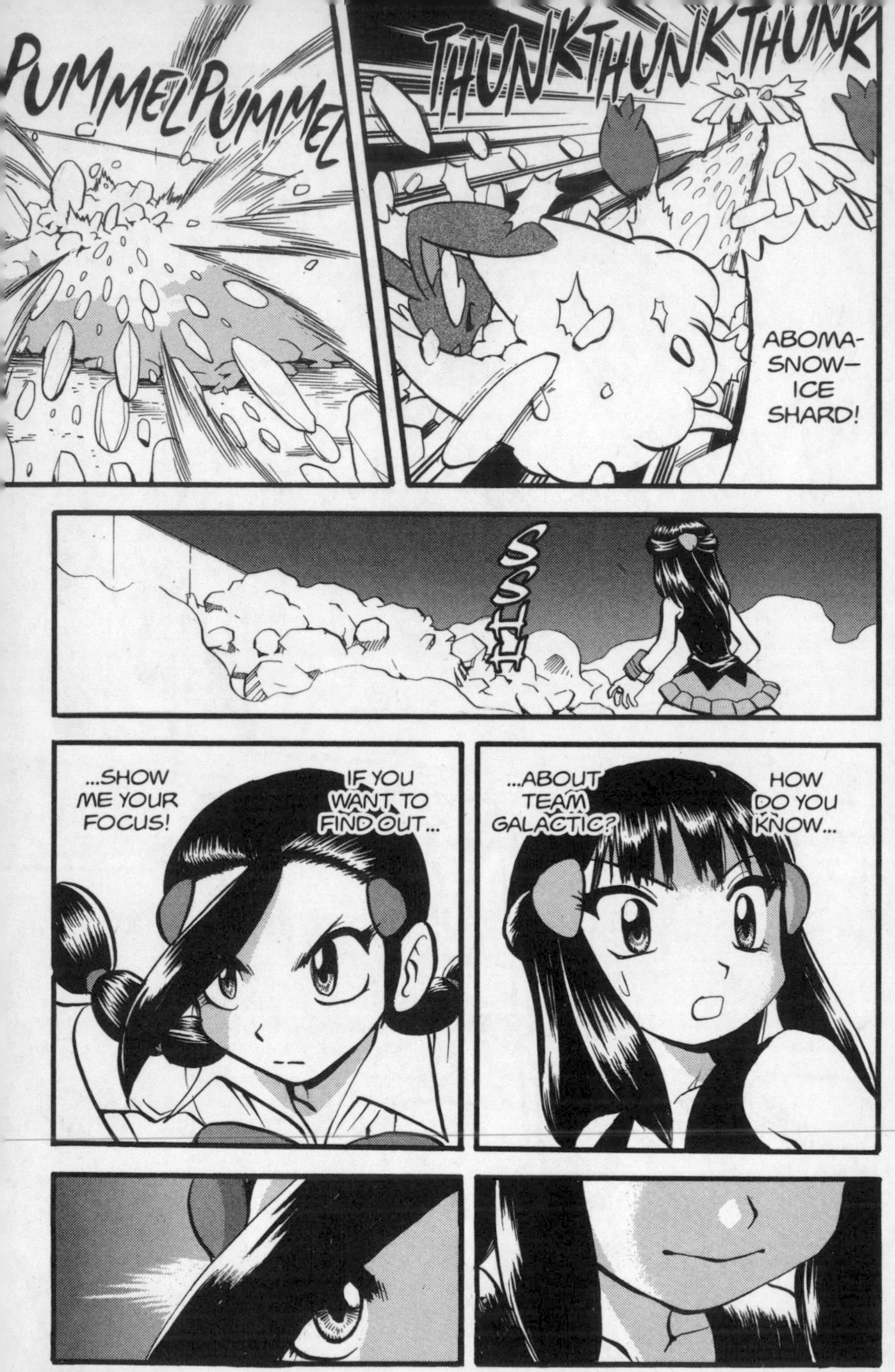
THUNK THUNK THUNK
ABOMA-SNOW—ICE SHARD!
PUMMEL PUMMEL
SSHH
HOW DO YOU KNOW...
...ABOUT TEAM GALACTIC?
IF YOU WANT TO FIND OUT...
...SHOW ME YOUR FOCUS!

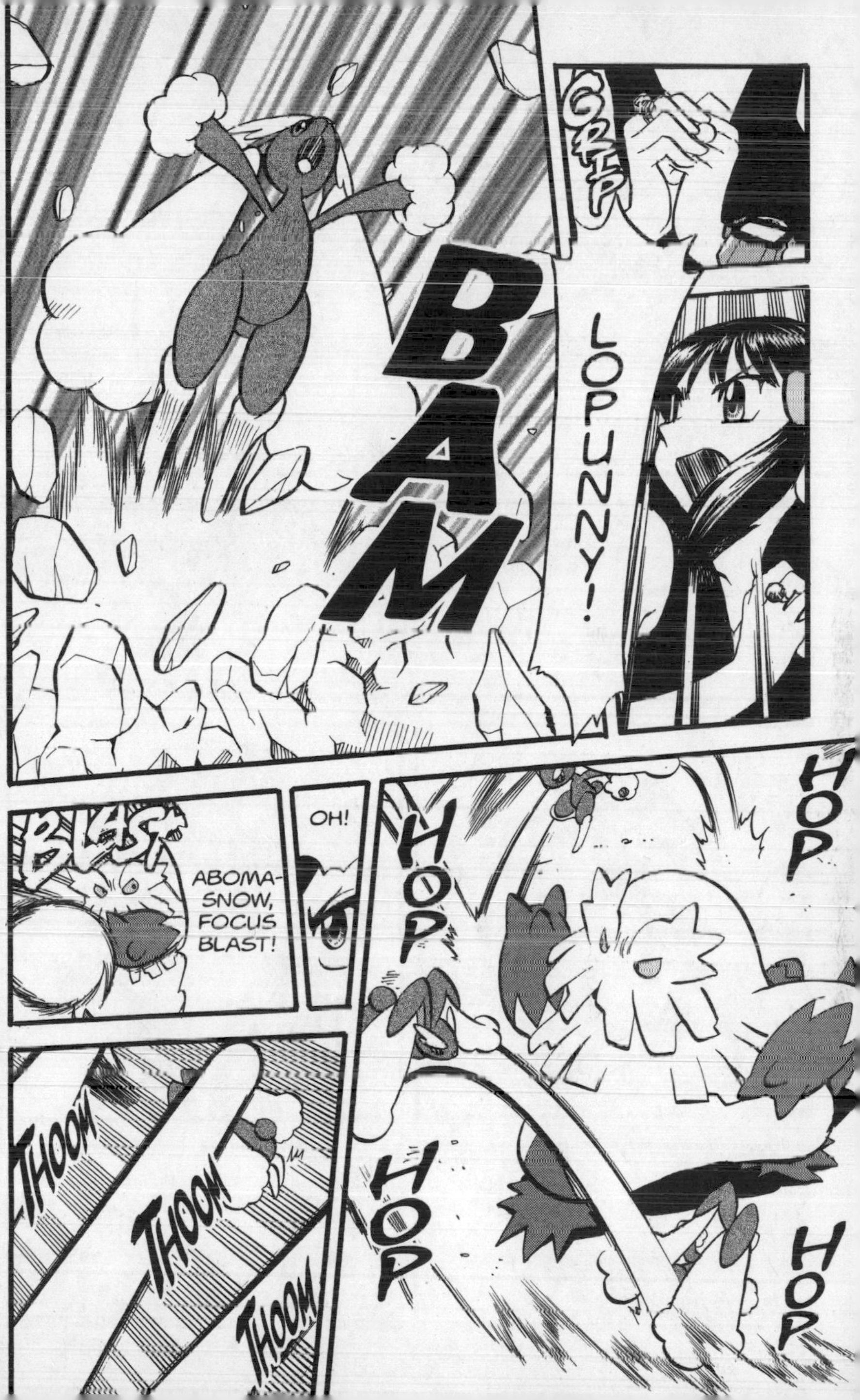
GRIP
LOPUNNY!
BAM
HOP
HOP
HOP
HOP
OH!
BLAST
ABOMASNOW, FOCUS BLAST!
THOOM
THOOM
THOOM

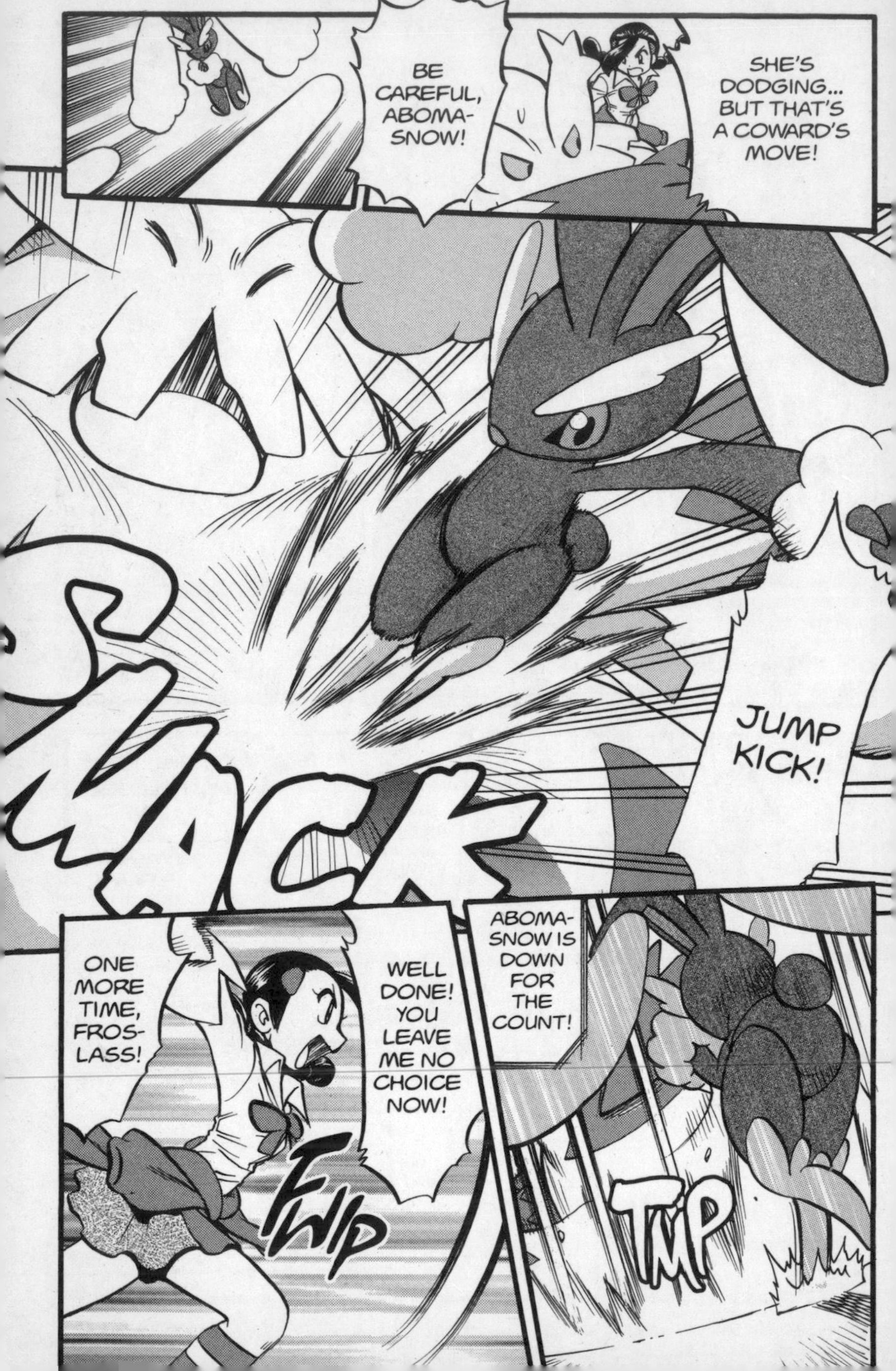
SHE'S DODGING... BUT THAT'S A COWARD'S MOVE!
BE CAREFUL, ABOMA-SNOW!
JUMP KICK!
SMACK
ABOMA-SNOW IS DOWN FOR THE COUNT!
TMP
WELL DONE! YOU LEAVE ME NO CHOICE NOW!
ONE MORE TIME, FROS-LASS!
FWIP

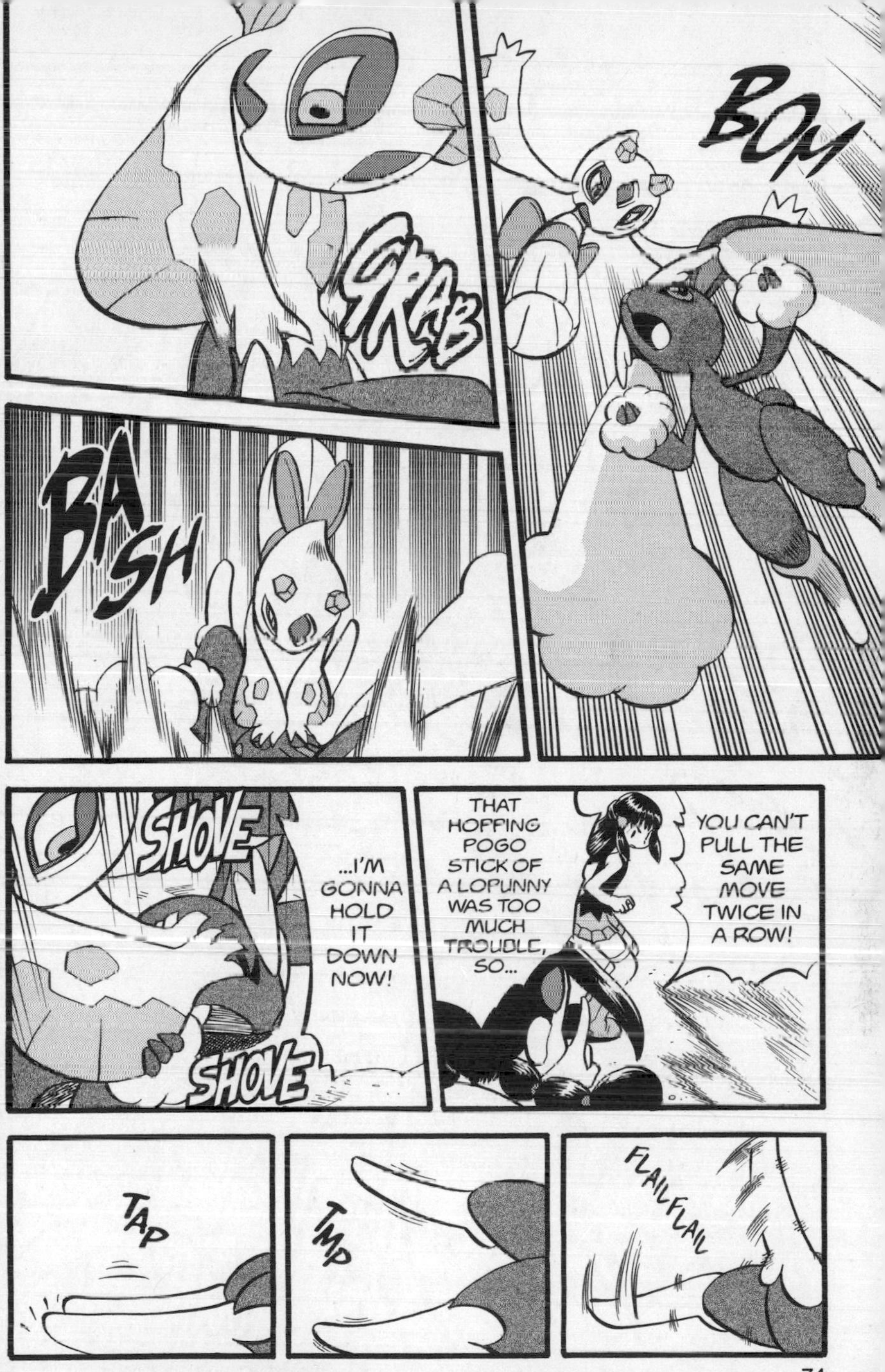
BOM
GRAB
BASH
YOU CAN'T PULL THE SAME MOVE TWICE IN A ROW!
THAT HOPPING POGO STICK OF A LOPUNNY WAS TOO MUCH TROUBLE, SO...
SHOVE
...I'M GONNA HOLD IT DOWN NOW!
SHOVE
FLAIL FLAIL
TMP
TAP

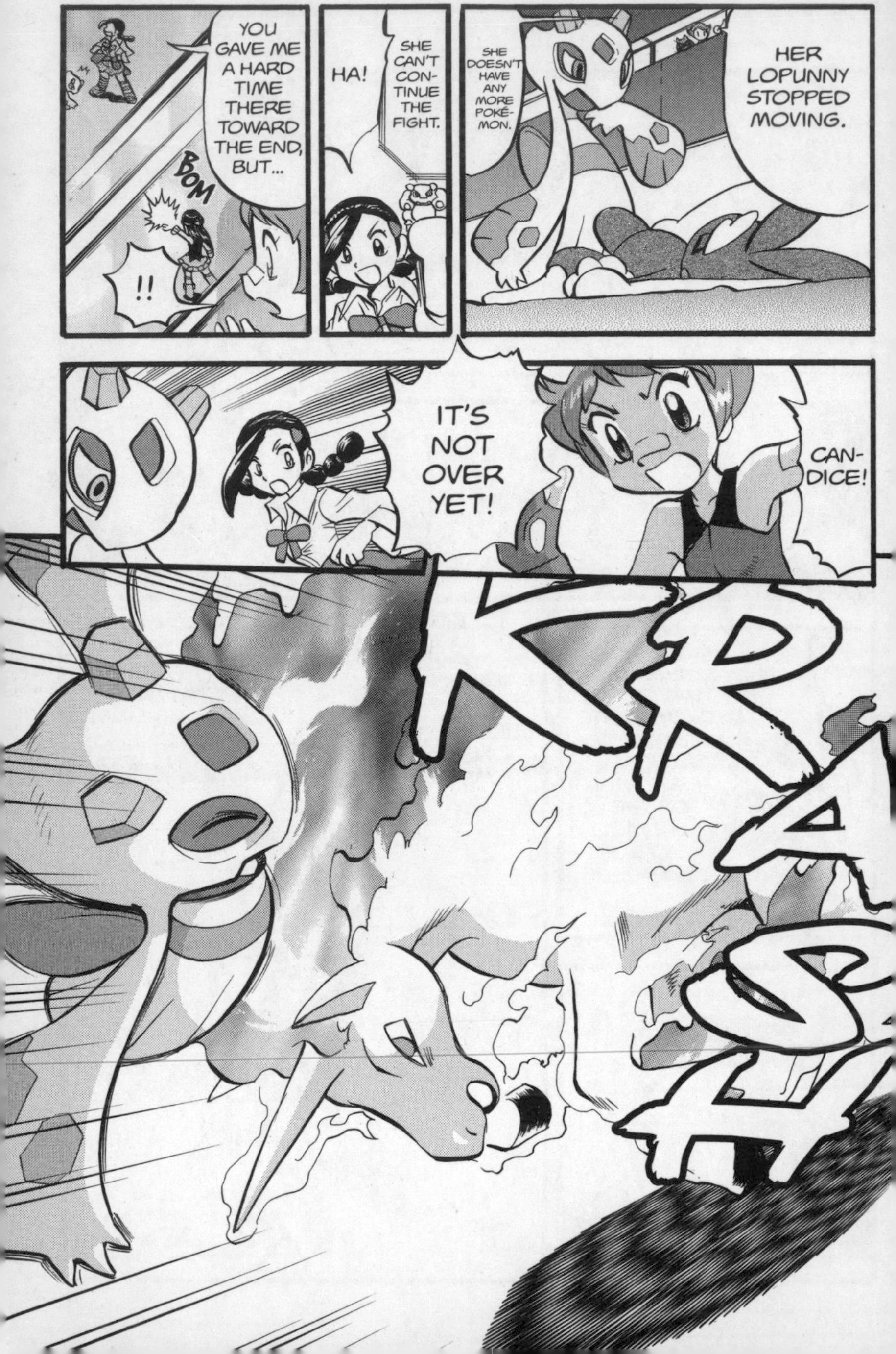
HER LOPUNNY STOPPED MOVING.
SHE DOESN'T HAVE ANY MORE POKÉMON.
SHE CAN'T CON-TINUE THE FIGHT.
HA!
YOU GAVE ME A HARD TIME THERE TOWARD THE END, BUT...
BOM
!!
CAN-DICE!
IT'S NOT OVER YET!
KRASSH

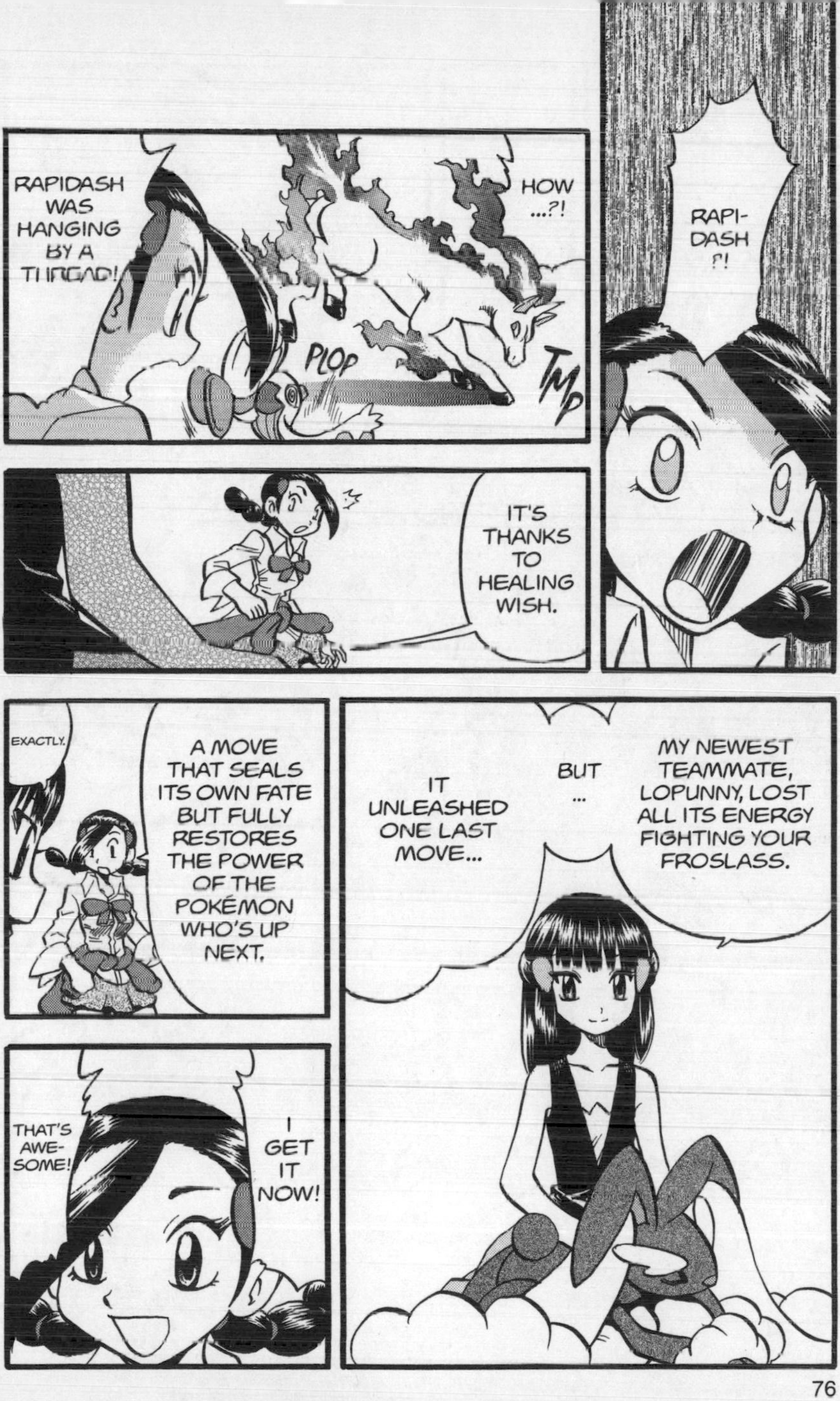
RAPI-DASH ?!
HOW ...?!
RAPIDASH WAS HANGING BY A THREAD!
TMP
PLOP
IT'S THANKS TO HEALING WISH.
MY NEWEST TEAMMATE, LOPUNNY, LOST ALL ITS ENERGY FIGHTING YOUR FROSLASS.
BUT ...
IT UNLEASHED ONE LAST MOVE...
A MOVE THAT SEALS ITS OWN FATE BUT FULLY RESTORES THE POWER OF THE POKÉMON WHO'S UP NEXT.
EXACTLY.
I GET IT NOW!
THAT'S AWE-SOME!

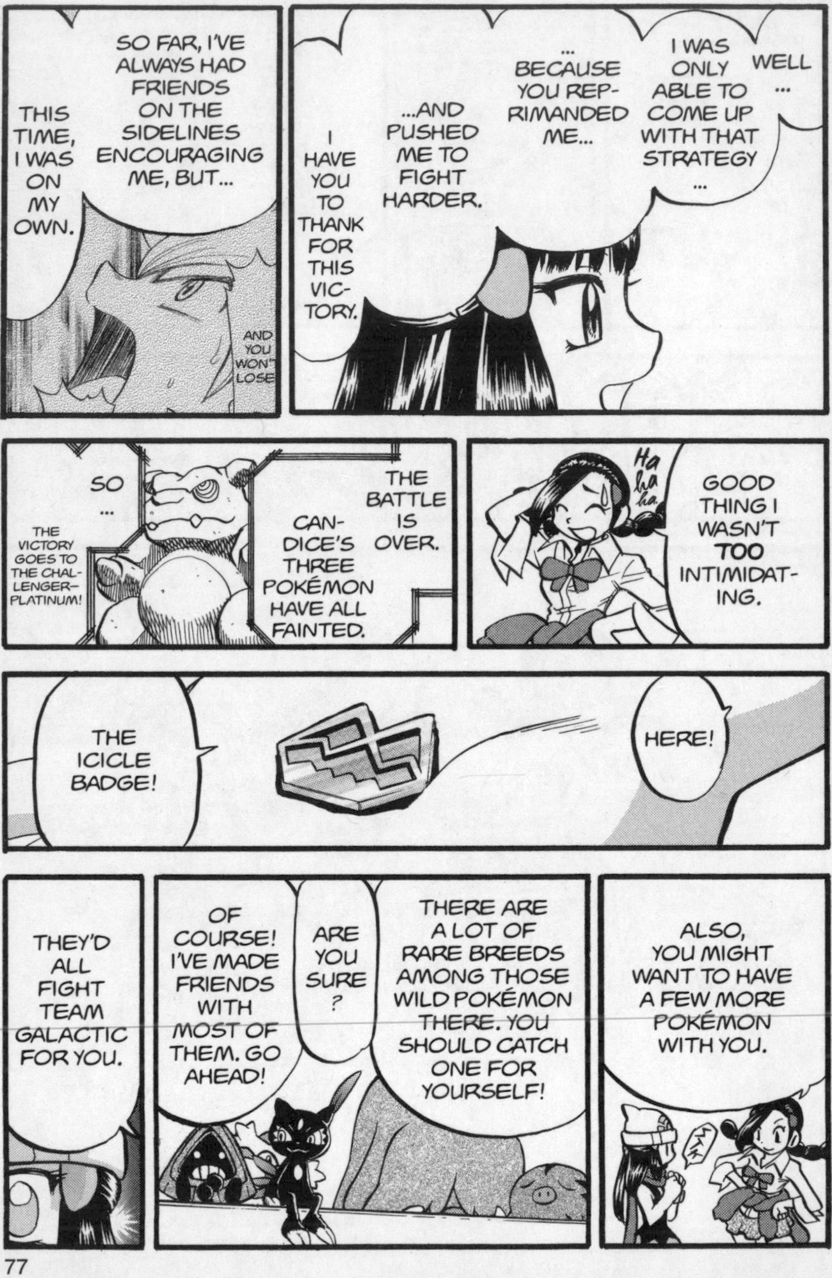
WELL ...
I WAS ONLY ABLE TO COME UP WITH THAT STRATEGY ...
... BECAUSE YOU REPRIMANDED ME...
...AND PUSHED ME TO FIGHT HARDER.
I HAVE YOU TO THANK FOR THIS VICTORY.
SO FAR, I'VE ALWAYS HAD FRIENDS ON THE SIDELINES ENCOURAGING ME, BUT...
THIS TIME, I WAS ON MY OWN.
AND YOU WON'T LOSE
Ha ha ha.
GOOD THING I WASN'T **TOO** INTIMIDATING.
THE BATTLE IS OVER.
CANDICE'S THREE POKÉMON HAVE ALL FAINTED.
SO ...
THE VICTORY GOES TO THE CHALLENGER—PLATINUM!
HERE!
THE ICICLE BADGE!
ALSO, YOU MIGHT WANT TO HAVE A FEW MORE POKÉMON WITH YOU.
THERE ARE A LOT OF RARE BREEDS AMONG THOSE WILD POKÉMON THERE. YOU SHOULD CATCH ONE FOR YOURSELF!
ARE YOU SURE?
OF COURSE! I'VE MADE FRIENDS WITH MOST OF THEM. GO AHEAD!
THEY'D ALL FIGHT TEAM GALACTIC FOR YOU.

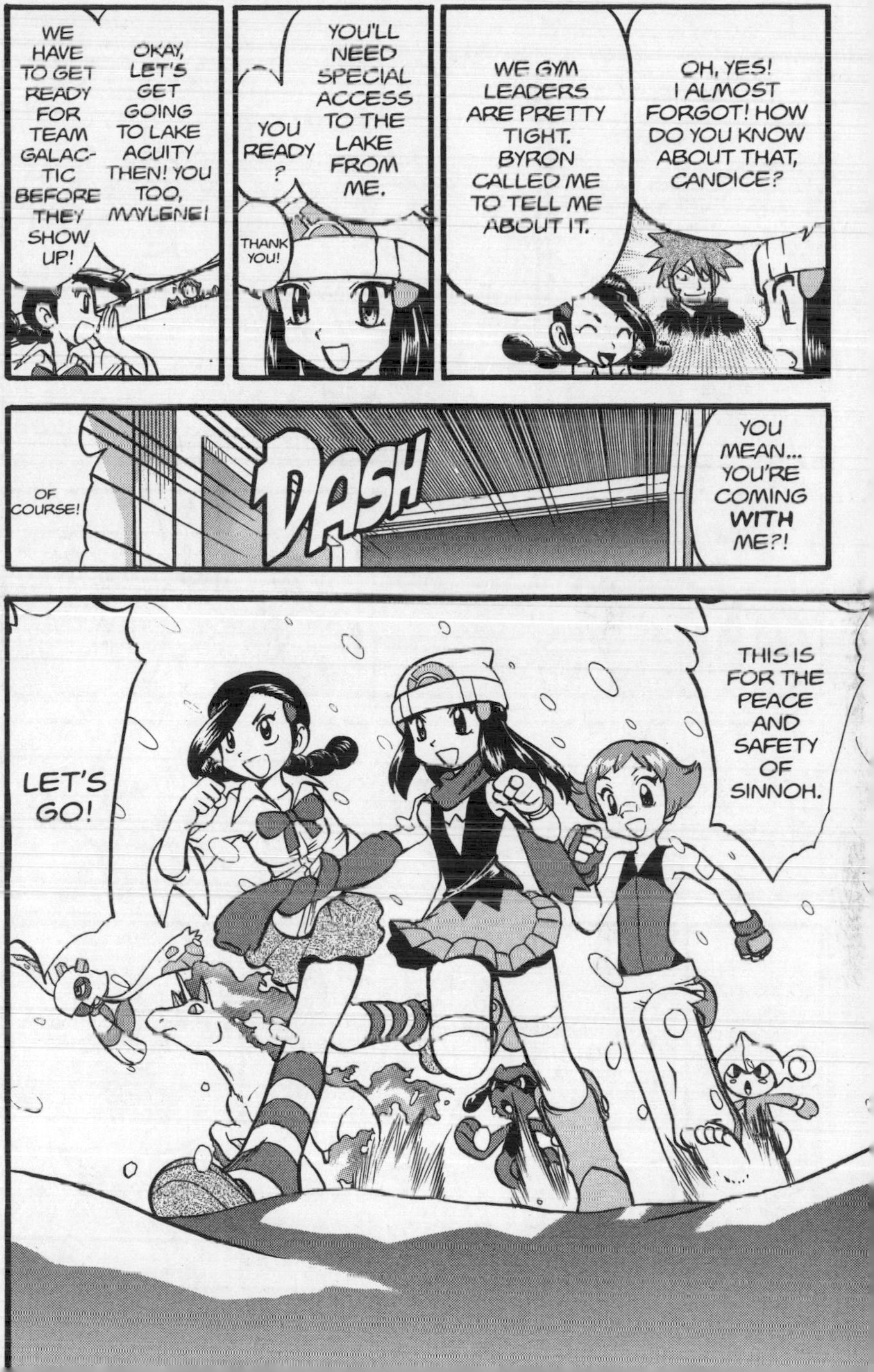
OH, YES! I ALMOST FORGOT! HOW DO YOU KNOW ABOUT THAT, CANDICE?
WE GYM LEADERS ARE PRETTY TIGHT. BYRON CALLED ME TO TELL ME ABOUT IT.
YOU'LL NEED SPECIAL ACCESS TO THE LAKE FROM ME.
YOU READY?
THANK YOU!
OKAY, LET'S GET GOING TO LAKE ACUITY THEN! YOU TOO, MAYLENE!
WE HAVE TO GET READY FOR TEAM GALACTIC BEFORE THEY SHOW UP!
YOU MEAN... YOU'RE COMING WITH ME?!
DASH
OF COURSE!
THIS IS FOR THE PEACE AND SAFETY OF SINNOH.
LET'S GO!

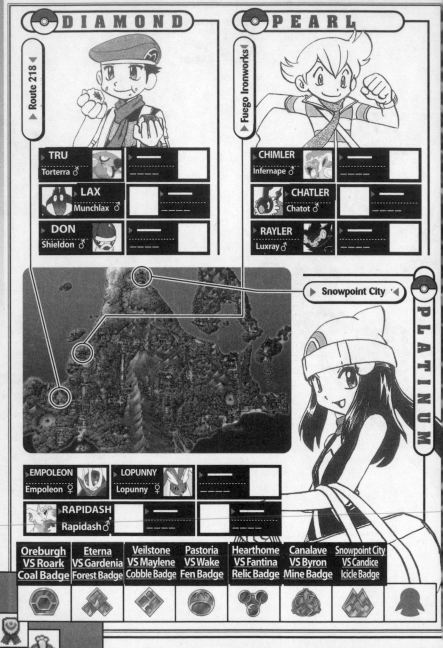

DIAMOND

▶ Route 218 ▼

TRU
Torterra ♂

LAX
Munchlax ♂

DON
Shieldon ♂

PEARL

▶ Fuego Ironworks◀

CHIMLER
Infernape ♂

CHATLER
Chatot ♂

RAYLER
Luxray ♂

▶ Snowpoint City ◀

PLATINUM

EMPOLEON
Empoleon ♀

LOPUNNY
Lopunny ♀

RAPIDASH
Rapidash ♂

Oreburgh VS Roark Coal Badge	Eterna VS Gardenia Forest Badge	Veilstone VS Maylene Cobble Badge	Pastoria VS Wake Fen Badge	Hearthome VS Fantina Relic Badge	Canalave VS Byron Mine Badge	Snowpoint City VS Candice Icicle Badge

52

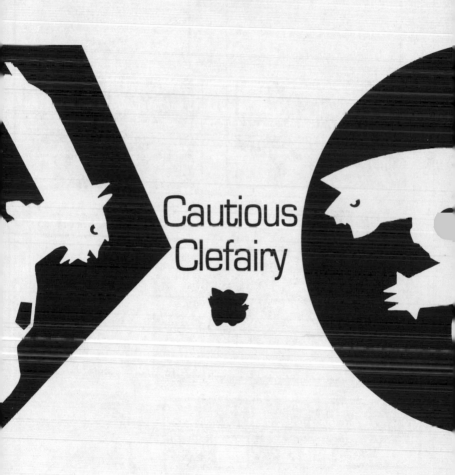

Cautious
Clefairy

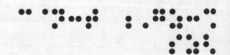

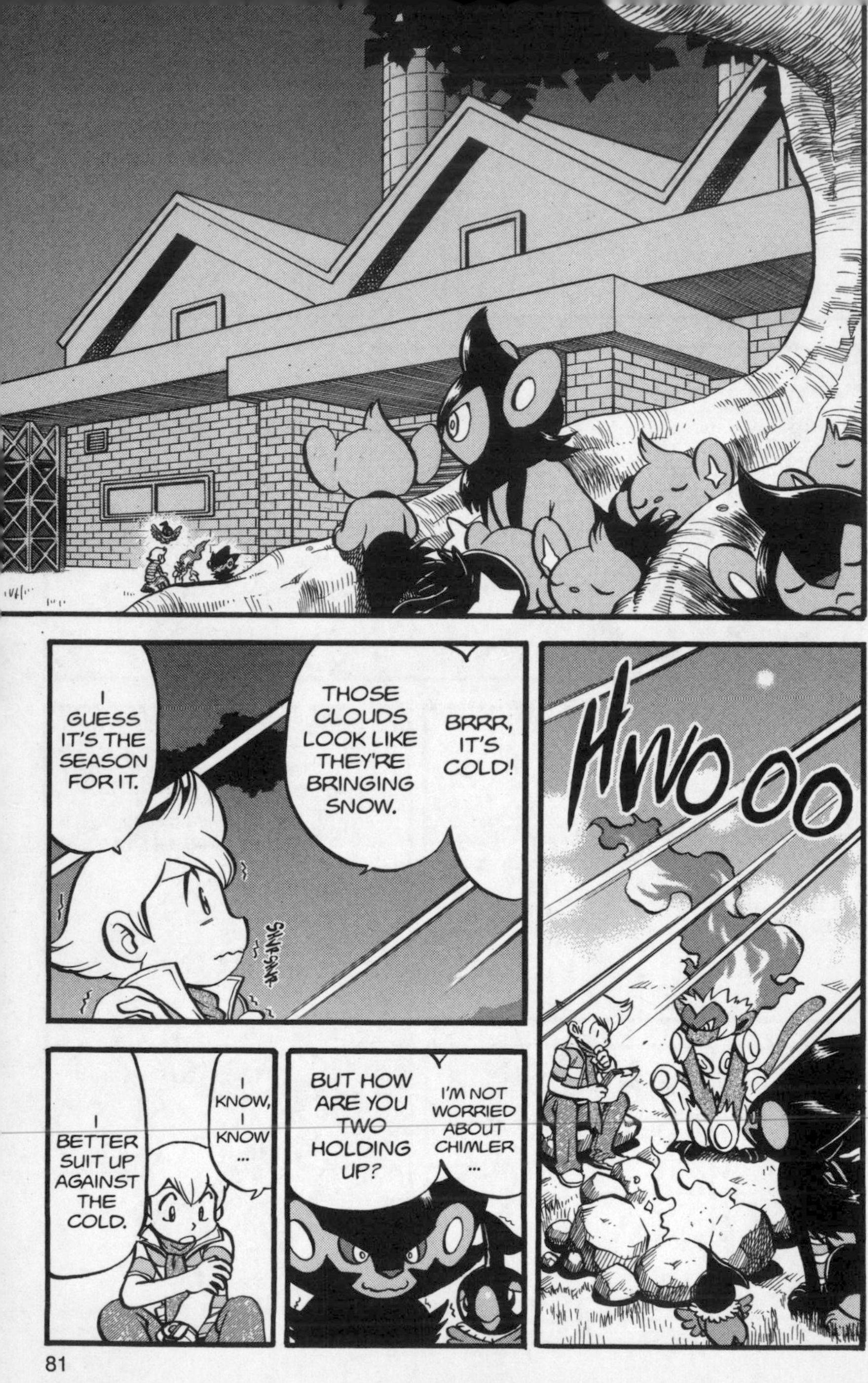
HWOOO
BRRR, IT'S COLD!
THOSE CLOUDS LOOK LIKE THEY'RE BRINGING SNOW.
I GUESS IT'S THE SEASON FOR IT.
I'M NOT WORRIED ABOUT CHIMLER ...
BUT HOW ARE YOU TWO HOLDING UP?
I KNOW, I KNOW ...
I BETTER SUIT UP AGAINST THE COLD.

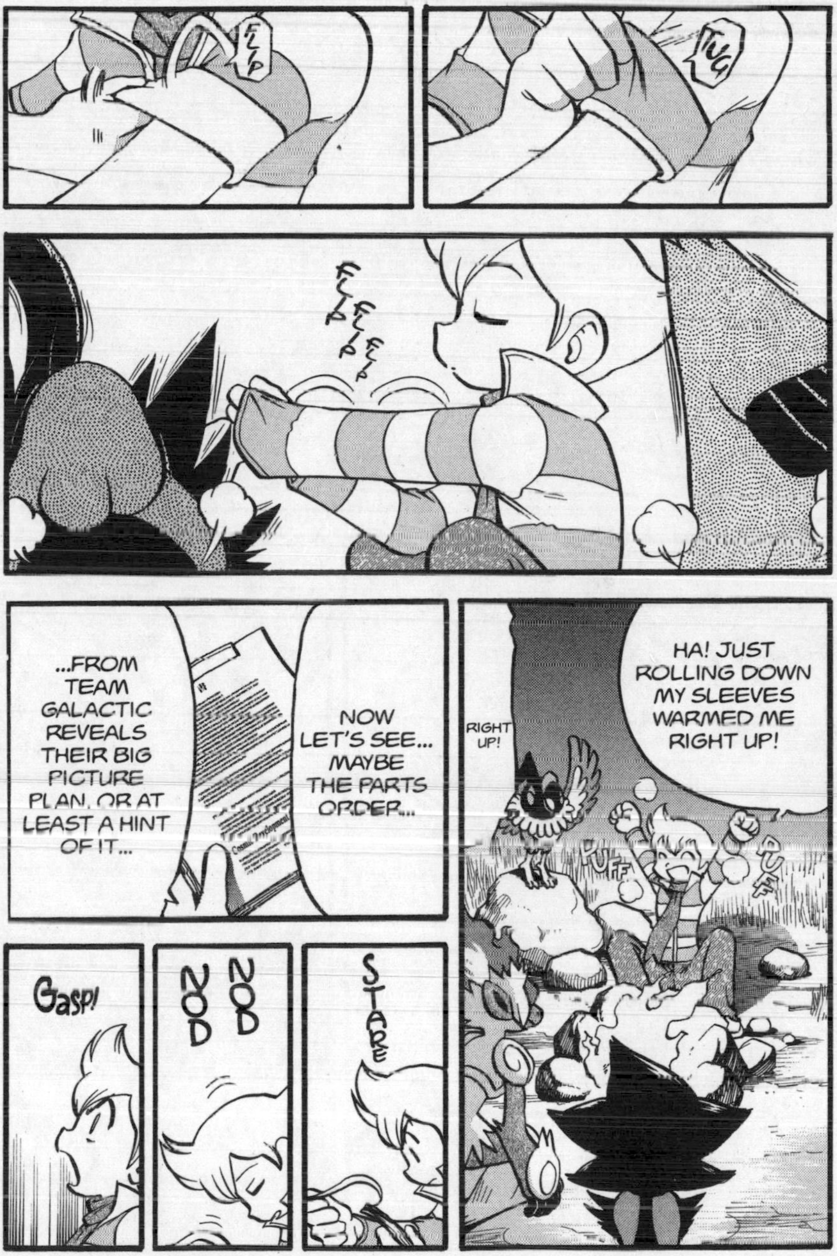
TUG
FLIP
FLIP FLIP FLIP
HA! JUST ROLLING DOWN MY SLEEVES WARMED ME RIGHT UP!
RIGHT UP!
PUFF
PUFF
NOW LET'S SEE... MAYBE THE PARTS ORDER...
...FROM TEAM GALACTIC REVEALS THEIR BIG PICTURE PLAN, OR AT LEAST A HINT OF IT...
STARE
NOD NOD
Gasp!

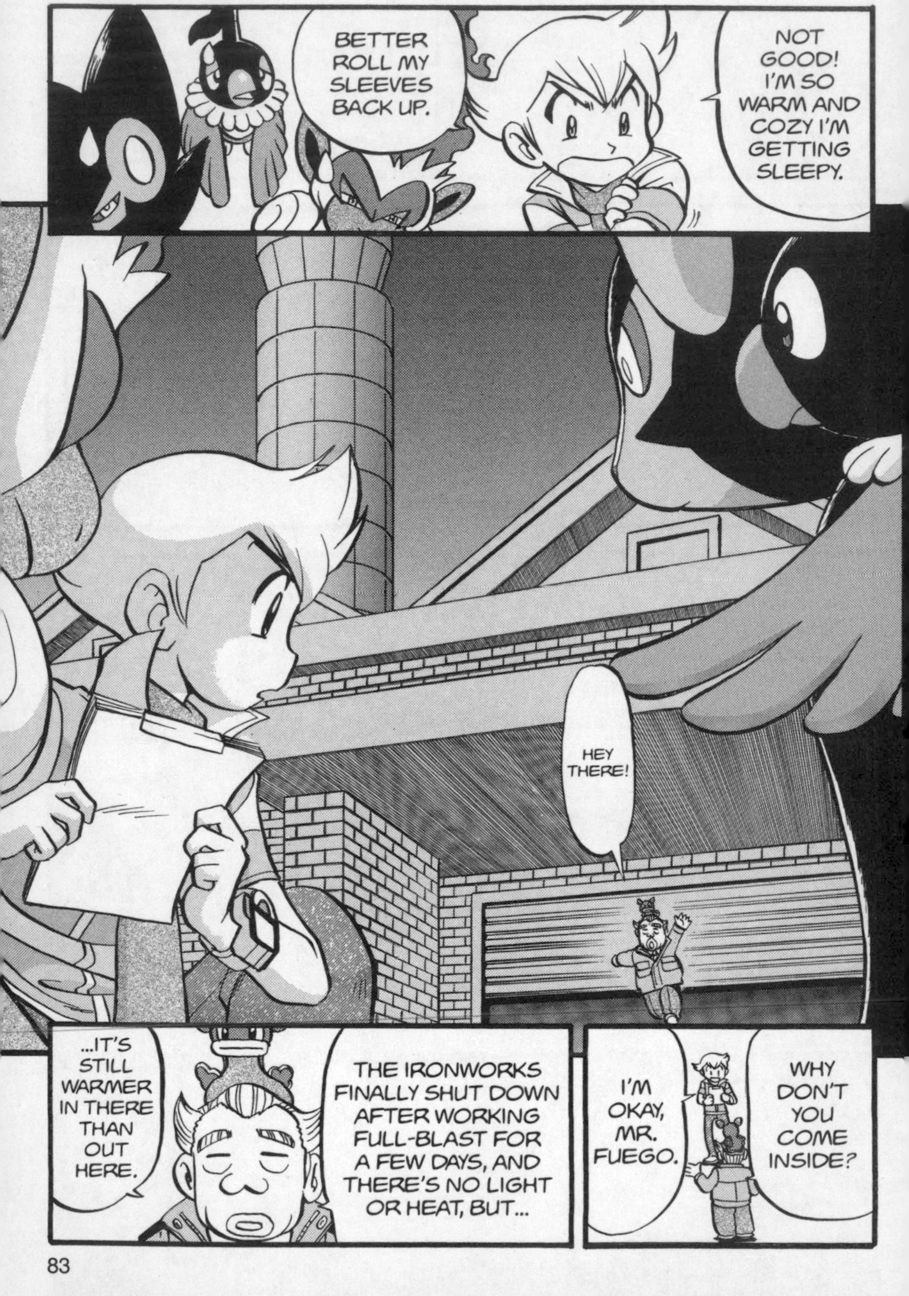
NOT GOOD! I'M SO WARM AND COZY I'M GETTING SLEEPY.
BETTER ROLL MY SLEEVES BACK UP.
HEY THERE!
WHY DON'T YOU COME INSIDE?
I'M OKAY, MR. FUEGO.
THE IRONWORKS FINALLY SHUT DOWN AFTER WORKING FULL-BLAST FOR A FEW DAYS, AND THERE'S NO LIGHT OR HEAT, BUT...
...IT'S STILL WARMER IN THERE THAN OUT HERE.

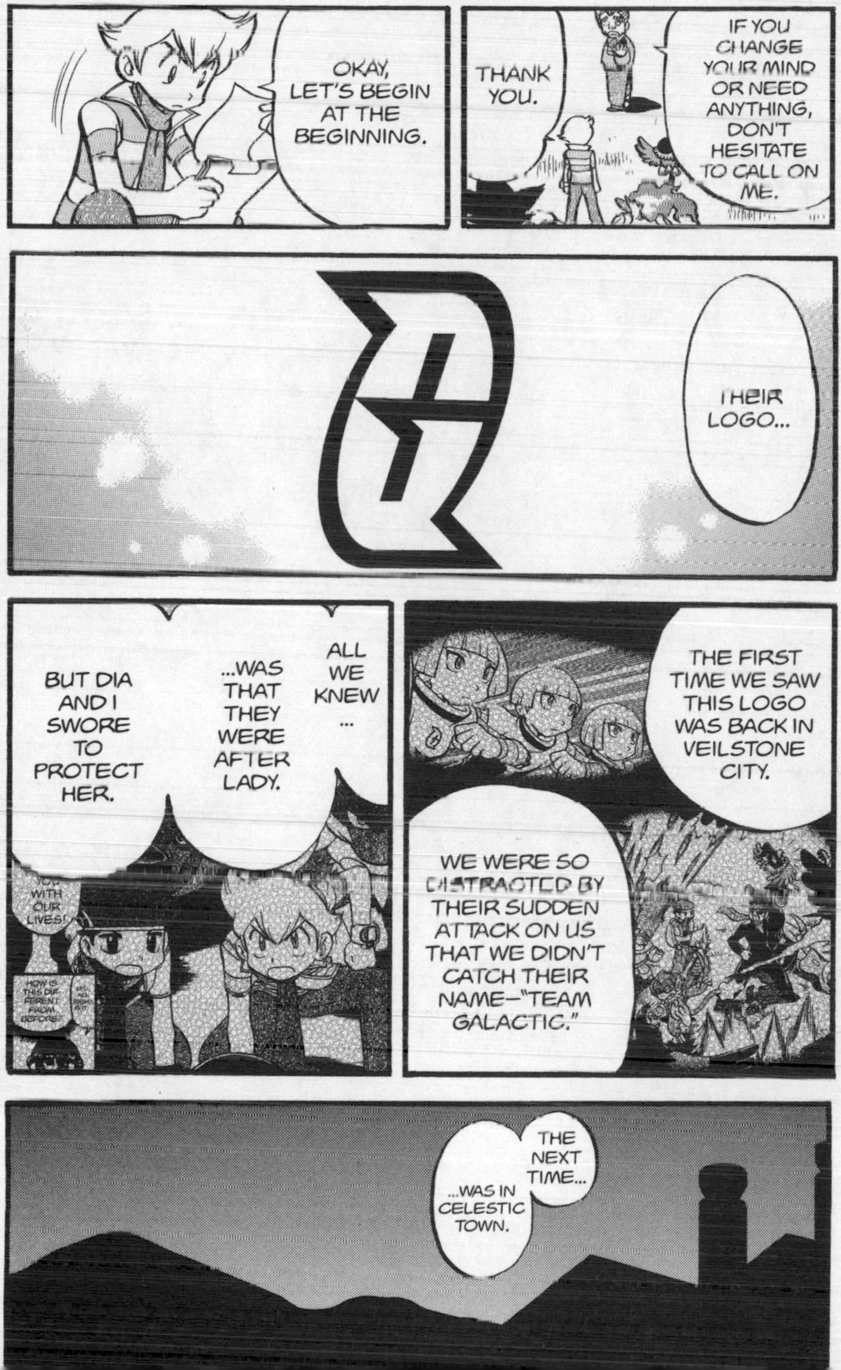
IF YOU CHANGE YOUR MIND OR NEED ANYTHING, DON'T HESITATE TO CALL ON ME.
THANK YOU.
OKAY, LET'S BEGIN AT THE BEGINNING.
THEIR LOGO...
THE FIRST TIME WE SAW THIS LOGO WAS BACK IN VEILSTONE CITY.
WE WERE SO DISTRACTED BY THEIR SUDDEN ATTACK ON US THAT WE DIDN'T CATCH THEIR NAME—"TEAM GALACTIC."
ALL WE KNEW ...
...WAS THAT THEY WERE AFTER LADY.
BUT DIA AND I SWORE TO PROTECT HER.
HOW IS THIS DIFFERENT FROM BEFORE?
THE NEXT TIME...
...WAS IN CELESTIC TOWN.

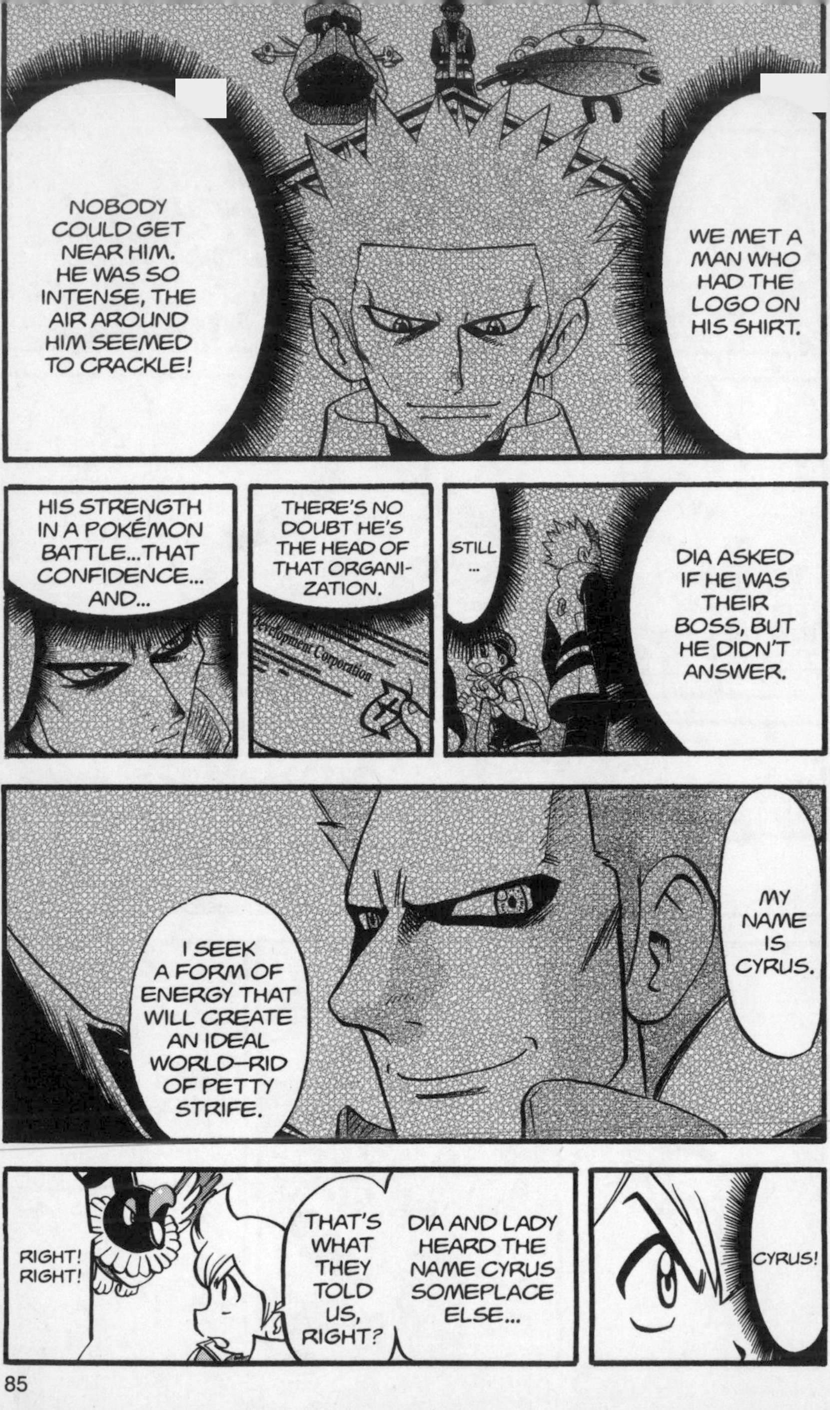
WE MET A MAN WHO HAD THE LOGO ON HIS SHIRT.
NOBODY COULD GET NEAR HIM. HE WAS SO INTENSE, THE AIR AROUND HIM SEEMED TO CRACKLE!
DIA ASKED IF HE WAS THEIR BOSS, BUT HE DIDN'T ANSWER.
STILL ...
THERE'S NO DOUBT HE'S THE HEAD OF THAT ORGANI-ZATION.
HIS STRENGTH IN A POKÉMON BATTLE...THAT CONFIDENCE... AND...
MY NAME IS CYRUS.
I SEEK A FORM OF ENERGY THAT WILL CREATE AN IDEAL WORLD—RID OF PETTY STRIFE.
CYRUS!
DIA AND LADY HEARD THE NAME CYRUS SOMEPLACE ELSE...
THAT'S WHAT THEY TOLD US, RIGHT?
RIGHT! RIGHT!

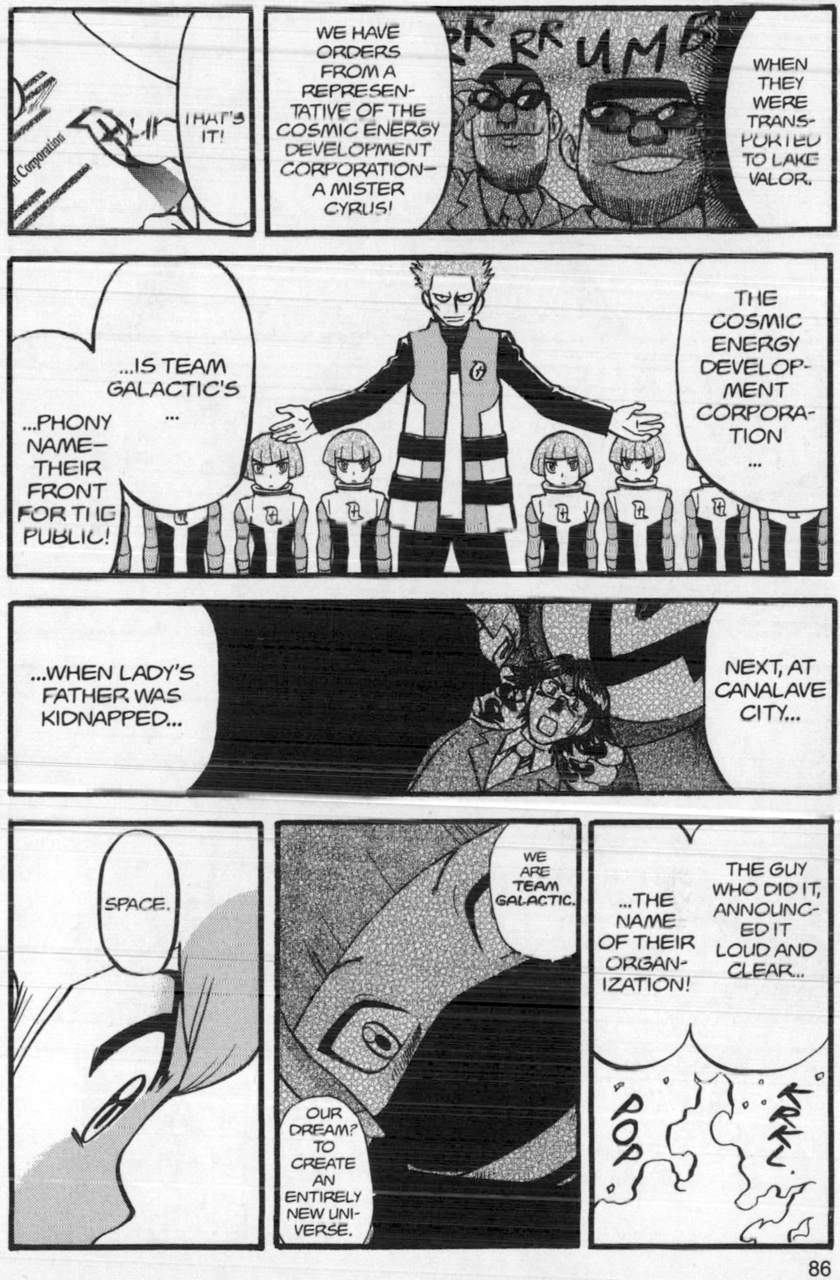
WHEN THEY WERE TRANSPORTED TO LAKE VALOR.
WE HAVE ORDERS FROM A REPRESENTATIVE OF THE COSMIC ENERGY DEVELOPMENT CORPORATION—A MISTER CYRUS!
THAT'S IT!
THE COSMIC ENERGY DEVELOPMENT CORPORATION...
...IS TEAM GALACTIC'S...
...PHONY NAME—THEIR FRONT FOR THE PUBLIC!
NEXT, AT CANALAVE CITY...
...WHEN LADY'S FATHER WAS KIDNAPPED...
THE GUY WHO DID IT, ANNOUNCED IT LOUD AND CLEAR...
...THE NAME OF THEIR ORGANIZATION!
KRKL
POP
WE ARE TEAM GALACTIC.
OUR DREAM? TO CREATE AN ENTIRELY NEW UNIVERSE.
SPACE.

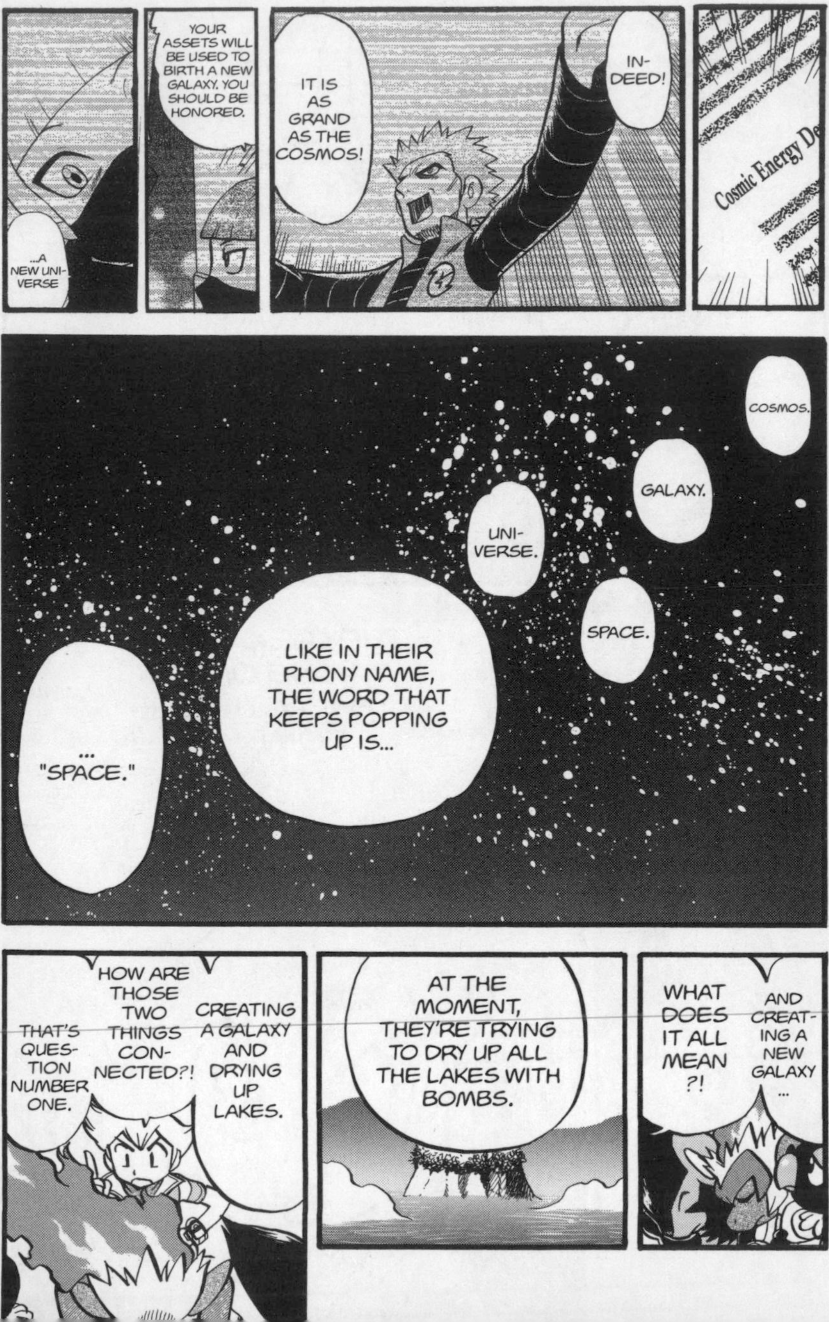
Cosmic Energy
IN-DEED!
IT IS AS GRAND AS THE COSMOS!
YOUR ASSETS WILL BE USED TO BIRTH A NEW GALAXY. YOU SHOULD BE HONORED.
...A NEW UNI-VERSE
COSMOS.
GALAXY.
UNI-VERSE.
SPACE.
LIKE IN THEIR PHONY NAME, THE WORD THAT KEEPS POPPING UP IS...
... "SPACE."
AND CREAT-ING A NEW GALAXY ...
WHAT DOES IT ALL MEAN ?!
AT THE MOMENT, THEY'RE TRYING TO DRY UP ALL THE LAKES WITH BOMBS.
CREATING A GALAXY AND DRYING UP LAKES.
HOW ARE THOSE TWO THINGS CON-NECTED?!
THAT'S QUES-TION NUMBER ONE.

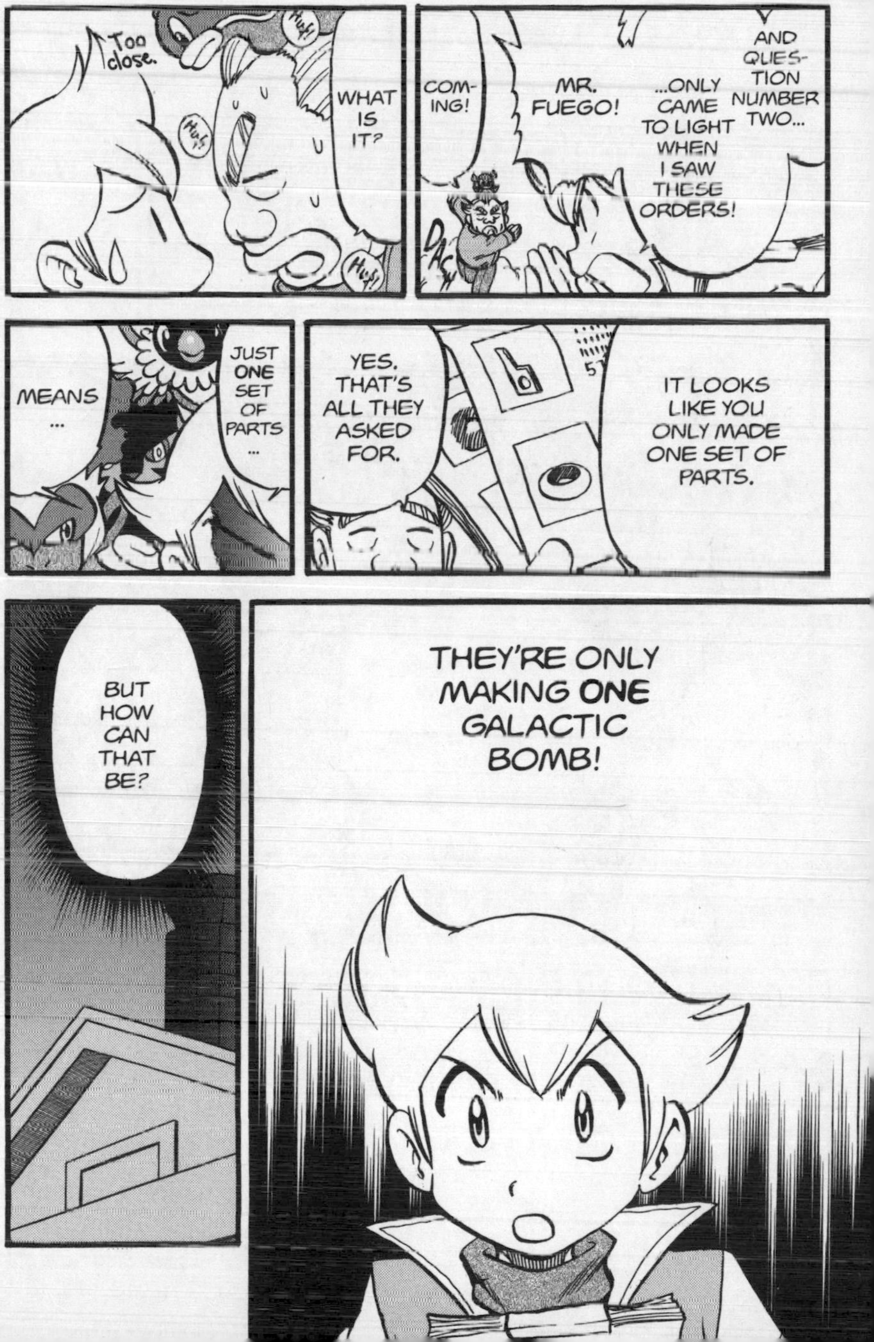
AND QUIES-TION NUMBER TWO...
...ONLY CAME TO LIGHT WHEN I SAW THESE ORDERS!
MR. FUEGO!
COM-ING!
WHAT IS IT?
Huff!
Huff!
Huff!
Too close.
IT LOOKS LIKE YOU ONLY MADE ONE SET OF PARTS.
YES. THAT'S ALL THEY ASKED FOR.
JUST ONE SET OF PARTS...
MEANS...
THEY'RE ONLY MAKING ONE GALACTIC BOMB!
BUT HOW CAN THAT BE?

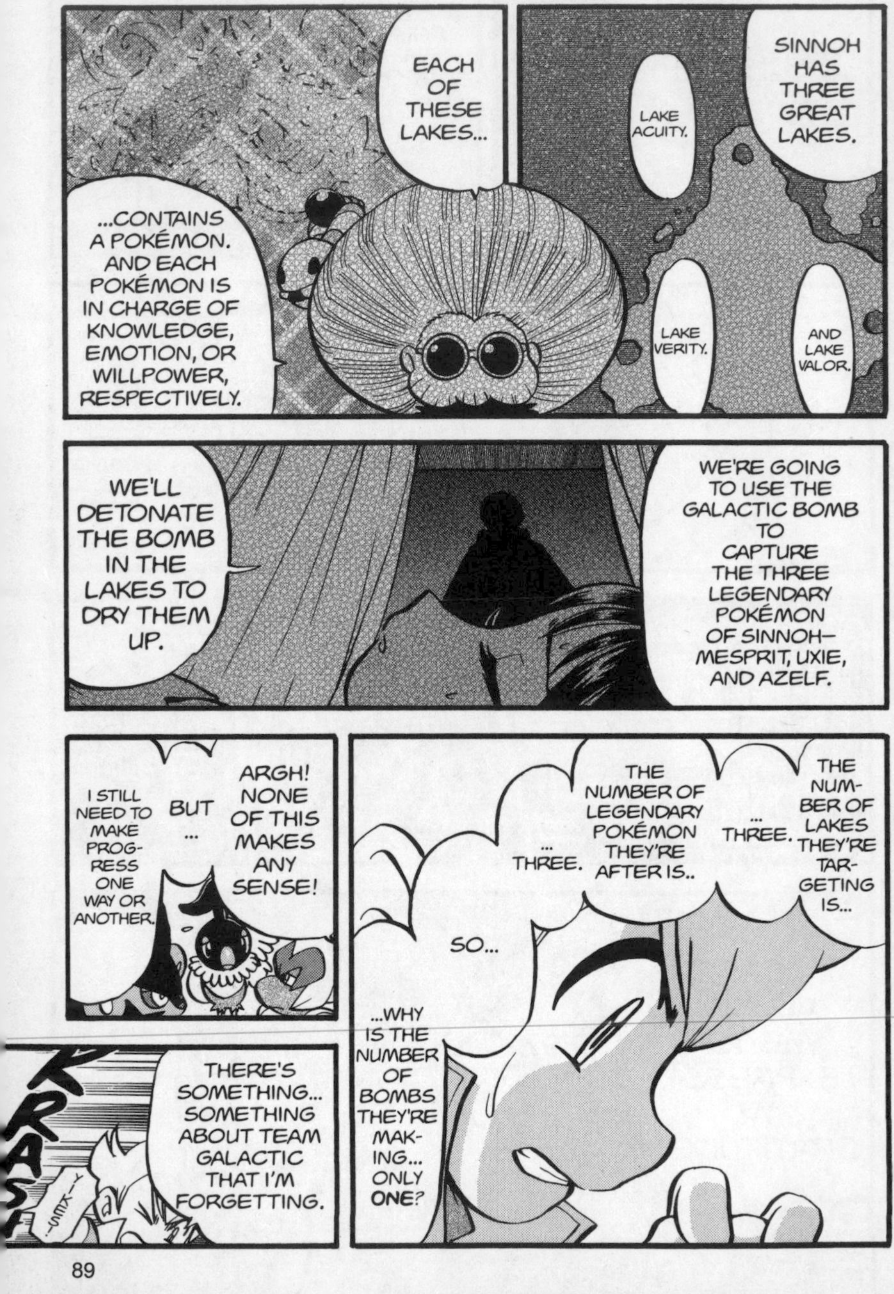
SINNOH HAS THREE GREAT LAKES.
LAKE ACUITY.
LAKE VERITY.
AND LAKE VALOR.
EACH OF THESE LAKES...
...CONTAINS A POKÉMON. AND EACH POKÉMON IS IN CHARGE OF KNOWLEDGE, EMOTION, OR WILLPOWER, RESPECTIVELY.
WE'RE GOING TO USE THE GALACTIC BOMB TO CAPTURE THE THREE LEGENDARY POKÉMON OF SINNOH—MESPRIT, UXIE, AND AZELF.
WE'LL DETONATE THE BOMB IN THE LAKES TO DRY THEM UP.
THE NUMBER OF LAKES THEY'RE TARGETING IS...
... THREE.
THE NUMBER OF LEGENDARY POKÉMON THEY'RE AFTER IS..
... THREE.
SO...
...WHY IS THE NUMBER OF BOMBS THEY'RE MAKING... ONLY ONE?
ARGH! NONE OF THIS MAKES ANY SENSE!
BUT ...
I STILL NEED TO MAKE PROGRESS ONE WAY OR ANOTHER.
THERE'S SOMETHING... SOMETHING ABOUT TEAM GALACTIC THAT I'M FORGETTING.
KRASH
YIKES!

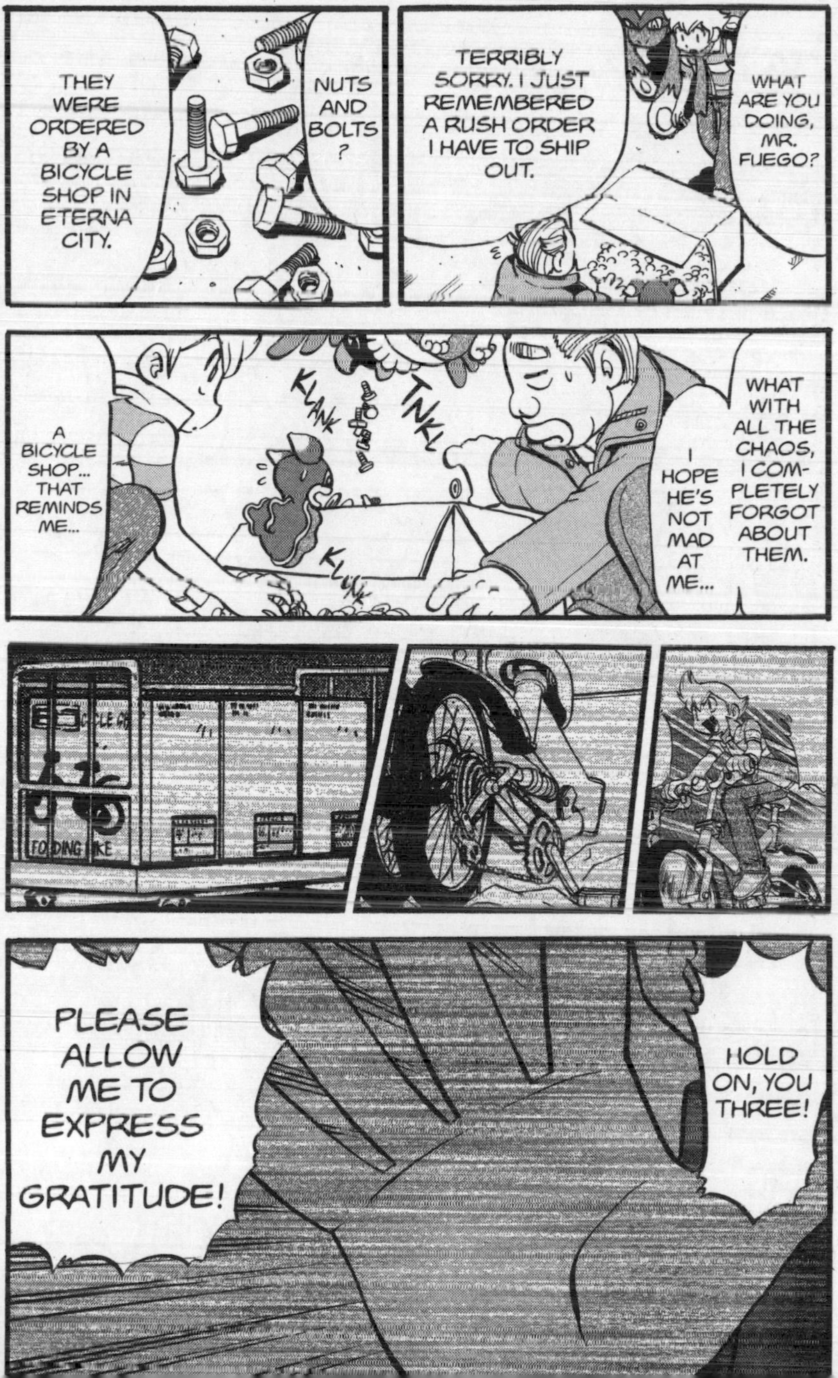
WHAT ARE YOU DOING, MR. FUEGO?
TERRIBLY SORRY. I JUST REMEMBERED A RUSH ORDER I HAVE TO SHIP OUT.
NUTS AND BOLTS?
THEY WERE ORDERED BY A BICYCLE SHOP IN ETERNA CITY.
WHAT WITH ALL THE CHAOS, I COMPLETELY FORGOT ABOUT THEM.
I HOPE HE'S NOT MAD AT ME...
TNKL
KLANK
KLANK
A BICYCLE SHOP... THAT REMINDS ME...
HOLD ON, YOU THREE!
PLEASE ALLOW ME TO EXPRESS MY GRATITUDE!

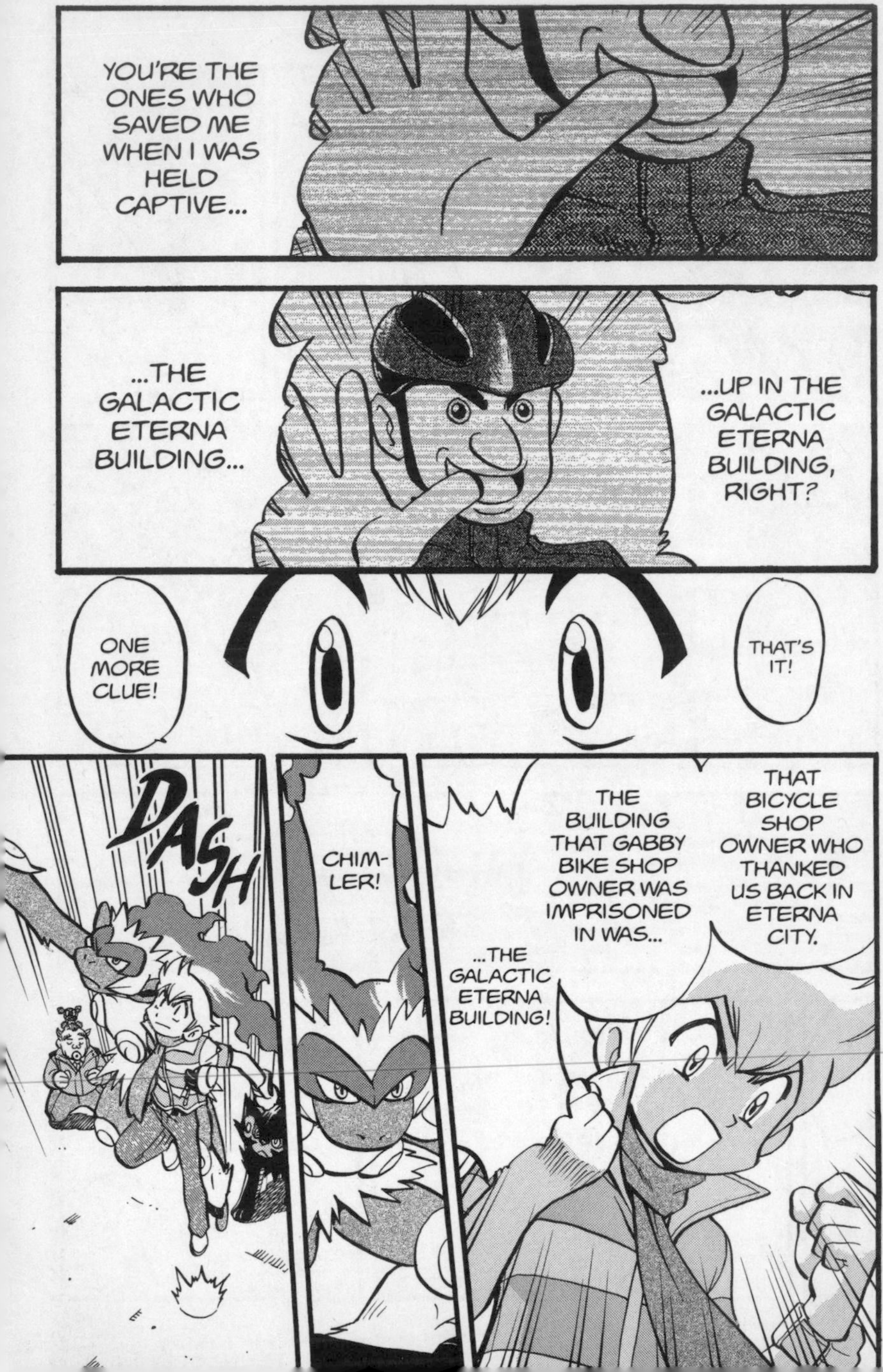
YOU'RE THE ONES WHO SAVED ME WHEN I WAS HELD CAPTIVE...
...UP IN THE GALACTIC ETERNA BUILDING, RIGHT?
...THE GALACTIC ETERNA BUILDING...
THAT'S IT!
ONE MORE CLUE!
THAT BICYCLE SHOP OWNER WHO THANKED US BACK IN ETERNA CITY.
THE BUILDING THAT GABBY BIKE SHOP OWNER WAS IMPRISONED IN WAS...
...THE GALACTIC ETERNA BUILDING!
CHIM-LER!
DASH

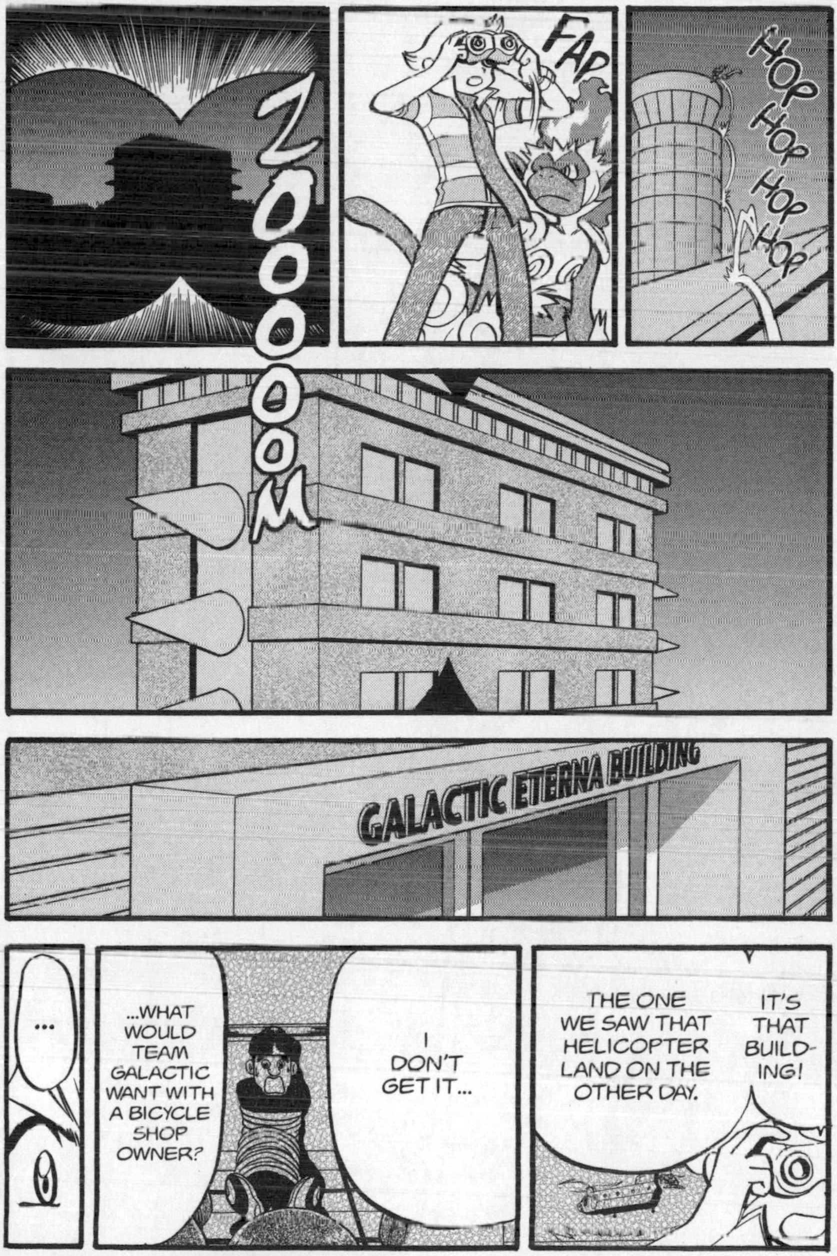
HOP HOP HOP HOP
FAP
ZOOOOOOM
GALACTIC ETERNA BUILDING
IT'S THAT BUILDING!
THE ONE WE SAW THAT HELICOPTER LAND ON THE OTHER DAY.
I DON'T GET IT...
...WHAT WOULD TEAM GALACTIC WANT WITH A BICYCLE SHOP OWNER?
...

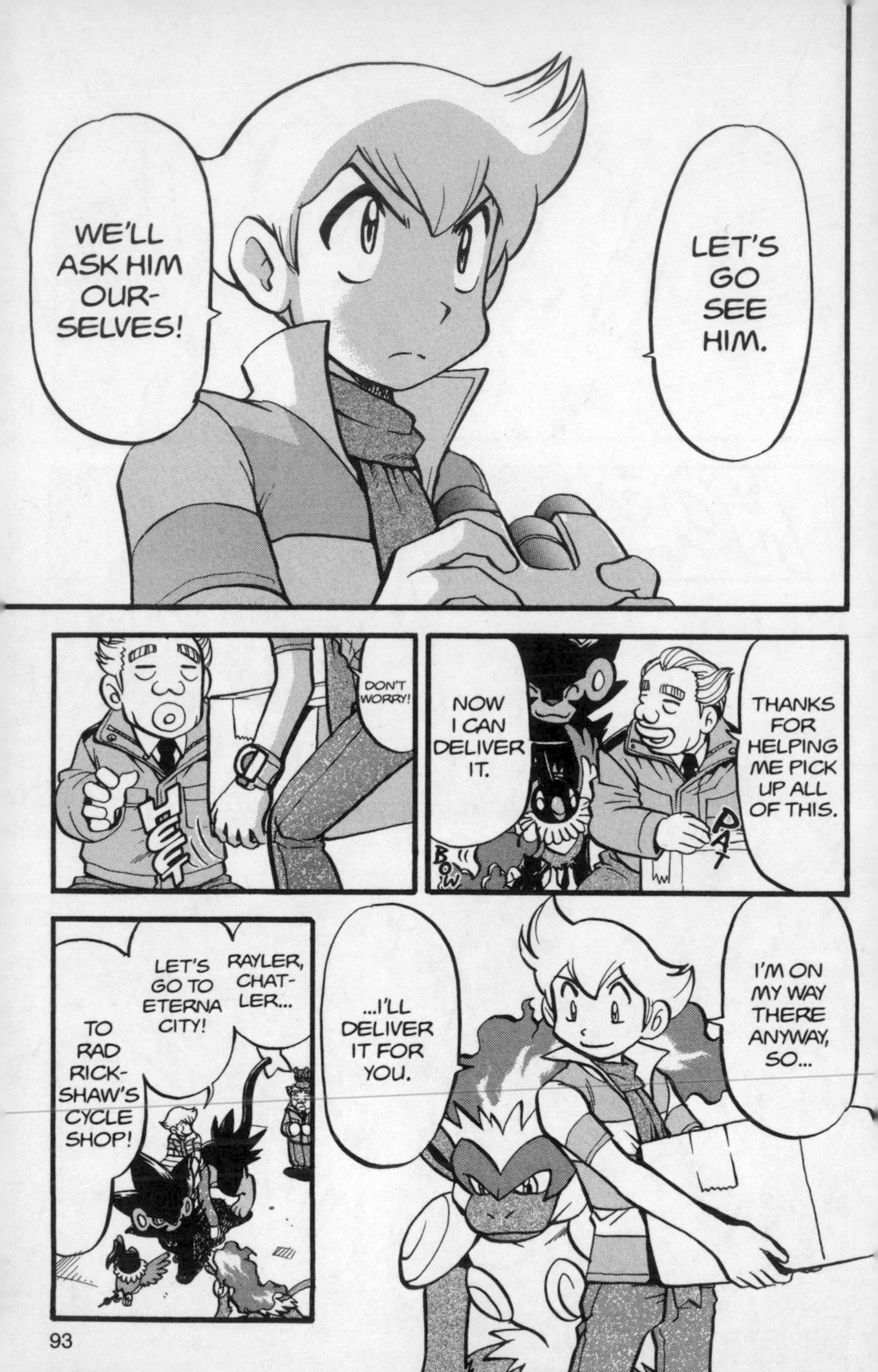
LET'S GO SEE HIM.
WE'LL ASK HIM OUR-SELVES!
THANKS FOR HELPING ME PICK UP ALL OF THIS.
PAT
NOW I CAN DELIVER IT.
BOW
DON'T WORRY!
I'M ON MY WAY THERE ANYWAY, SO...
...I'LL DELIVER IT FOR YOU.
RAYLER, CHAT-LER...
LET'S GO TO ETERNA CITY!
TO RAD RICK-SHAW'S CYCLE SHOP!

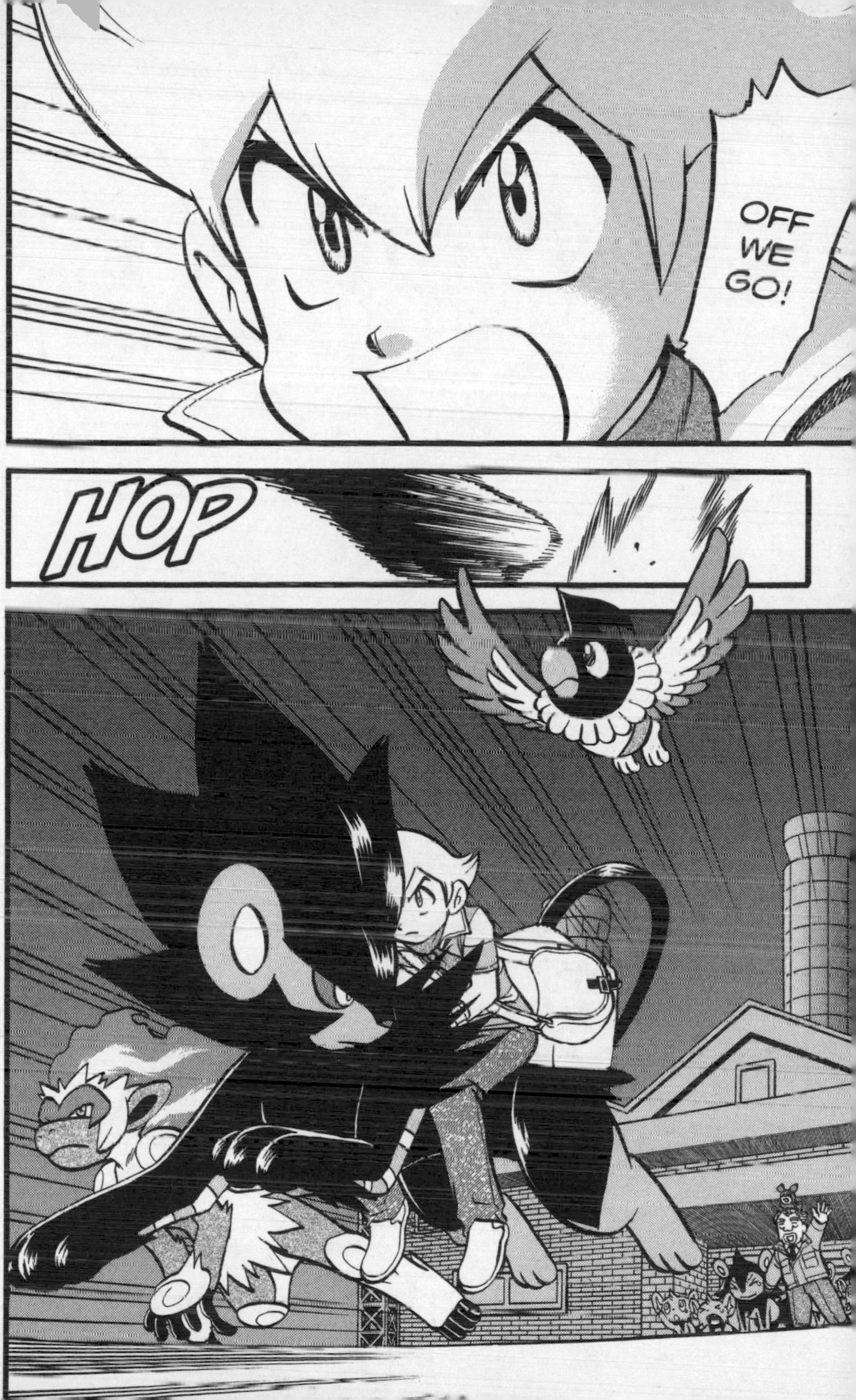
OFF WE GO!
HOP

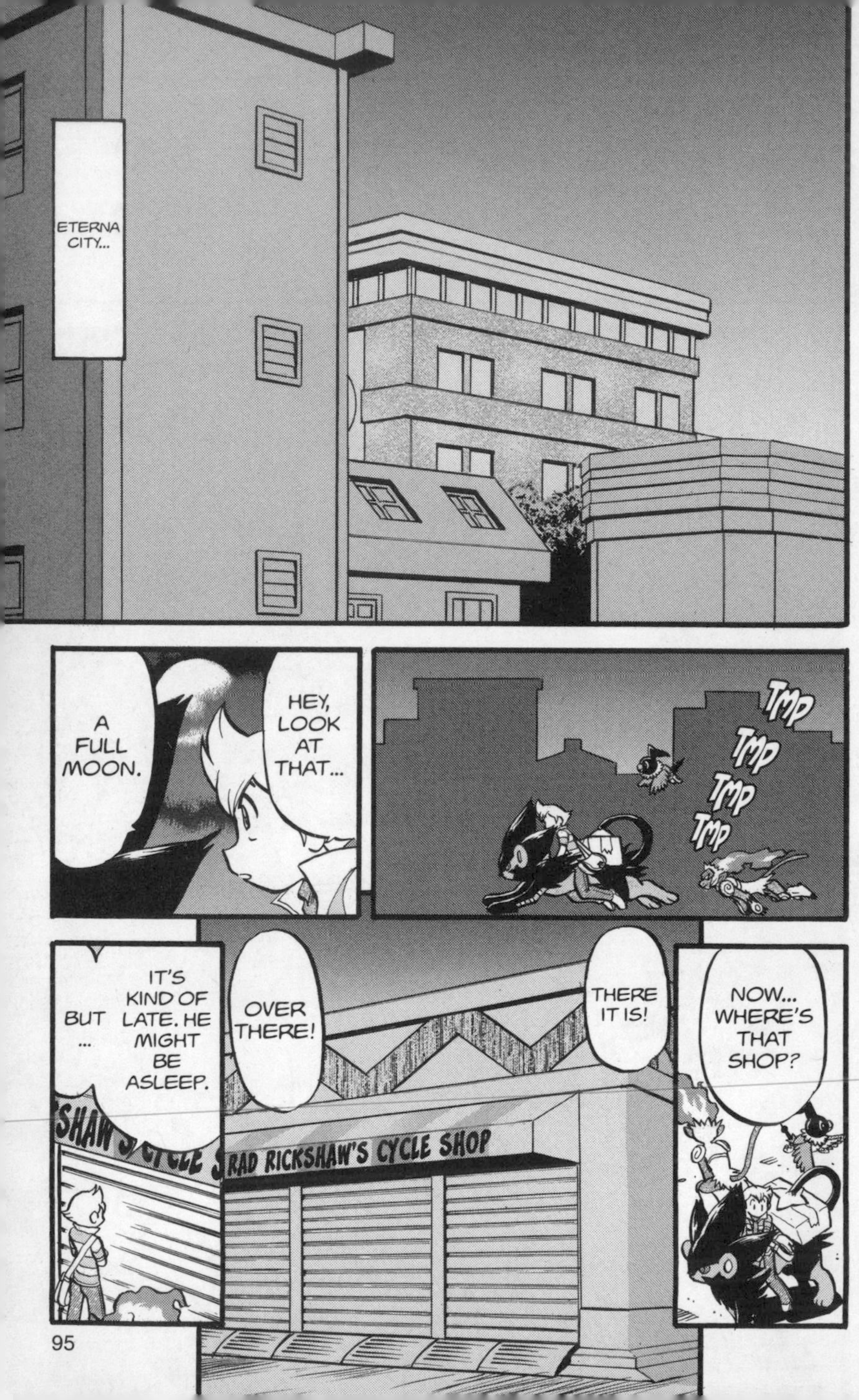
ETERNA CITY...
TMP
TMP
TMP
TMP
HEY, LOOK AT THAT...
A FULL MOON.
NOW... WHERE'S THAT SHOP?
THERE IT IS!
OVER THERE!
RAD RICKSHAW'S CYCLE SHOP
IT'S KIND OF LATE. HE MIGHT BE ASLEEP.
BUT ...

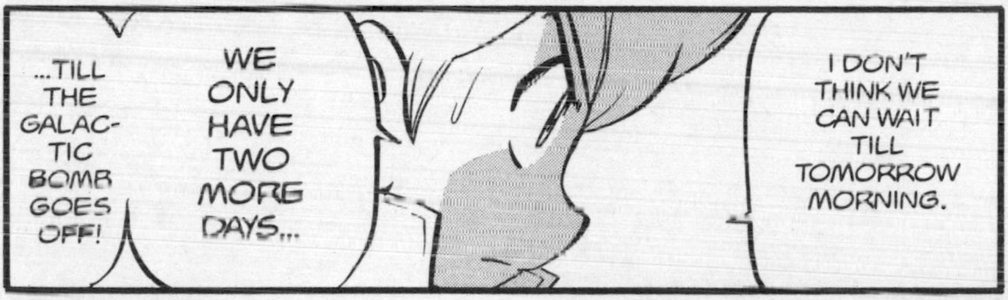
I DON'T THINK WE CAN WAIT TILL TOMORROW MORNING.
WE ONLY HAVE TWO MORE DAYS...
...TILL THE GALACTIC BOMB GOES OFF!

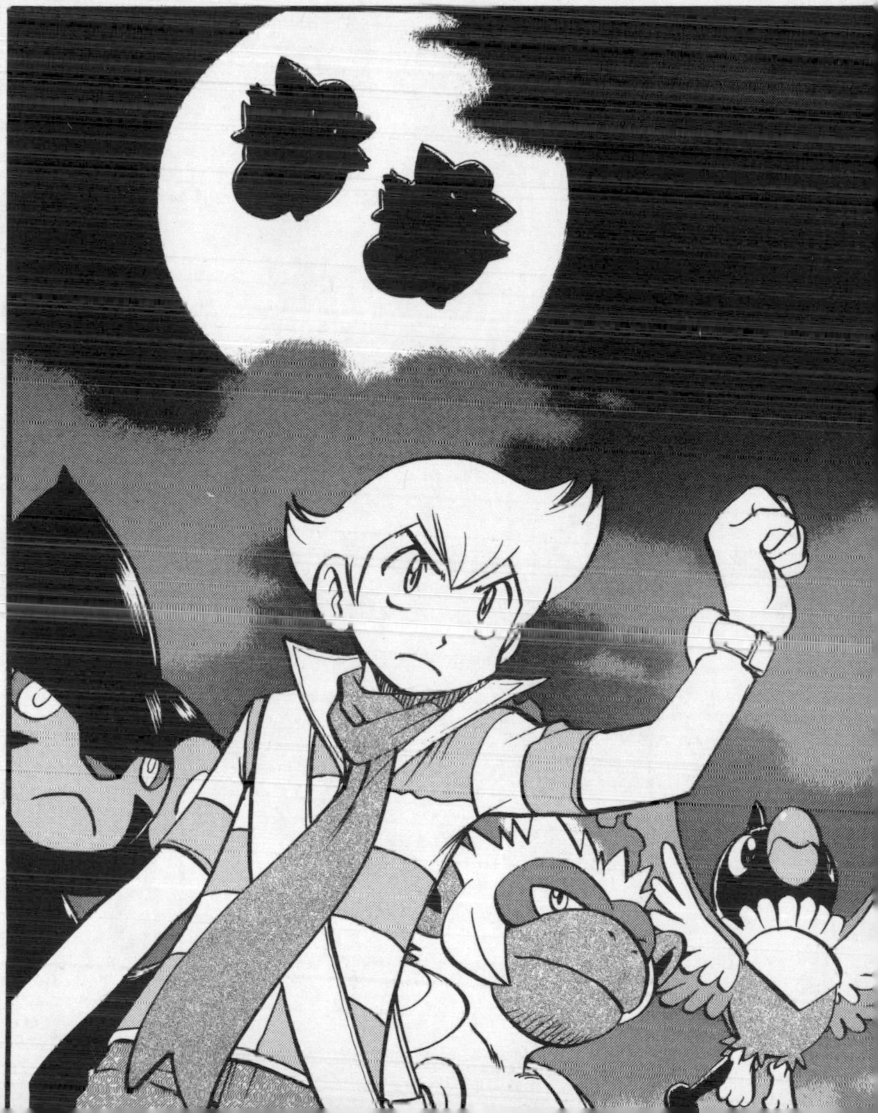

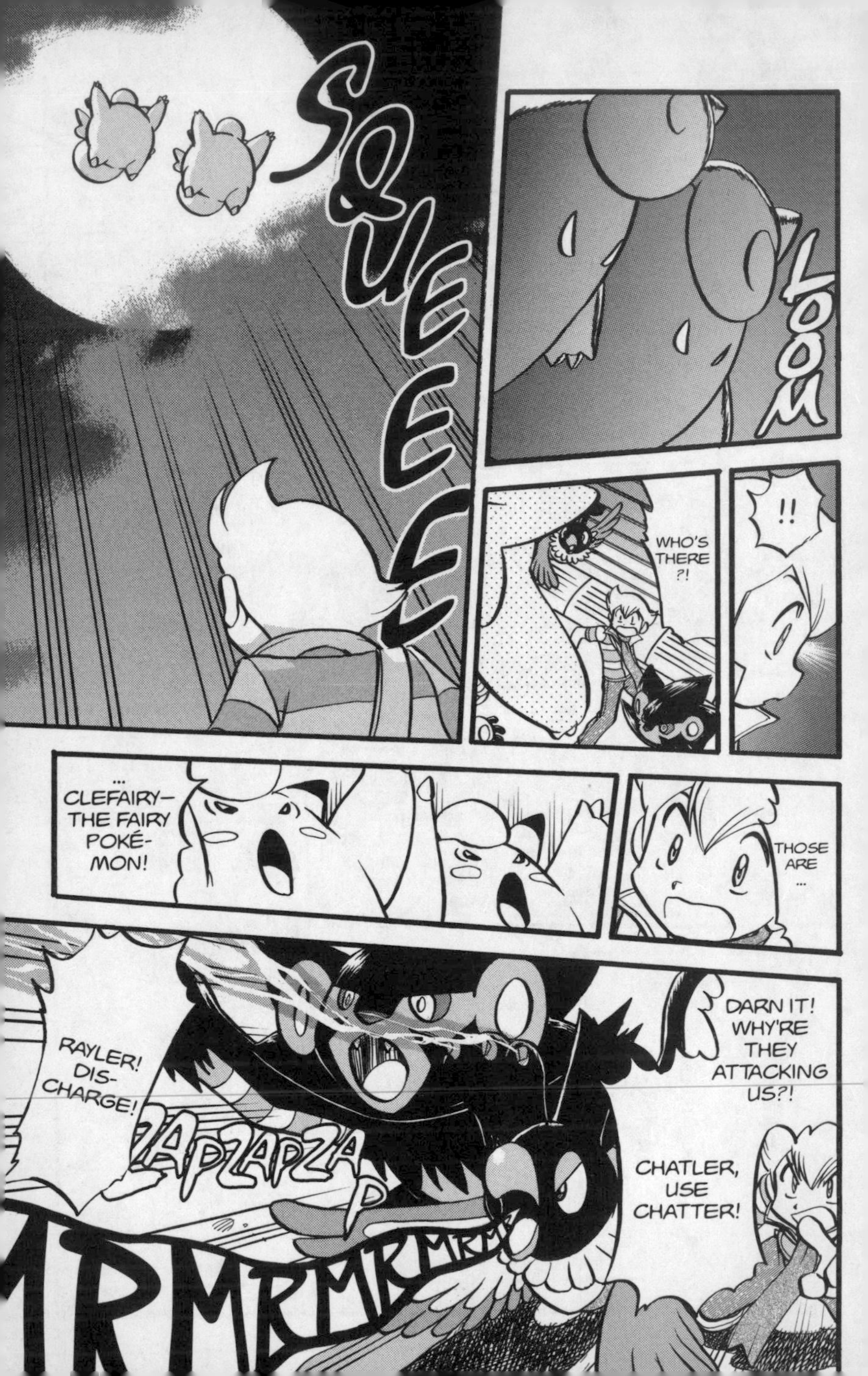
LOOOM
!!
WHO'S THERE ?!
SQUEEEEE
THOSE ARE ...
... CLEFAIRY— THE FAIRY POKÉMON!
DARN IT! WHY'RE THEY ATTACKING US?!
RAYLER! DIS- CHARGE!
ZAPZAPZAPZAP
CHATLER, USE CHATTER!
MRMRMRMRMRM

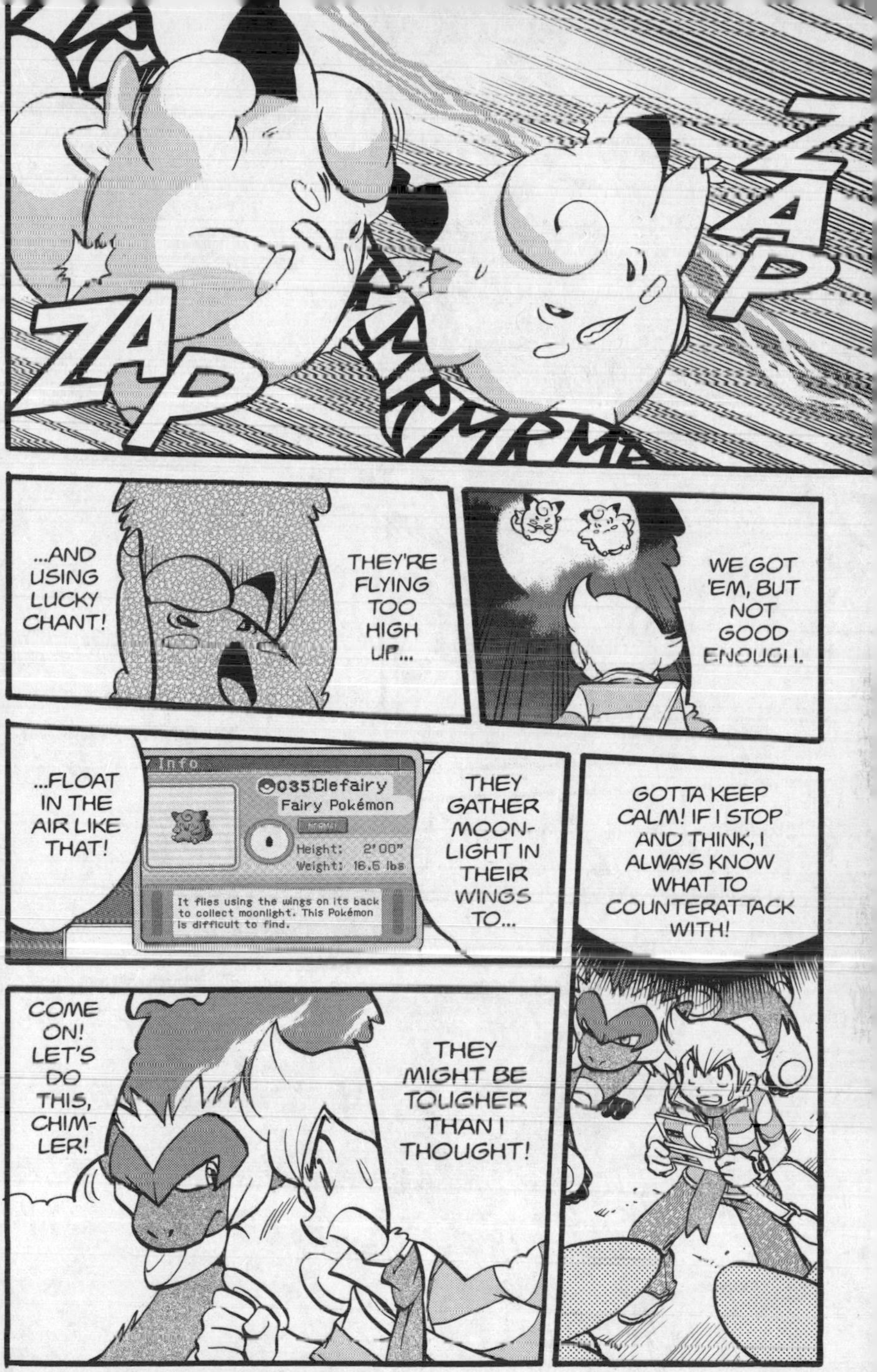
ZAP
ZAP
WE GOT 'EM, BUT NOT GOOD ENOUGH!
THEY'RE FLYING TOO HIGH UP...
...AND USING LUCKY CHANT!
GOTTA KEEP CALM! IF I STOP AND THINK, I ALWAYS KNOW WHAT TO COUNTERATTACK WITH!
THEY GATHER MOONLIGHT IN THEIR WINGS TO...
Info
035 Clefairy
Fairy Pokémon
Height: 2'00"
Weight: 16.5 lbs
It flies using the wings on its back to collect moonlight. This Pokémon is difficult to find.
...FLOAT IN THE AIR LIKE THAT!
THEY MIGHT BE TOUGHER THAN I THOUGHT!
COME ON! LET'S DO THIS, CHIMLER!

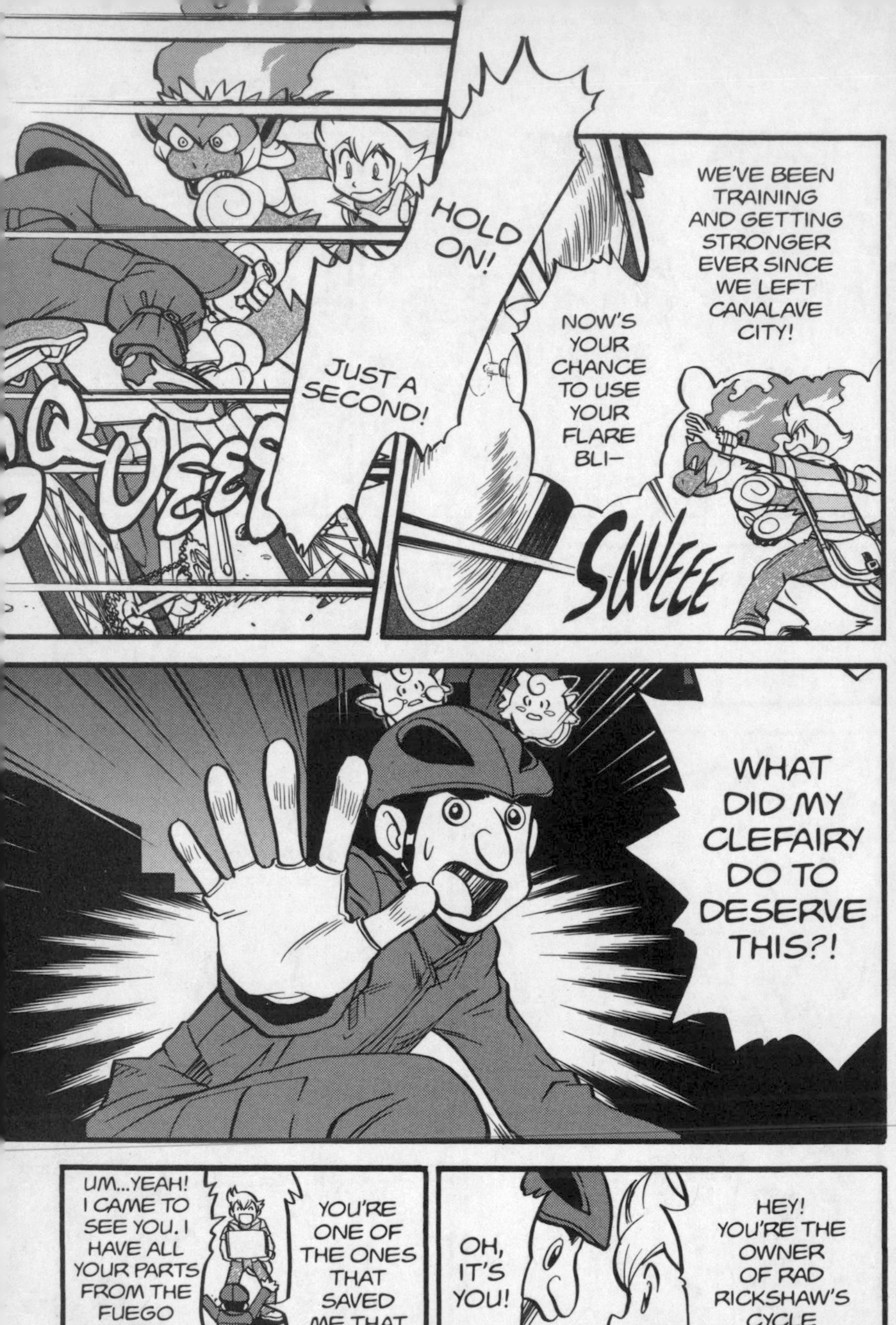
WE'VE BEEN TRAINING AND GETTING STRONGER EVER SINCE WE LEFT CANALAVE CITY!
NOW'S YOUR CHANCE TO USE YOUR FLARE BLI–
SQUEEE
HOLD ON!
JUST A SECOND!
WHAT DID MY CLEFAIRY DO TO DESERVE THIS?!
HEY! YOU'RE THE OWNER OF RAD RICKSHAW'S CYCLE SHOP!
OH, IT'S YOU!
YOU'RE ONE OF THE ONES THAT SAVED ME THAT TIME!
UM...YEAH! I CAME TO SEE YOU. I HAVE ALL YOUR PARTS FROM THE FUEGO IRON-WORKS.

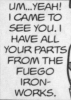

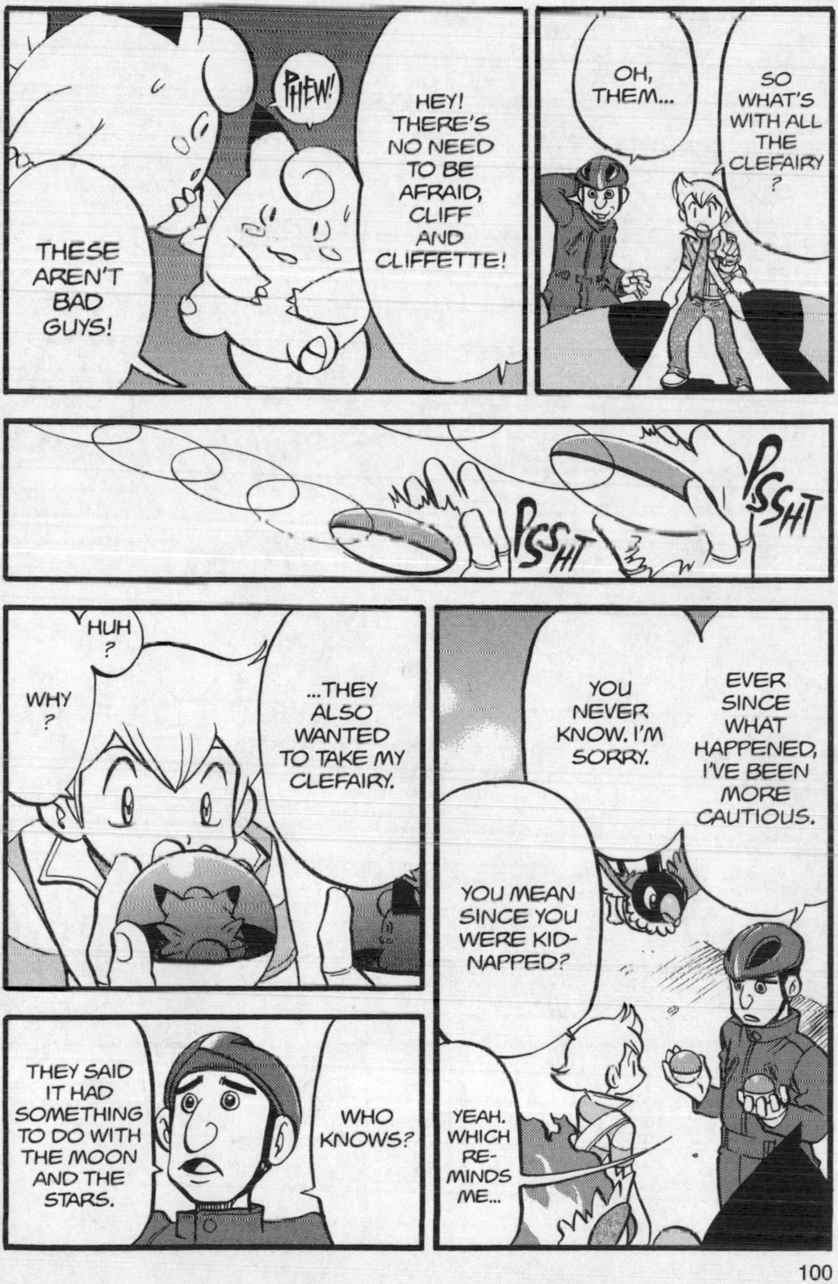
SO WHAT'S WITH ALL THE CLEFAIRY?
OH, THEM...
HEY! THERE'S NO NEED TO BE AFRAID, CLIFF AND CLIFFETTE!
PHEW!
THESE AREN'T BAD GUYS!
PSSHT
PSSHT
EVER SINCE WHAT HAPPENED, I'VE BEEN MORE CAUTIOUS.
YOU NEVER KNOW. I'M SORRY.
YOU MEAN SINCE YOU WERE KID-NAPPED?
YEAH. WHICH RE-MINDS ME...
...THEY ALSO WANTED TO TAKE MY CLEFAIRY.
HUH?
WHY?
WHO KNOWS?
THEY SAID IT HAD SOMETHING TO DO WITH THE MOON AND THE STARS.

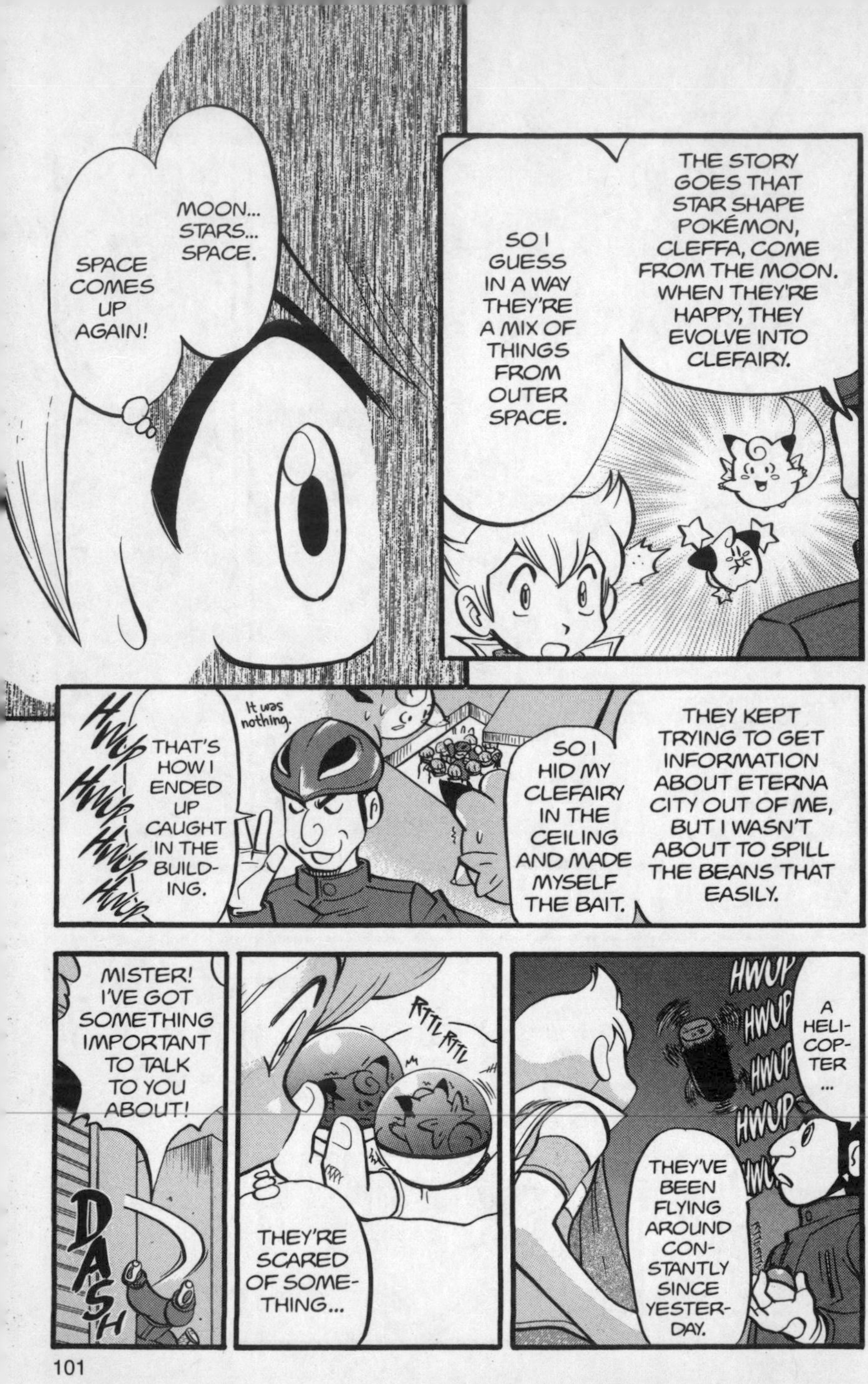
THE STORY GOES THAT STAR SHAPE POKÉMON, CLEFFA, COME FROM THE MOON. WHEN THEY'RE HAPPY, THEY EVOLVE INTO CLEFAIRY.
SO I GUESS IN A WAY THEY'RE A MIX OF THINGS FROM OUTER SPACE.
MOON... STARS... SPACE.
SPACE COMES UP AGAIN!
THEY KEPT TRYING TO GET INFORMATION ABOUT ETERNA CITY OUT OF ME, BUT I WASN'T ABOUT TO SPILL THE BEANS THAT EASILY.
SO I HID MY CLEFAIRY IN THE CEILING AND MADE MYSELF THE BAIT.
It was nothing.
THAT'S HOW I ENDED UP CAUGHT IN THE BUILD-ING.
HWUP HWUP HWUP HWUP
A HELI-COP-TER...
HWUP HWUP HWUP HWUP
THEY'VE BEEN FLYING AROUND CON-STANTLY SINCE YESTER-DAY.
RTTL RTTL
THEY'RE SCARED OF SOME-THING...
MISTER! I'VE GOT SOMETHING IMPORTANT TO TALK TO YOU ABOUT!
DASH

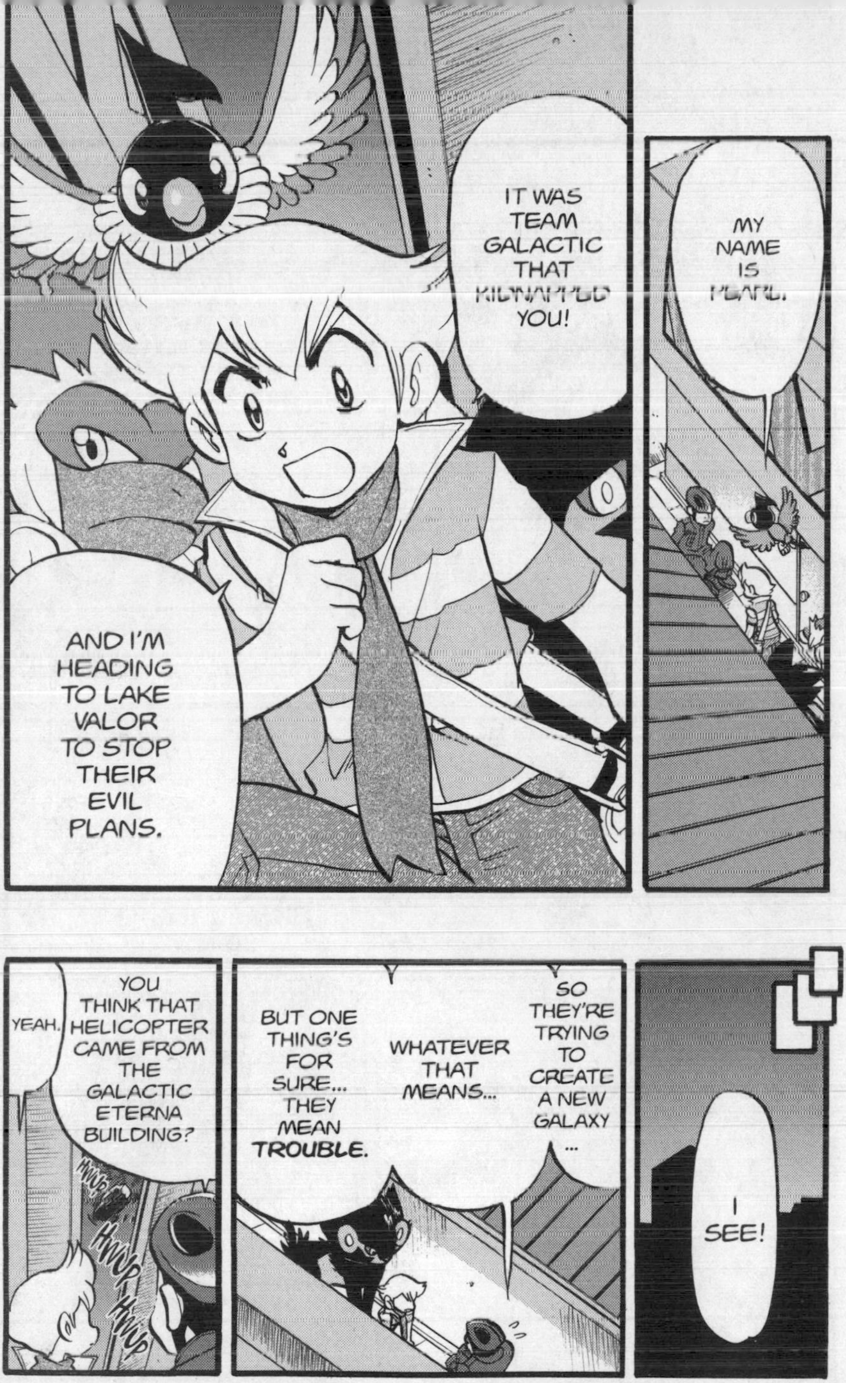
MY NAME IS PEARL.
IT WAS TEAM GALACTIC THAT KIDNAPPED YOU!
AND I'M HEADING TO LAKE VALOR TO STOP THEIR EVIL PLANS.
I SEE!
SO THEY'RE TRYING TO CREATE A NEW GALAXY ...
WHATEVER THAT MEANS...
BUT ONE THING'S FOR SURE... THEY MEAN **TROUBLE**.
YOU THINK THAT HELICOPTER CAME FROM THE GALACTIC ETERNA BUILDING?
YEAH.

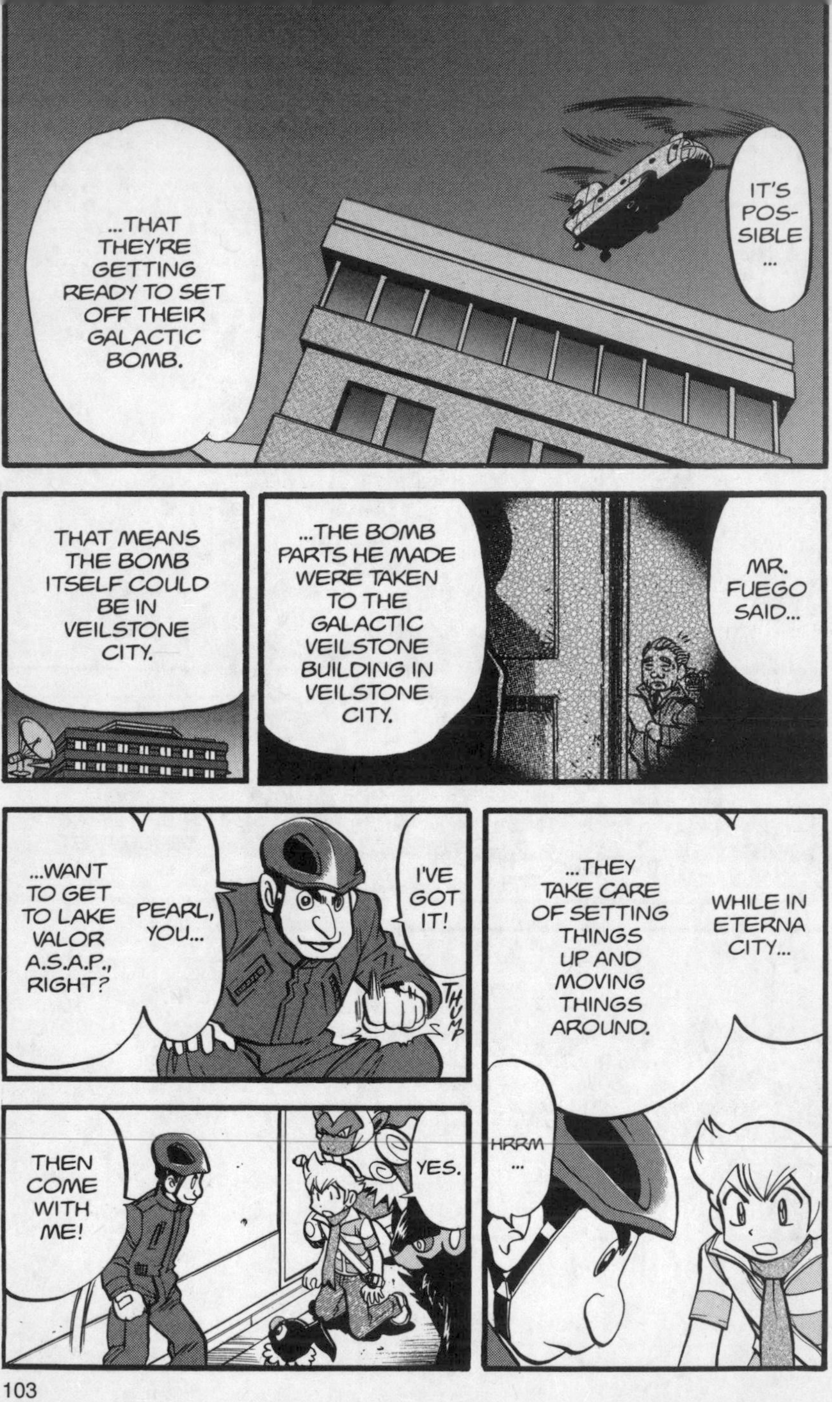
IT'S POS-SIBLE...
...THAT THEY'RE GETTING READY TO SET OFF THEIR GALACTIC BOMB.
MR. FUEGO SAID...
...THE BOMB PARTS HE MADE WERE TAKEN TO THE GALACTIC VEILSTONE BUILDING IN VEILSTONE CITY.
THAT MEANS THE BOMB ITSELF COULD BE IN VEILSTONE CITY.
WHILE IN ETERNA CITY...
...THEY TAKE CARE OF SETTING THINGS UP AND MOVING THINGS AROUND.
HRRM...
I'VE GOT IT!
THUMP
PEARL, YOU...
...WANT TO GET TO LAKE VALOR A.S.A.P., RIGHT?
YES.
THEN COME WITH ME!

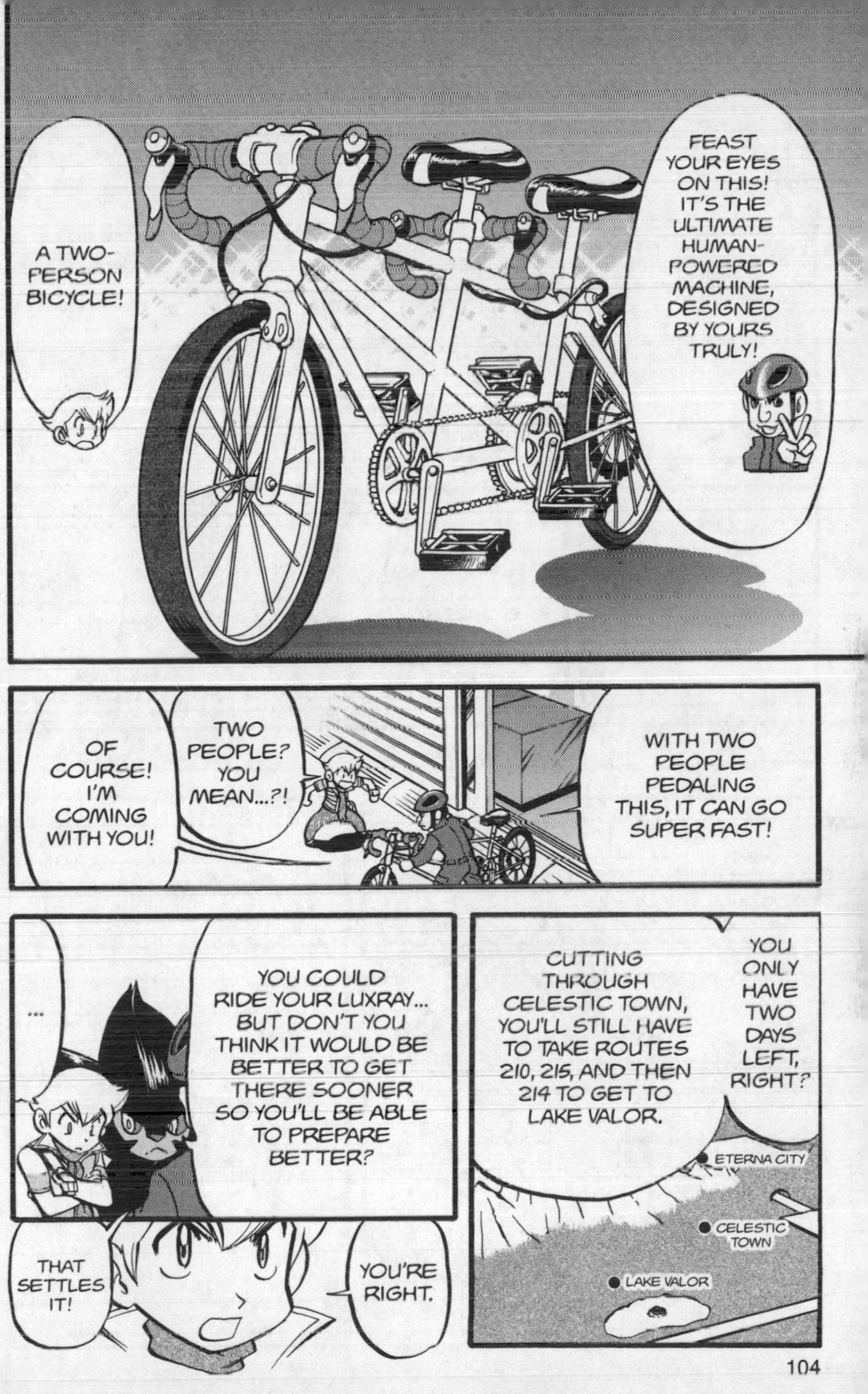
FEAST YOUR EYES ON THIS! IT'S THE ULTIMATE HUMAN-POWERED MACHINE, DESIGNED BY YOURS TRULY!
A TWO-PERSON BICYCLE!
WITH TWO PEOPLE PEDALING THIS, IT CAN GO SUPER FAST!
TWO PEOPLE? YOU MEAN...?!
OF COURSE! I'M COMING WITH YOU!
YOU ONLY HAVE TWO DAYS LEFT, RIGHT?
CUTTING THROUGH CELESTIC TOWN, YOU'LL STILL HAVE TO TAKE ROUTES 210, 215, AND THEN 214 TO GET TO LAKE VALOR.
ETERNA CITY
CELESTIC TOWN
LAKE VALOR
YOU COULD RIDE YOUR LUXRAY... BUT DON'T YOU THINK IT WOULD BE BETTER TO GET THERE SOONER SO YOU'LL BE ABLE TO PREPARE BETTER?
...
YOU'RE RIGHT.
THAT SETTLES IT!

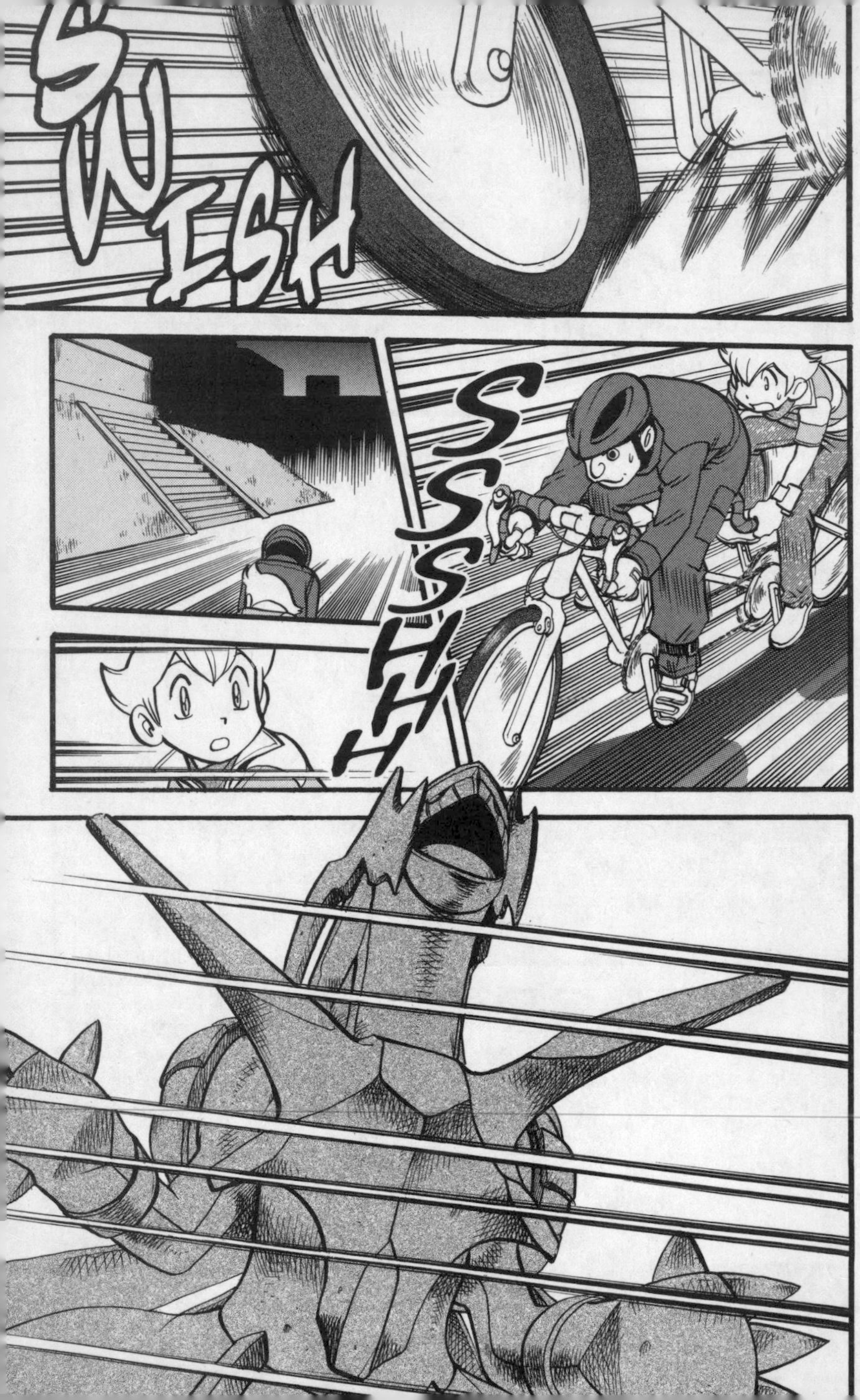
SWISH
SSSHHH

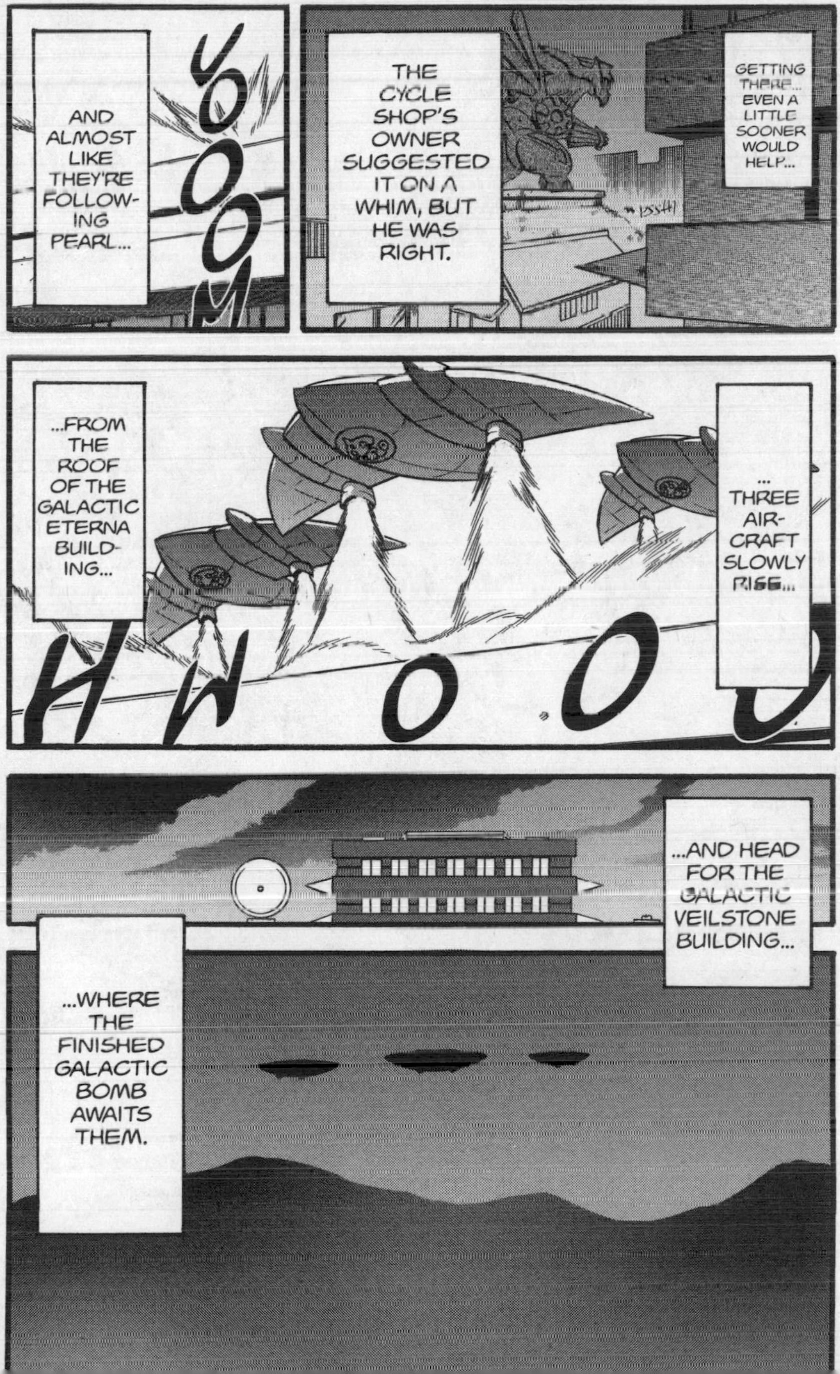
GETTING THERE... EVEN A LITTLE SOONER WOULD HELP...
THE CYCLE SHOP'S OWNER SUGGESTED IT ON A WHIM, BUT HE WAS RIGHT.
AND ALMOST LIKE THEY'RE FOLLOW-ING PEARL...
... THREE AIR-CRAFT SLOWLY RISE...
...FROM THE ROOF OF THE GALACTIC ETERNA BUILD-ING...
...AND HEAD FOR THE GALACTIC VEILSTONE BUILDING...
...WHERE THE FINISHED GALACTIC BOMB AWAITS THEM.

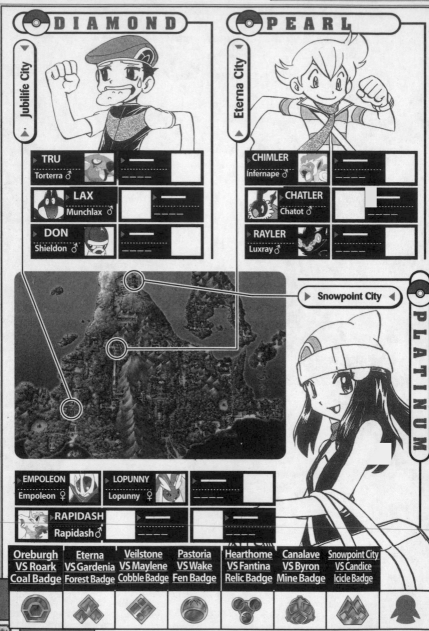

ADVENTURE MAP

DIAMOND

Jubilife City

TRU Torterra ♂		— — — —
LAX Munchlax ♂		—
DON Shieldon ♂		— — — —

PEARL

Eterna City

CHIMLER Infernape ♂		— — — —
CHATLER Chatot ♂		— — — —
RAYLER Luxray ♂		— — — —

▶ Snowpoint City ◀

PLATINUM

EMPOLEON Empoleon ♀	**LOPUNNY** Lopunny ♀	— — — —
RAPIDASH Rapidash ♂		— — — —

Oreburgh VS Roark Coal Badge	Eterna VS Gardenia Forest Badge	Veilstone VS Maylene Cobble Badge	Pastoria VS Wake Fen Badge	Hearthome VS Fantina Relic Badge	Canalave VS Byron Mine Badge	Snowpoint City VS Candice Icicle Badge

53

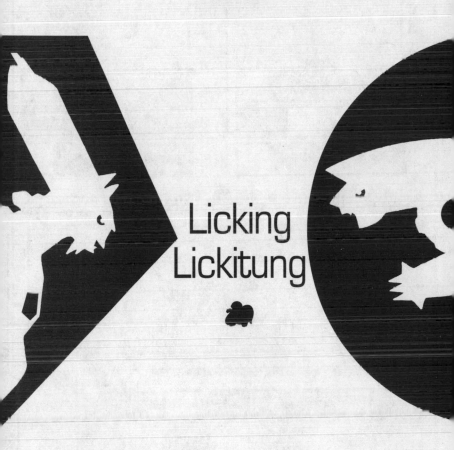

Licking
Lickitung

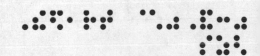

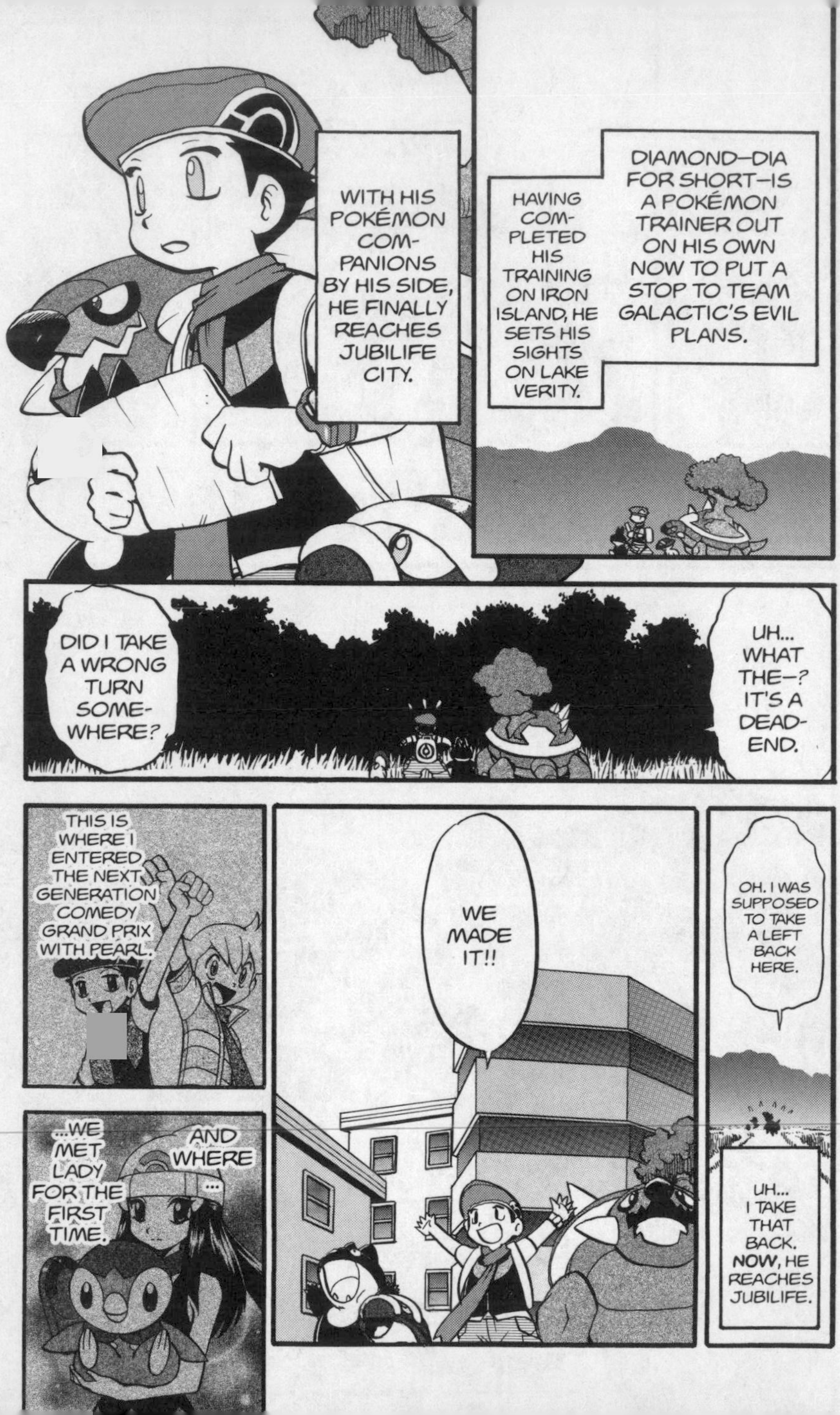
DIAMOND—DIA FOR SHORT—IS A POKÉMON TRAINER OUT ON HIS OWN NOW TO PUT A STOP TO TEAM GALACTIC'S EVIL PLANS.
HAVING COM-PLETED HIS TRAINING ON IRON ISLAND, HE SETS HIS SIGHTS ON LAKE VERITY.
WITH HIS POKÉMON COM-PANIONS BY HIS SIDE, HE FINALLY REACHES JUBILIFE CITY.
UH... WHAT THE—? IT'S A DEAD-END.
DID I TAKE A WRONG TURN SOME-WHERE?
OH. I WAS SUPPOSED TO TAKE A LEFT BACK HERE.
UH... I TAKE THAT BACK. **NOW**, HE REACHES JUBILIFE.
WE MADE IT!!
THIS IS WHERE I ENTERED THE NEXT GENERATION COMEDY GRAND PRIX WITH PEARL.
AND WHERE
...WE MET LADY FOR THE FIRST TIME.
...

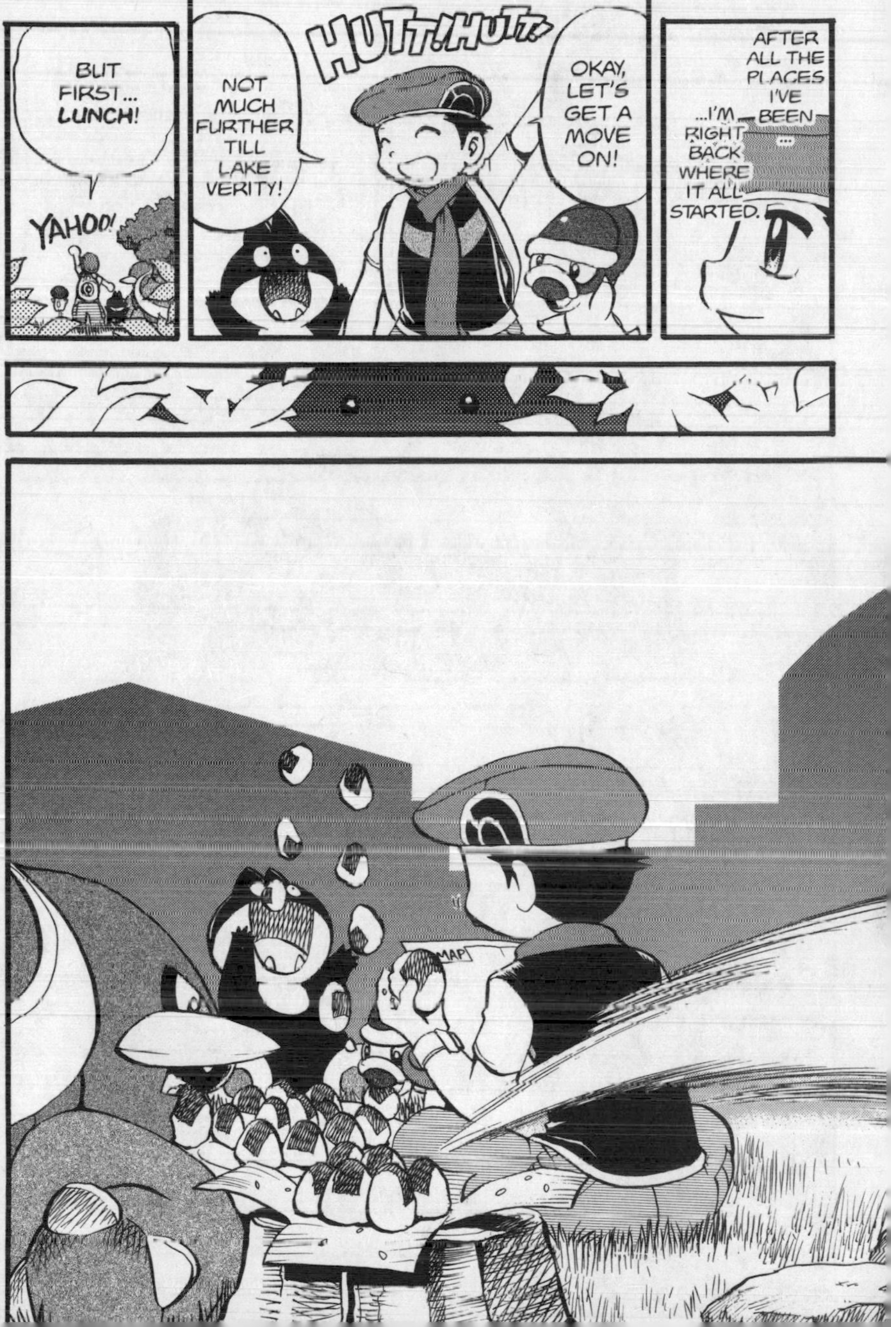
AFTER ALL THE PLACES I'VE BEEN...
...I'M RIGHT BACK WHERE IT ALL STARTED.
OKAY, LET'S GET A MOVE ON!
HUTT! HUTT!
NOT MUCH FURTHER TILL LAKE VERITY!
BUT FIRST... LUNCH!
YAHOO!
MAP

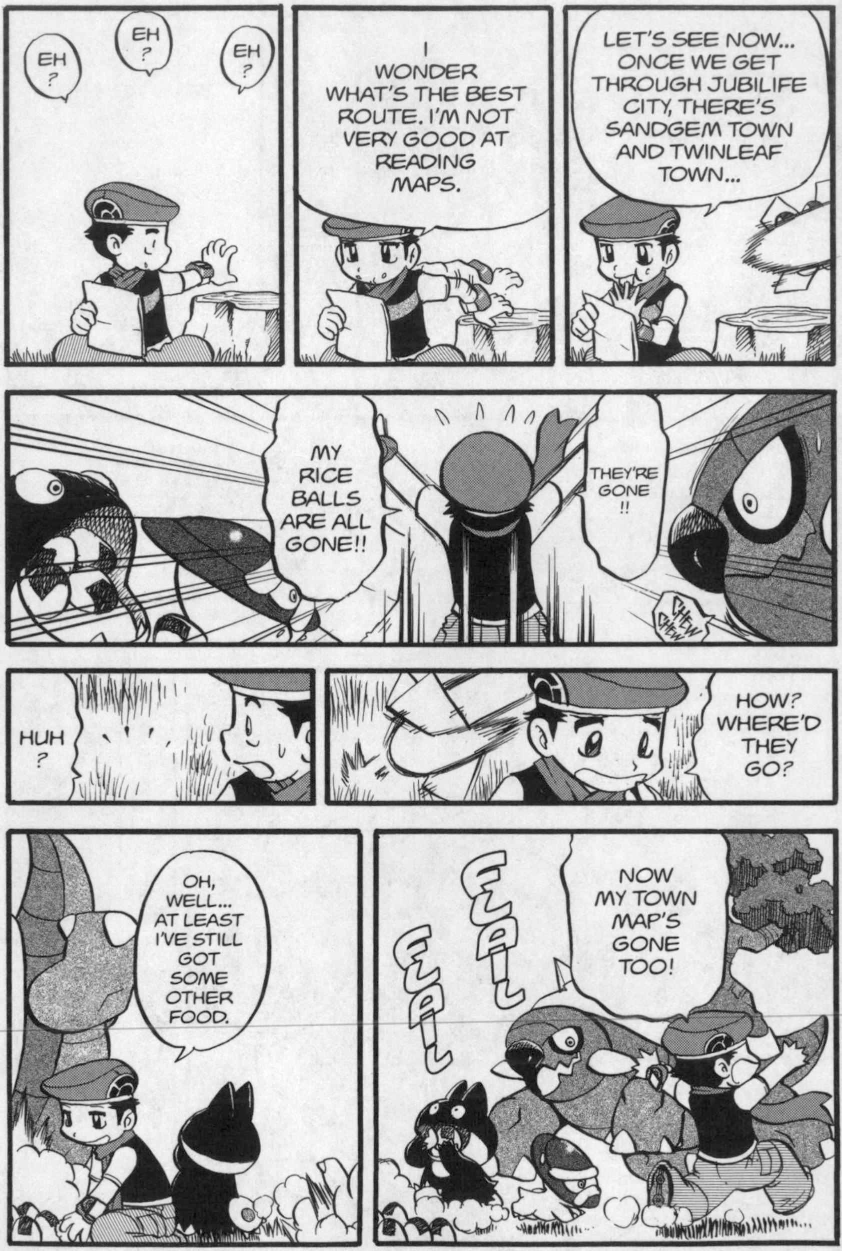
LET'S SEE NOW... ONCE WE GET THROUGH JUBILIFE CITY, THERE'S SANDGEM TOWN AND TWINLEAF TOWN...
I WONDER WHAT'S THE BEST ROUTE. I'M NOT VERY GOOD AT READING MAPS.
EH?
EH?
EH?
THEY'RE GONE!!
MY RICE BALLS ARE ALL GONE!!
CHEW CHEW
HOW? WHERE'D THEY GO?
HUH?
NOW MY TOWN MAP'S GONE TOO!
FLAIL
FLAIL
OH, WELL... AT LEAST I'VE STILL GOT SOME OTHER FOOD.

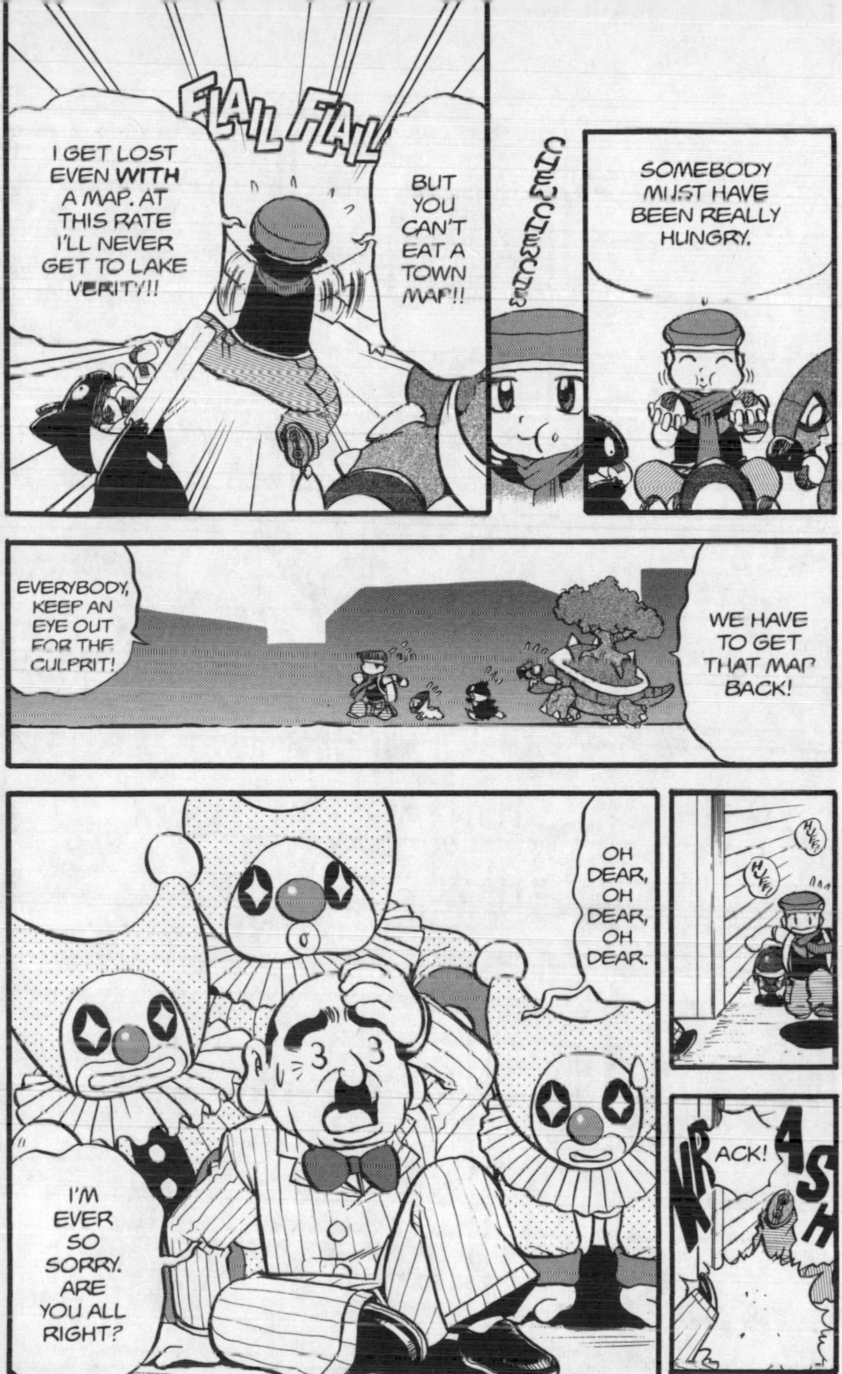
SOMEBODY MUST HAVE BEEN REALLY HUNGRY.
CHEW CHEW CHEW
BUT YOU CAN'T EAT A TOWN MAP!!
FLAIL FLAIL
I GET LOST EVEN WITH A MAP. AT THIS RATE I'LL NEVER GET TO LAKE VERITY!!
WE HAVE TO GET THAT MAP BACK!
EVERYBODY, KEEP AN EYE OUT FOR THE CULPRIT!
KRASH
ACK!
OH DEAR, OH DEAR, OH DEAR.
I'M EVER SO SORRY. ARE YOU ALL RIGHT?

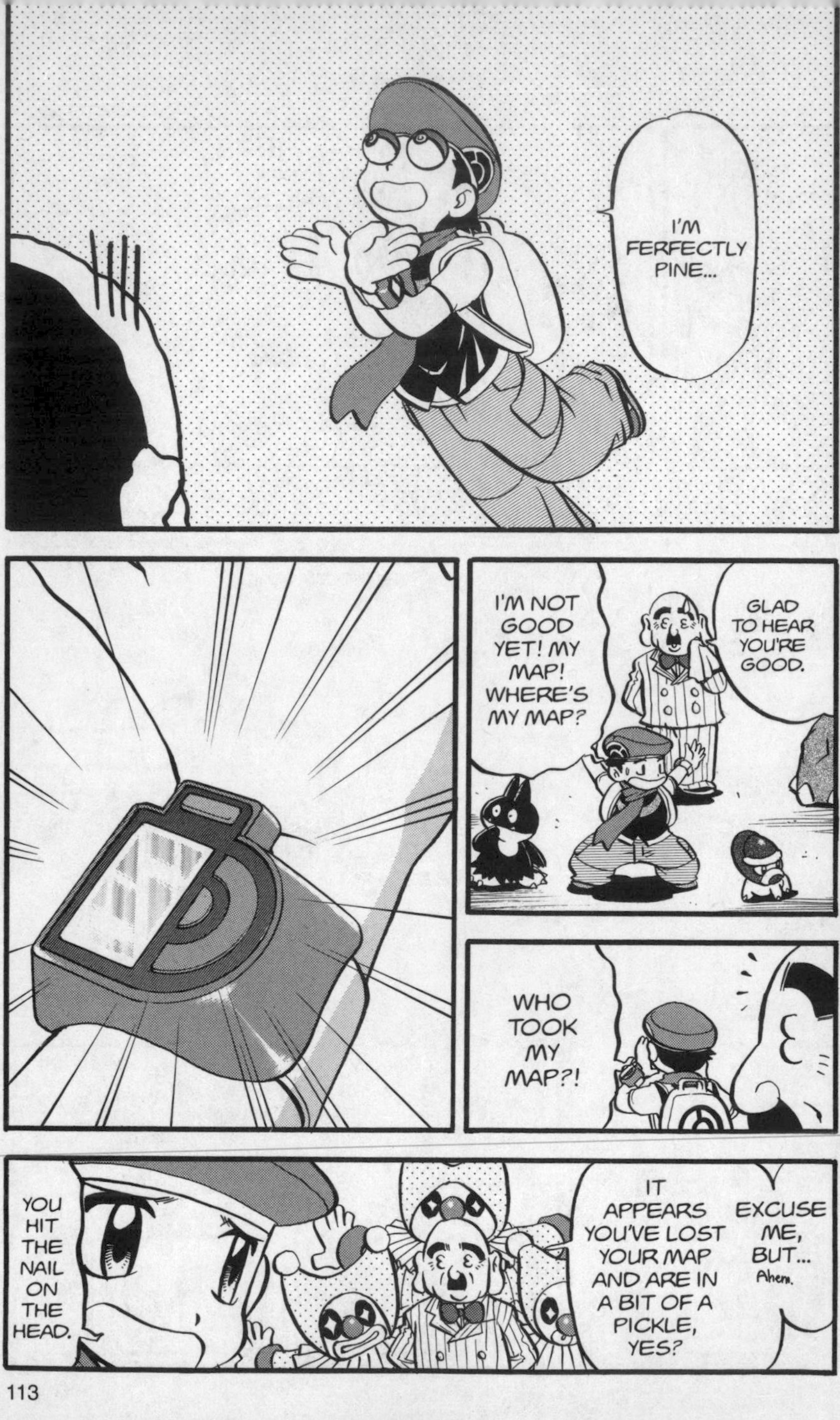
I'M FERFECTLY PINE...
GLAD TO HEAR YOU'RE GOOD.
I'M NOT GOOD YET! MY MAP! WHERE'S MY MAP?
WHO TOOK MY MAP?!
EXCUSE ME, BUT...
Ahem.
IT APPEARS YOU'VE LOST YOUR MAP AND ARE IN A BIT OF A PICKLE, YES?
YOU HIT THE NAIL ON THE HEAD.

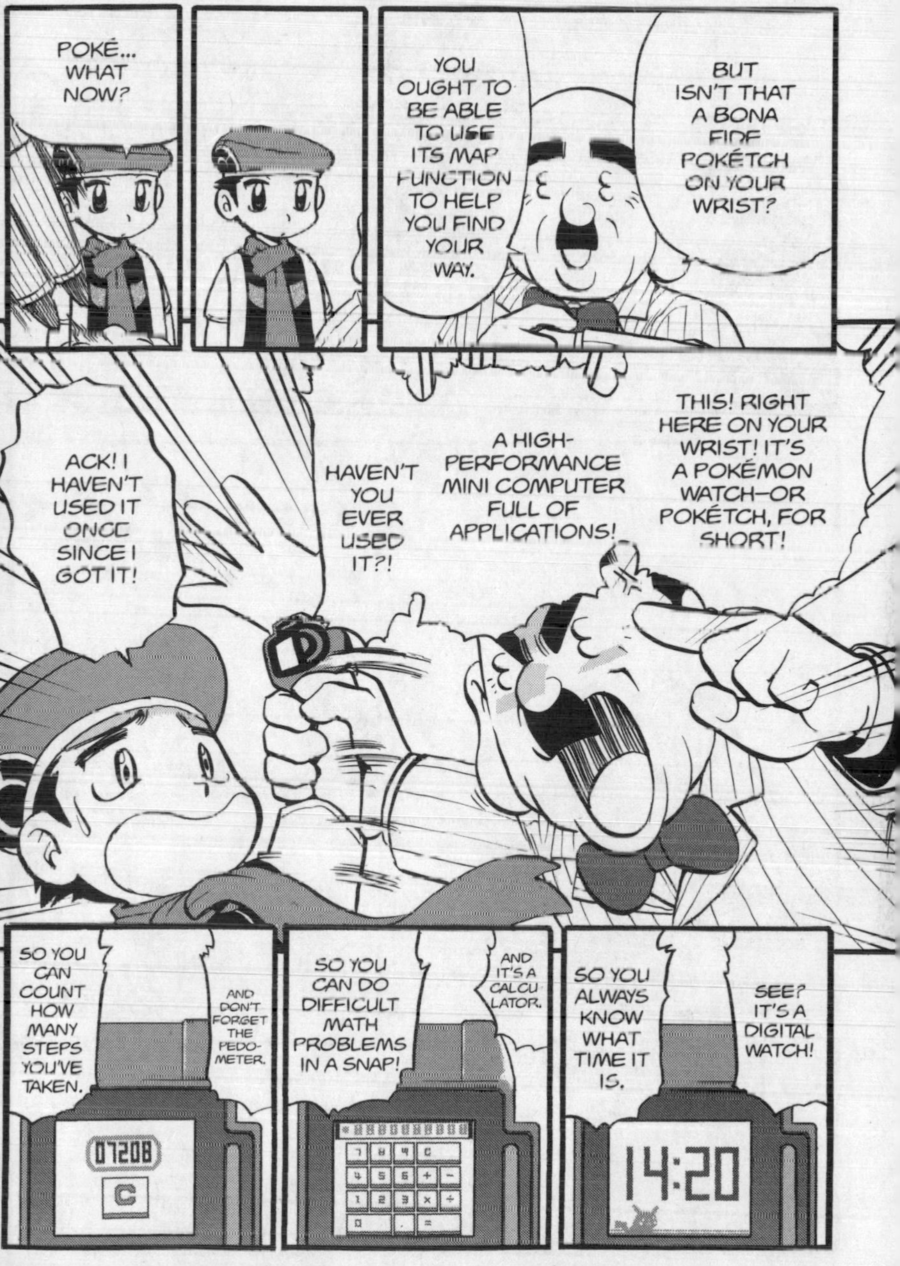
BUT ISN'T THAT A BONA FIDE POKÉTCH ON YOUR WRIST?
YOU OUGHT TO BE ABLE TO USE ITS MAP FUNCTION TO HELP YOU FIND YOUR WAY.
POKÉ... WHAT NOW?
THIS! RIGHT HERE ON YOUR WRIST! IT'S A POKÉMON WATCH—OR POKÉTCH, FOR SHORT!
A HIGH-PERFORMANCE MINI COMPUTER FULL OF APPLICATIONS!
HAVEN'T YOU EVER USED IT?!
ACK! I HAVEN'T USED IT ONCE SINCE I GOT IT!
SEE? IT'S A DIGITAL WATCH!
SO YOU ALWAYS KNOW WHAT TIME IT IS.
14:20
AND IT'S A CALCULATOR.
SO YOU CAN DO DIFFICULT MATH PROBLEMS IN A SNAP!
AND DON'T FORGET THE PEDOMETER.
SO YOU CAN COUNT HOW MANY STEPS YOU'VE TAKEN.
07208

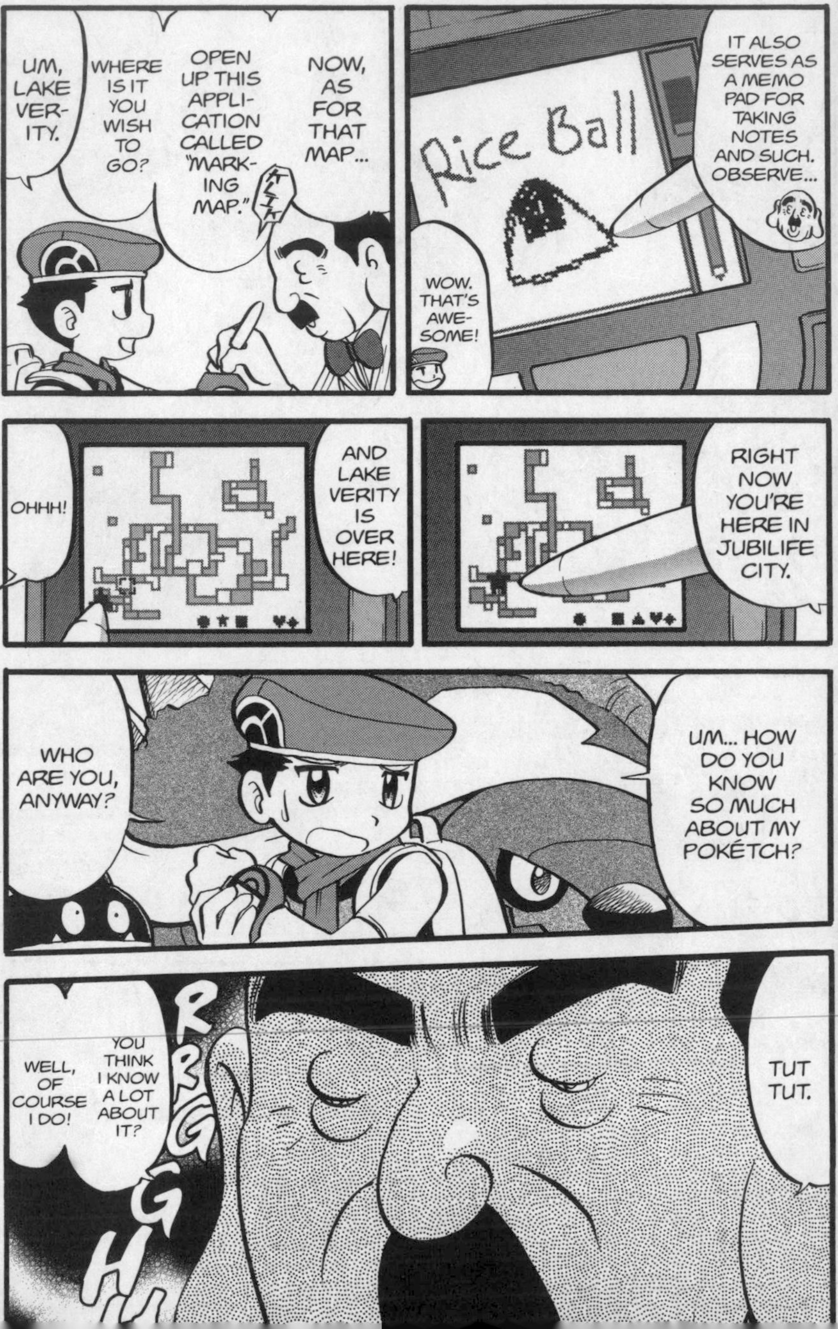
IT ALSO SERVES AS A MEMO PAD FOR TAKING NOTES AND SUCH. OBSERVE...
Rice Ball
WOW. THAT'S AWE-SOME!
NOW, AS FOR THAT MAP...
OPEN UP THIS APPLI-CATION CALLED "MARK-ING MAP."
WHERE IS IT YOU WISH TO GO?
UM, LAKE VER-ITY.
RIGHT NOW YOU'RE HERE IN JUBILIFE CITY.
AND LAKE VERITY IS OVER HERE!
OHHH!
UM... HOW DO YOU KNOW SO MUCH ABOUT MY POKÉTCH?
WHO ARE YOU, ANYWAY?
TUT TUT.
YOU THINK I KNOW A LOT ABOUT IT?
WELL, OF COURSE I DO!
RRGGH

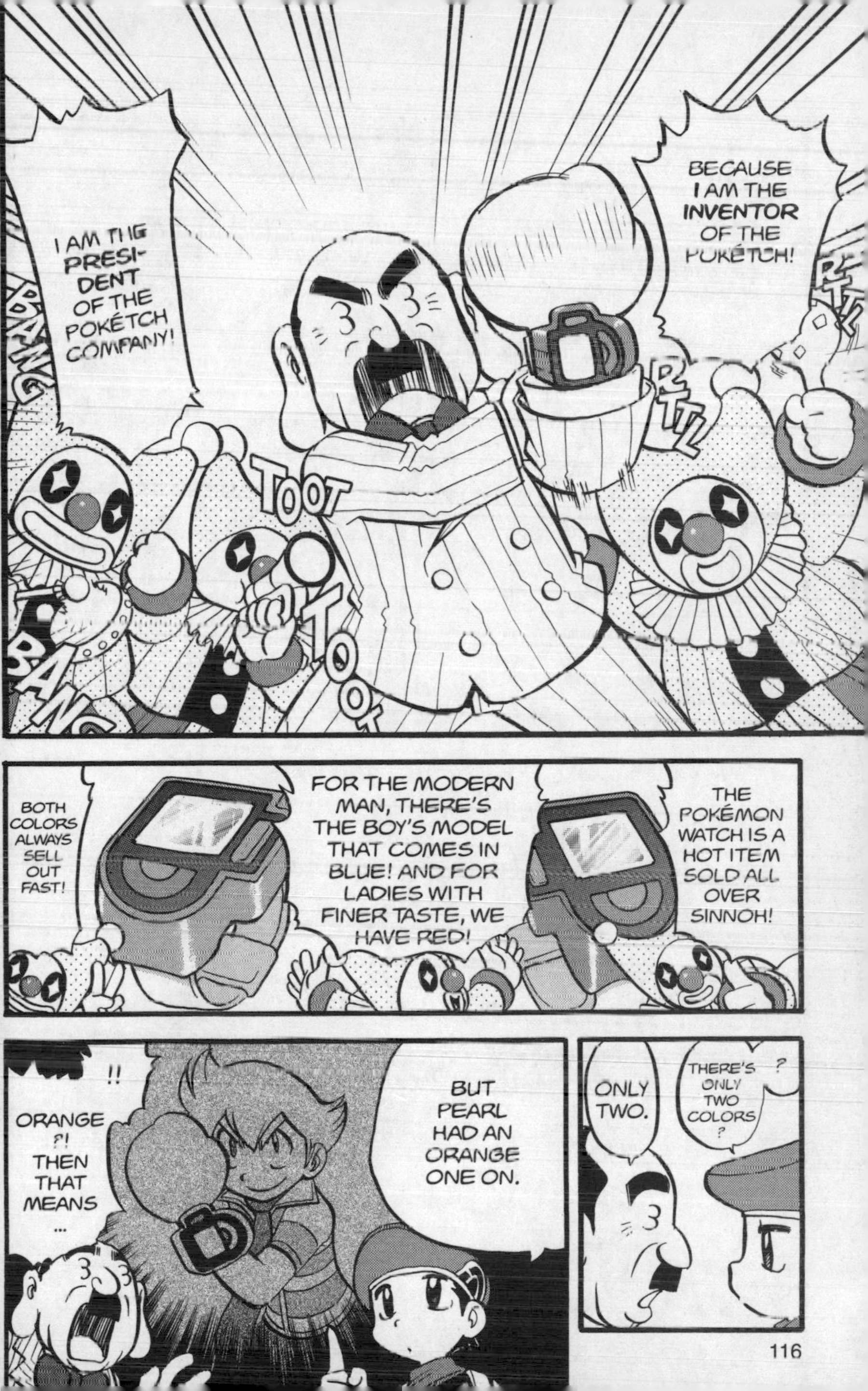
BECAUSE I AM THE INVENTOR OF THE POKÉTCH!
RTTL
RTTL
I AM THE PRESIDENT OF THE POKÉTCH COMPANY!
TOOT
TOOT TOOT
BANG
BANG
THE POKÉMON WATCH IS A HOT ITEM SOLD ALL OVER SINNOH!
FOR THE MODERN MAN, THERE'S THE BOY'S MODEL THAT COMES IN BLUE! AND FOR LADIES WITH FINER TASTE, WE HAVE RED!
BOTH COLORS ALWAYS SELL OUT FAST!
THERE'S ONLY TWO COLORS?
ONLY TWO.
BUT PEARL HAD AN ORANGE ONE ON.
!!
ORANGE?! THEN THAT MEANS...

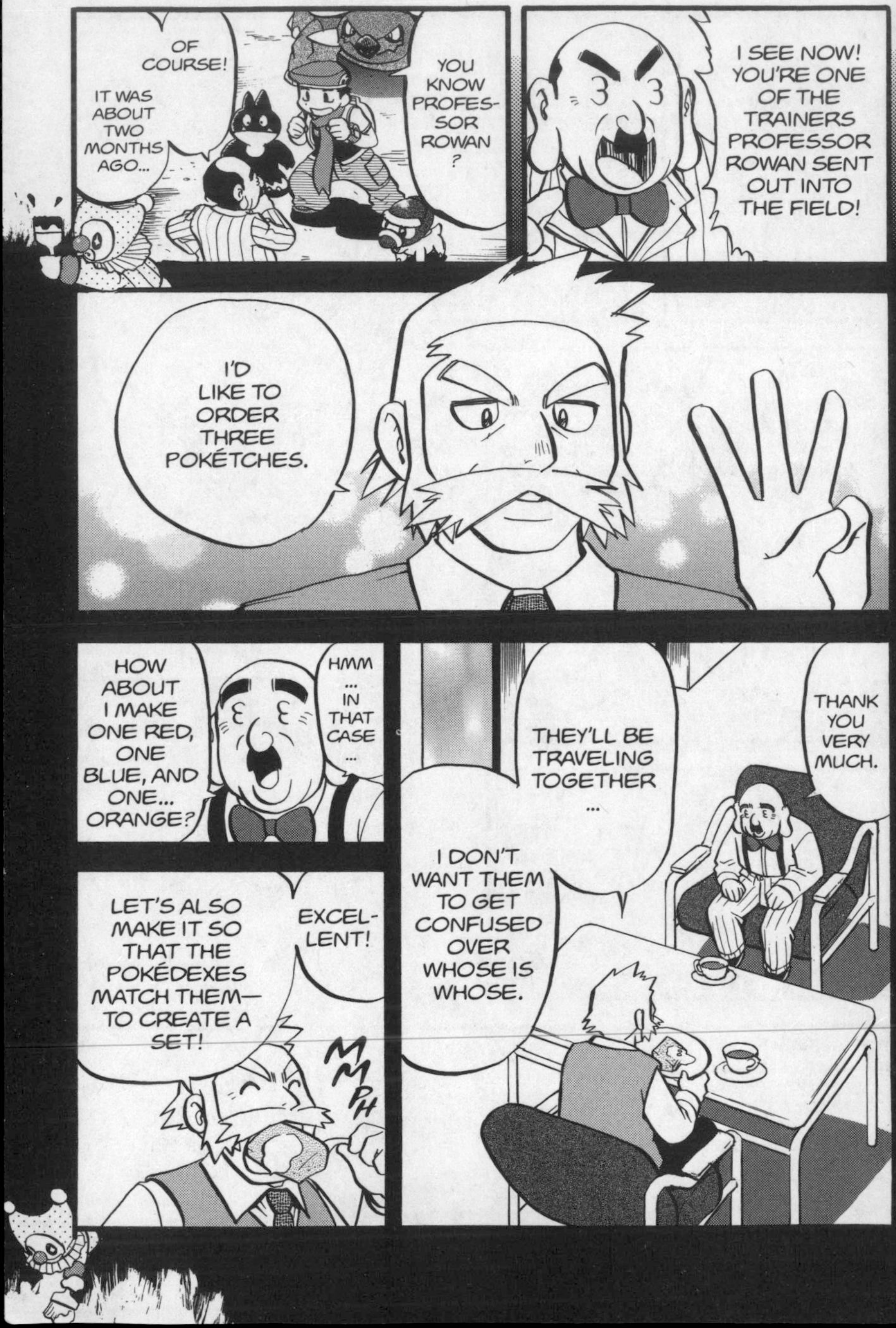
I SEE NOW! YOU'RE ONE OF THE TRAINERS PROFESSOR ROWAN SENT OUT INTO THE FIELD!
YOU KNOW PROFESSOR ROWAN?
OF COURSE!
IT WAS ABOUT TWO MONTHS AGO...
I'D LIKE TO ORDER THREE POKÉTCHES.
THANK YOU VERY MUCH.
THEY'LL BE TRAVELING TOGETHER...
I DON'T WANT THEM TO GET CONFUSED OVER WHOSE IS WHOSE.
HMM... IN THAT CASE...
HOW ABOUT I MAKE ONE RED, ONE BLUE, AND ONE... ORANGE?
EXCELLENT!
LET'S ALSO MAKE IT SO THAT THE POKÉDEXES MATCH THEM—TO CREATE A SET!
MMPH

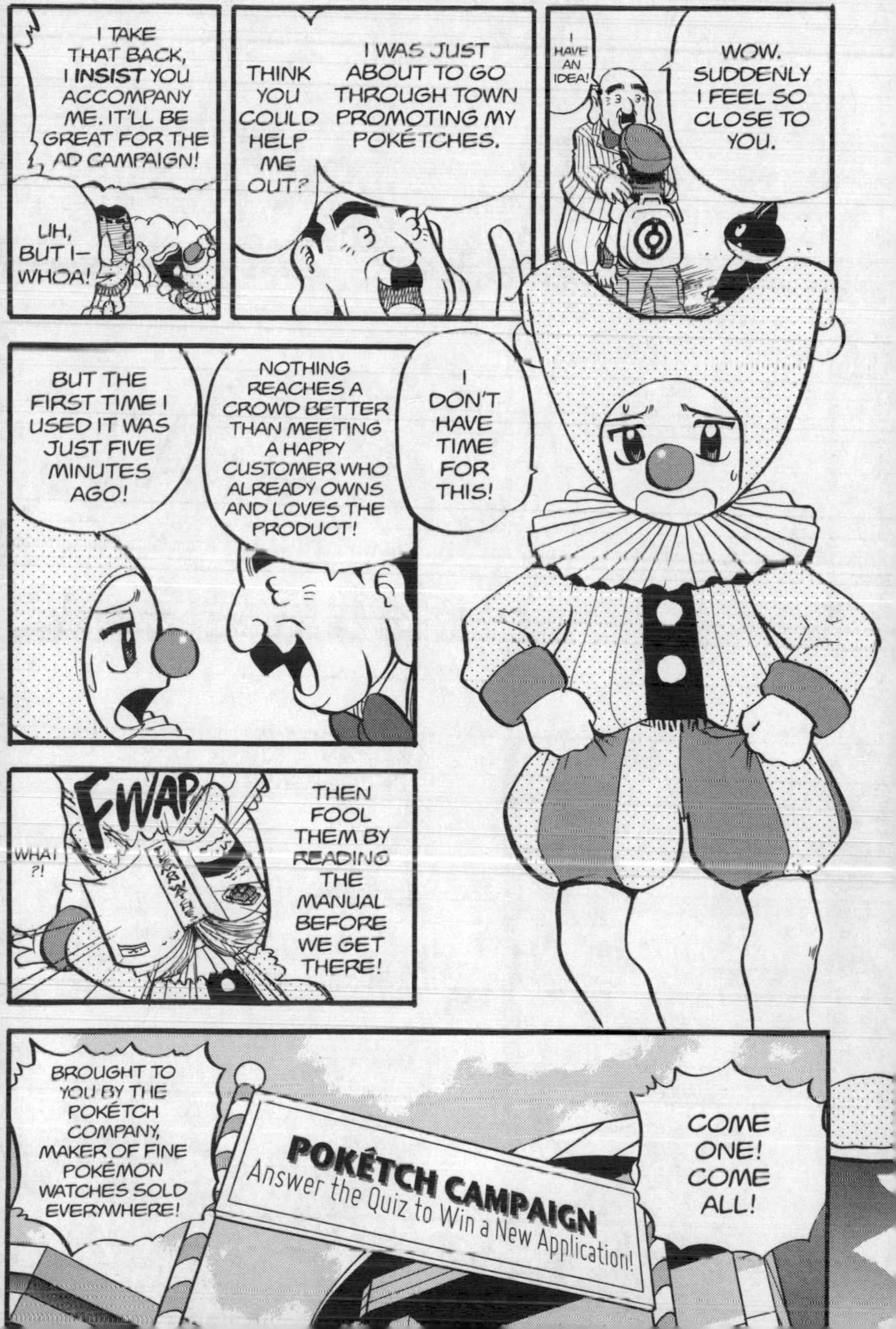
WOW. SUDDENLY I FEEL SO CLOSE TO YOU.
I HAVE AN IDEA!
I WAS JUST ABOUT TO GO THROUGH TOWN PROMOTING MY POKÉTCHES.
THINK YOU COULD HELP ME OUT?
I TAKE THAT BACK, I **INSIST** YOU ACCOMPANY ME. IT'LL BE GREAT FOR THE AD CAMPAIGN!
UH, BUT I— WHOA!
I DON'T HAVE TIME FOR THIS!
NOTHING REACHES A CROWD BETTER THAN MEETING A HAPPY CUSTOMER WHO ALREADY OWNS AND LOVES THE PRODUCT!
BUT THE FIRST TIME I USED IT WAS JUST FIVE MINUTES AGO!
THEN FOOL THEM BY READING THE MANUAL BEFORE WE GET THERE!
FWAP
WHAT ?!
COME ONE! COME ALL!
POKÉTCH CAMPAIGN
Answer the Quiz to Win a New Application!
BROUGHT TO YOU BY THE POKÉTCH COMPANY, MAKER OF FINE POKÉMON WATCHES SOLD EVERYWHERE!

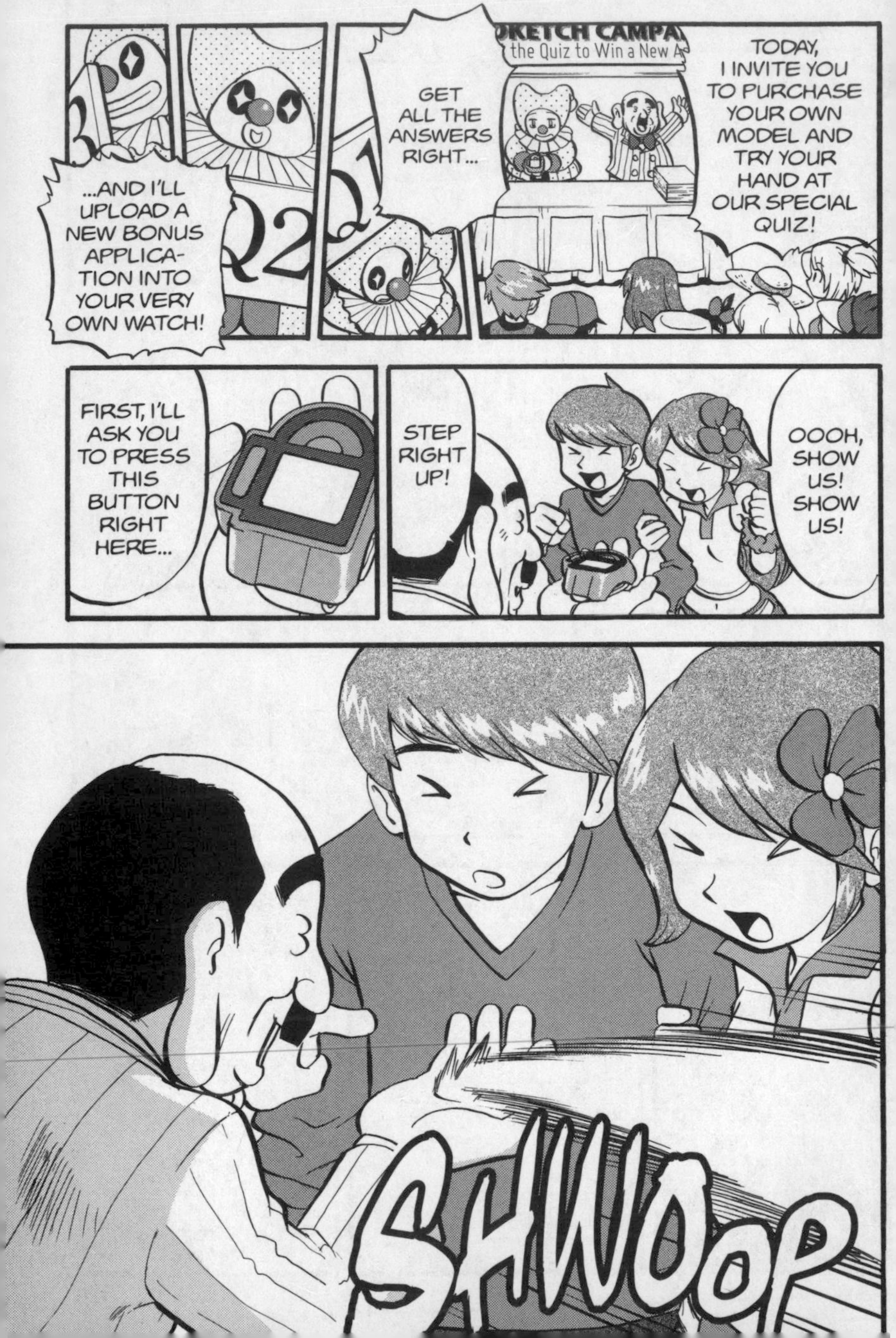
OKETCH CAMPA
the Quiz to Win a New A
TODAY, I INVITE YOU TO PURCHASE YOUR OWN MODEL AND TRY YOUR HAND AT OUR SPECIAL QUIZ!
GET ALL THE ANSWERS RIGHT...
Q2
...AND I'LL UPLOAD A NEW BONUS APPLICA-TION INTO YOUR VERY OWN WATCH!
OOOH, SHOW US! SHOW US!
STEP RIGHT UP!
FIRST, I'LL ASK YOU TO PRESS THIS BUTTON RIGHT HERE...
SHWOOP

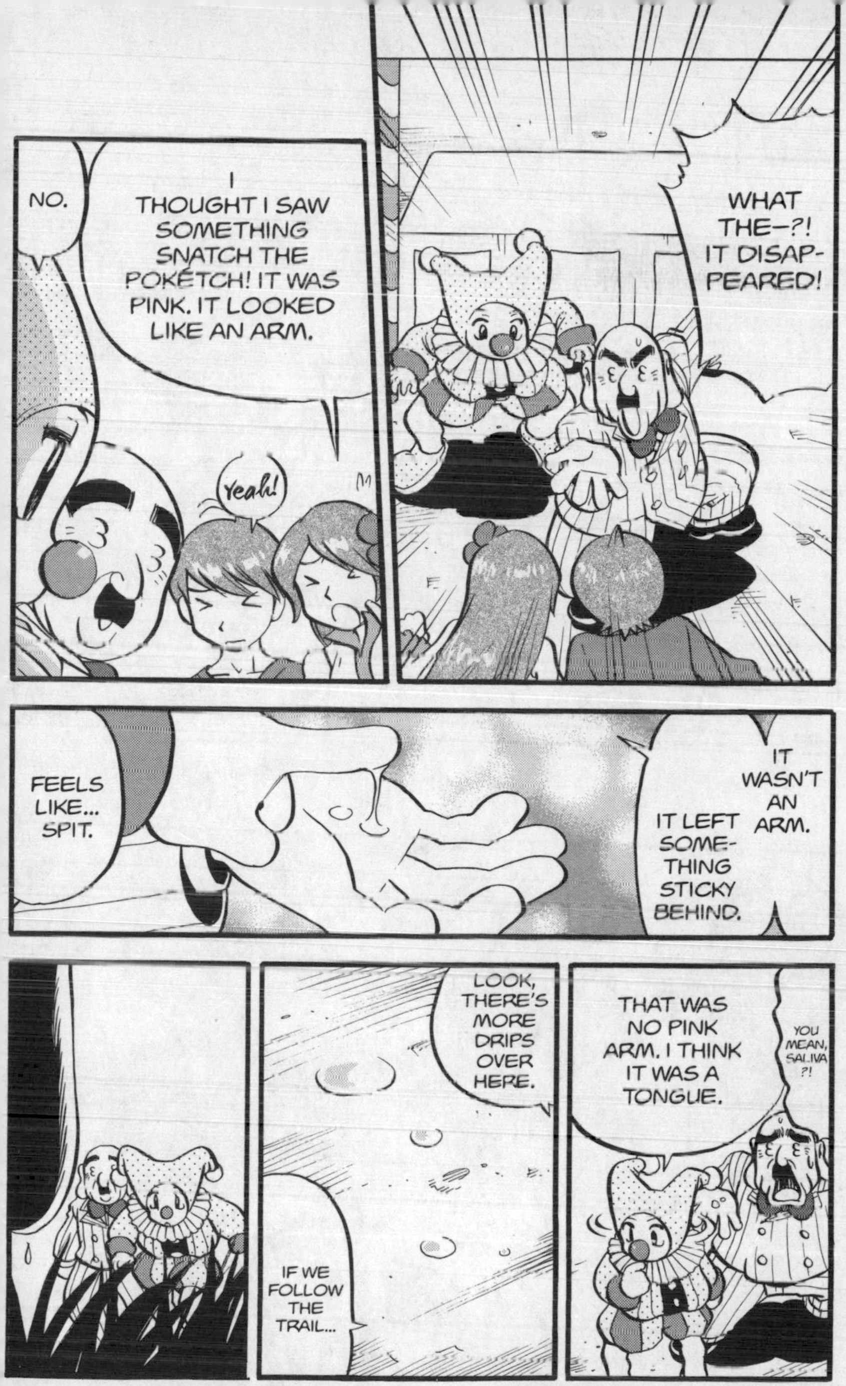
WHAT THE–?! IT DISAPPEARED!
I THOUGHT I SAW SOMETHING SNATCH THE POKÉTCH! IT WAS PINK. IT LOOKED LIKE AN ARM.
NO.
Yeah!
IT WASN'T AN ARM.
IT LEFT SOMETHING STICKY BEHIND.
FEELS LIKE... SPIT.
YOU MEAN, SALIVA?!
THAT WAS NO PINK ARM. I THINK IT WAS A TONGUE.
LOOK, THERE'S MORE DRIPS OVER HERE.
IF WE FOLLOW THE TRAIL...

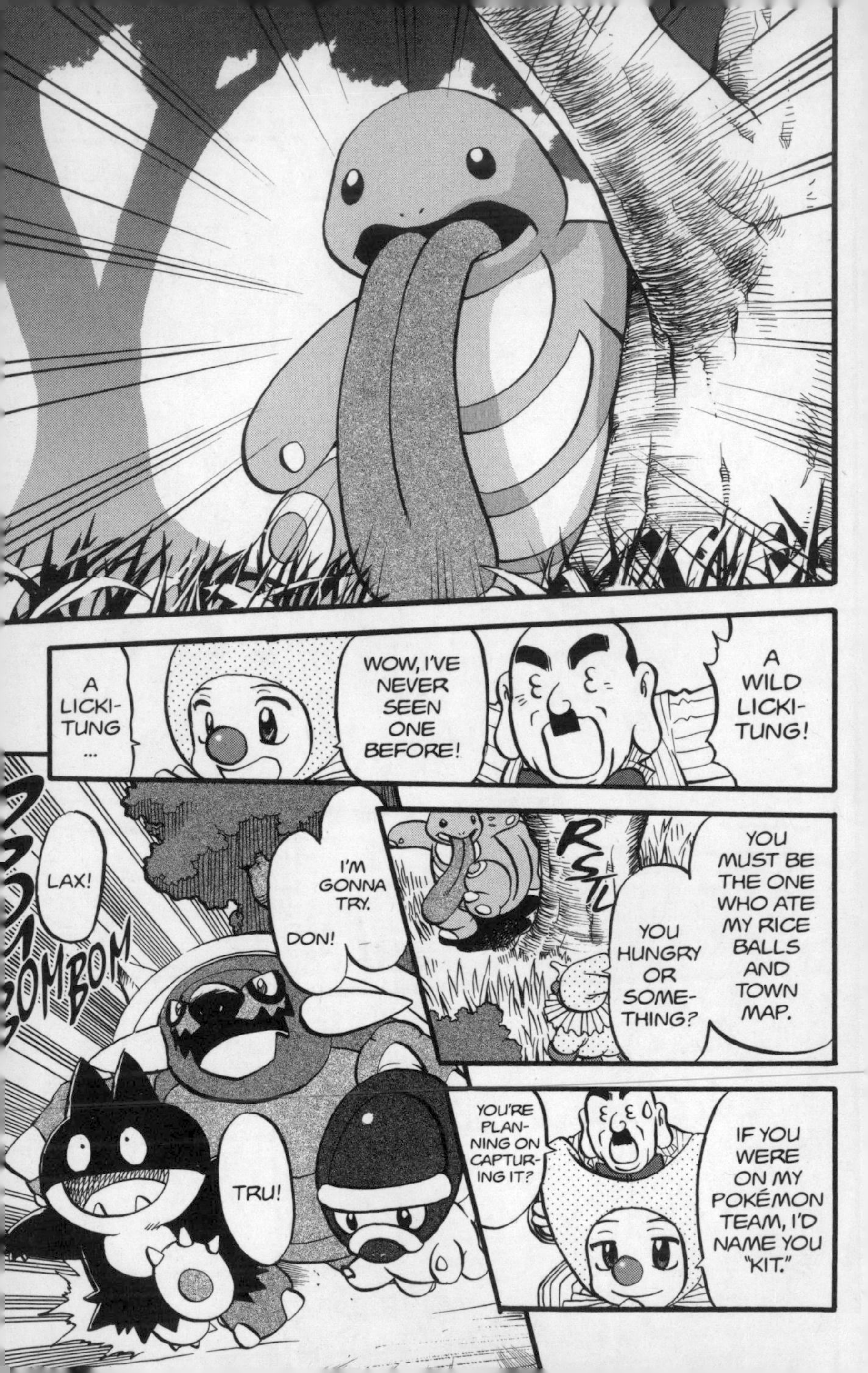
A WILD LICKI-TUNG!
WOW, I'VE NEVER SEEN ONE BEFORE!
A LICKI-TUNG ...
YOU MUST BE THE ONE WHO ATE MY RICE BALLS AND TOWN MAP.
YOU HUNGRY OR SOME-THING?
RSTL
IF YOU WERE ON MY POKÉMON TEAM, I'D NAME YOU "KIT."
YOU'RE PLAN-NING ON CAPTUR-ING IT?
I'M GONNA TRY.
DON!
LAX!
BOMBOM
TRU!

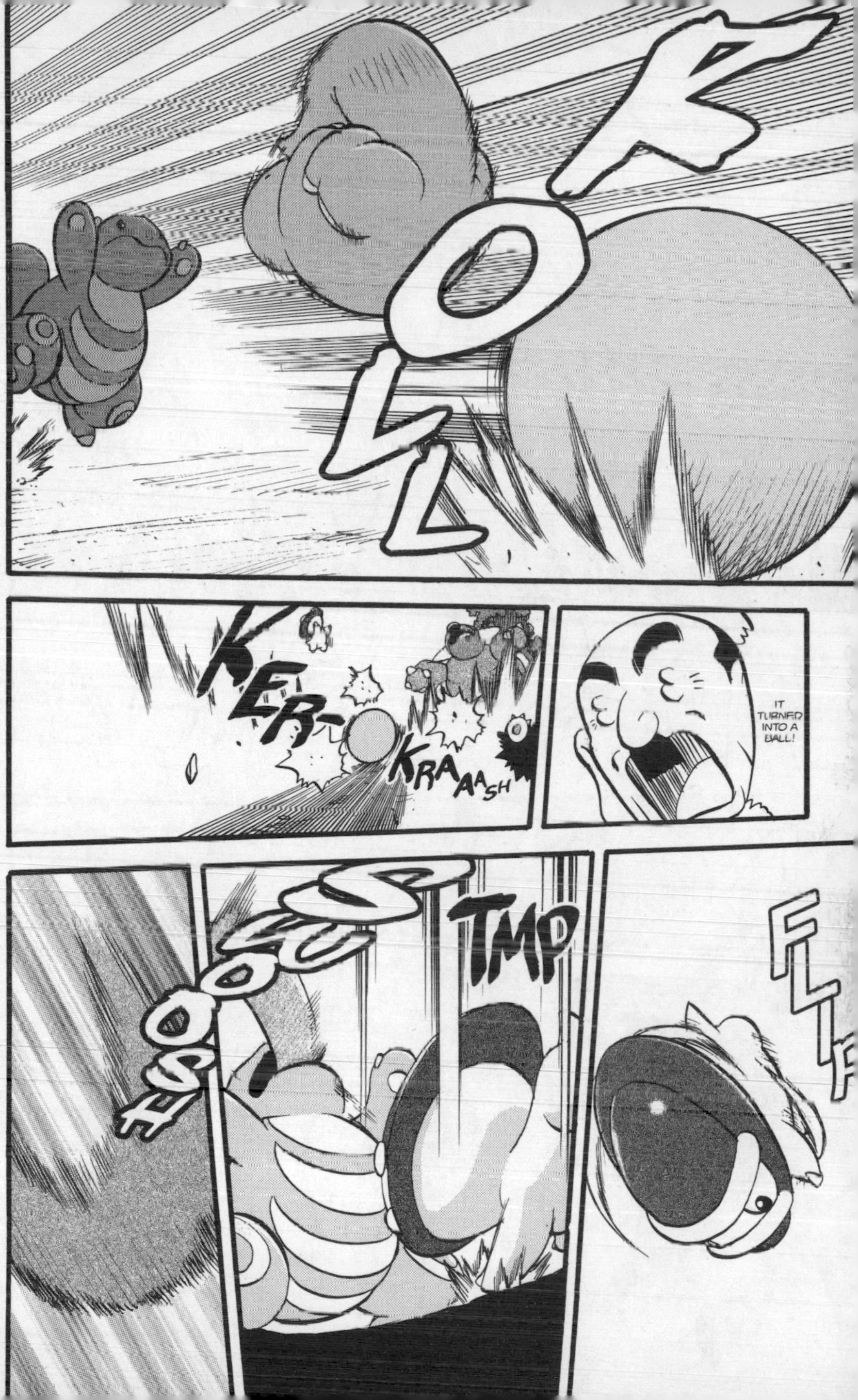
ROLL
IT TURNED INTO A BALL!
KER-KRAAASH
FLIP
TMP
SWOOSH

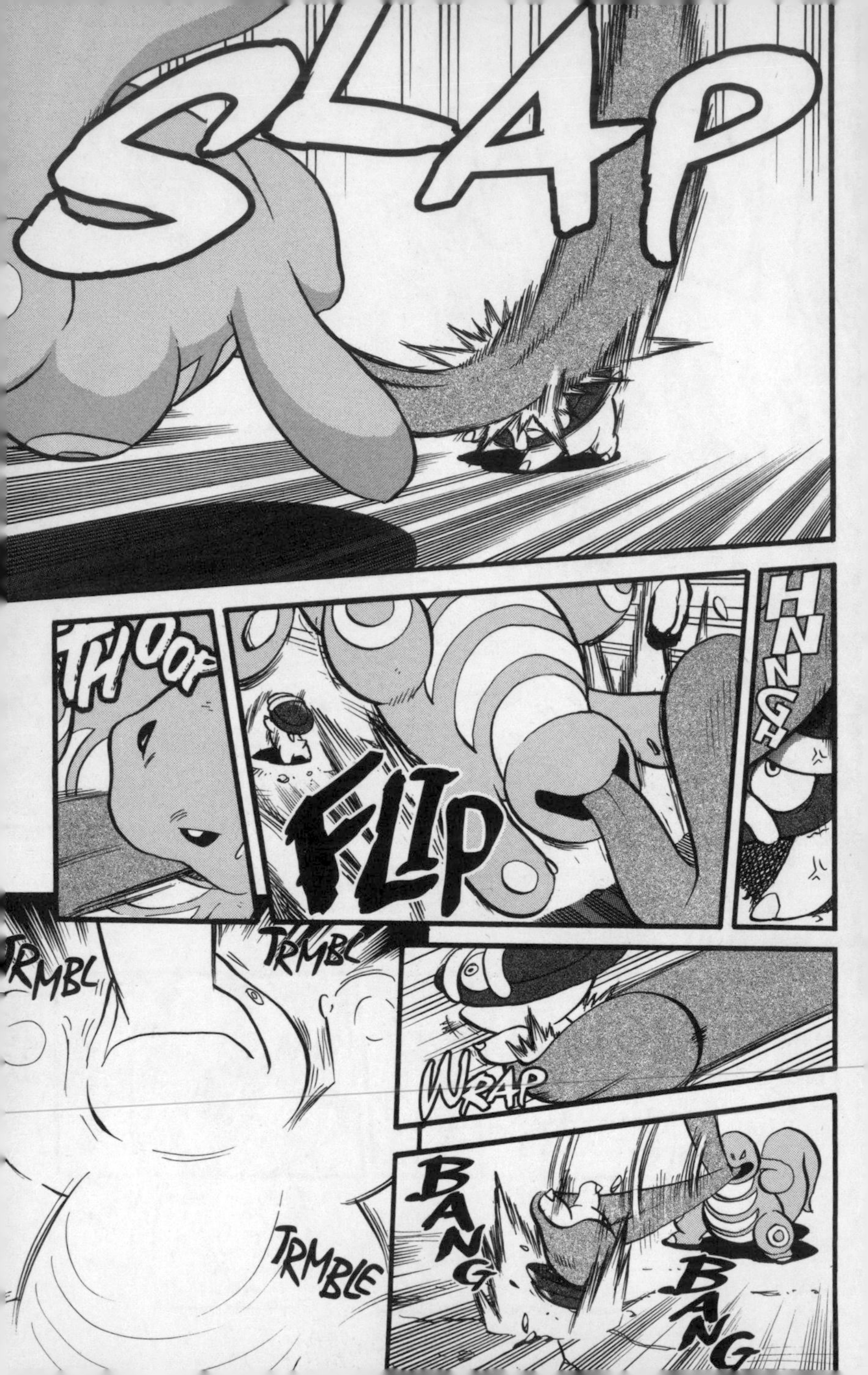
SLAP
HNNGH
FLIP
THOOT
WRAP
BANG
BANG
TRMBL
TRMBL
TRMBLE

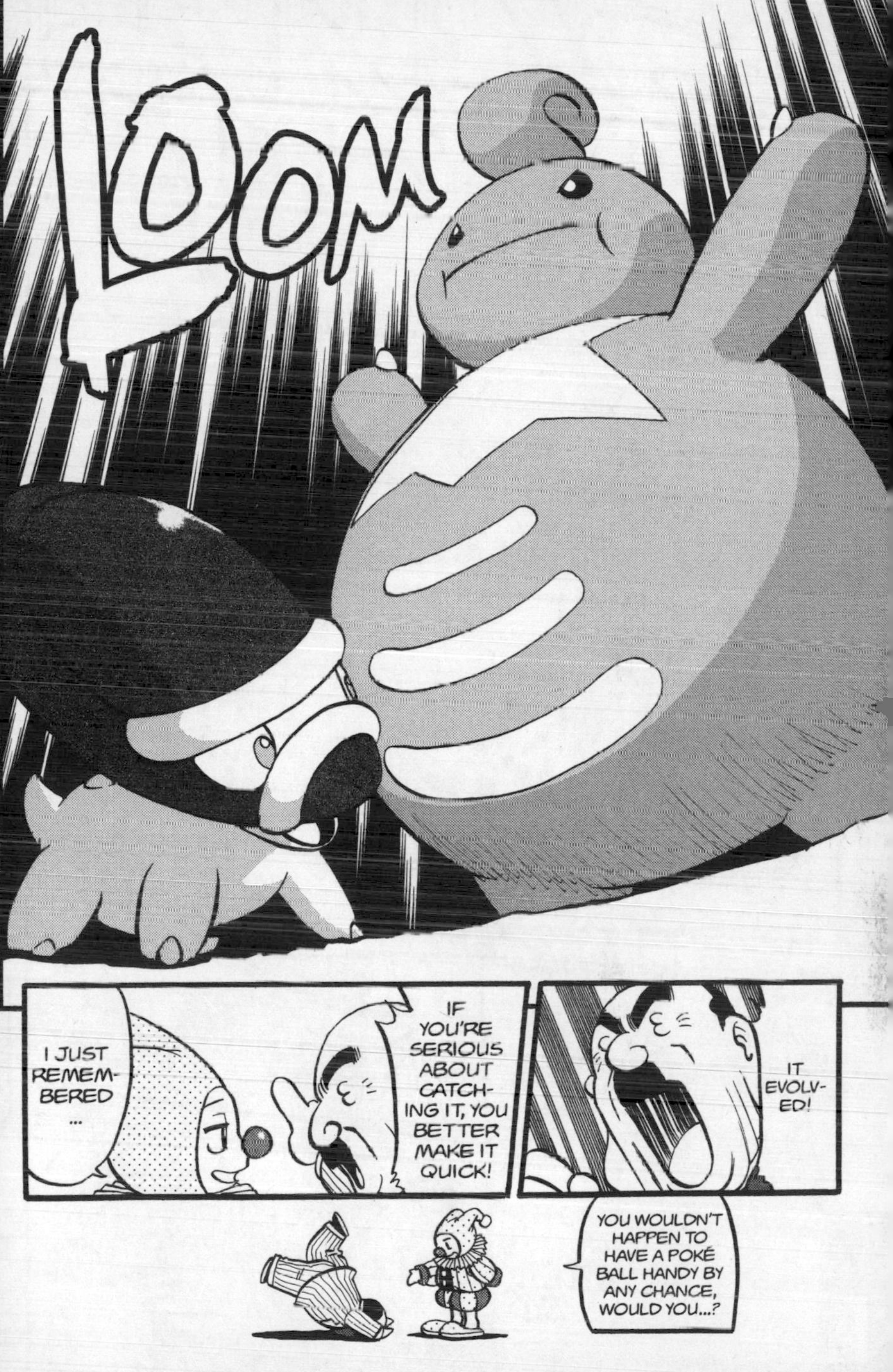
LOOM
IT EVOLV-ED!
IF YOU'RE SERIOUS ABOUT CATCH-ING IT, YOU BETTER MAKE IT QUICK!
I JUST REMEM-BERED ...
YOU WOULDN'T HAPPEN TO HAVE A POKÉ BALL HANDY BY ANY CHANCE, WOULD YOU...?

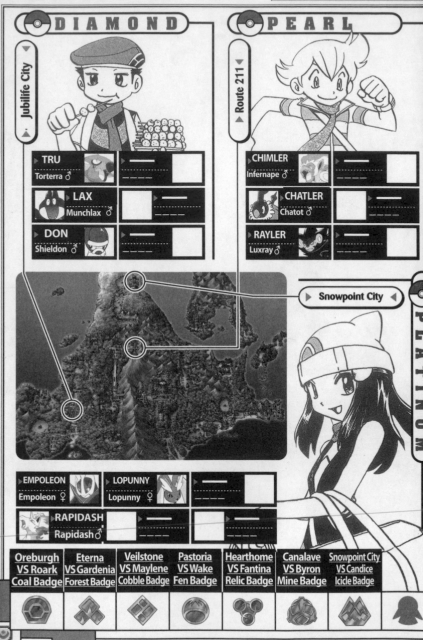

DIAMOND

Jubilife City

TRU	Torterra ♂
LAX	Munchlax ♂
DON	Shieldon ♂

PEARL

Route 211

CHIMLER	Infernape ♂
CHATLER	Chatot ♂
RAYLER	Luxray ♂

Snowpoint City

PLATINUM

EMPOLEON	Empoleon ♀
LOPUNNY	Lopunny ♀
RAPIDASH	Rapidash ♂

Oreburgh VS Roark Coal Badge	Eterna VS Gardenia Forest Badge	Veilstone VS Maylene Cobble Badge	Pastoria VS Wake Fen Badge	Hearthome VS Fantina Relic Badge	Canalave VS Byron Mine Badge	Snowpoint City VS Candice Icicle Badge

54

Luring in a Lickilicky

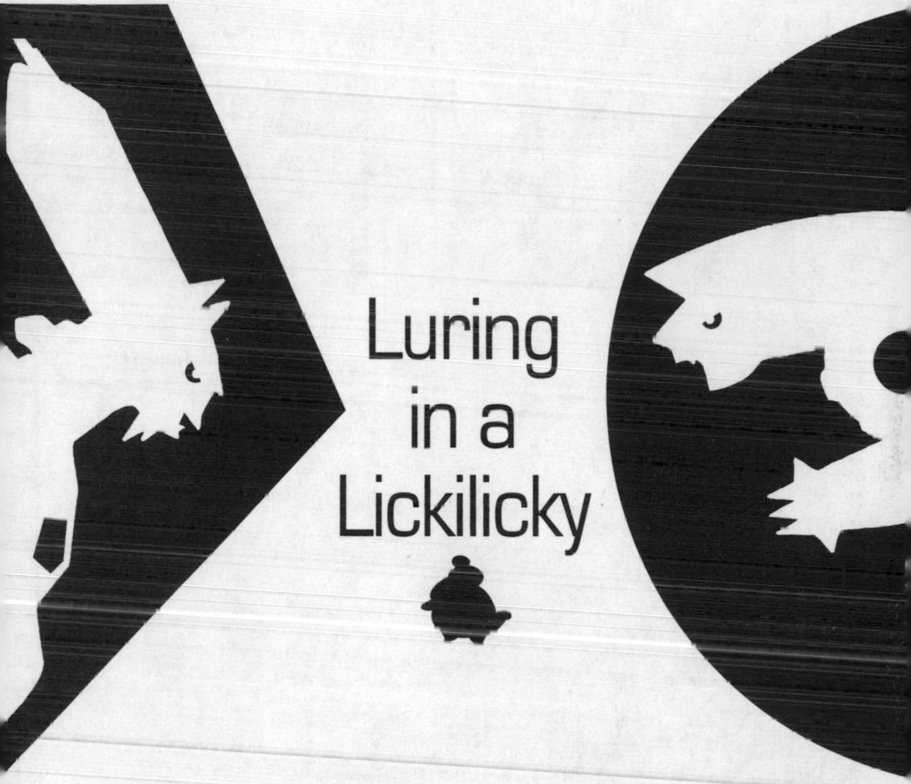

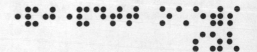

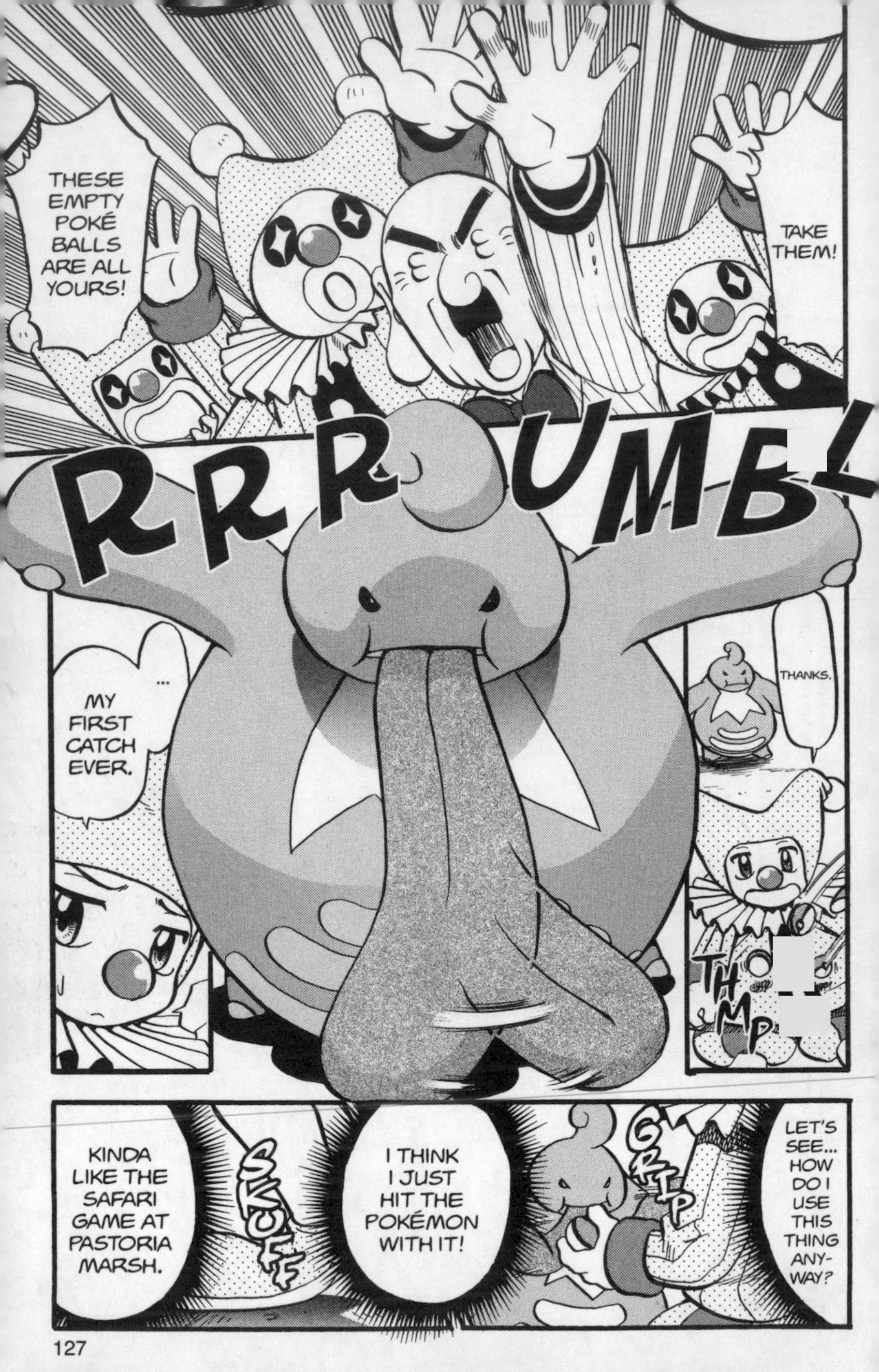
THESE EMPTY POKÉ BALLS ARE ALL YOURS!
TAKE THEM!
RRRUMB!
THANKS.
THMP
...
MY FIRST CATCH EVER.
LET'S SEE... HOW DO I USE THIS THING ANY-WAY?
GRIP
I THINK I JUST HIT THE POKÉMON WITH IT!
SKOFF
KINDA LIKE THE SAFARI GAME AT PASTORIA MARSH.

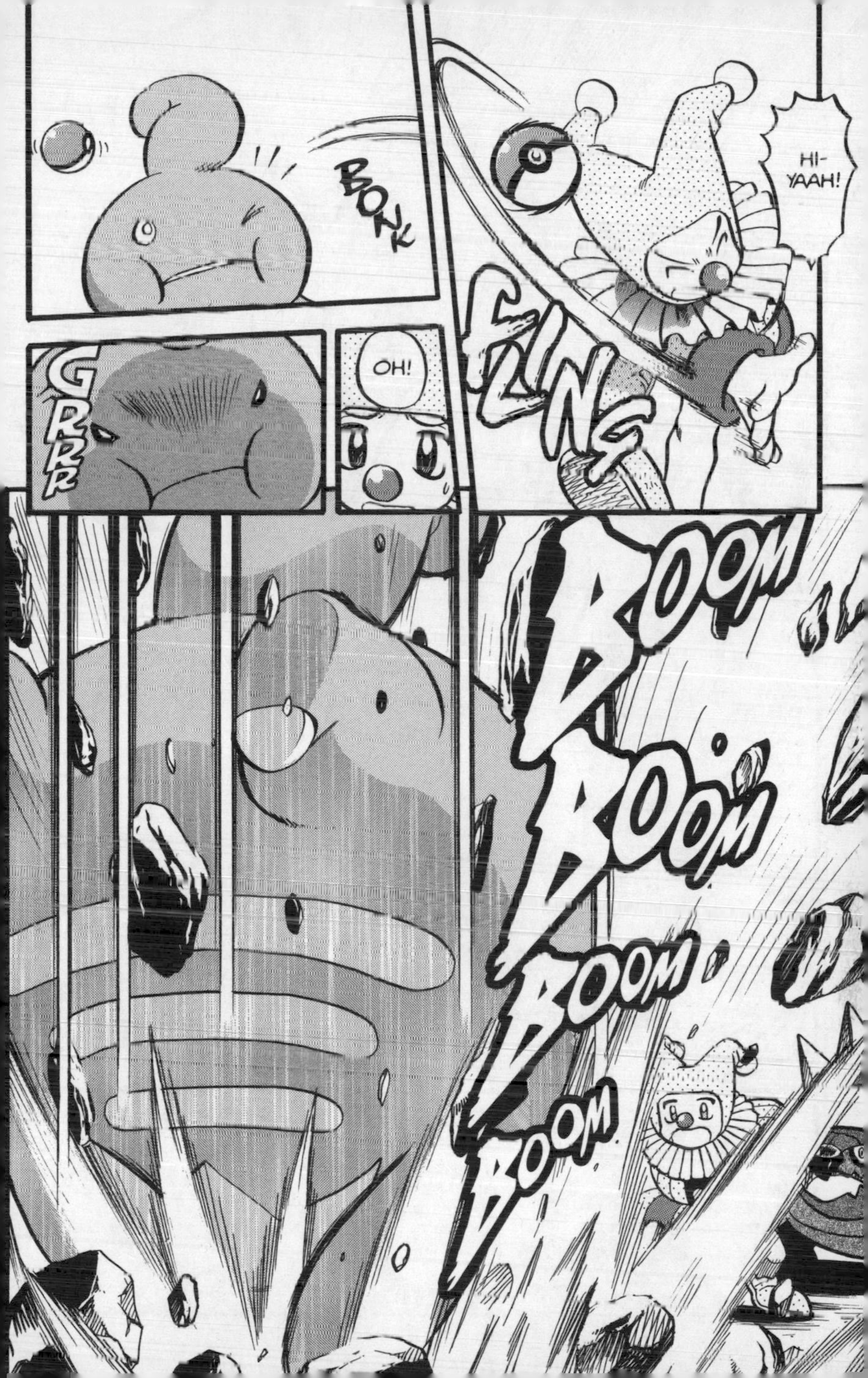
HI-YAAH!
FLING
BONK
OH!
GRRR
BOOM
BOOM
BOOM
BOOM

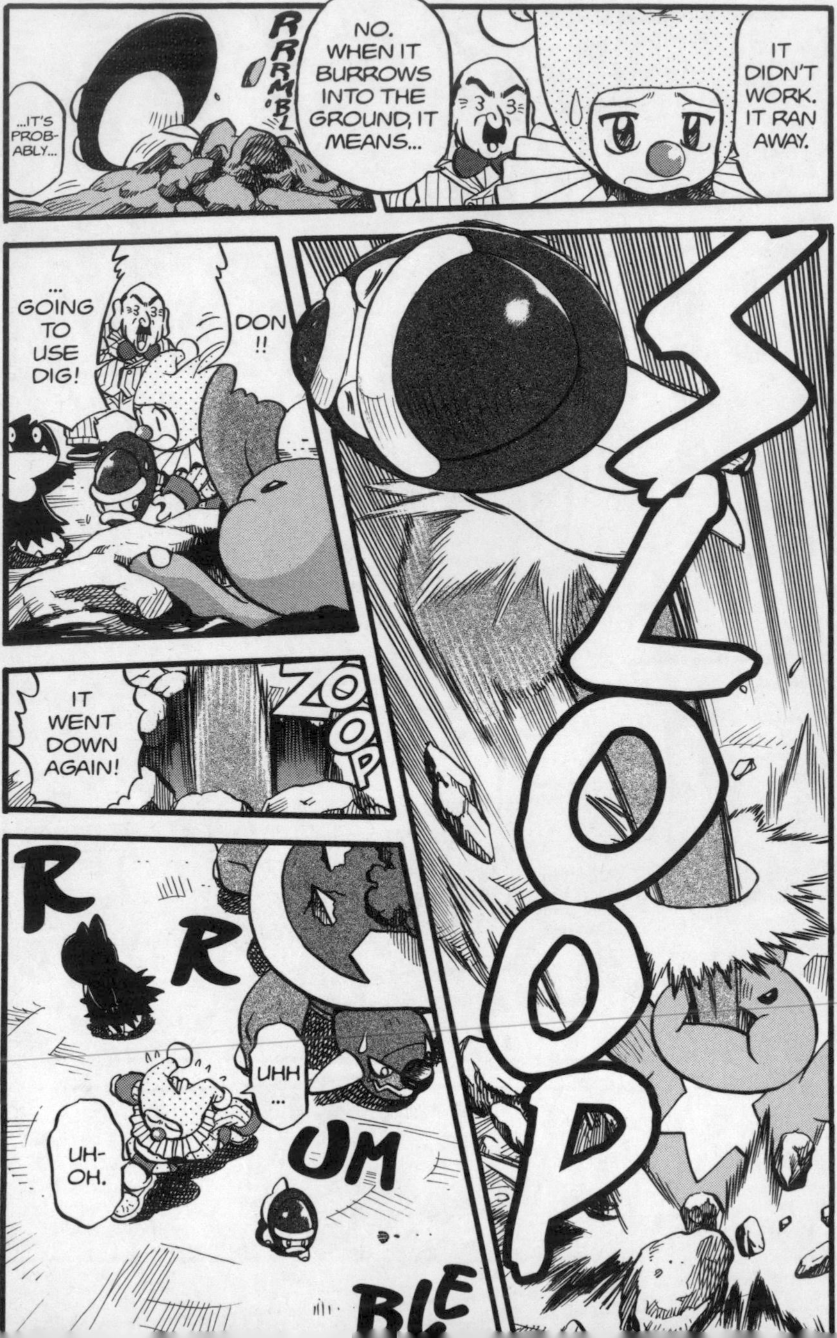

IT DIDN'T WORK. IT RAN AWAY.
NO. WHEN IT BURROWS INTO THE GROUND, IT MEANS...
RRRMBL
...IT'S PROBABLY...
ZOOP
... GOING TO USE DIG!
DON !!
ZOOP
IT WENT DOWN AGAIN!
R
R
UHH ...
UH-OH.
UM
BLE

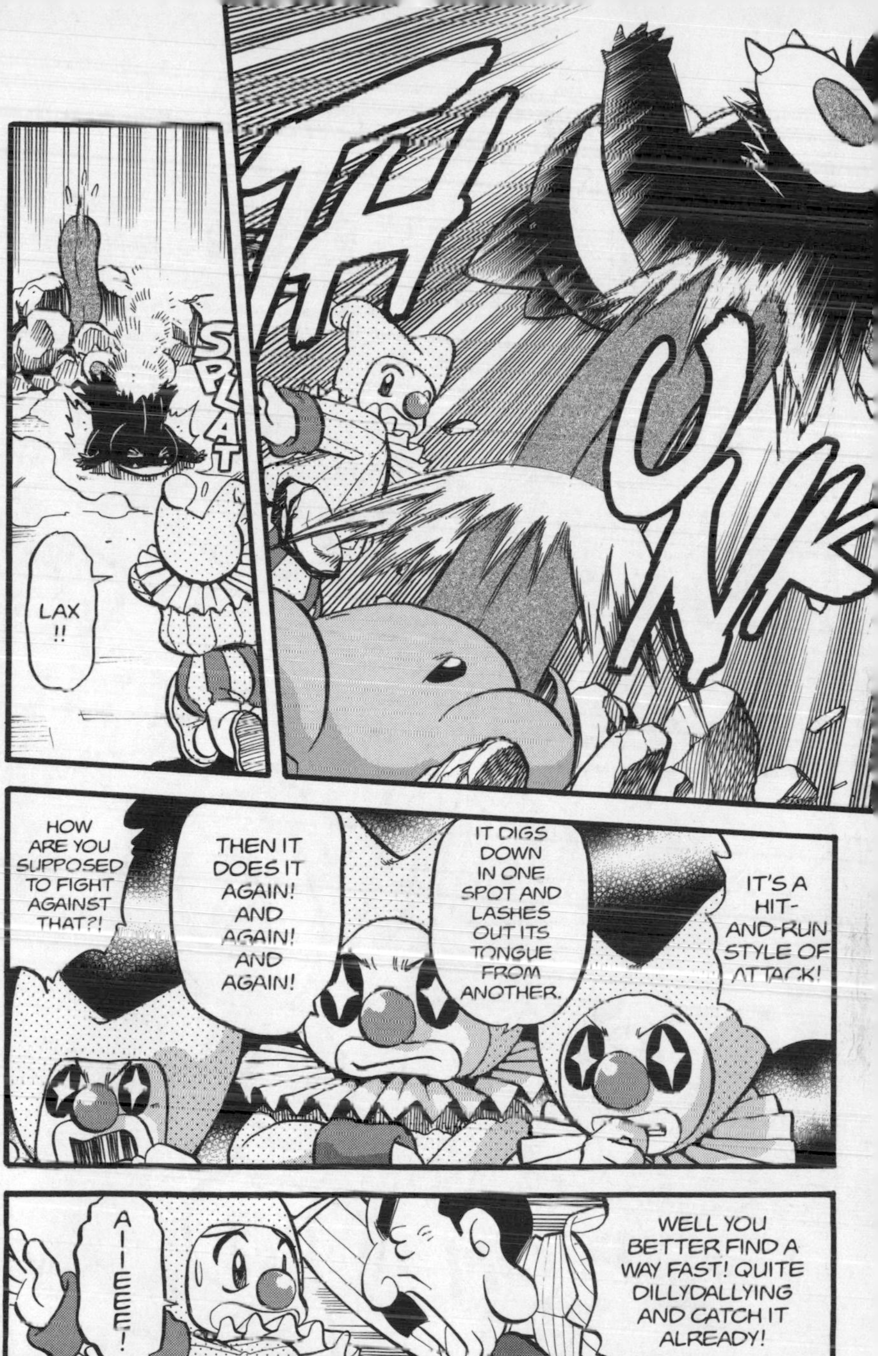
SPLAT
LAX !!
IT'S A HIT-AND-RUN STYLE OF ATTACK!
IT DIGS DOWN IN ONE SPOT AND LASHES OUT ITS TONGUE FROM ANOTHER.
THEN IT DOES IT AGAIN! AND AGAIN! AND AGAIN!
HOW ARE YOU SUPPOSED TO FIGHT AGAINST THAT?!
WELL YOU BETTER FIND A WAY FAST! QUITE DILLYDALLYING AND CATCH IT ALREADY!
AIIEEE!

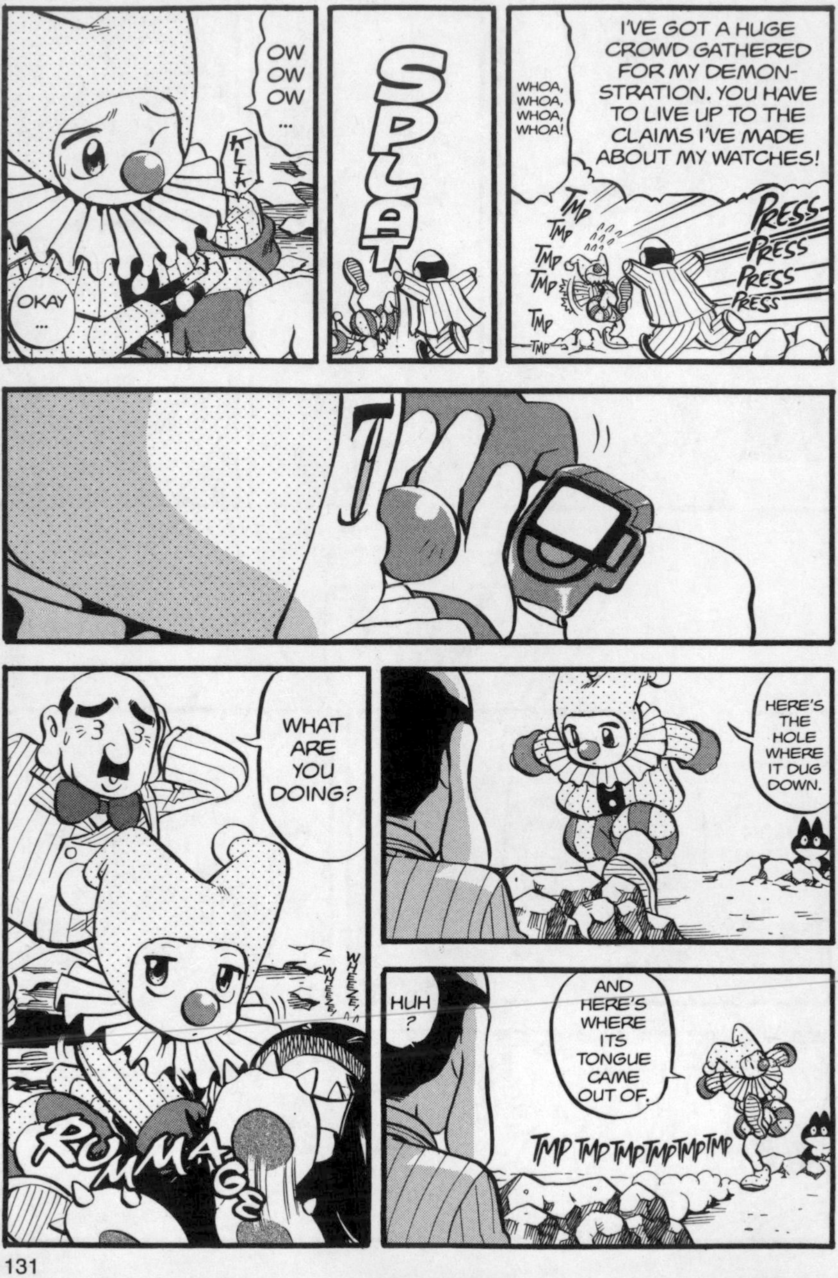
I'VE GOT A HUGE CROWD GATHERED FOR MY DEMONSTRATION. YOU HAVE TO LIVE UP TO THE CLAIMS I'VE MADE ABOUT MY WATCHES!
WHOA, WHOA, WHOA, WHOA!
PRESS PRESS PRESS PRESS
TMP TMP TMP TMP TMP TMP
SPLAT
OW OW OW ...
KLIK
OKAY ...
HERE'S THE HOLE WHERE IT DUG DOWN.
AND HERE'S WHERE ITS TONGUE CAME OUT OF.
HUH?
TMP TMP TMP TMP TMP TMP
WHAT ARE YOU DOING?
WHEEZE, WHEEZE,
RUMMAGE

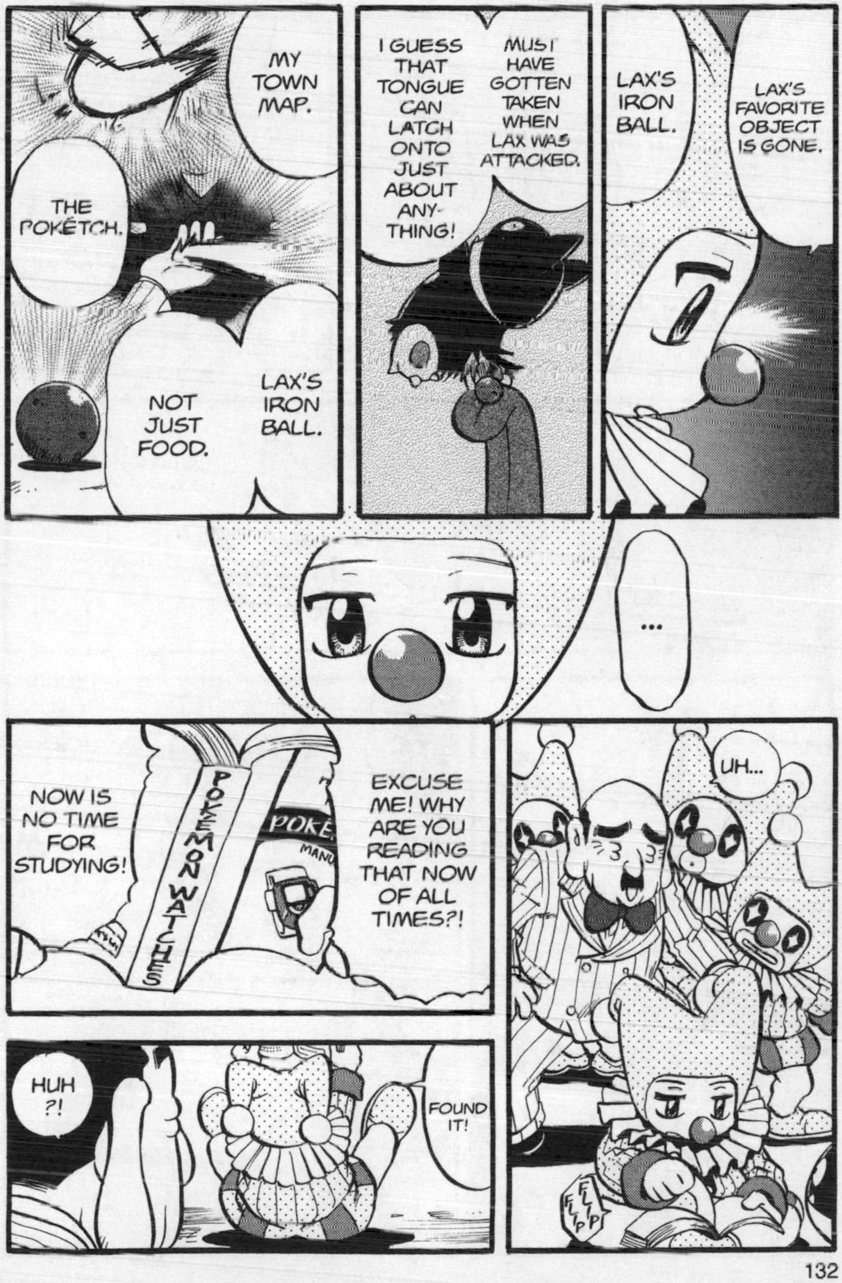
LAX'S FAVORITE OBJECT IS GONE.
LAX'S IRON BALL.
MUST HAVE GOTTEN TAKEN WHEN LAX WAS ATTACKED.
I GUESS THAT TONGUE CAN LATCH ONTO JUST ABOUT ANYTHING!
MY TOWN MAP.
THE POKÉTCH.
LAX'S IRON BALL.
NOT JUST FOOD.
...
UH...
FLIP FLIP
EXCUSE ME! WHY ARE YOU READING THAT NOW OF ALL TIMES?!
POKÉMON WATCHES
NOW IS NO TIME FOR STUDYING!
FOUND IT!
HUH ?!

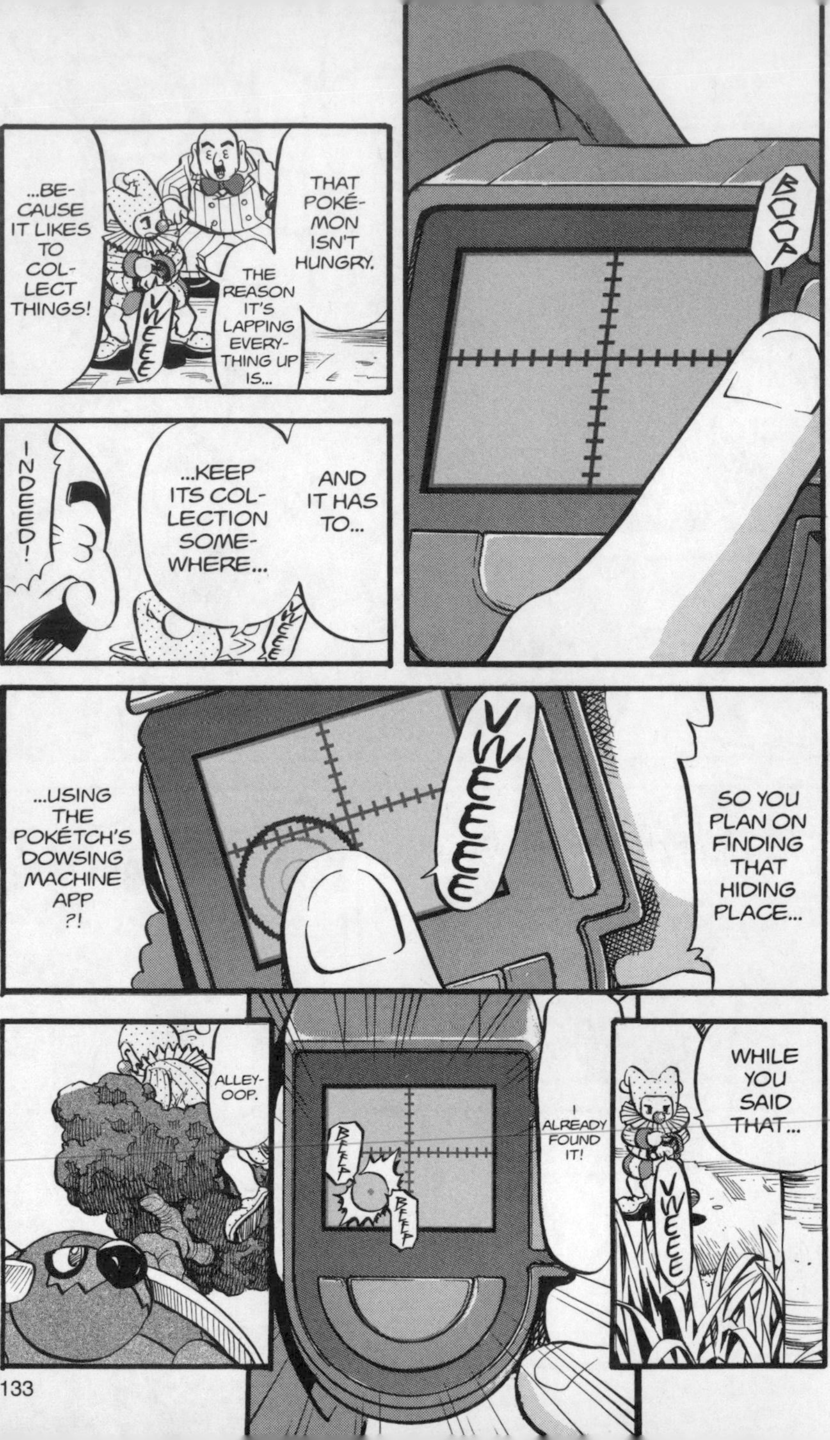
BOOP
THAT POKÉMON ISN'T HUNGRY.
THE REASON IT'S LAPPING EVERYTHING UP IS...
...BECAUSE IT LIKES TO COLLECT THINGS!
VWEEE
AND IT HAS TO...
...KEEP ITS COLLECTION SOMEWHERE...
INDEED!
VWEEE
SO YOU PLAN ON FINDING THAT HIDING PLACE...
VWEEEEE
...USING THE POKÉTCH'S DOWSING MACHINE APP ?!
WHILE YOU SAID THAT...
VWEEE
I ALREADY FOUND IT!
BEEP
BEEP
ALLEY-OOP.

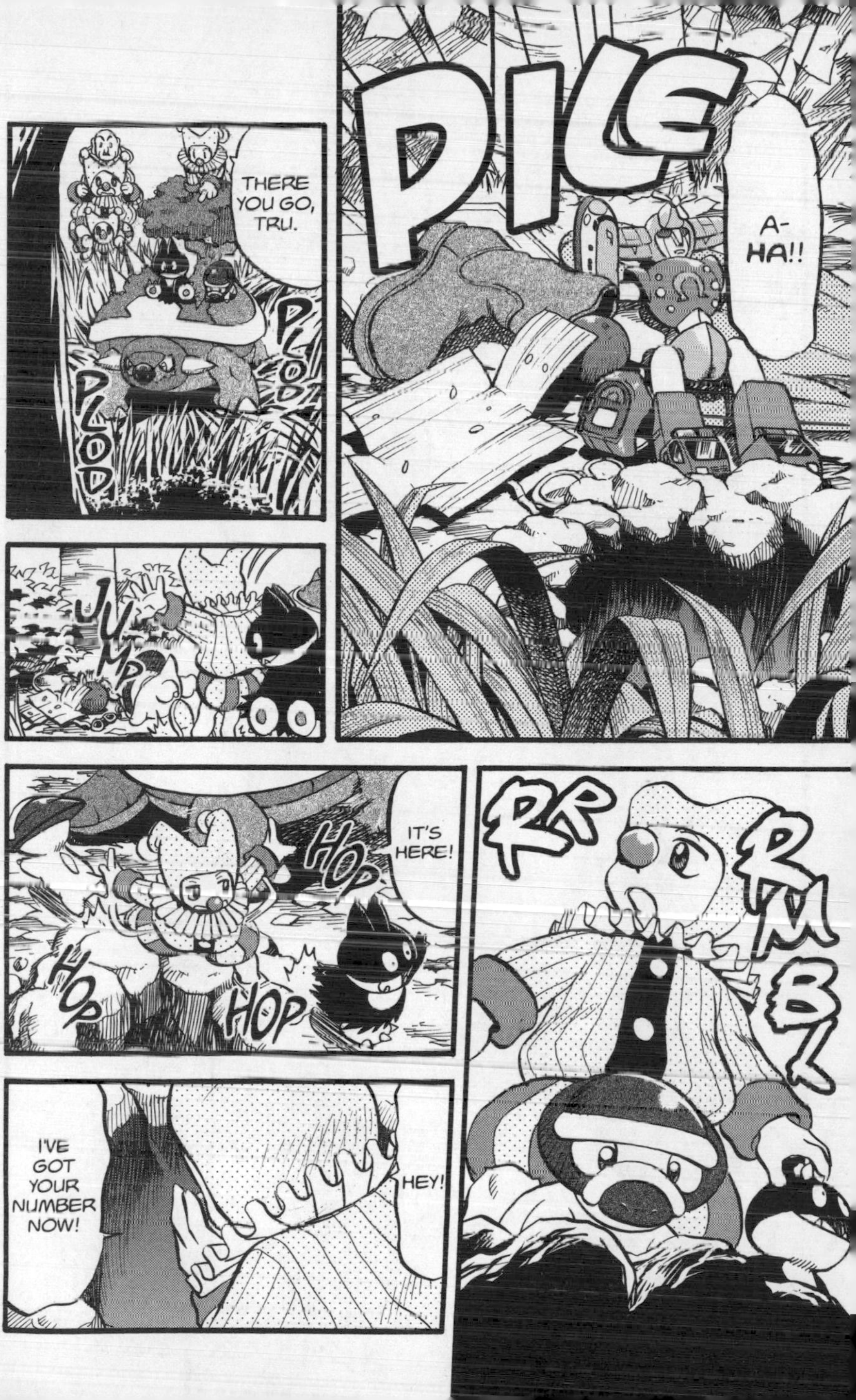
PIC
A-HA!!
THERE YOU GO, TRU.
PLOD
PLOD
JUMP
RR
RMBL
IT'S HERE!
HOP
HOP
HOP
HEY!
I'VE GOT YOUR NUMBER NOW!

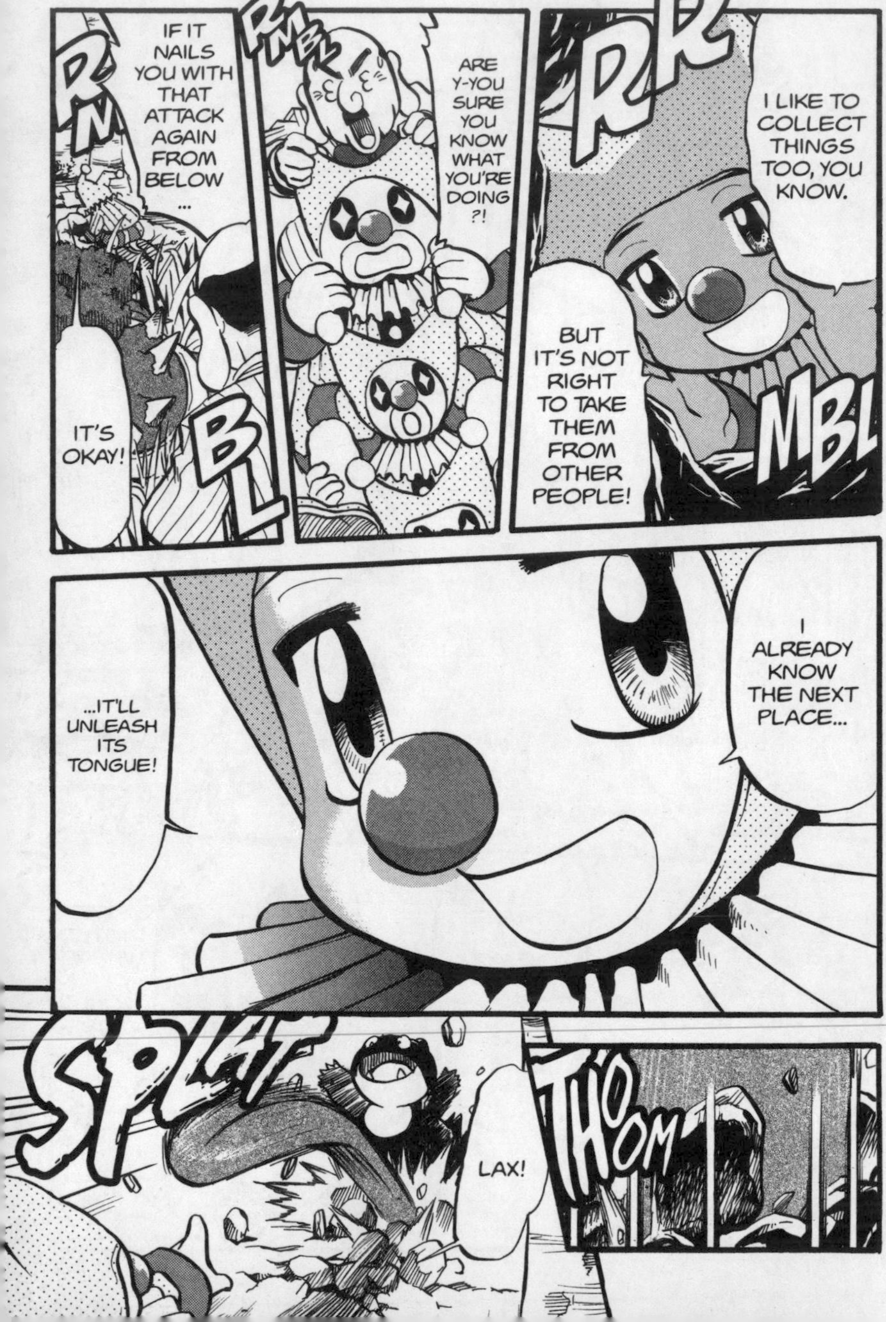
RR
I LIKE TO COLLECT THINGS TOO, YOU KNOW.
BUT IT'S NOT RIGHT TO TAKE THEM FROM OTHER PEOPLE!
MBL
RMBL
ARE Y-YOU SURE YOU KNOW WHAT YOU'RE DOING?!
RN
IF IT NAILS YOU WITH THAT ATTACK AGAIN FROM BELOW...
IT'S OKAY!
BL
I ALREADY KNOW THE NEXT PLACE...
...IT'LL UNLEASH ITS TONGUE!
THOOM
LAX!
SPLAT

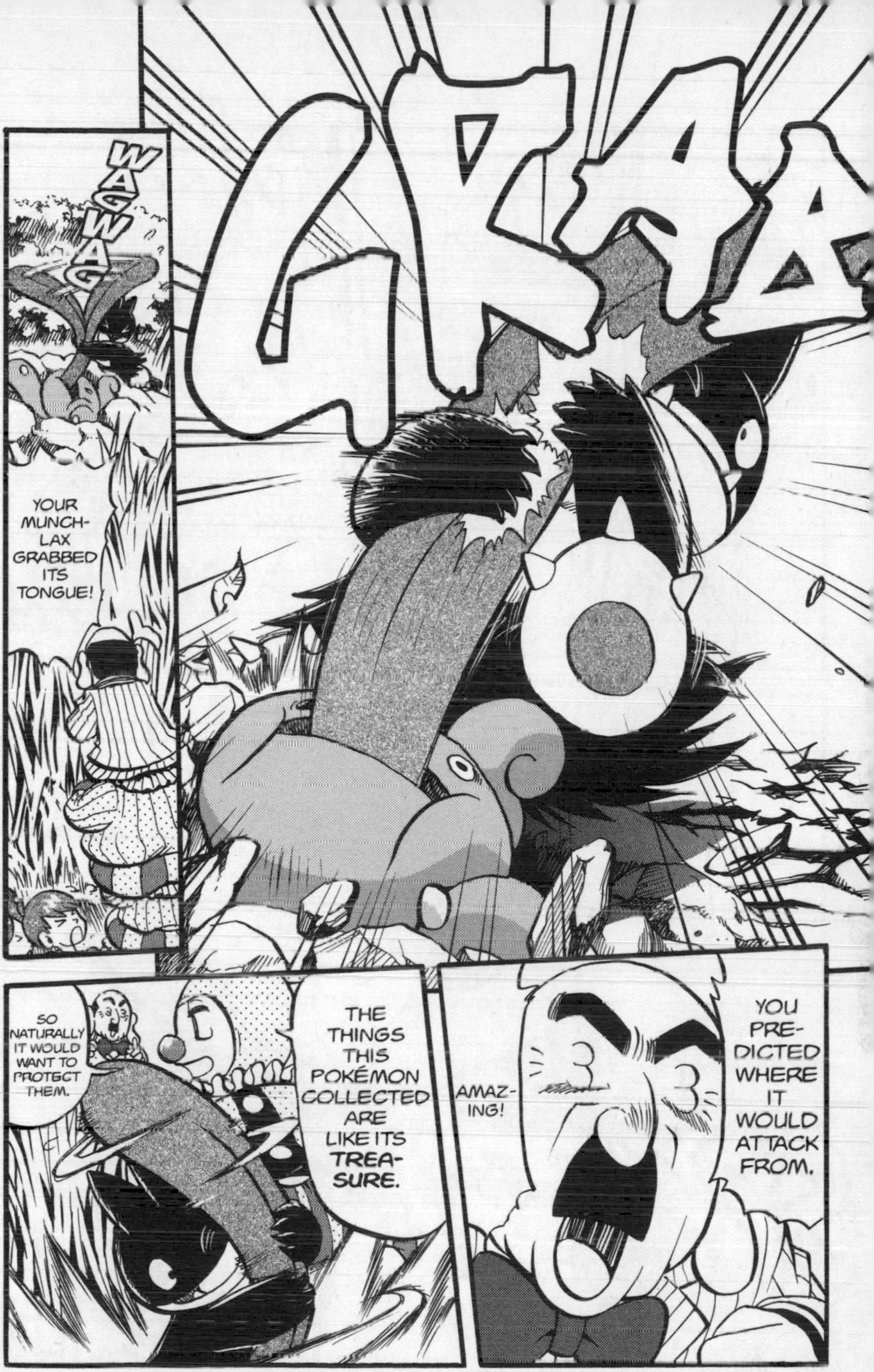
WAG WAG
YOUR MUNCH-LAX GRABBED ITS TONGUE!
YOU PRE-DICTED WHERE IT WOULD ATTACK FROM.
AMAZ-ING!
THE THINGS THIS POKÉMON COLLECTED ARE LIKE ITS TREASURE.
SO NATURALLY IT WOULD WANT TO PROTECT THEM.

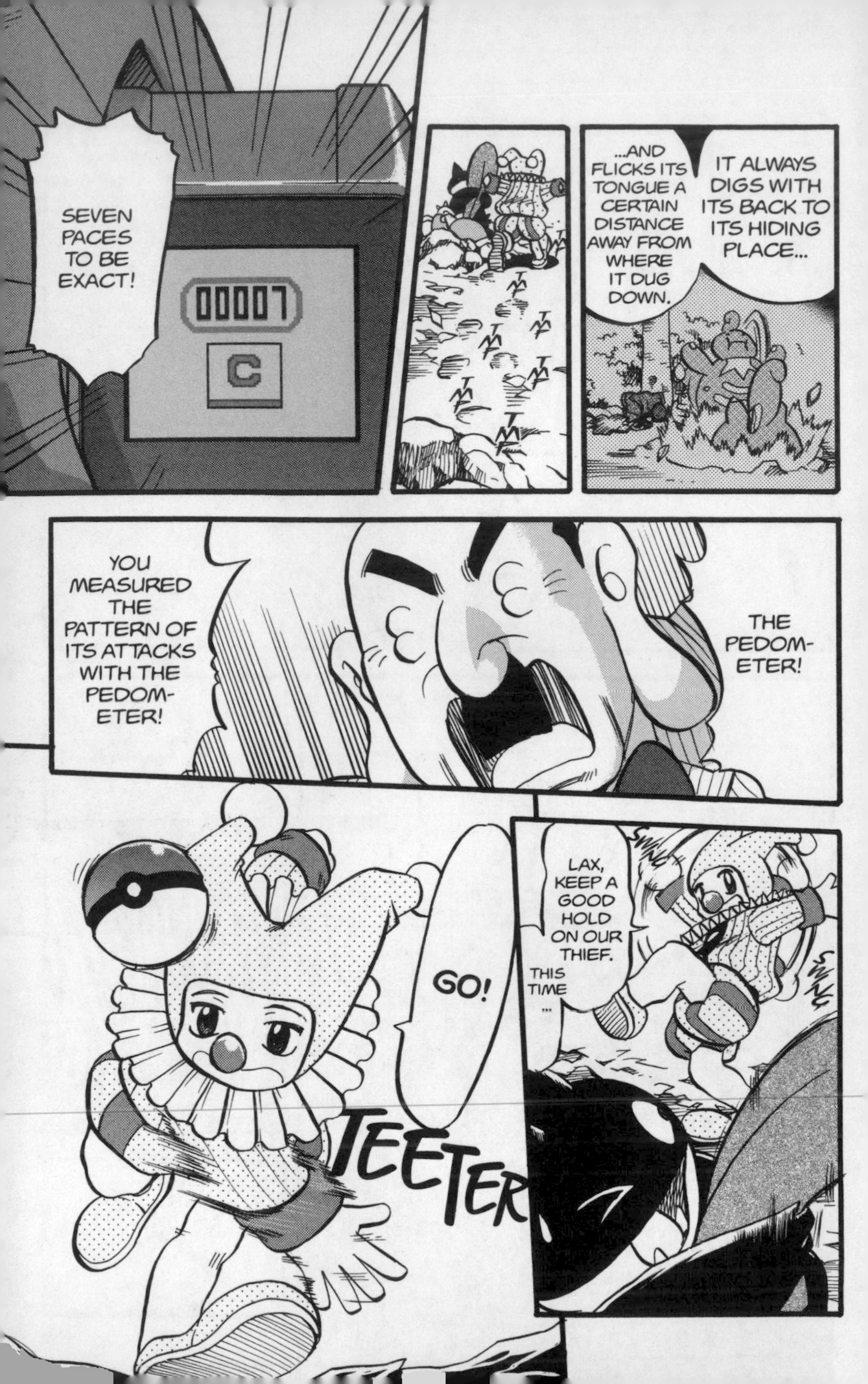
IT ALWAYS DIGS WITH ITS BACK TO ITS HIDING PLACE...
...AND FLICKS ITS TONGUE A CERTAIN DISTANCE AWAY FROM WHERE IT DUG DOWN.
TMP
00007
C
SEVEN PACES TO BE EXACT!
THE PEDOM-ETER!
YOU MEASURED THE PATTERN OF ITS ATTACKS WITH THE PEDOM-ETER!
SWING
LAX, KEEP A GOOD HOLD ON OUR THIEF.
THIS TIME ...
SWING
GO!
TEETER

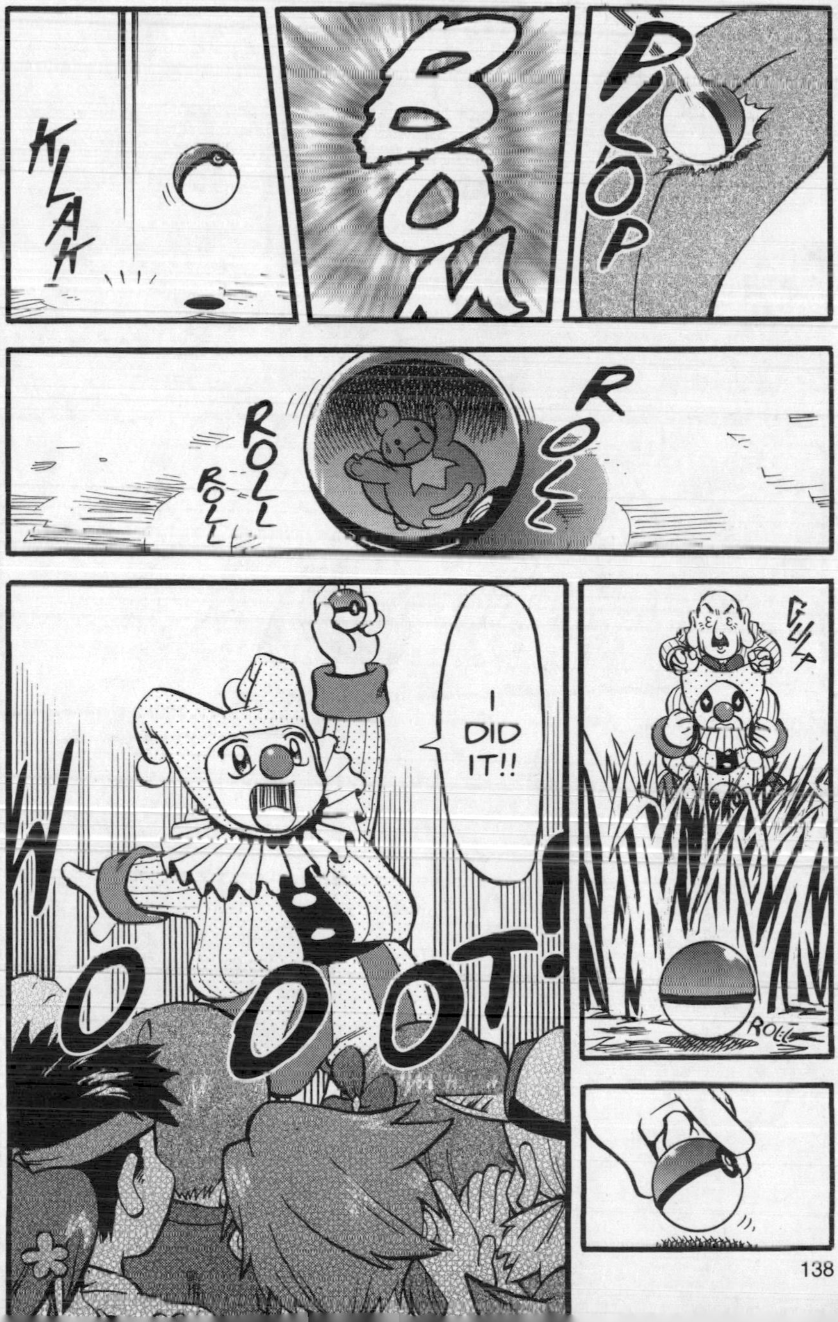
PLOP
BOOM
KLAK!
ROLL
ROLL
ROLL
GULP
ROLL
I DID IT!!
WOOOT!

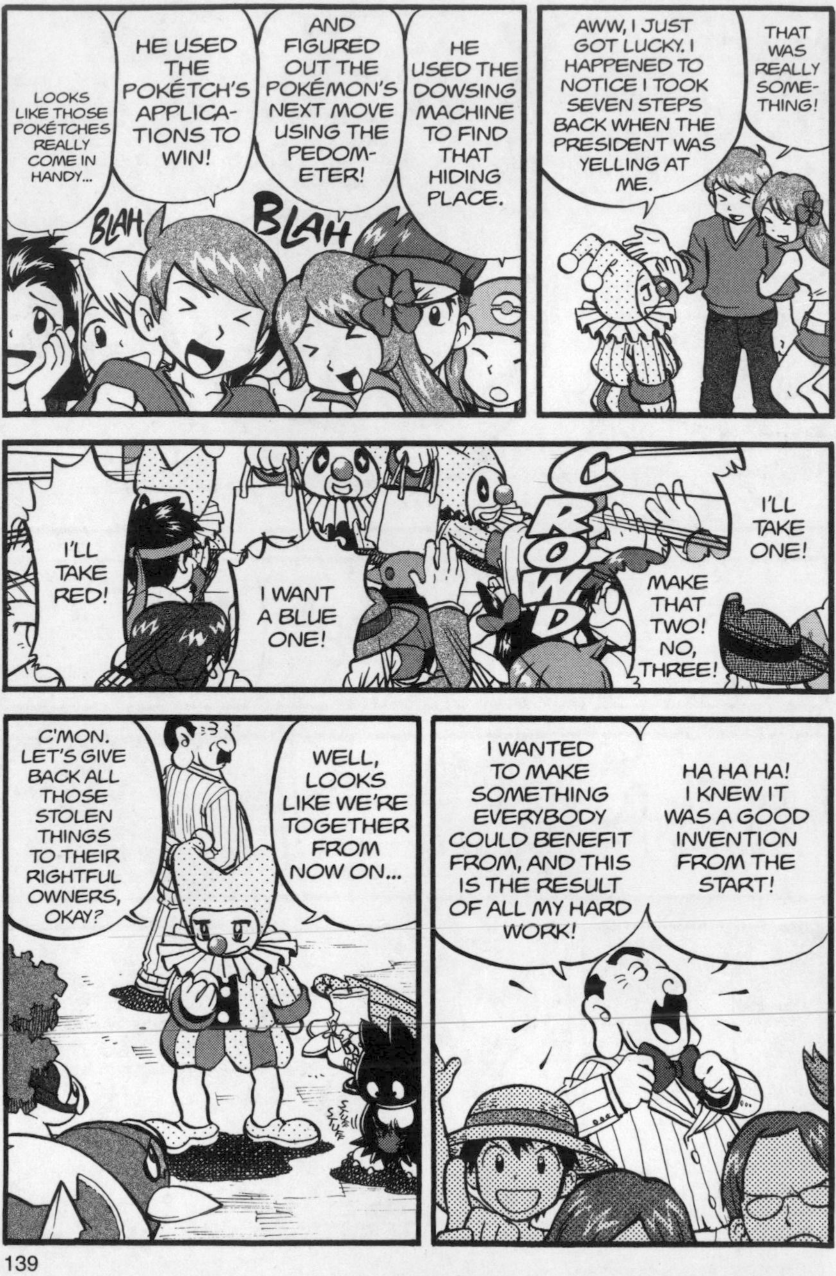
THAT WAS REALLY SOME-THING!
AWW, I JUST GOT LUCKY. I HAPPENED TO NOTICE I TOOK SEVEN STEPS BACK WHEN THE PRESIDENT WAS YELLING AT ME.
HE USED THE DOWSING MACHINE TO FIND THAT HIDING PLACE.
AND FIGURED OUT THE POKÉMON'S NEXT MOVE USING THE PEDOM-ETER!
BLAH
HE USED THE POKÉTCH'S APPLICA-TIONS TO WIN!
BLAH
LOOKS LIKE THOSE POKÉTCHES REALLY COME IN HANDY...
I'LL TAKE ONE!
MAKE THAT TWO! NO, THREE!
CROWD
I WANT A BLUE ONE!
I'LL TAKE RED!
HA HA HA! I KNEW IT WAS A GOOD INVENTION FROM THE START!
I WANTED TO MAKE SOMETHING EVERYBODY COULD BENEFIT FROM, AND THIS IS THE RESULT OF ALL MY HARD WORK!
WELL, LOOKS LIKE WE'RE TOGETHER FROM NOW ON...
C'MON. LET'S GIVE BACK ALL THOSE STOLEN THINGS TO THEIR RIGHTFUL OWNERS, OKAY?

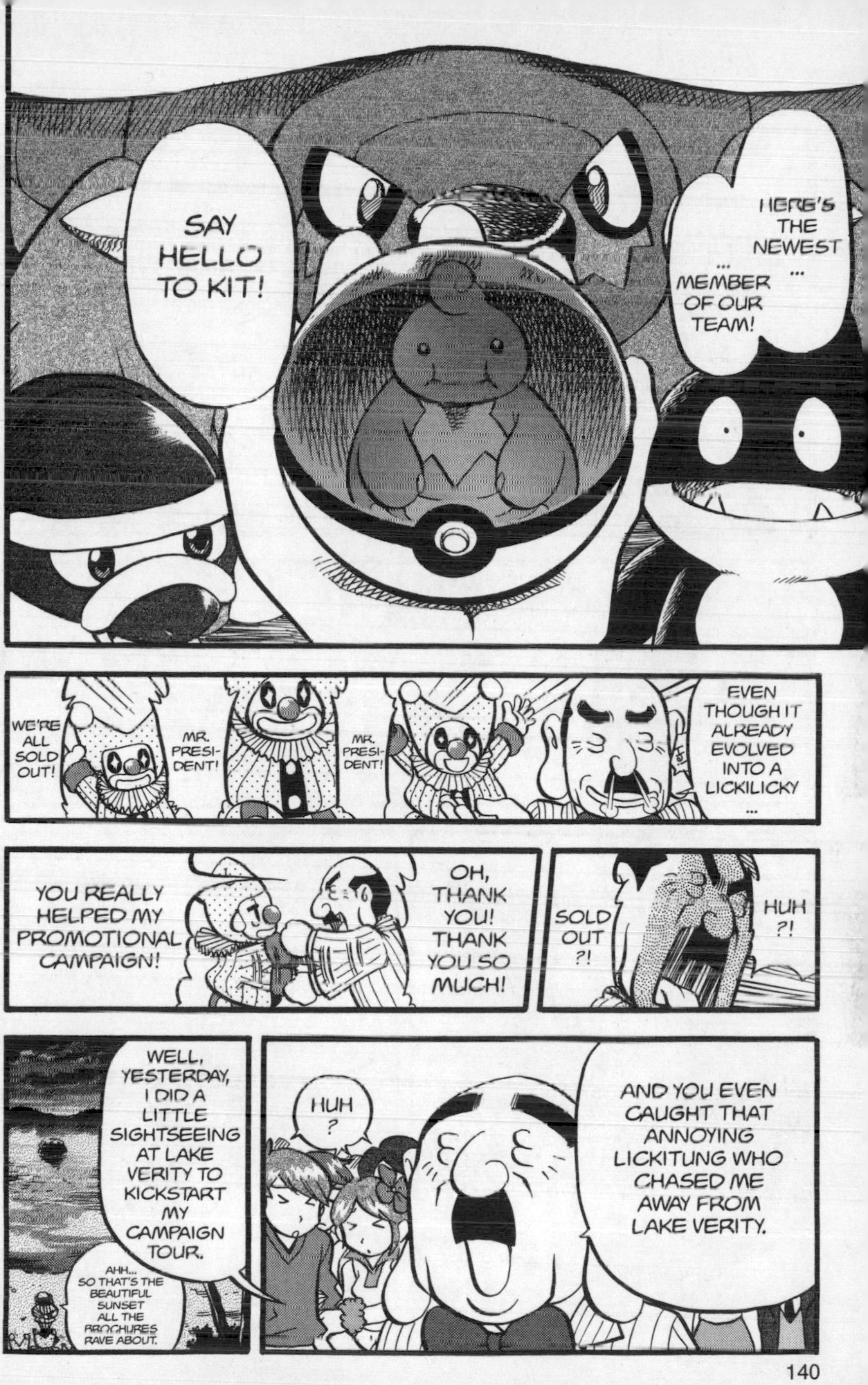
HERE'S THE NEWEST ... MEMBER OF OUR TEAM!
SAY HELLO TO KIT!
EVEN THOUGH IT ALREADY EVOLVED INTO A LICKILICKY ...
MR. PRESIDENT!
MR. PRESIDENT!
WE'RE ALL SOLD OUT!
HUH ?!
SOLD OUT ?!
OH, THANK YOU! THANK YOU SO MUCH!
YOU REALLY HELPED MY PROMOTIONAL CAMPAIGN!
AND YOU EVEN CAUGHT THAT ANNOYING LICKITUNG WHO CHASED ME AWAY FROM LAKE VERITY.
HUH ?
WELL, YESTERDAY, I DID A LITTLE SIGHTSEEING AT LAKE VERITY TO KICKSTART MY CAMPAIGN TOUR.
AHH... SO THAT'S THE BEAUTIFUL SUNSET ALL THE BROCHURES RAVE ABOUT.

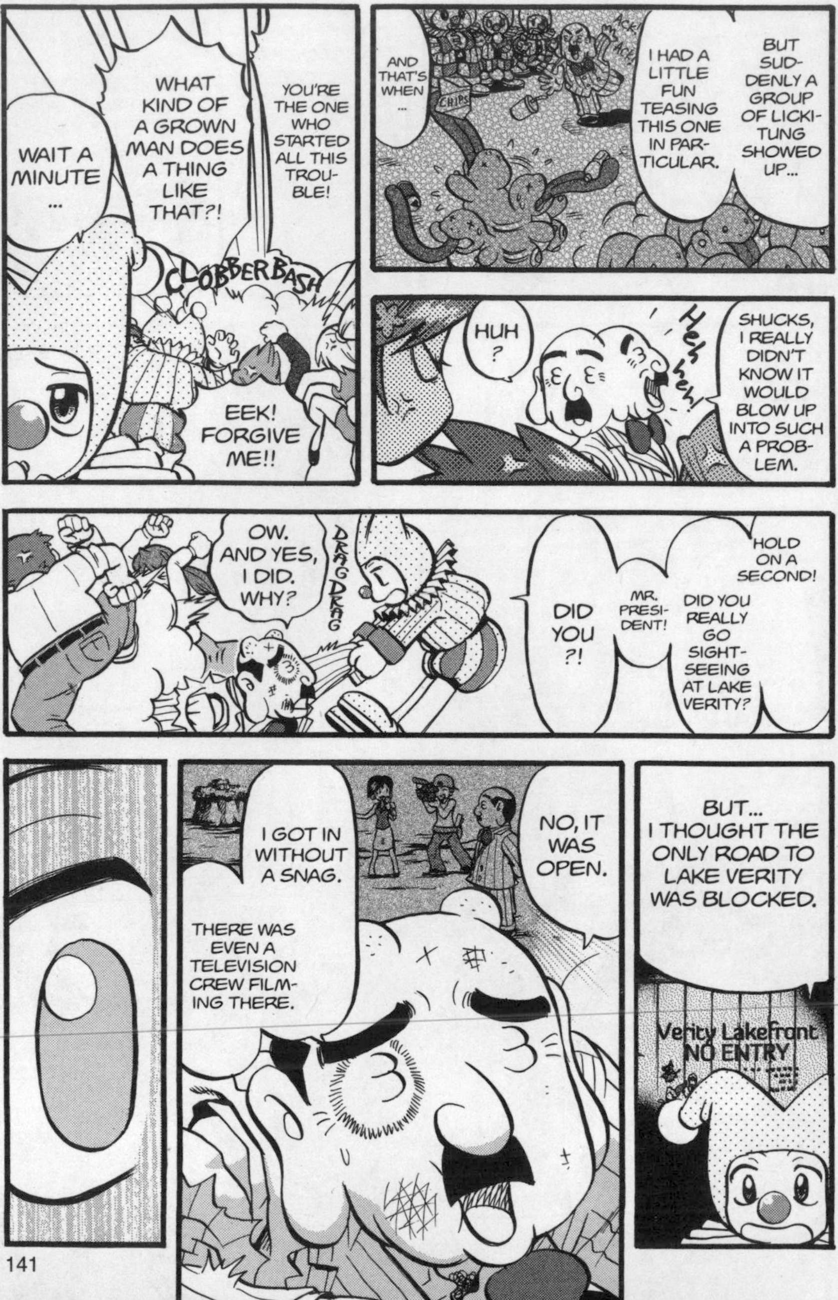
BUT SUDDENLY A GROUP OF LICKITUNG SHOWED UP...
I HAD A LITTLE FUN TEASING THIS ONE IN PARTICULAR.
AND THAT'S WHEN ...
CHIPS
SHUCKS, I REALLY DIDN'T KNOW IT WOULD BLOW UP INTO SUCH A PROBLEM.
Heh heh!
HUH?
YOU'RE THE ONE WHO STARTED ALL THIS TROUBLE!
WHAT KIND OF A GROWN MAN DOES A THING LIKE THAT?!
WAIT A MINUTE ...
CLOBBER BASH
EEK! FORGIVE ME!!
HOLD ON A SECOND!
DID YOU REALLY GO SIGHTSEEING AT LAKE VERITY?
MR. PRESIDENT!
DID YOU ?!
DRAG DRAG
OW. AND YES, I DID. WHY?
BUT... I THOUGHT THE ONLY ROAD TO LAKE VERITY WAS BLOCKED.
Verity Lakefront NO ENTRY
NO, IT WAS OPEN.
I GOT IN WITHOUT A SNAG.
THERE WAS EVEN A TELEVISION CREW FILMING THERE.

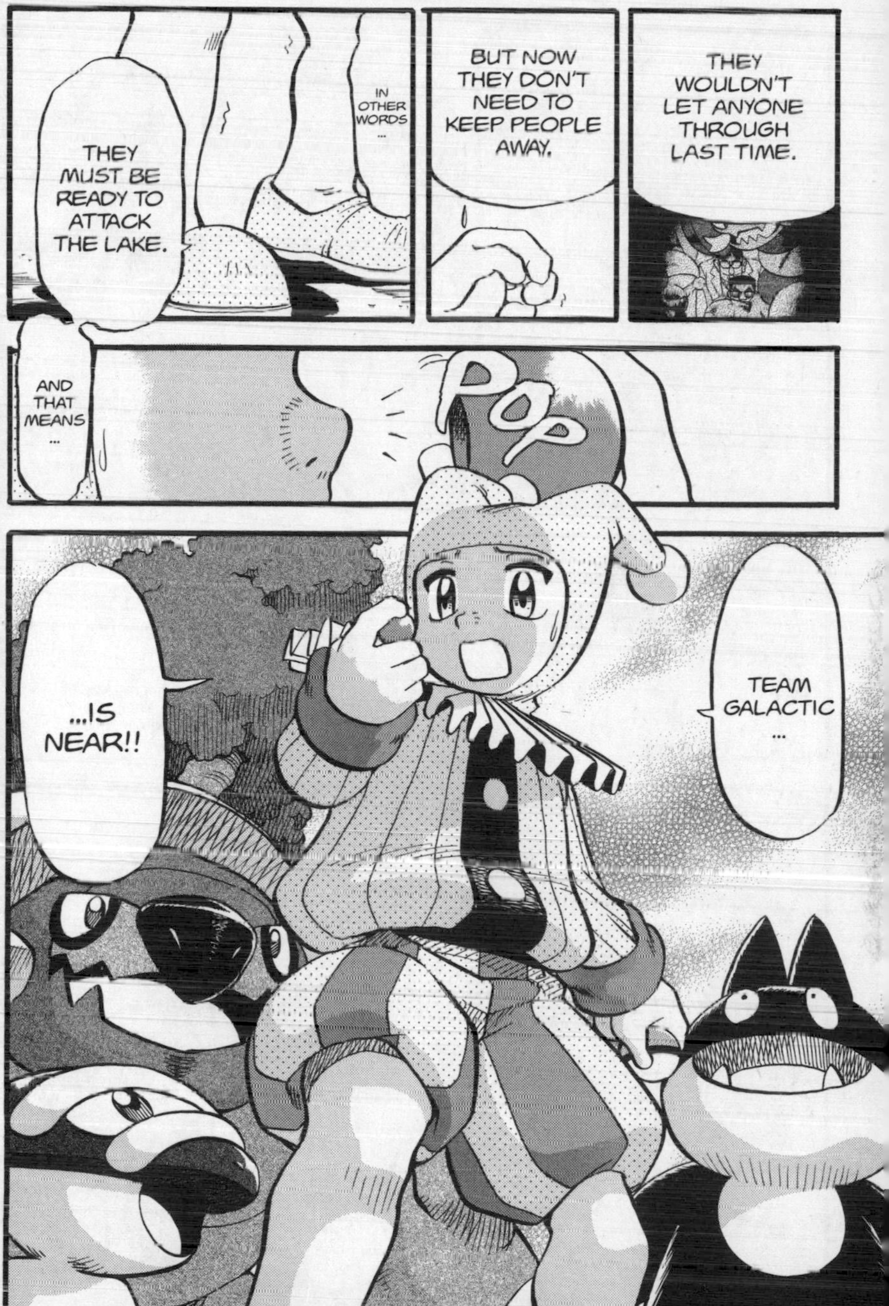
THEY WOULDN'T LET ANYONE THROUGH LAST TIME.
BUT NOW THEY DON'T NEED TO KEEP PEOPLE AWAY.
IN OTHER WORDS ...
THEY MUST BE READY TO ATTACK THE LAKE.
AND THAT MEANS ...
POP
TEAM GALACTIC ...
...IS NEAR!!

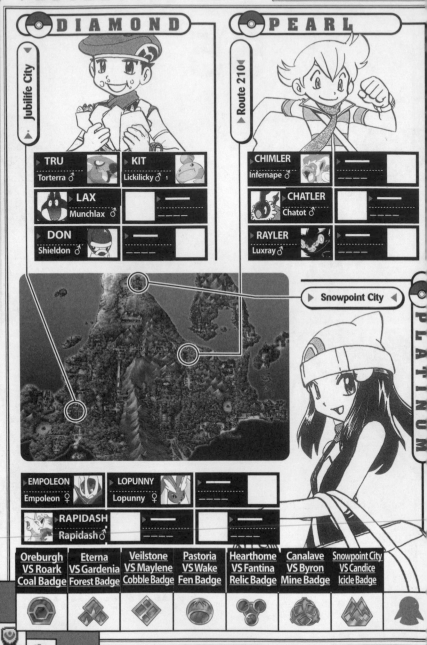

◦ DIAMOND

▲ Jubilife City ▲

▸ TRU Torterra ♂	▸ KIT Lickilicky ♂ 1	
▸ LAX Munchlax ♂		
▸ DON Shieldon ♂		

◦ PEARL

▲ Route 210 ◄

▸ CHIMLER Infernape ♂		
▸ CHATLER Chatot ♂		
▸ RAYLER Luxray ♂		

▸ Snowpoint City ◄

PLATINUM

▸ EMPOLEON Empoleon ♀	▸ LOPUNNY Lopunny ♀	
▸ RAPIDASH Rapidash ♂		

| Oreburgh
VS Roark
Coal Badge | Eterna
VS Gardenia
Forest Badge | Veilstone
VS Maylene
Cobble Badge | Pastoria
VS Wake
Fen Badge | Hearthome
VS Fantina
Relic Badge | Canalave
VS Byron
Mine Badge | Snowpoint City
VS Candice
Icicle Badge | |

55

Well Met, Weepinbell

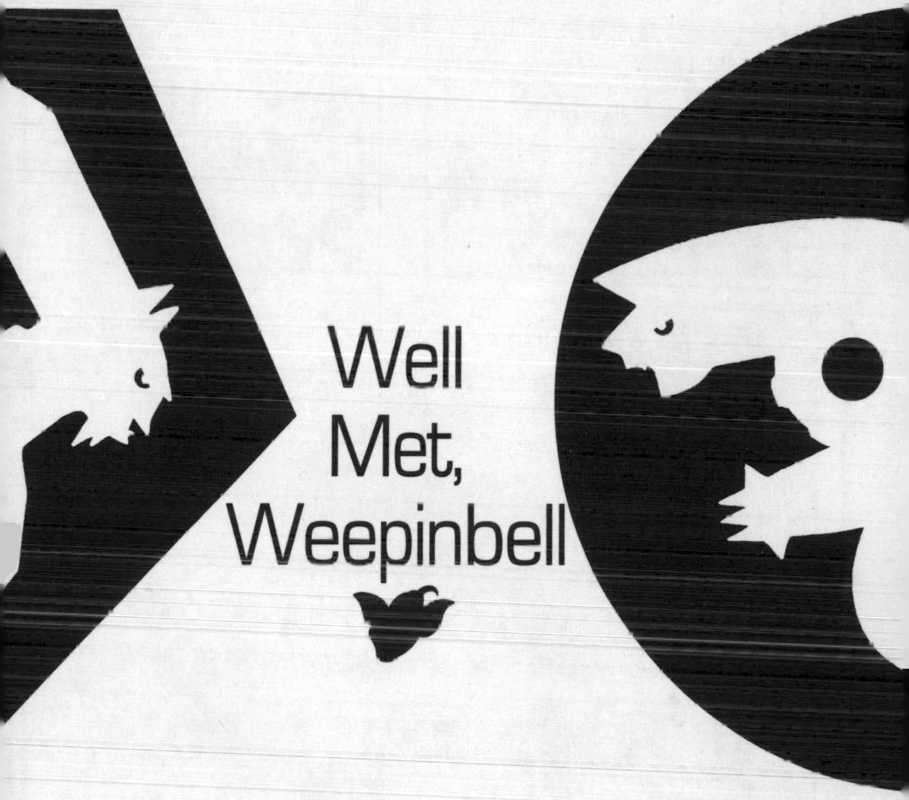

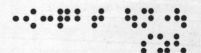

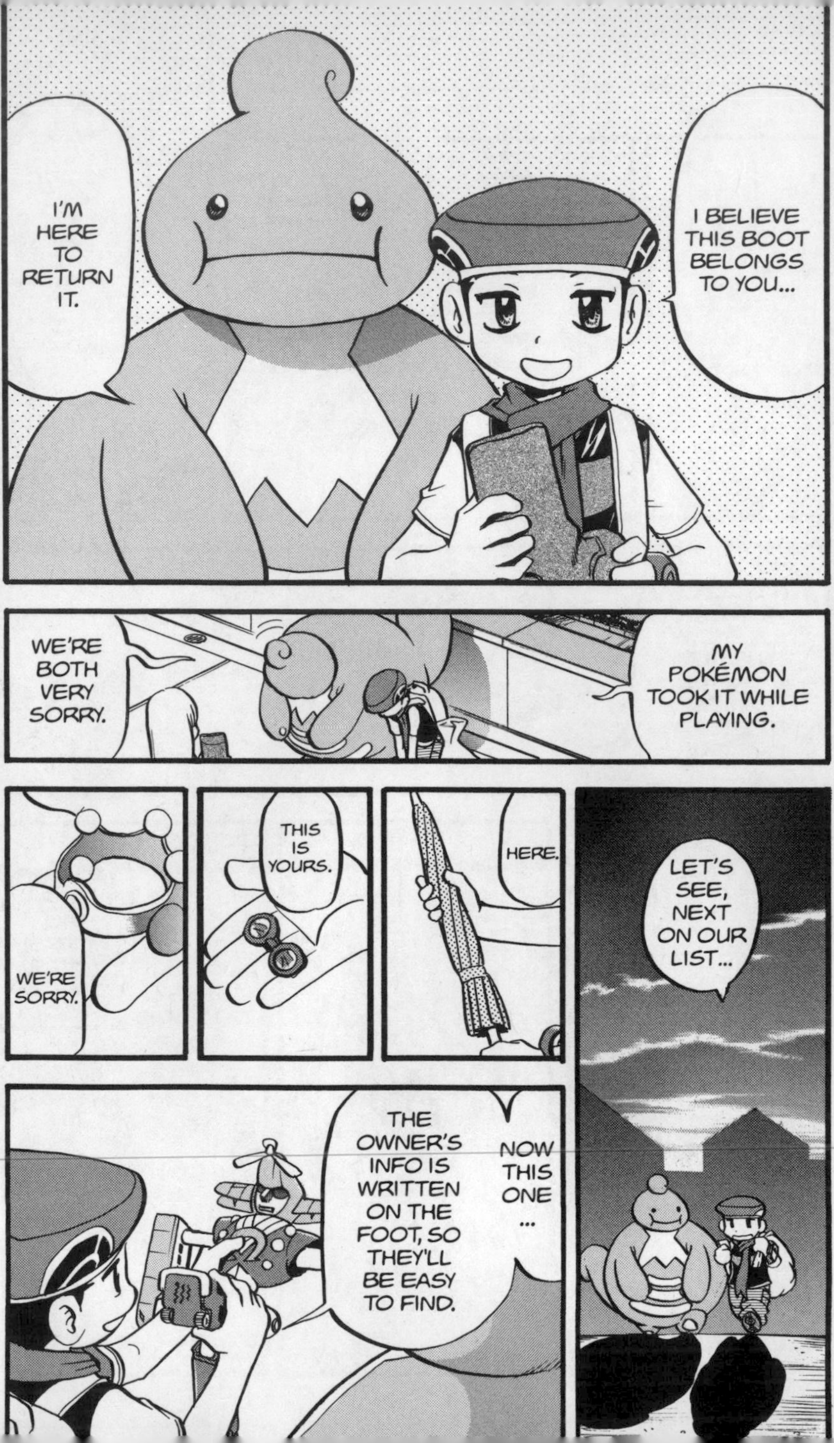
I BELIEVE THIS BOOT BELONGS TO YOU...
I'M HERE TO RETURN IT.
MY POKÉMON TOOK IT WHILE PLAYING.
WE'RE BOTH VERY SORRY.
LET'S SEE, NEXT ON OUR LIST...
HERE.
THIS IS YOURS.
WE'RE SORRY.
NOW THIS ONE ...
THE OWNER'S INFO IS WRITTEN ON THE FOOT, SO THEY'LL BE EASY TO FIND.

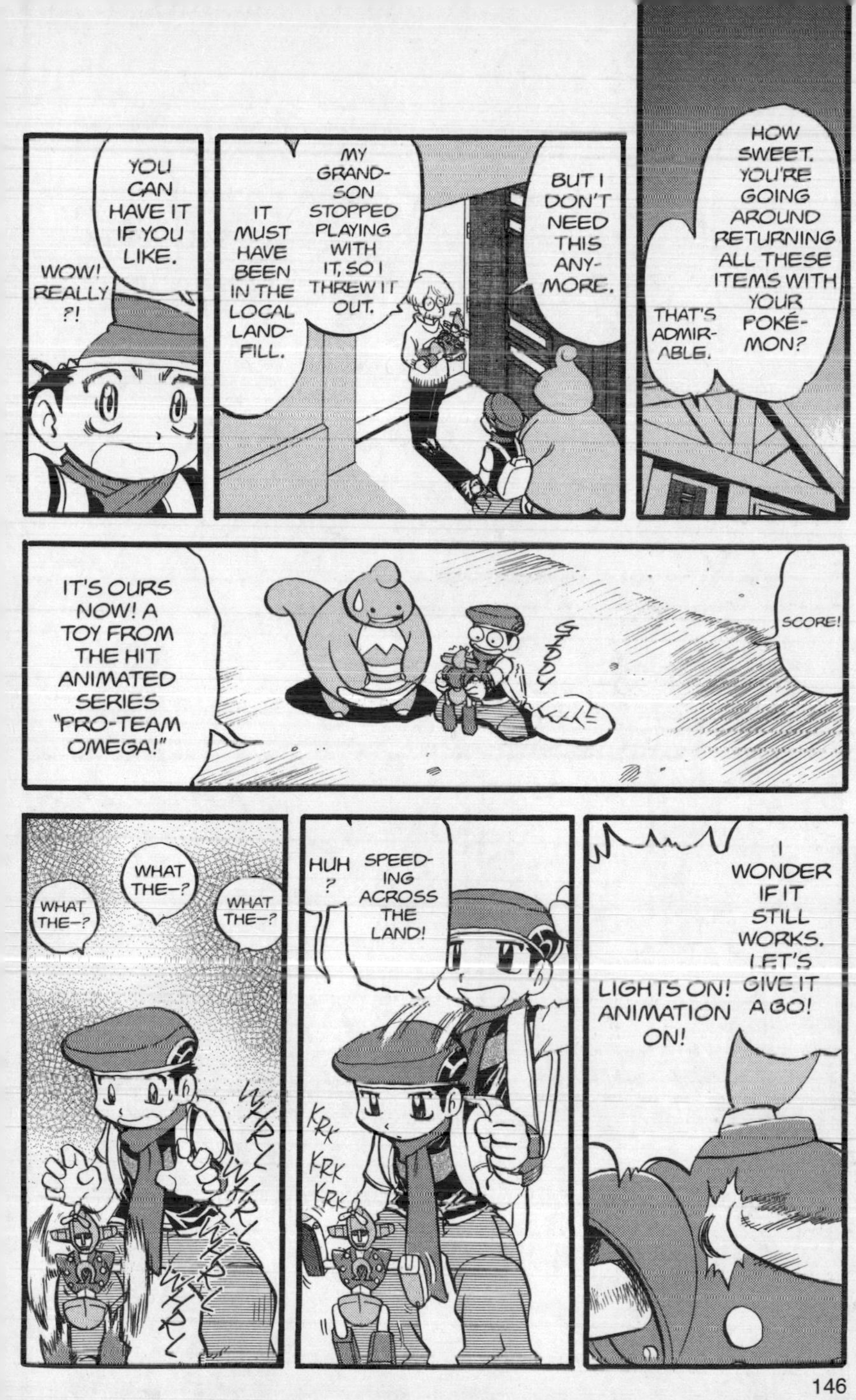
HOW SWEET. YOU'RE GOING AROUND RETURNING ALL THESE ITEMS WITH YOUR POKÉMON?
THAT'S ADMIRABLE.
BUT I DON'T NEED THIS ANYMORE.
MY GRANDSON STOPPED PLAYING WITH IT, SO I THREW IT OUT.
IT MUST HAVE BEEN IN THE LOCAL LANDFILL.
YOU CAN HAVE IT IF YOU LIKE.
WOW! REALLY?!
SCORE!
GIDDY
IT'S OURS NOW! A TOY FROM THE HIT ANIMATED SERIES "PRO-TEAM OMEGA!"
I WONDER IF IT STILL WORKS. LET'S GIVE IT A GO!
LIGHTS ON! ANIMATION ON!
SPEEDING ACROSS THE LAND!
HUH?
KRK KRK KRK
WHAT THE-?
WHAT THE-?
WHAT THE-?
WHRL WHRL WHRL WHRL

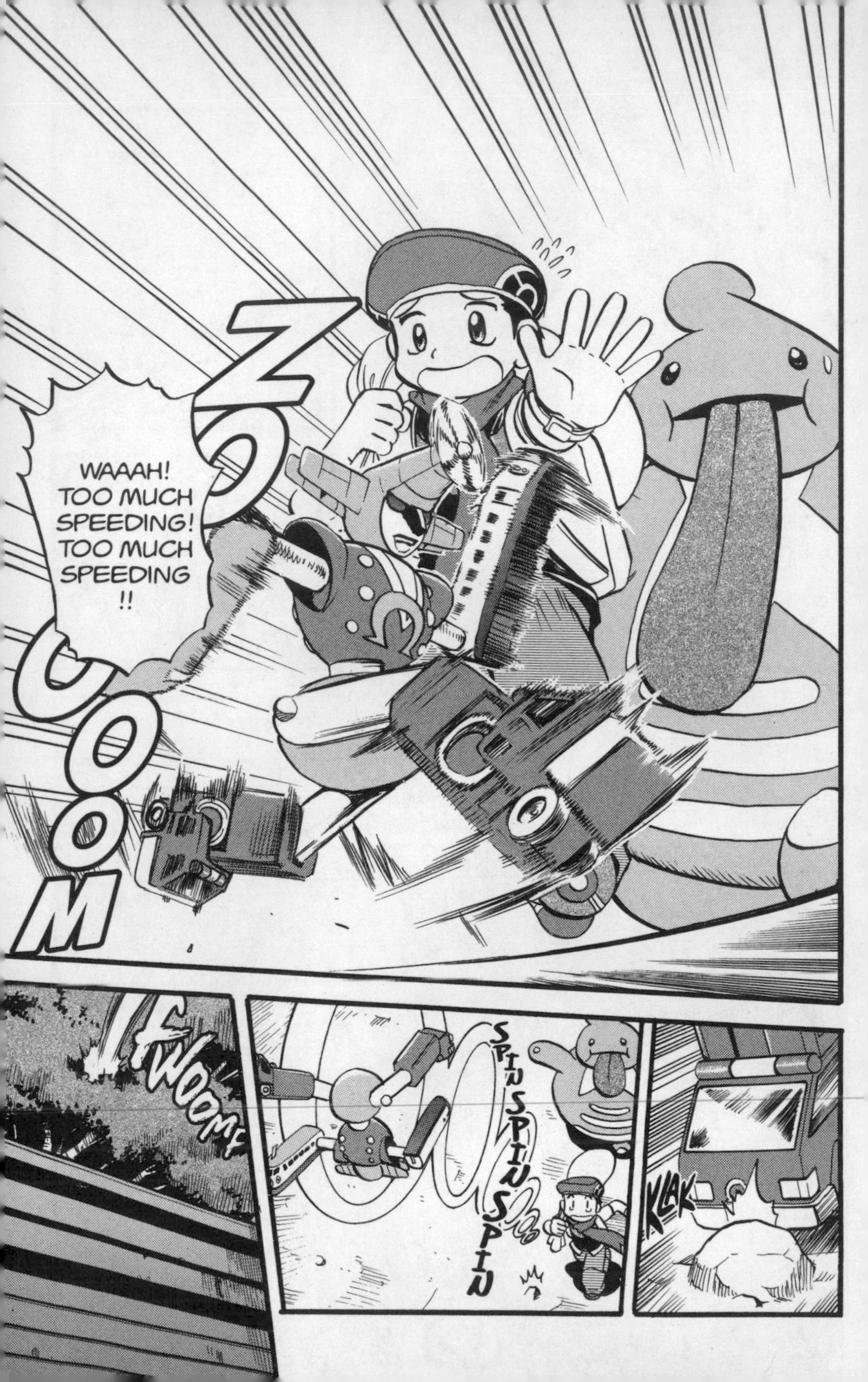
WAAAH! TOO MUCH SPEEDING! TOO MUCH SPEEDING !!
ZOOOOOM
KLAK
SPIN SPIN SPIN SPIN
FWOOM

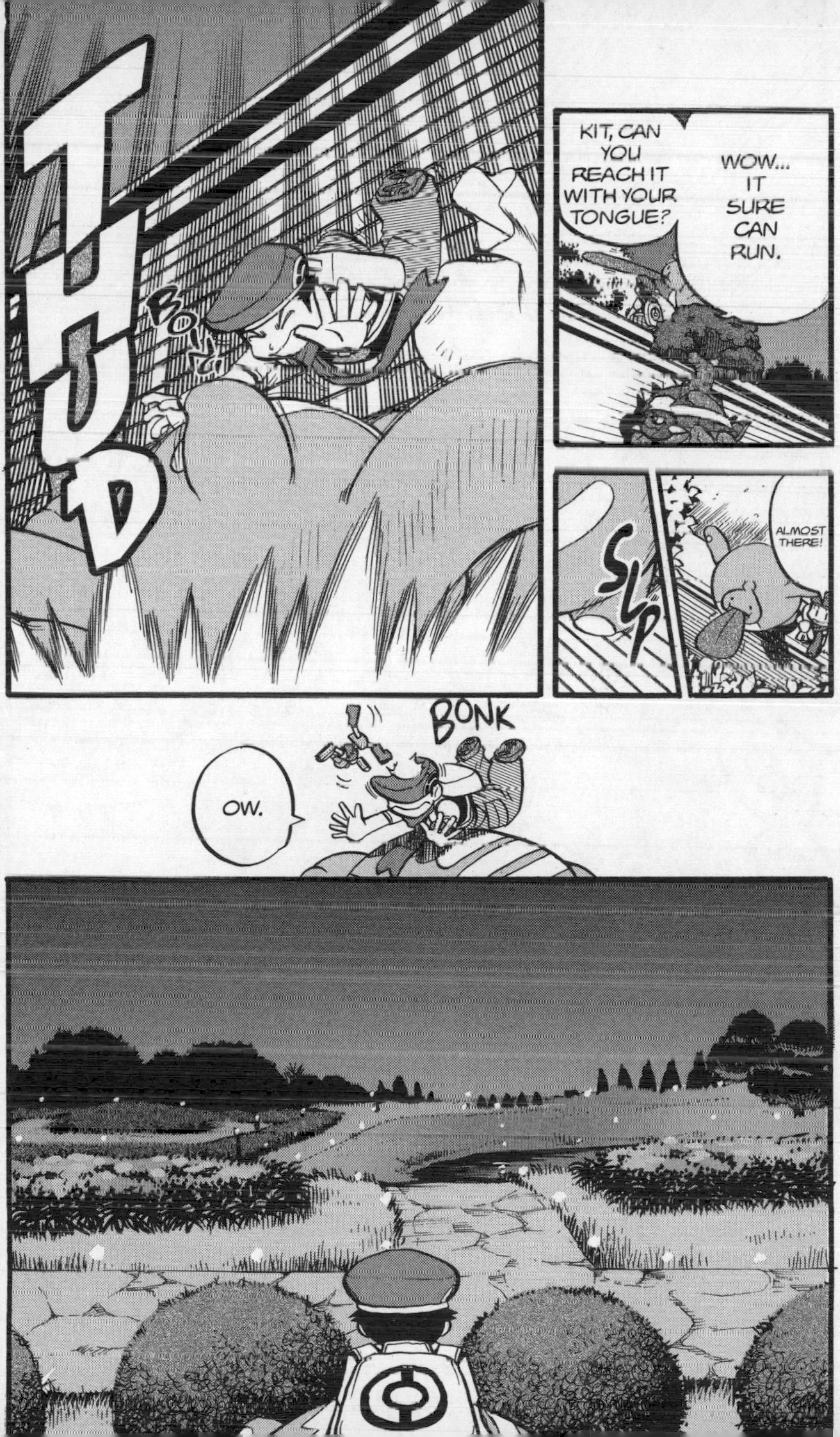
WOW... IT SURE CAN RUN.
KIT, CAN YOU REACH IT WITH YOUR TONGUE?
ALMOST THERE!
SLP
THUD
BOING
BONK
OW.

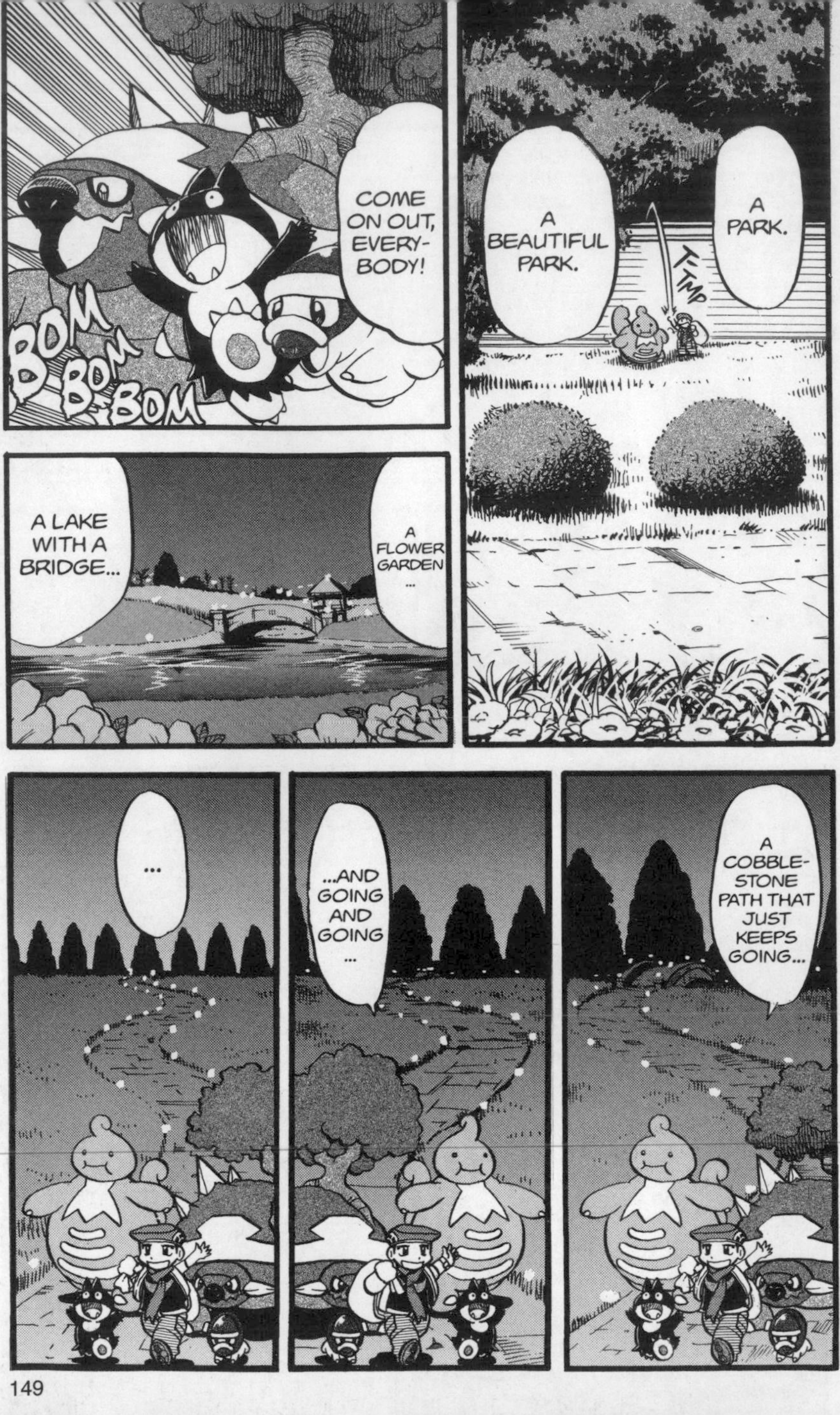
A PARK.
A BEAUTIFUL PARK.
T-TMP
COME ON OUT, EVERY-BODY!
BOM BOM BOM BOM
A FLOWER GARDEN ...
A LAKE WITH A BRIDGE...
A COBBLE-STONE PATH THAT JUST KEEPS GOING...
...AND GOING AND GOING ...
...

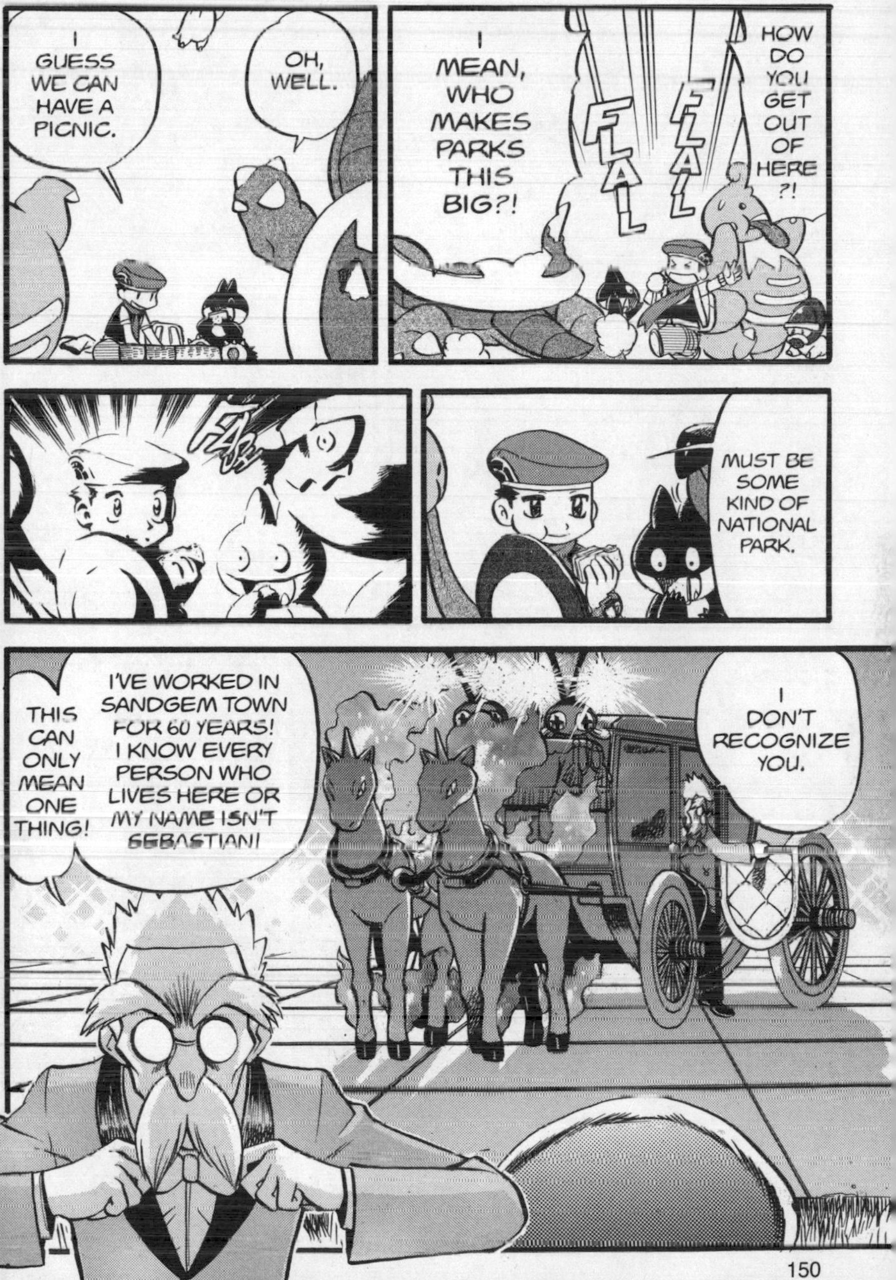
HOW DO YOU GET OUT OF HERE?!
FLALL
FLALL
I MEAN, WHO MAKES PARKS THIS BIG?!
OH, WELL.
I GUESS WE CAN HAVE A PICNIC.
MUST BE SOME KIND OF NATIONAL PARK.
I DON'T RECOGNIZE YOU.
I'VE WORKED IN SANDGEM TOWN FOR 60 YEARS! I KNOW EVERY PERSON WHO LIVES HERE OR MY NAME ISN'T SEBASTIAN!
THIS CAN ONLY MEAN ONE THING!

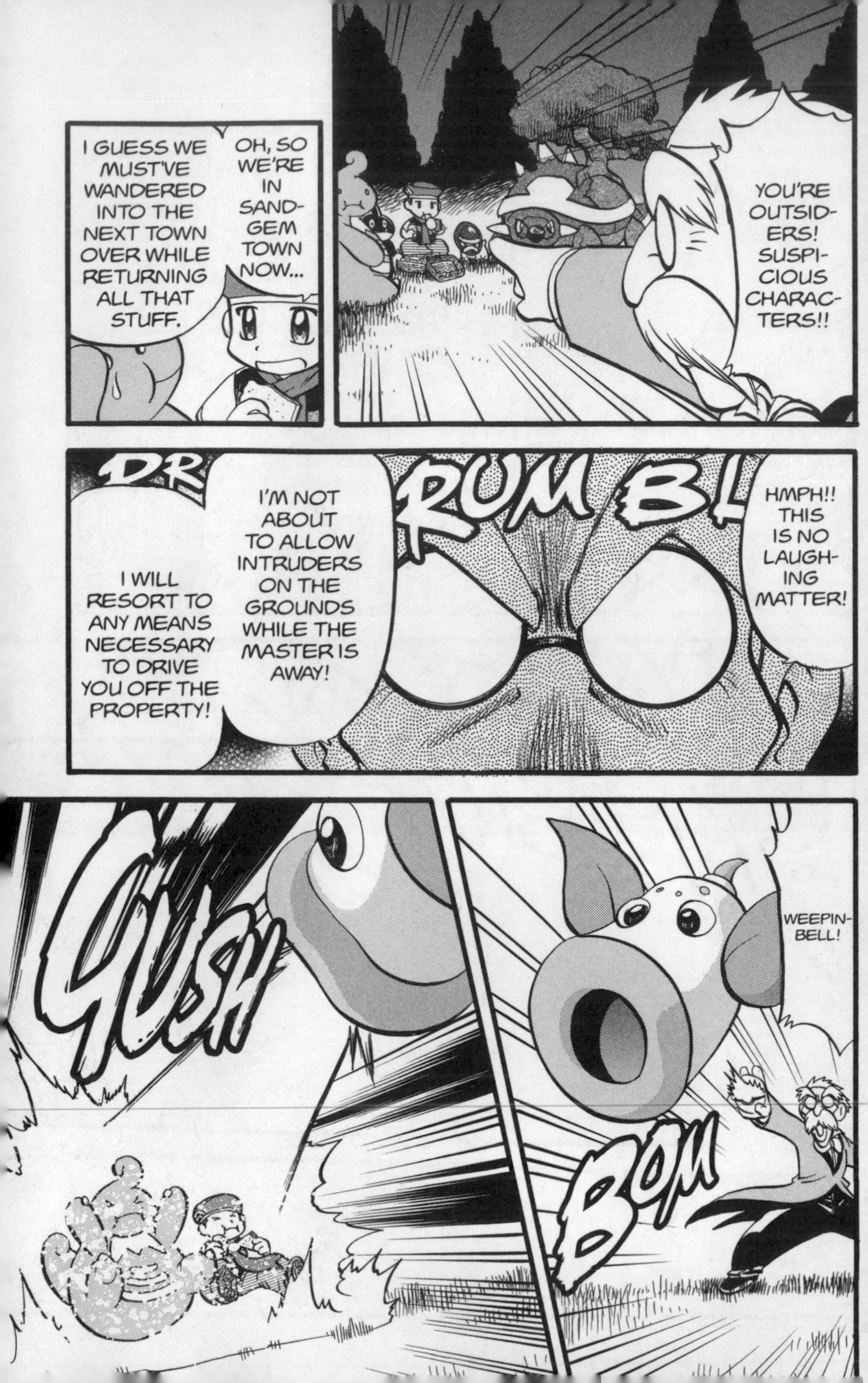

YOU'RE OUTSIDERS! SUSPICIOUS CHARACTERS!!
OH, SO WE'RE IN SANDGEM TOWN NOW...
I GUESS WE MUST'VE WANDERED INTO THE NEXT TOWN OVER WHILE RETURNING ALL THAT STUFF.
HMPH!! THIS IS NO LAUGHING MATTER!
DR RUM BL
I'M NOT ABOUT TO ALLOW INTRUDERS ON THE GROUNDS WHILE THE MASTER IS AWAY!
I WILL RESORT TO ANY MEANS NECESSARY TO DRIVE YOU OFF THE PROPERTY!
WEEPINBELL!
BOM
GUSH

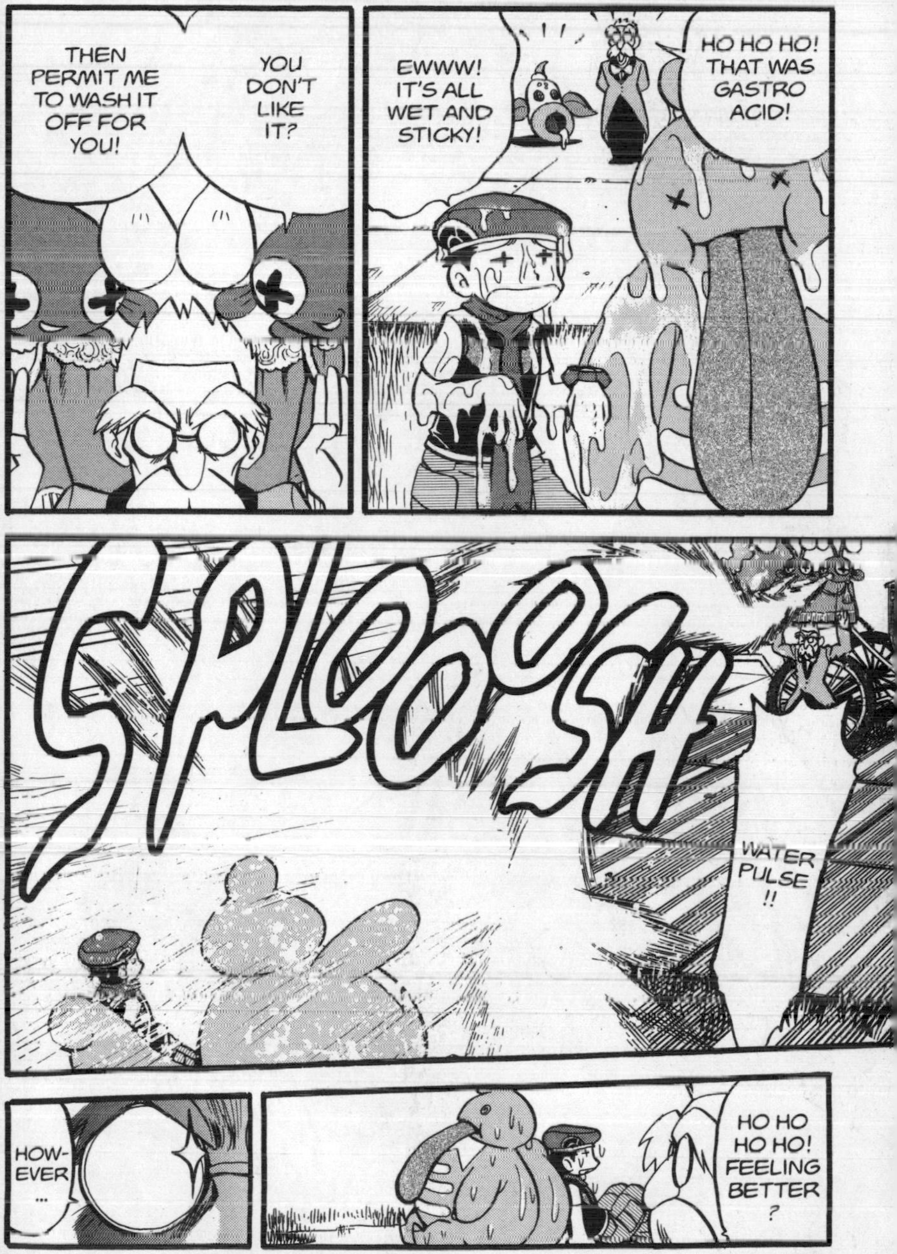
HO HO HO! THAT WAS GASTRO ACID!
EWWW! IT'S ALL WET AND STICKY!
YOU DON'T LIKE IT?
THEN PERMIT ME TO WASH IT OFF FOR YOU!
SPLOOOSH
WATER PULSE !!
HO HO HO HO! FEELING BETTER ?
HOW-EVER ...

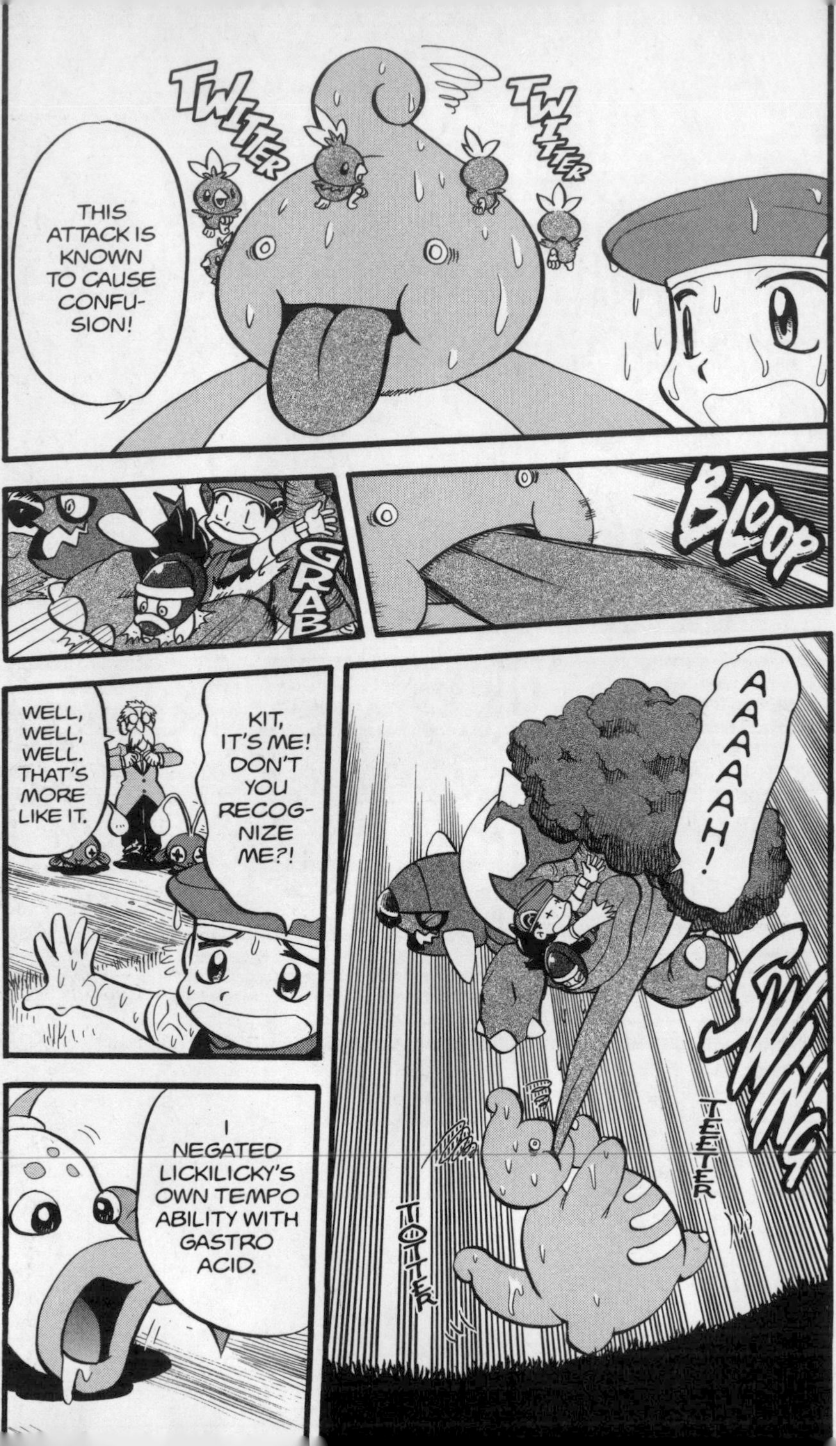
TWITTER
TWITTER
THIS ATTACK IS KNOWN TO CAUSE CONFU- SION!
BLOOP
GRAB
AAAAAH!
SWING
TEETER
TOTTER
KIT, IT'S ME! DON'T YOU RECOG- NIZE ME?!
WELL, WELL, WELL. THAT'S MORE LIKE IT.
I NEGATED LICKILICKY'S OWN TEMPO ABILITY WITH GASTRO ACID.

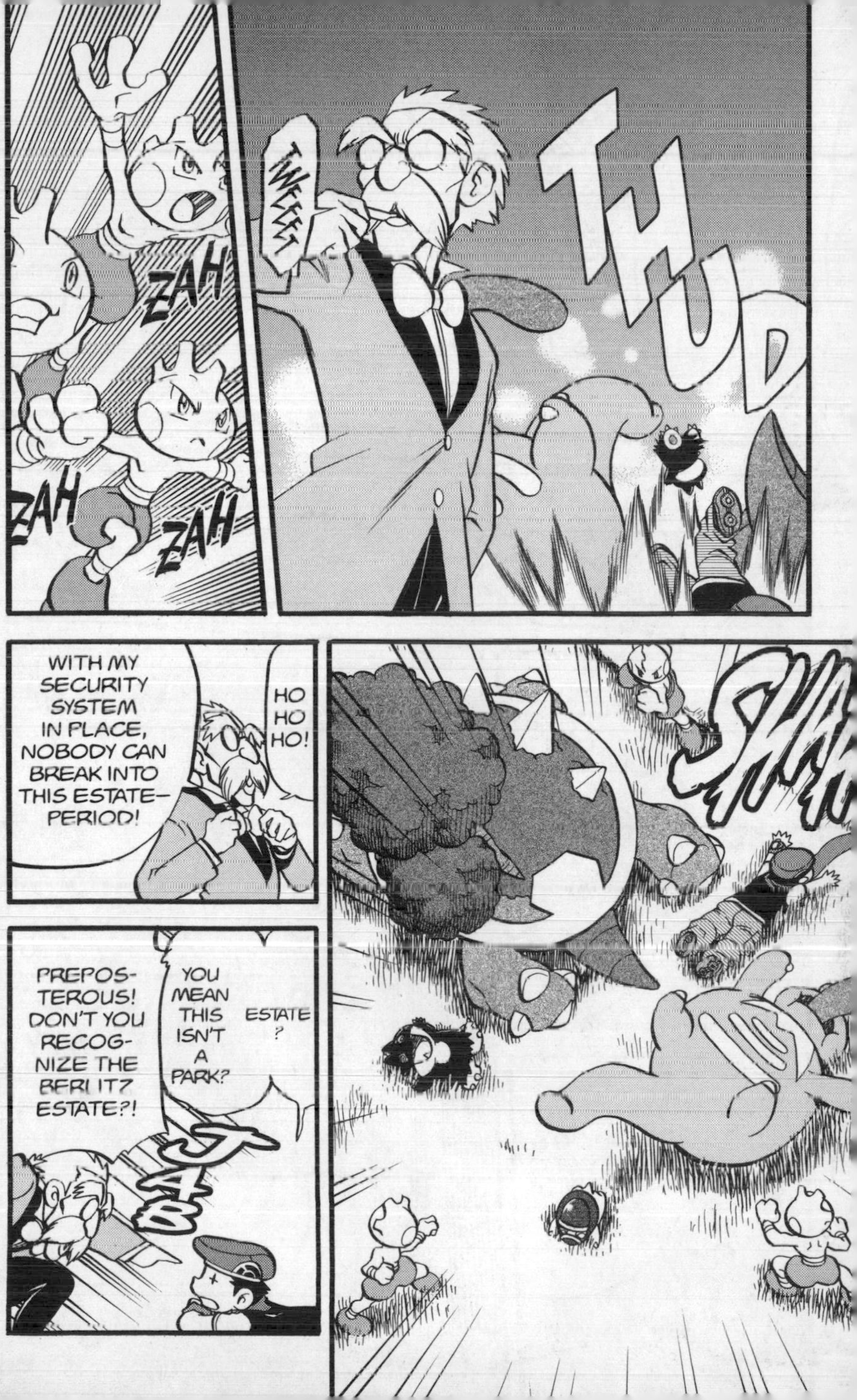
TWEEEET
THUD
ZAH
ZAH
ZAH
HO HO HO!
WITH MY SECURITY SYSTEM IN PLACE, NOBODY CAN BREAK INTO THIS ESTATE—PERIOD!
ESTATE?
YOU MEAN THIS ISN'T A PARK?
PREPOSTEROUS! DON'T YOU RECOGNIZE THE BERLITZ ESTATE?!
JAB

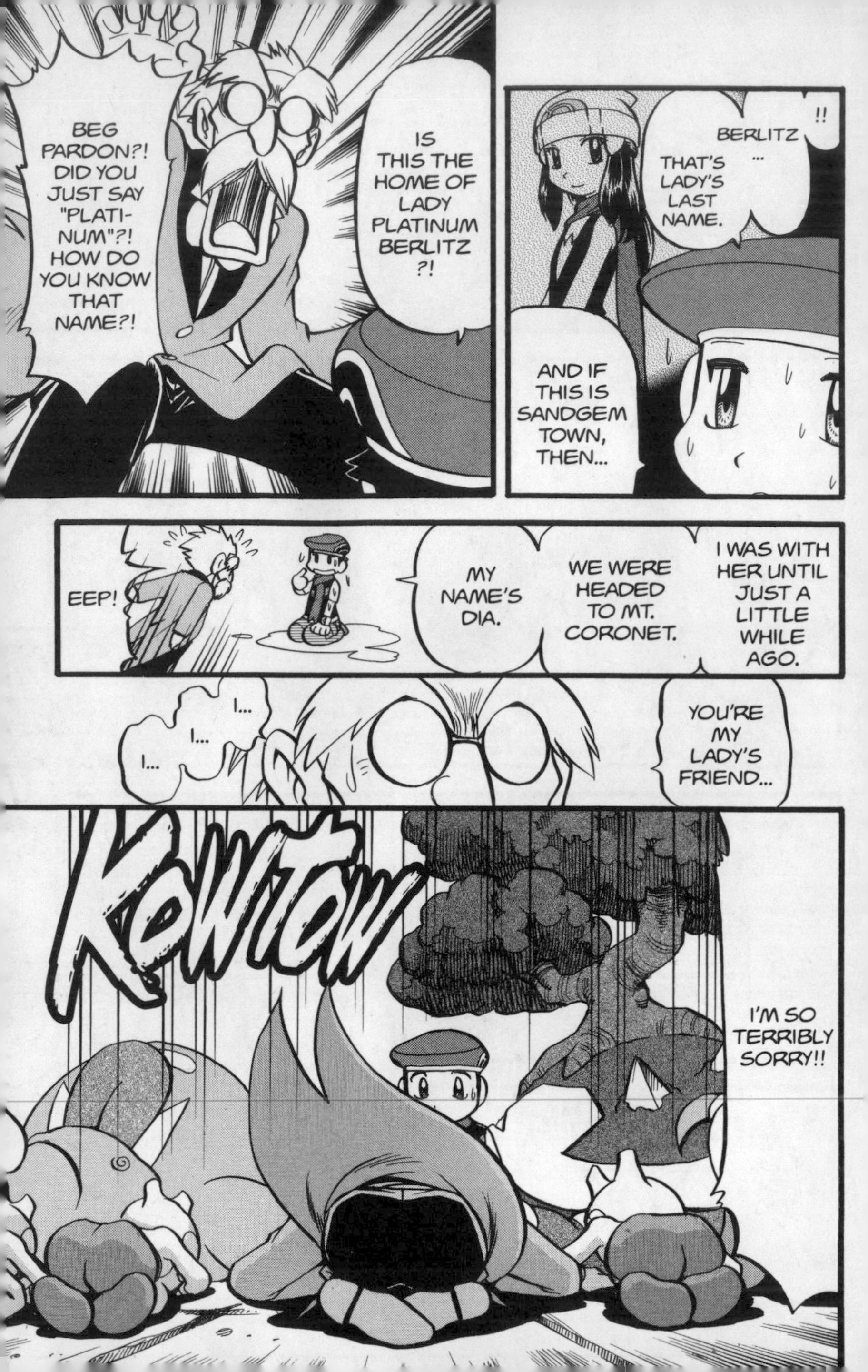
!!
BERLITZ ... THAT'S LADY'S LAST NAME.
AND IF THIS IS SANDGEM TOWN, THEN...
IS THIS THE HOME OF LADY PLATINUM BERLITZ ?!
BEG PARDON?! DID YOU JUST SAY "PLATI-NUM"?! HOW DO YOU KNOW THAT NAME?!
I WAS WITH HER UNTIL JUST A LITTLE WHILE AGO.
WE WERE HEADED TO MT. CORONET.
MY NAME'S DIA.
EEP!
YOU'RE MY LADY'S FRIEND...
I... I... I...
I'M SO TERRIBLY SORRY!!
KOWTOW

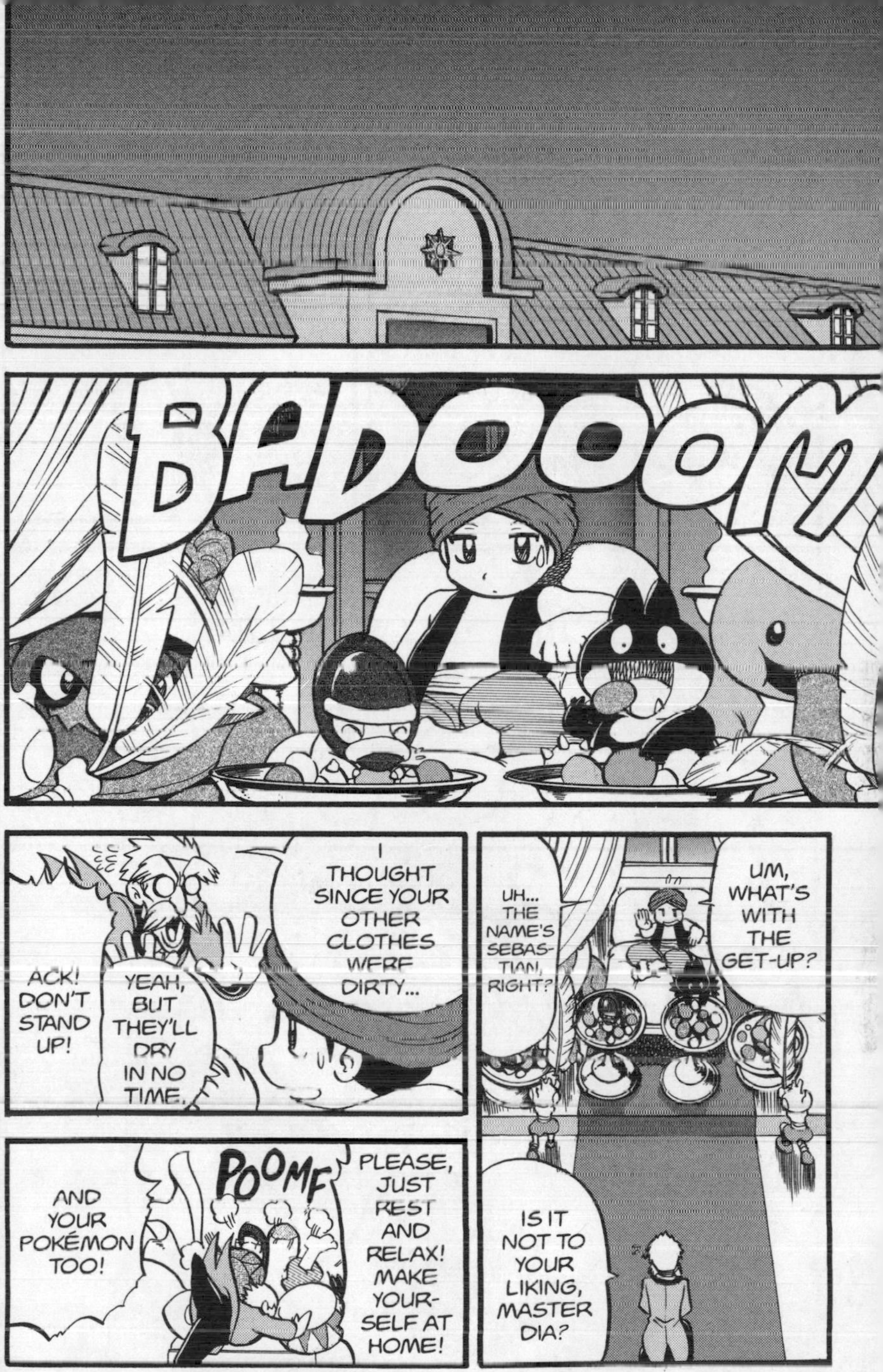
BADOOOM
UM, WHAT'S WITH THE GET-UP?
UH... THE NAME'S SEBAS-TIAN, RIGHT?
IS IT NOT TO YOUR LIKING, MASTER DIA?
I THOUGHT SINCE YOUR OTHER CLOTHES WERE DIRTY...
YEAH, BUT THEY'LL DRY IN NO TIME.
ACK! DON'T STAND UP!
POOMF
PLEASE, JUST REST AND RELAX! MAKE YOUR-SELF AT HOME!
AND YOUR POKÉMON TOO!

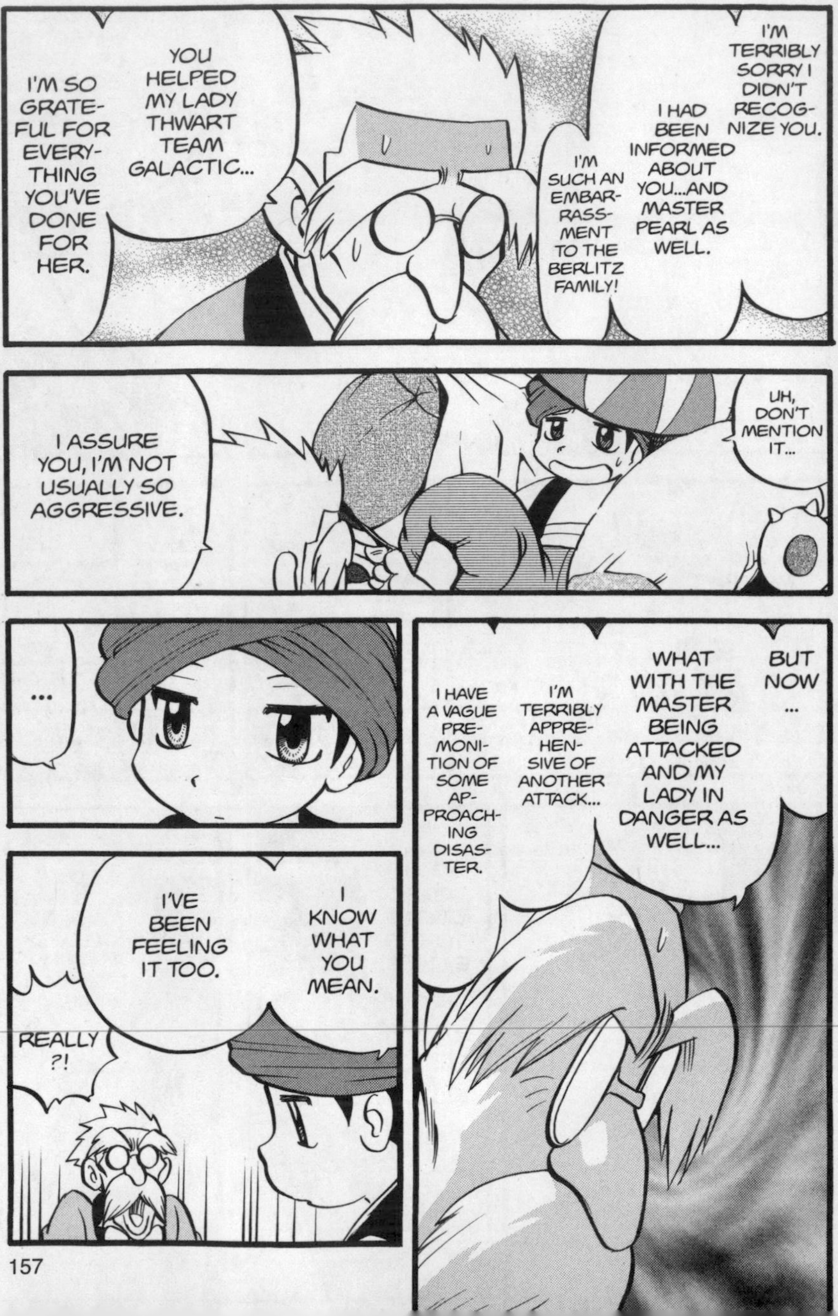
I'M TERRIBLY SORRY I DIDN'T RECOGNIZE YOU.
I HAD BEEN INFORMED ABOUT YOU...AND MASTER PEARL AS WELL.
I'M SUCH AN EMBARRASSMENT TO THE BERLITZ FAMILY!
YOU HELPED MY LADY THWART TEAM GALACTIC...
I'M SO GRATEFUL FOR EVERYTHING YOU'VE DONE FOR HER.
UH, DON'T MENTION IT...
I ASSURE YOU, I'M NOT USUALLY SO AGGRESSIVE.
BUT NOW...
WHAT WITH THE MASTER BEING ATTACKED AND MY LADY IN DANGER AS WELL...
I'M TERRIBLY APPREHENSIVE OF ANOTHER ATTACK...
I HAVE A VAGUE PREMONITION OF SOME APPROACHING DISASTER.
...
I KNOW WHAT YOU MEAN.
I'VE BEEN FEELING IT TOO.
REALLY?!

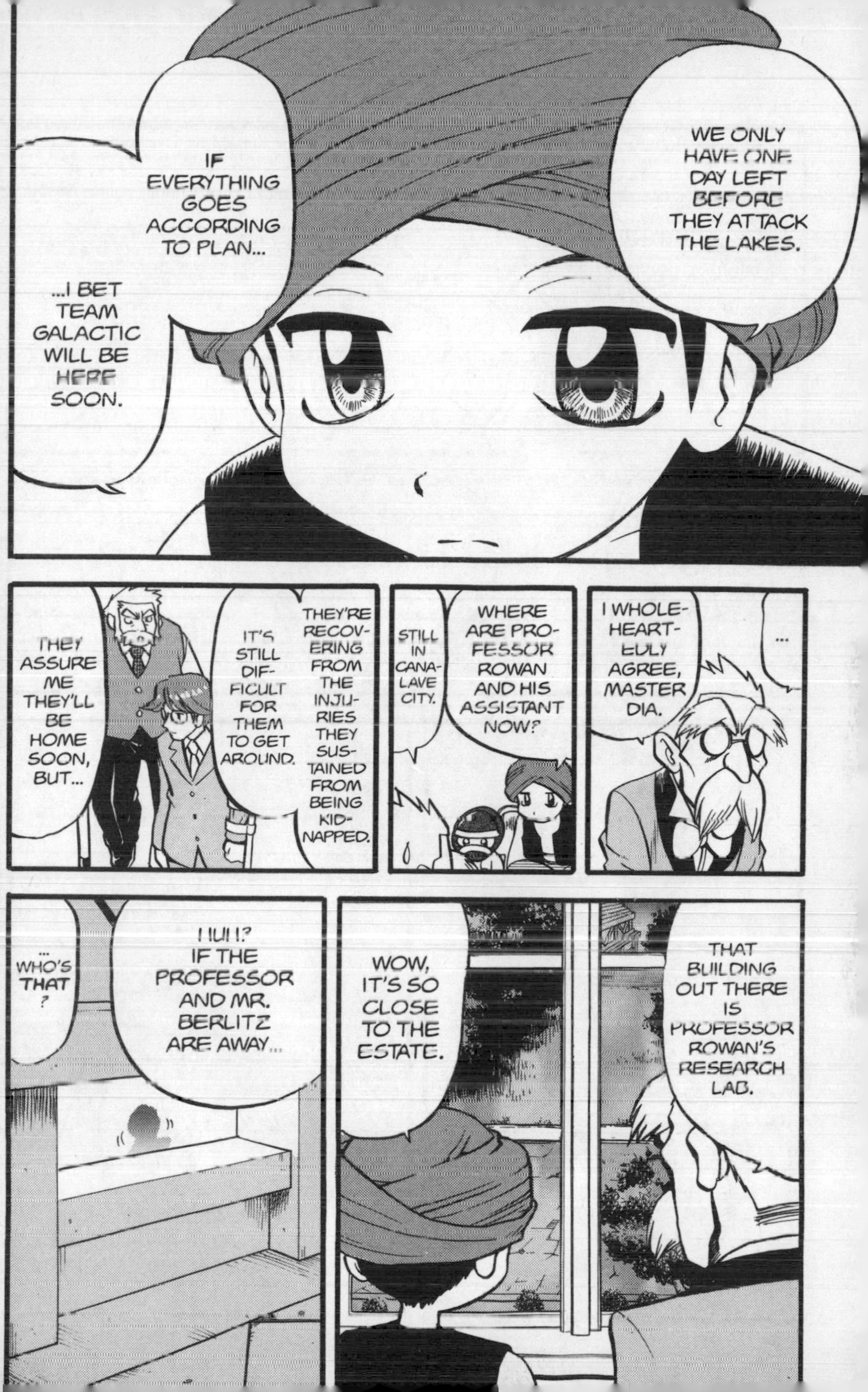
WE ONLY HAVE ONE DAY LEFT BEFORE THEY ATTACK THE LAKES.
IF EVERYTHING GOES ACCORDING TO PLAN...
...I BET TEAM GALACTIC WILL BE HERE SOON.
...
I WHOLEHEARTEDLY AGREE, MASTER DIA.
WHERE ARE PROFESSOR ROWAN AND HIS ASSISTANT NOW?
STILL IN CANALAVE CITY.
THEY'RE RECOVERING FROM THE INJURIES THEY SUSTAINED FROM BEING KIDNAPPED.
IT'S STILL DIFFICULT FOR THEM TO GET AROUND.
THEY ASSURE ME THEY'LL BE HOME SOON, BUT...
THAT BUILDING OUT THERE IS PROFESSOR ROWAN'S RESEARCH LAB.
WOW, IT'S SO CLOSE TO THE ESTATE.
HUH!? IF THE PROFESSOR AND MR. BERLITZ ARE AWAY...
...WHO'S THAT?

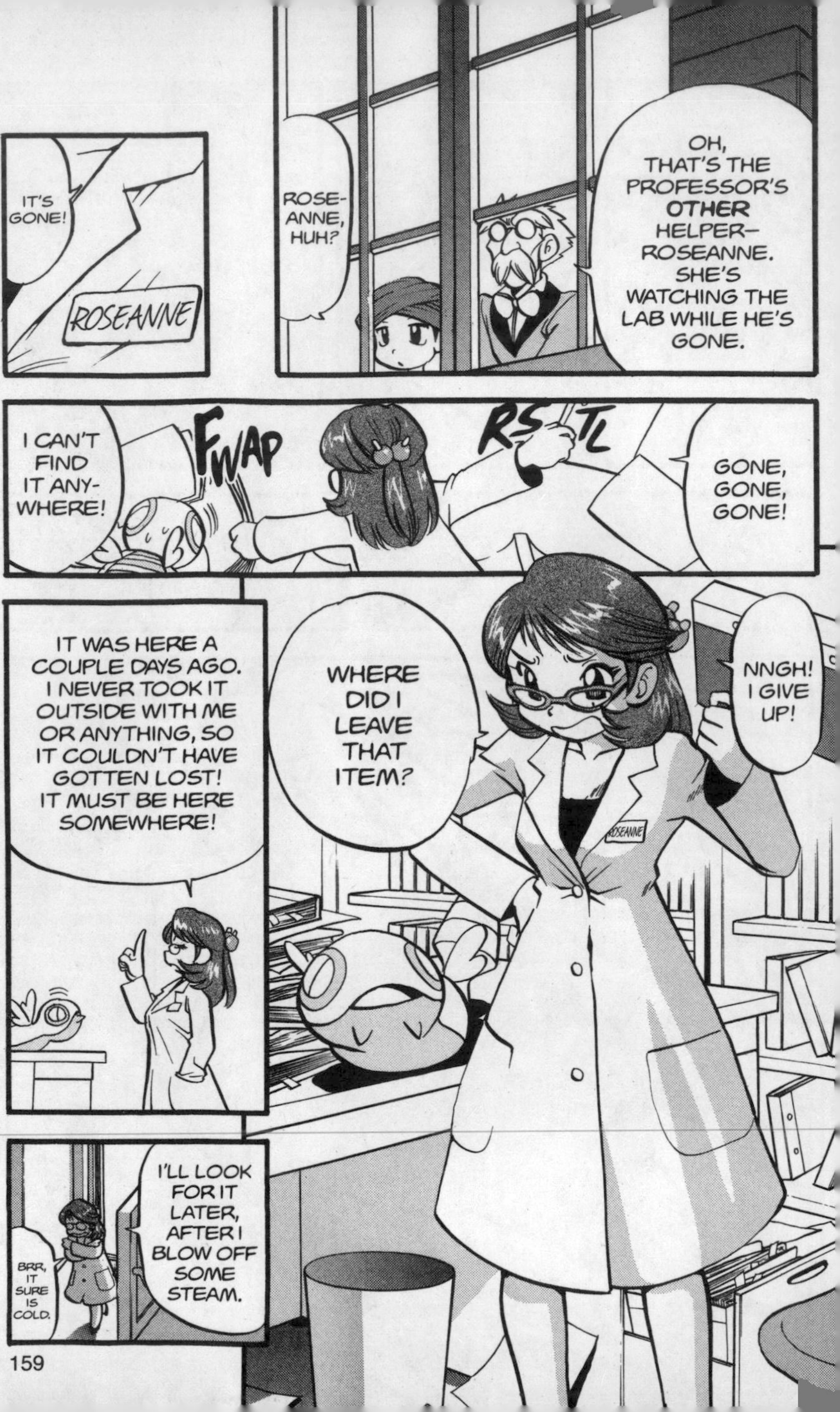
OH, THAT'S THE PROFESSOR'S **OTHER** HELPER— ROSEANNE. SHE'S WATCHING THE LAB WHILE HE'S GONE.
ROSE-ANNE, HUH?
IT'S GONE!
ROSEANNE
RSTL
GONE, GONE, GONE!
FWAP
I CAN'T FIND IT ANY-WHERE!
NNGH! I GIVE UP!
WHERE DID I LEAVE THAT ITEM?
ROSEANNE
IT WAS HERE A COUPLE DAYS AGO. I NEVER TOOK IT OUTSIDE WITH ME OR ANYTHING, SO IT COULDN'T HAVE GOTTEN LOST! IT MUST BE HERE SOMEWHERE!
I'LL LOOK FOR IT LATER, AFTER I BLOW OFF SOME STEAM.
BRR, IT SURE IS COLD.

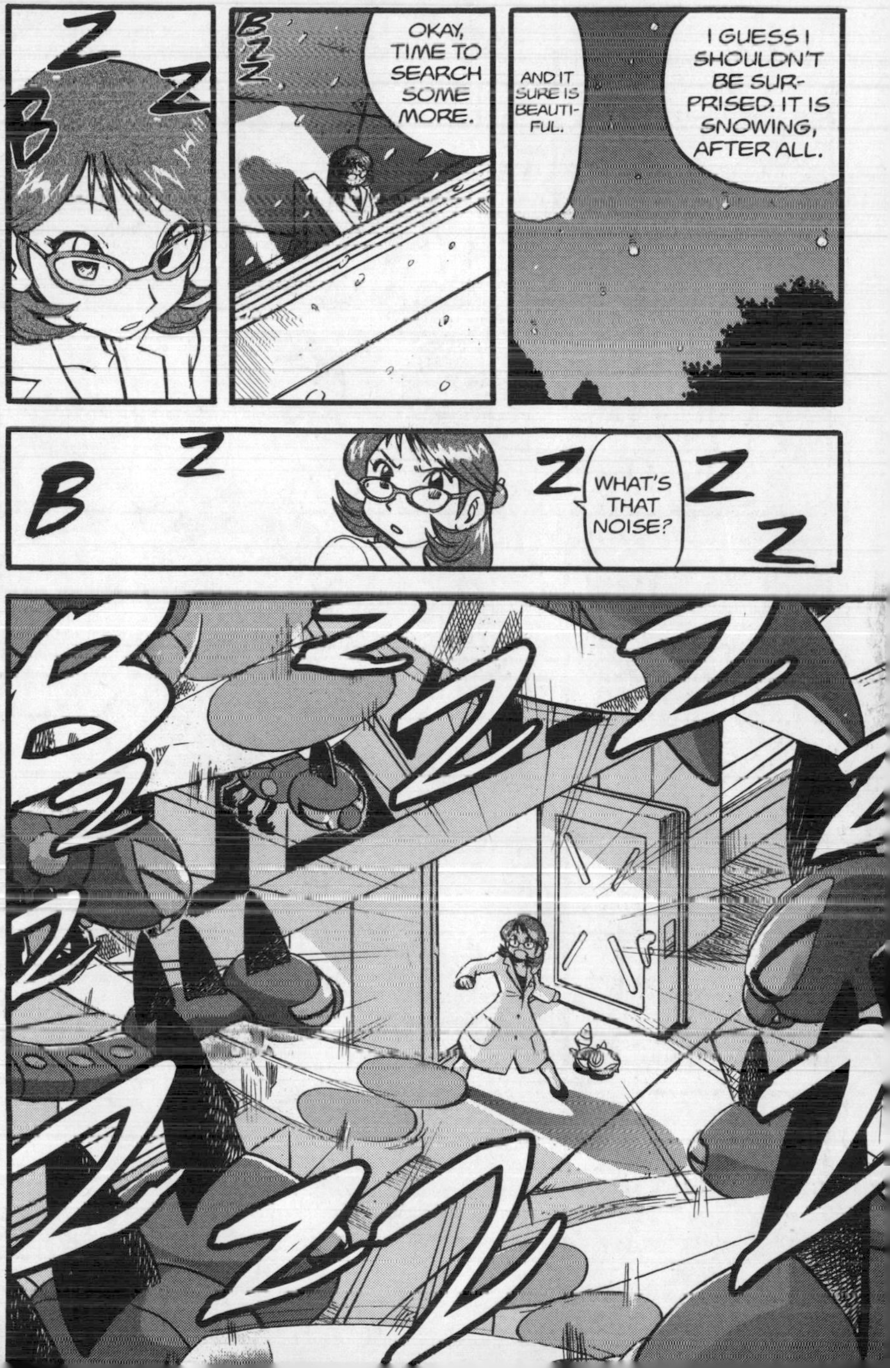
I GUESS I SHOULDN'T BE SURPRISED. IT IS SNOWING, AFTER ALL.
AND IT SURE IS BEAUTIFUL.
BZZ
OKAY, TIME TO SEARCH SOME MORE.
BZZ
BZZZZ
WHAT'S THAT NOISE?
BZZZZZ

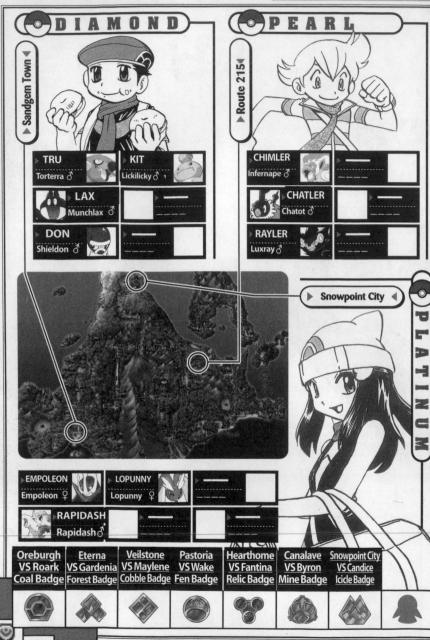

ADVENTURE MAP

DIAMOND

▲ Sandgem Town ▼

TRU		KIT	
Torterra ♂		Lickilicky ♂	

	LAX		
	Munchlax ♂		

	DON		
	Shieldon ♂		

PEARL

▶ Route 215 ◀

CHIMLER			
Infernape ♂			

	CHATLER		
	Chatot ♂		

	RAYLER		
	Luxray ♂		

▶ Snowpoint City ◀

PLATINUM

▶ EMPOLEON		LOPUNNY	
Empoleon ♀		Lopunny ♀	

	RAPIDASH		
	Rapidash ♂		

Oreburgh **VS Roark** Coal Badge	Eterna **VS Gardenia** Forest Badge	Veilstone **VS Maylene** Cobble Badge	Pastoria **VS Wake** Fen Badge	Hearthome **VS Fantina** Relic Badge	Canalave **VS Byron** Mine Badge	Snowpoint City **VS Candice** Icicle Badge

56

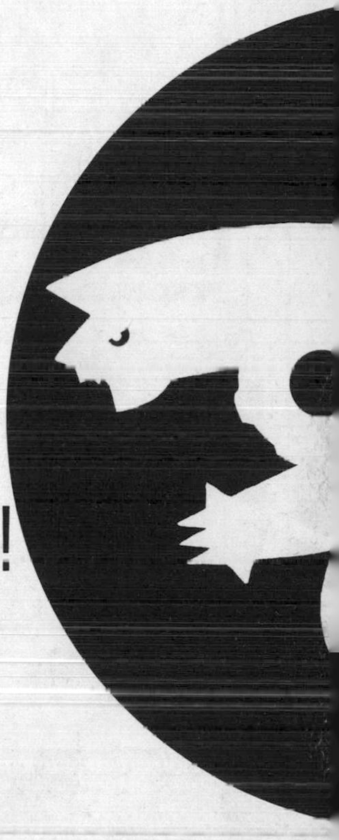

Yikes, Yanmega! I

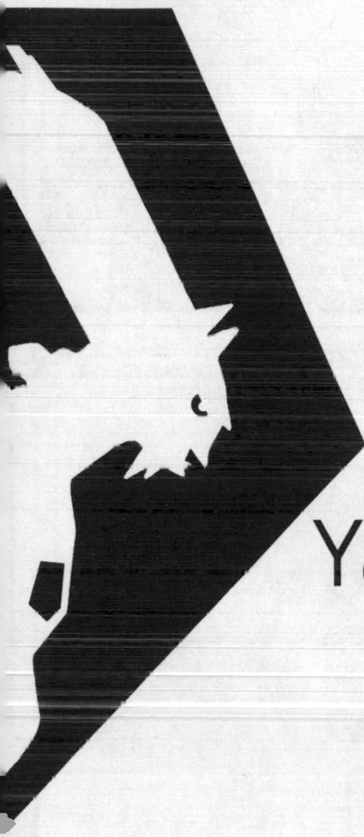

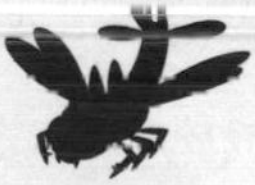

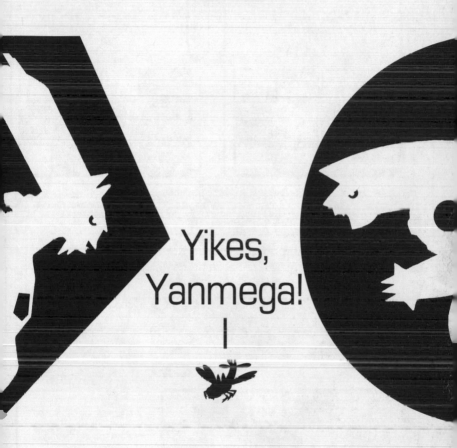

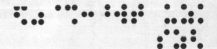

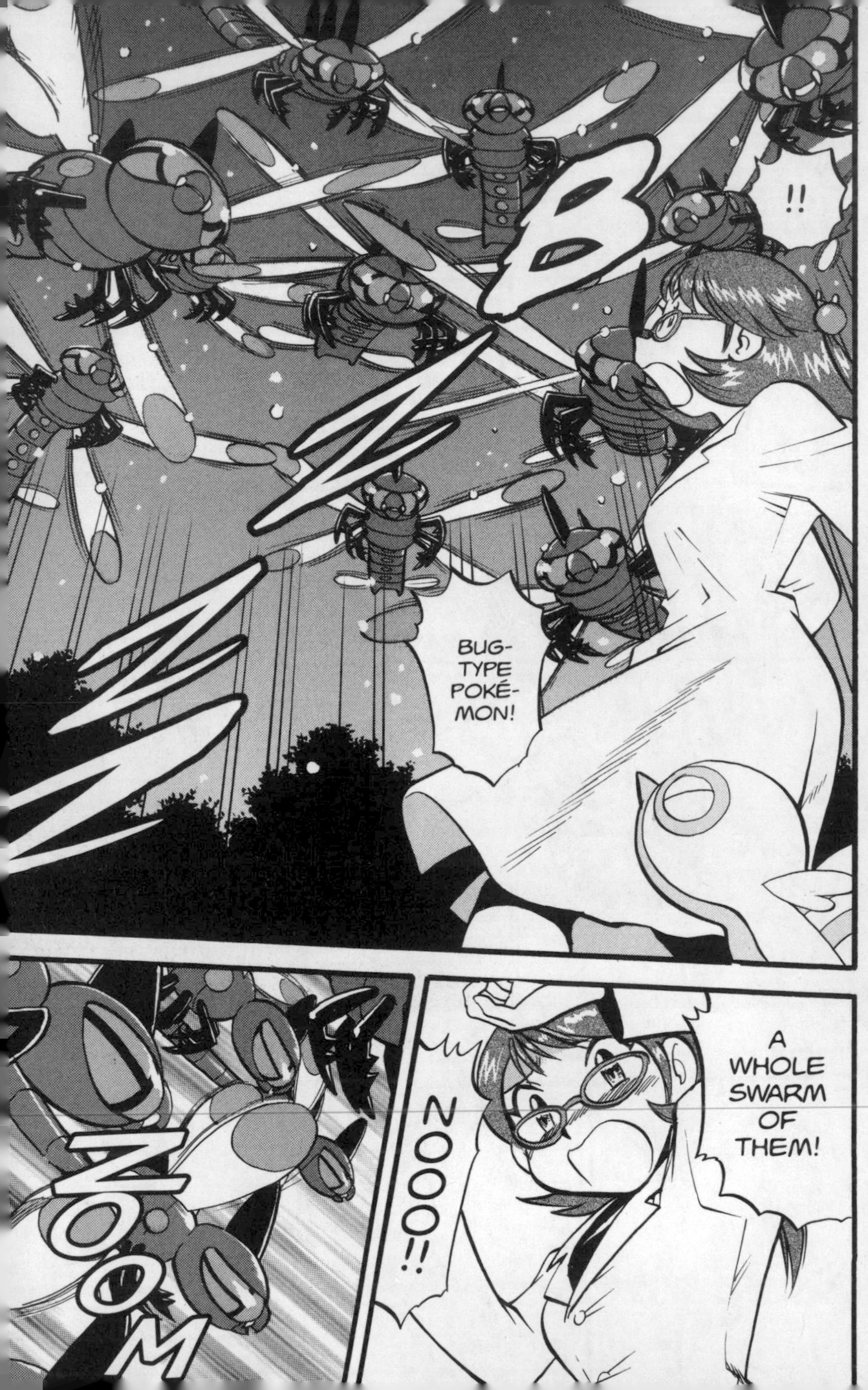
!!
BZZZ
BUG-TYPE POKÉMON!
A WHOLE SWARM OF THEM!
NOOOO!!
ZOOOM

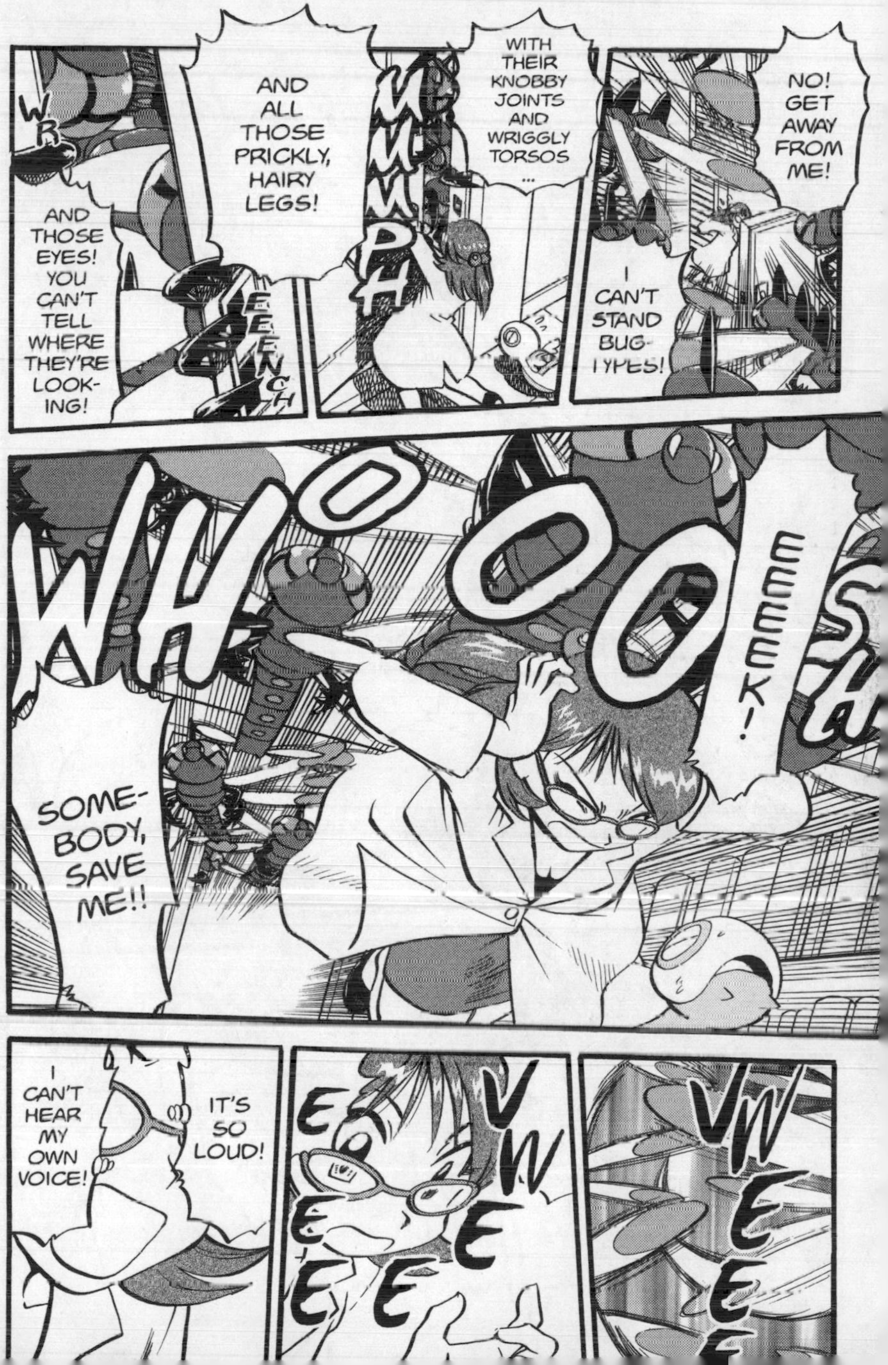
NO! GET AWAY FROM ME!
I CAN'T STAND BUG-TYPES!
WITH THEIR KNOBBY JOINTS AND WRIGGLY TORSOS ...
AND ALL THOSE PRICKLY, HAIRY LEGS!
AND THOSE EYES! YOU CAN'T TELL WHERE THEY'RE LOOKING!
EEEEEK!
WHOOOOSH
SOMEBODY, SAVE ME!!
IT'S SO LOUD!
I CAN'T HEAR MY OWN VOICE!

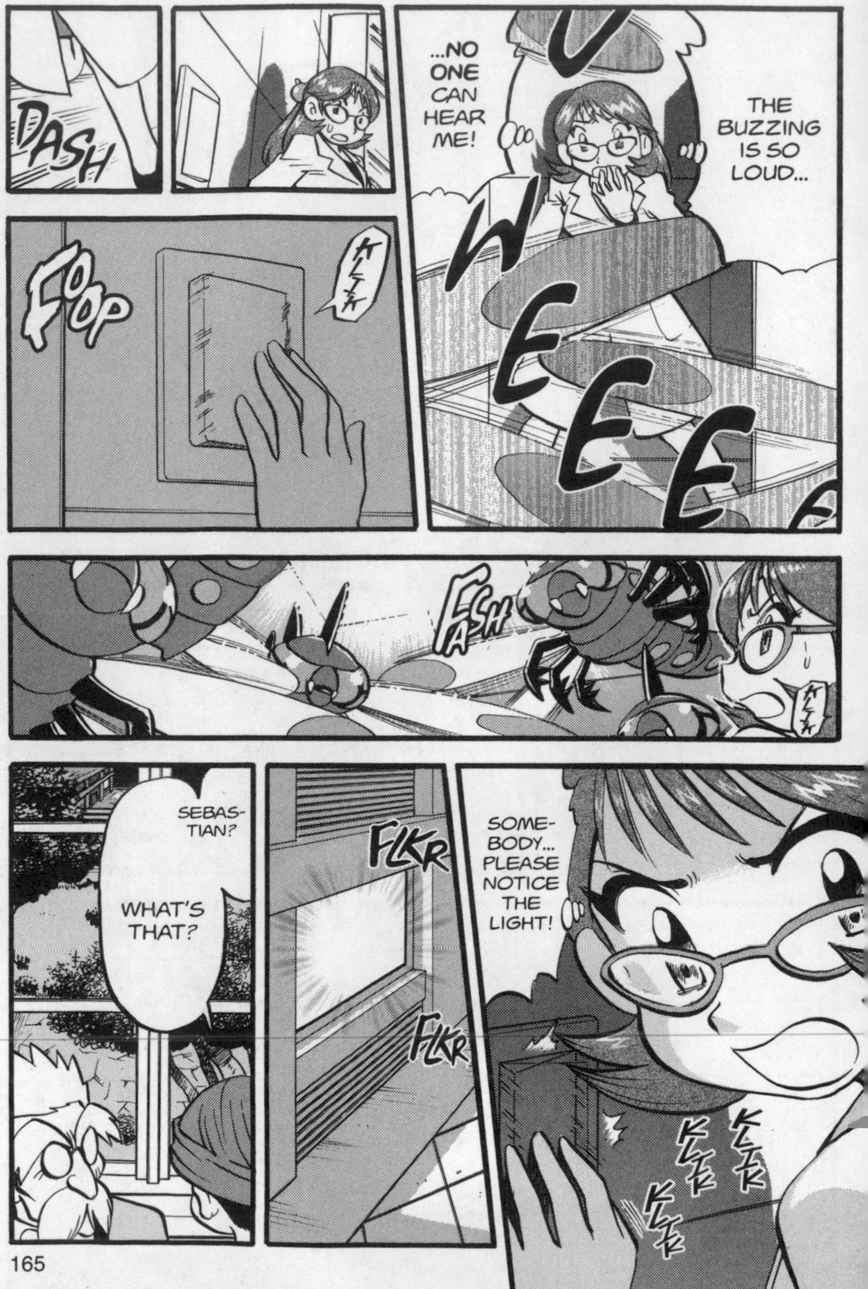
THE BUZZING IS SO LOUD...
...NO ONE CAN HEAR ME!
WEEEEE
DASH
FOOP
KLIK
FASH
KLIK
SOME-BODY... PLEASE NOTICE THE LIGHT!
KLIK KLIK
KLIK KLIK
FLKR
FLKR
SEBAS-TIAN?
WHAT'S THAT?

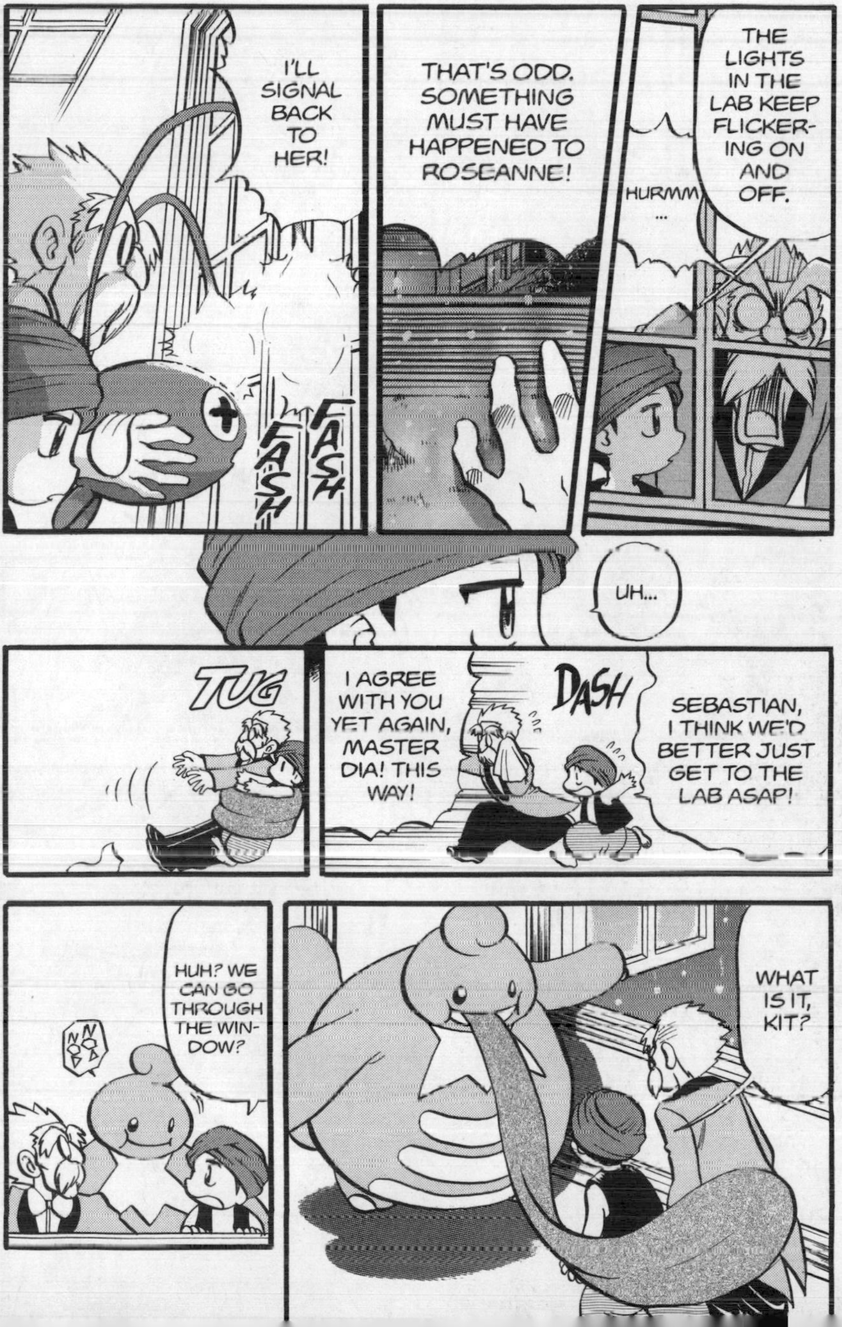
THE LIGHTS IN THE LAB KEEP FLICKER-ING ON AND OFF.
HURMM ...
THAT'S ODD. SOMETHING MUST HAVE HAPPENED TO ROSEANNE!
I'LL SIGNAL BACK TO HER!
FASH
FASH
UH...
SEBASTIAN, I THINK WE'D BETTER JUST GET TO THE LAB ASAP!
DASH
I AGREE WITH YOU YET AGAIN, MASTER DIA! THIS WAY!
TUG
WHAT IS IT, KIT?
HUH? WE CAN GO THROUGH THE WIN-DOW?
NOD NOD

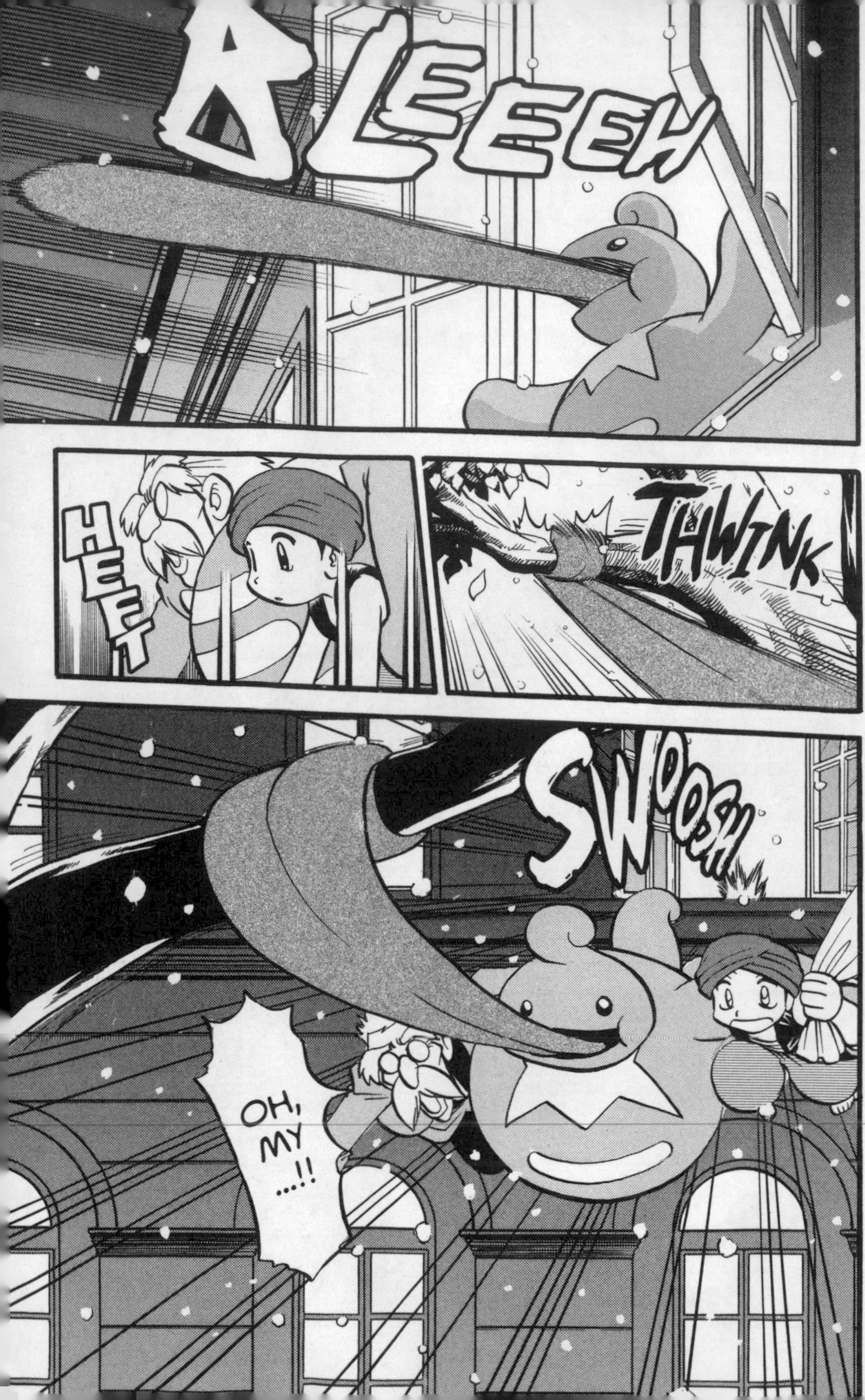
BLEEEH
THWINK
HEEFT
SWOOSH
OH, MY ...!!

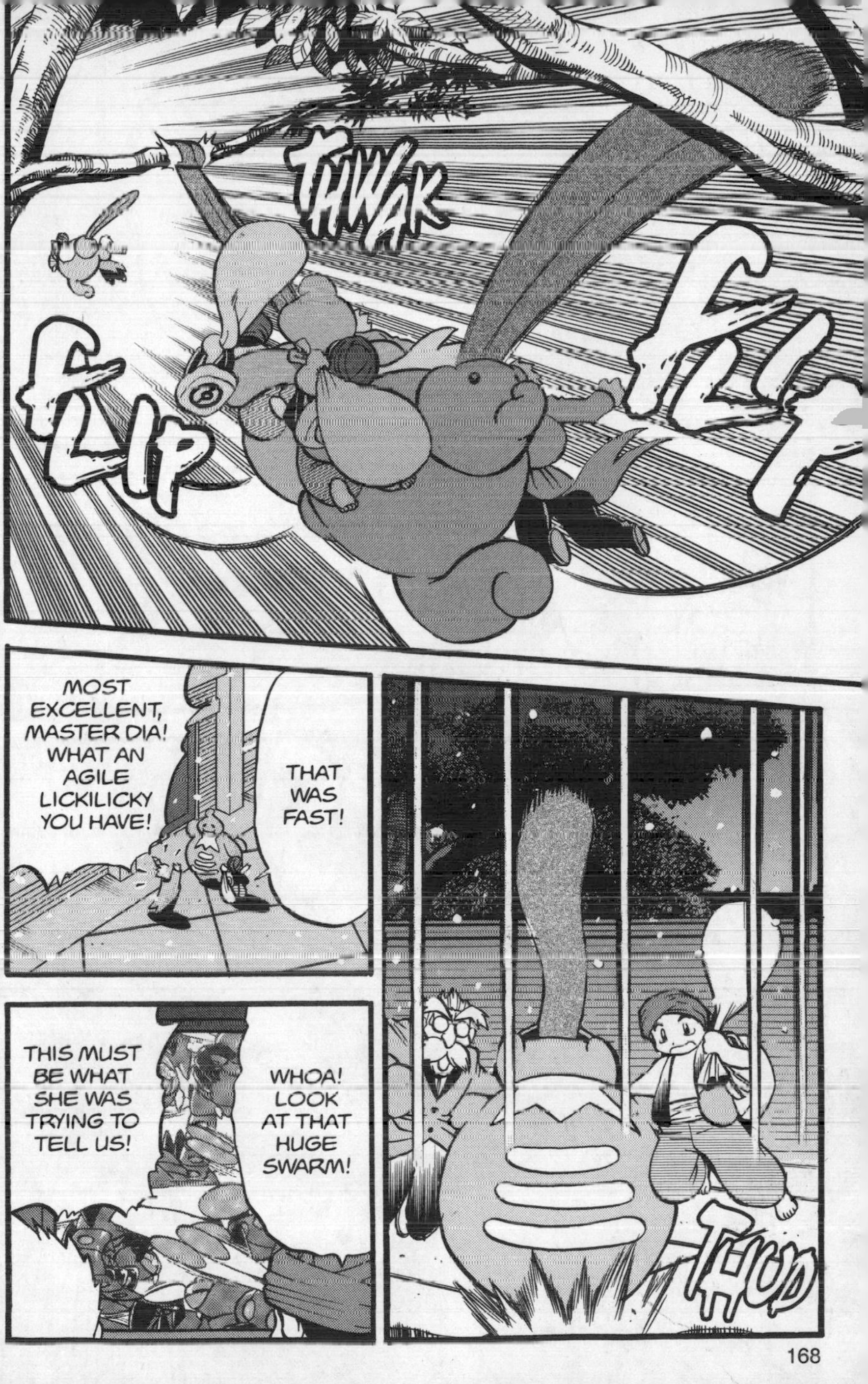
FLI
THWAK
FLIP
THUD
THAT WAS FAST!
MOST EXCELLENT, MASTER DIA! WHAT AN AGILE LICKILICKY YOU HAVE!
WHOA! LOOK AT THAT HUGE SWARM!
THIS MUST BE WHAT SHE WAS TRYING TO TELL US!

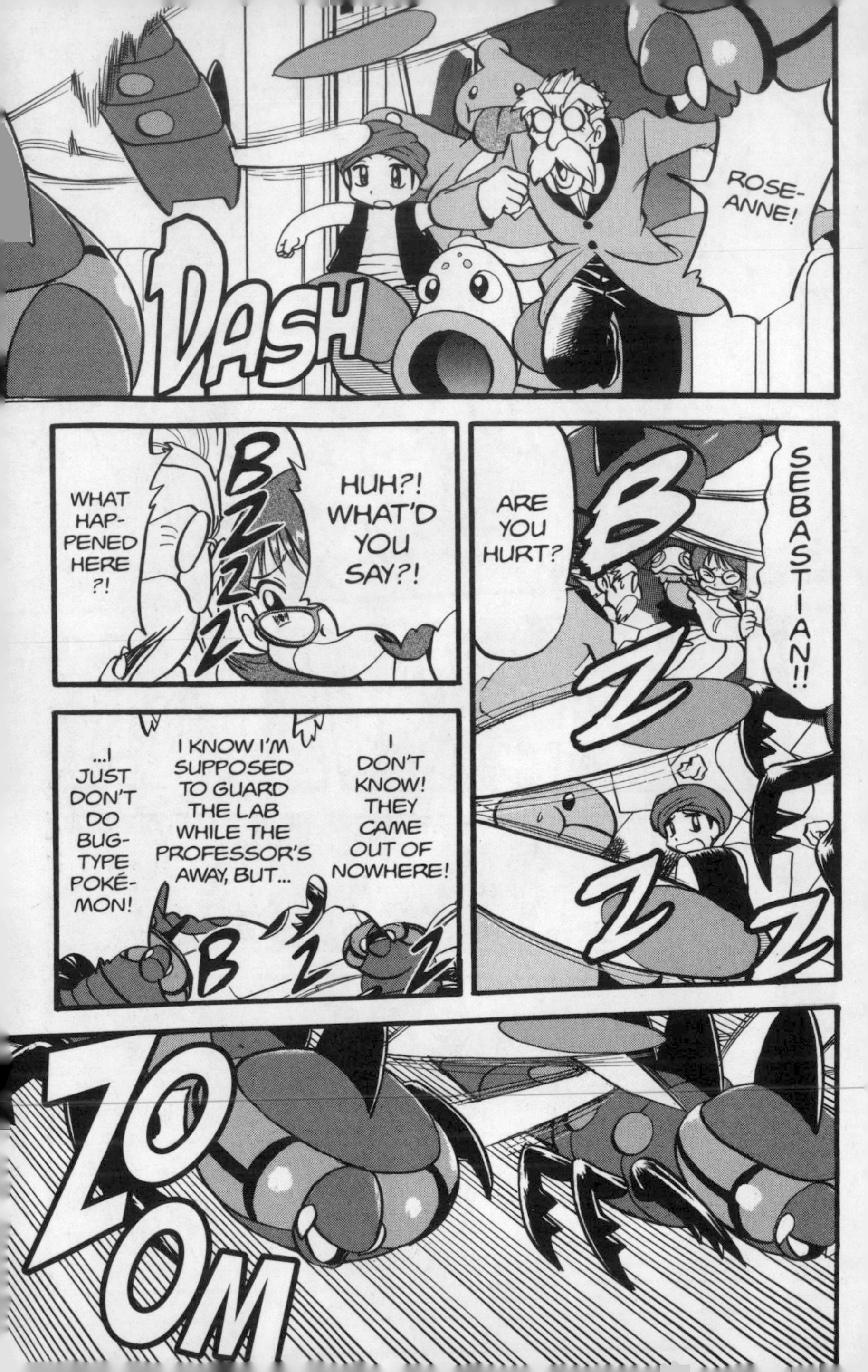
ROSE-ANNE!
DASH
SEBASTIAN!!
ARE YOU HURT?
BZZZ
HUH?! WHAT'D YOU SAY?!
WHAT HAP-PENED HERE?!
BZZZZ
I DON'T KNOW! THEY CAME OUT OF NOWHERE!
I KNOW I'M SUPPOSED TO GUARD THE LAB WHILE THE PROFESSOR'S AWAY, BUT...
...I JUST DON'T DO BUG-TYPE POKÉMON!
BZZ
ZOOM

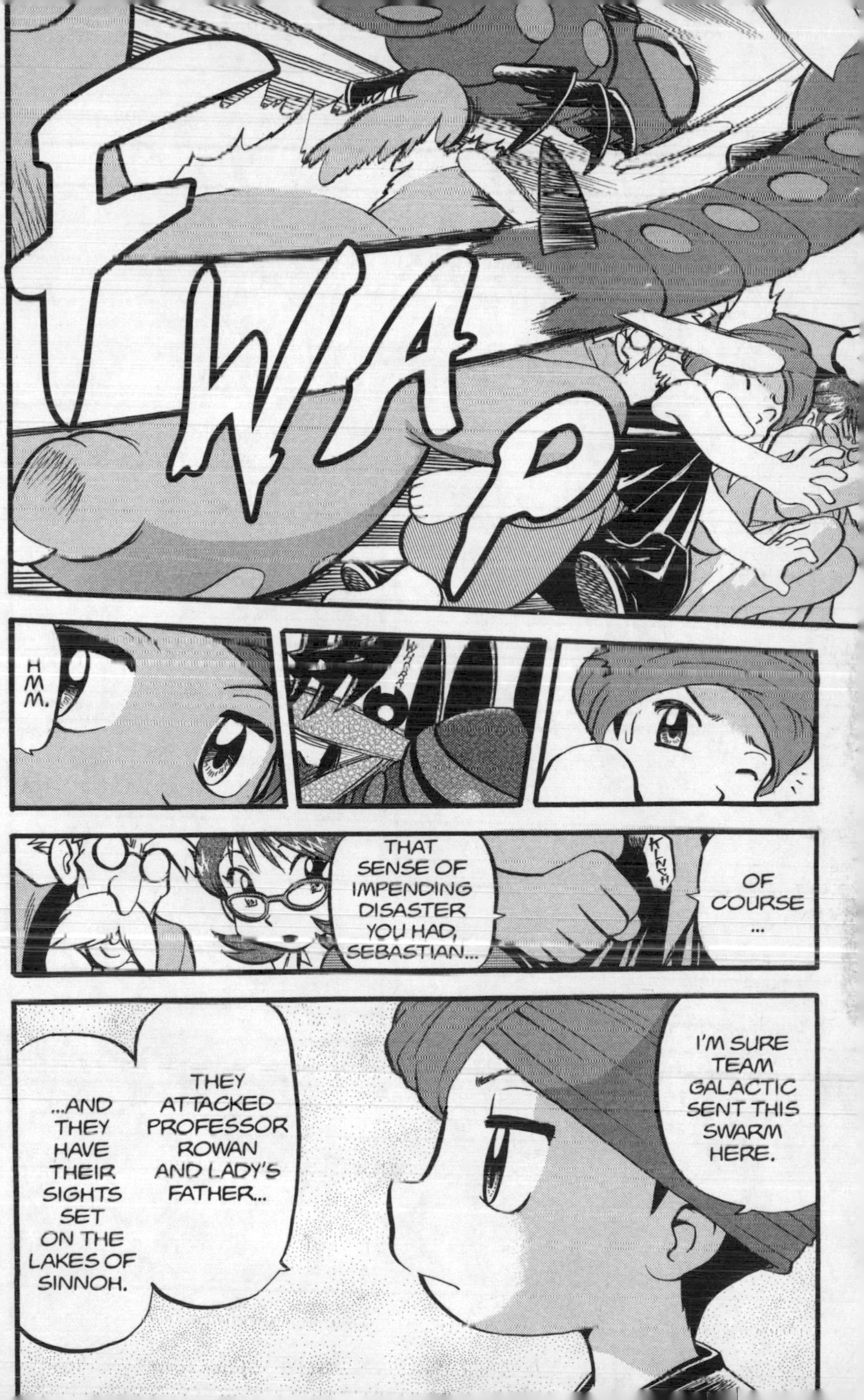
FWAP
WHIRR
HMM.
OF COURSE ...
KLNCH
THAT SENSE OF IMPENDING DISASTER YOU HAD, SEBASTIAN...
I'M SURE TEAM GALACTIC SENT THIS SWARM HERE.
THEY ATTACKED PROFESSOR ROWAN AND LADY'S FATHER...
...AND THEY HAVE THEIR SIGHTS SET ON THE LAKES OF SINNOH.

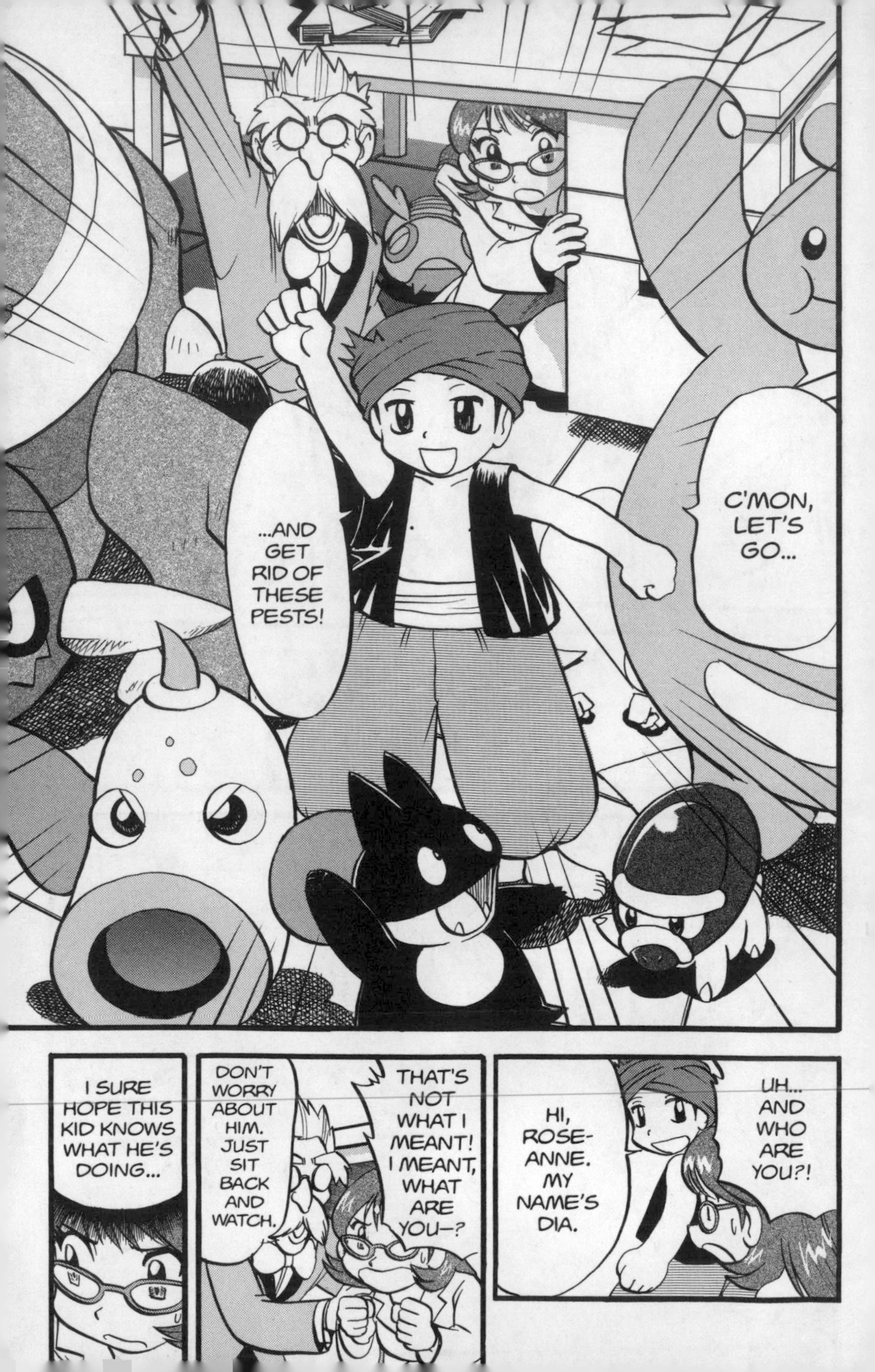
C'MON, LET'S GO...
...AND GET RID OF THESE PESTS!
UH... AND WHO ARE YOU?!
HI, ROSE-ANNE. MY NAME'S DIA.
DON'T WORRY ABOUT HIM. JUST SIT BACK AND WATCH.
THAT'S NOT WHAT I MEANT! I MEANT, WHAT ARE YOU—?
I SURE HOPE THIS KID KNOWS WHAT HE'S DOING...

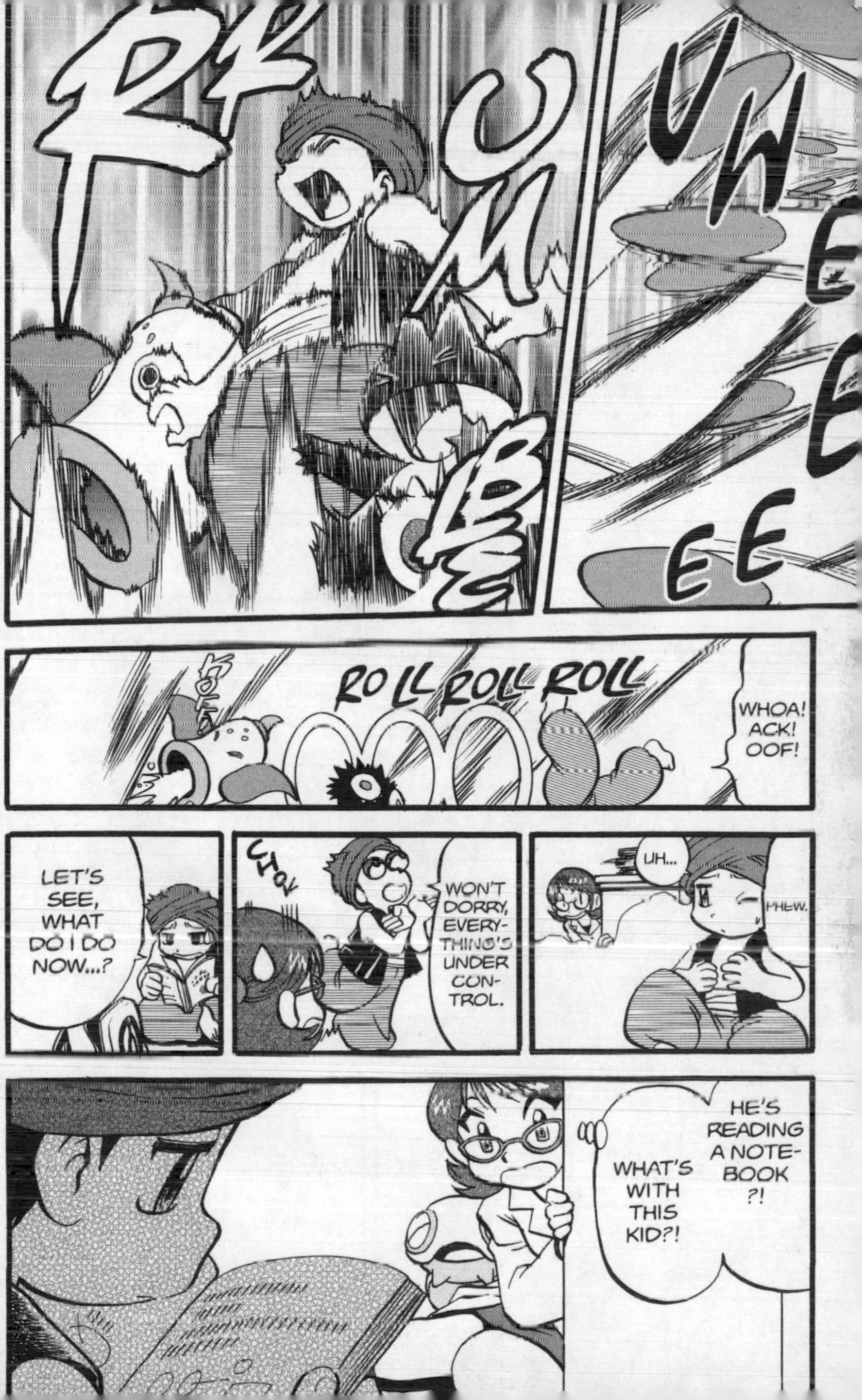
WHEEEEE
ROLL ROLL ROLL
WHOA! ACK! OOF!
UH...
PHEW.
DON'T WORRY, EVERYTHING'S UNDER CONTROL.
LET'S SEE, WHAT DO I DO NOW...?
HE'S READING A NOTEBOOK?!
WHAT'S WITH THIS KID?!

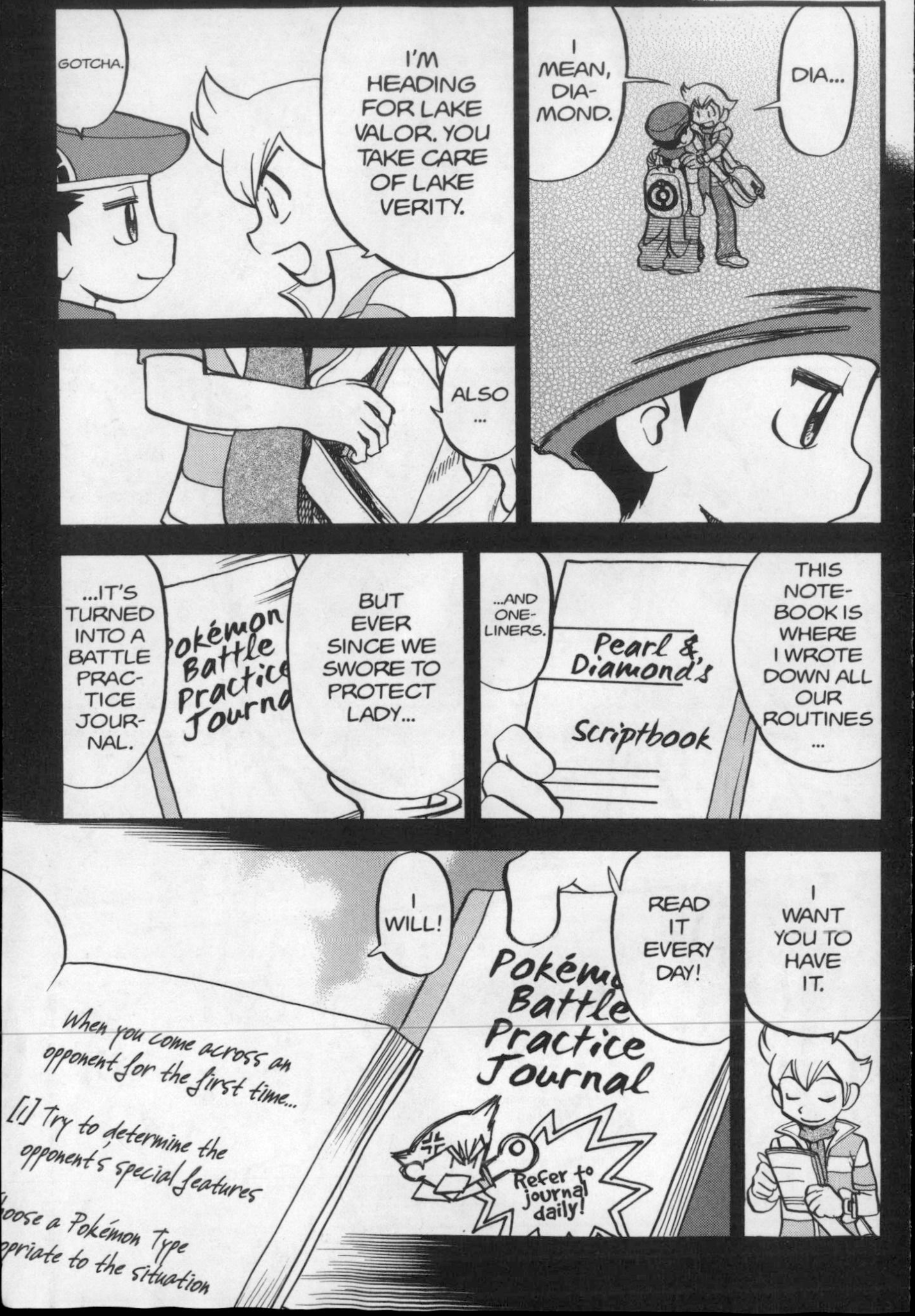
DIA...
I MEAN, DIA-MOND.
I'M HEADING FOR LAKE VALOR. YOU TAKE CARE OF LAKE VERITY.
GOTCHA.
ALSO ...
THIS NOTE-BOOK IS WHERE I WROTE DOWN ALL OUR ROUTINES ...
...AND ONE-LINERS.
Pearl & Diamond's Scriptbook
BUT EVER SINCE WE SWORE TO PROTECT LADY...
...IT'S TURNED INTO A BATTLE PRAC-TICE JOUR-NAL.
I WANT YOU TO HAVE IT.
READ IT EVERY DAY!
I WILL!
Battle Practice Journal
Refer to journal daily!
When you come across an opponent for the first time...
[1] Try to determine the opponent's special features

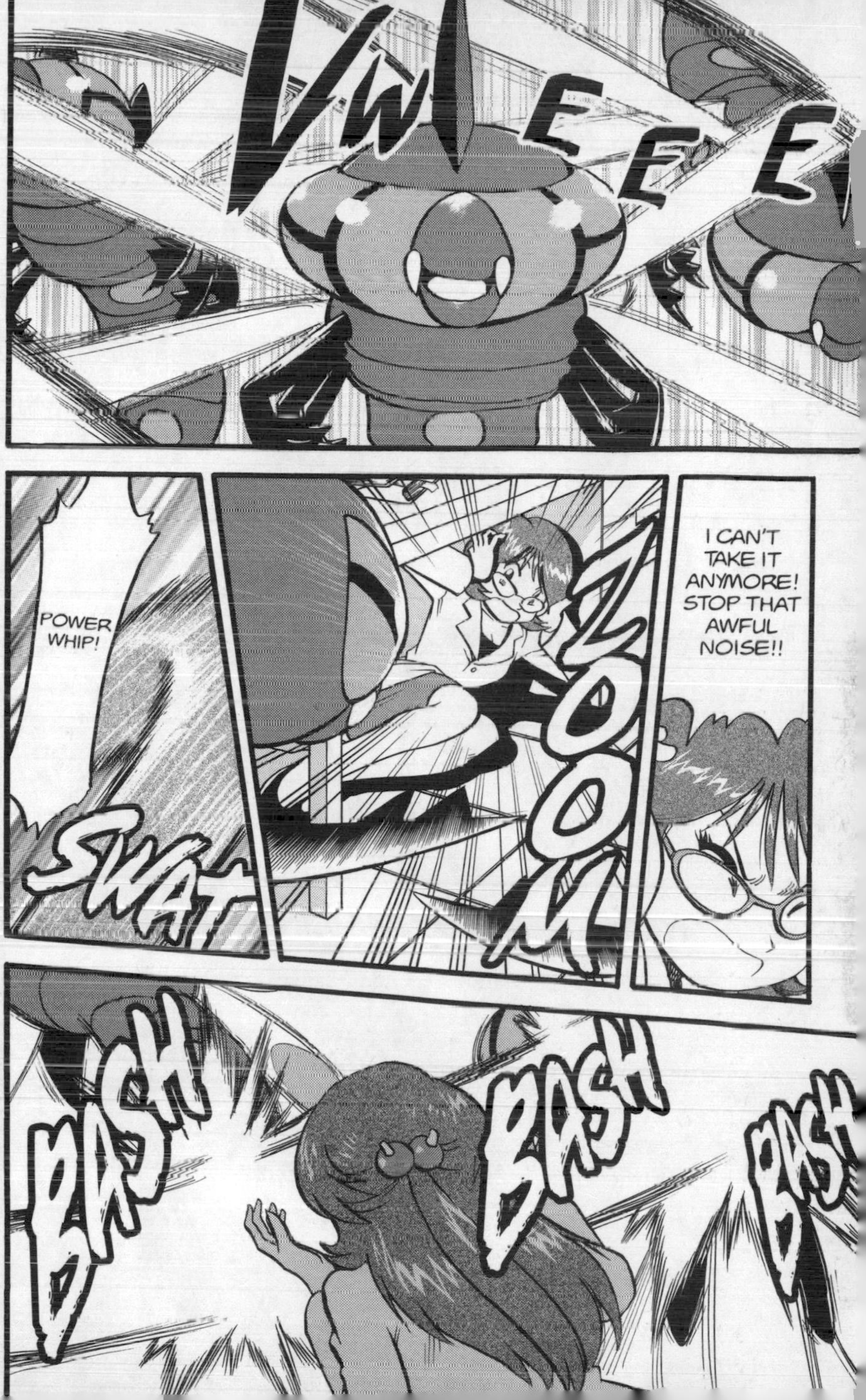
VWEEE
I CAN'T TAKE IT ANYMORE! STOP THAT AWFUL NOISE!!
ZOOOM
POWER WHIP!
SWAT
BASH
BASH
BASH

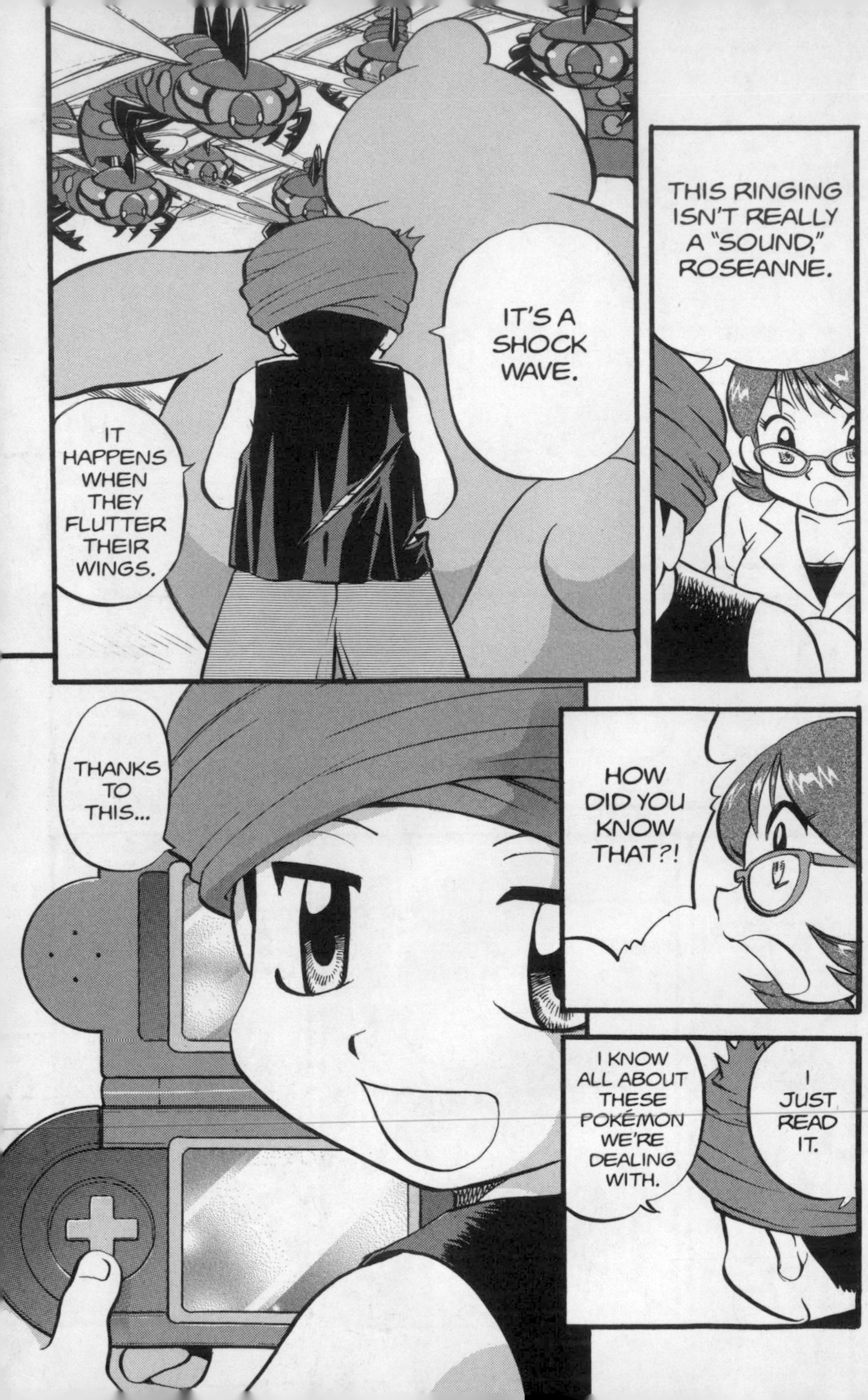
THIS RINGING ISN'T REALLY A "SOUND," ROSEANNE.
IT'S A SHOCK WAVE.
IT HAPPENS WHEN THEY FLUTTER THEIR WINGS.
HOW DID YOU KNOW THAT?!
I JUST READ IT.
I KNOW ALL ABOUT THESE POKÉMON WE'RE DEALING WITH.
THANKS TO THIS...

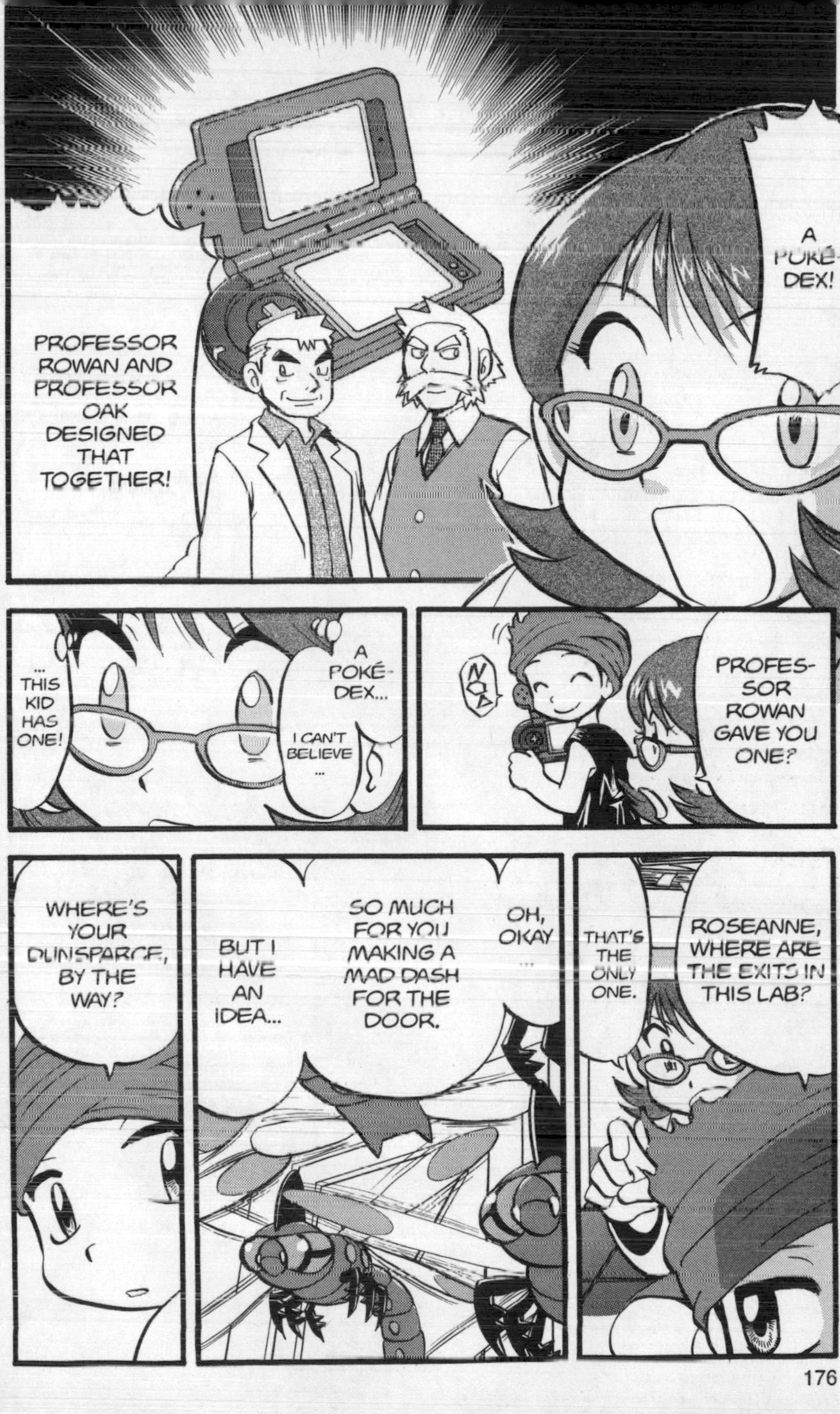
A POKÉ-DEX!
PROFESSOR ROWAN AND PROFESSOR OAK DESIGNED THAT TOGETHER!
PROFES-SOR ROWAN GAVE YOU ONE?
NOD
A POKÉ-DEX...
I CAN'T BELIEVE ...
... THIS KID HAS ONE!
ROSEANNE, WHERE ARE THE EXITS IN THIS LAB?
THAT'S THE ONLY ONE.
OH, OKAY ...
SO MUCH FOR YOU MAKING A MAD DASH FOR THE DOOR.
BUT I HAVE AN IDEA...
WHERE'S YOUR DUNSPARCE, BY THE WAY?

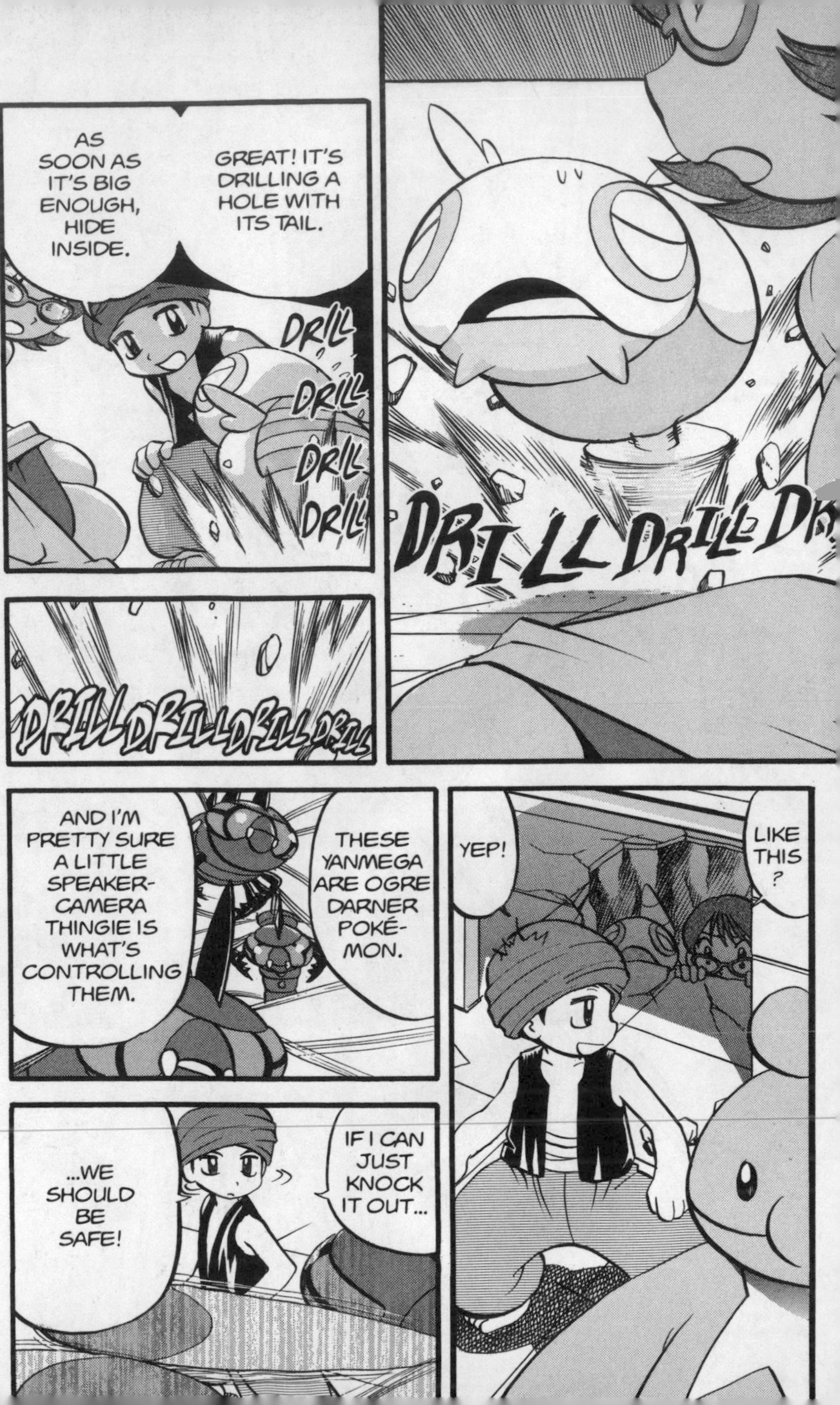
DRILL DRILL DR
GREAT! IT'S DRILLING A HOLE WITH ITS TAIL.
AS SOON AS IT'S BIG ENOUGH, HIDE INSIDE.
DRILL DRILL DRILL DRILL
DRILL DRILL DRILL DRILL
LIKE THIS?
YEP!
THESE YANMEGA ARE OGRE DARNER POKÉMON.
AND I'M PRETTY SURE A LITTLE SPEAKER-CAMERA THINGIE IS WHAT'S CONTROLLING THEM.
IF I CAN JUST KNOCK IT OUT...
...WE SHOULD BE SAFE!

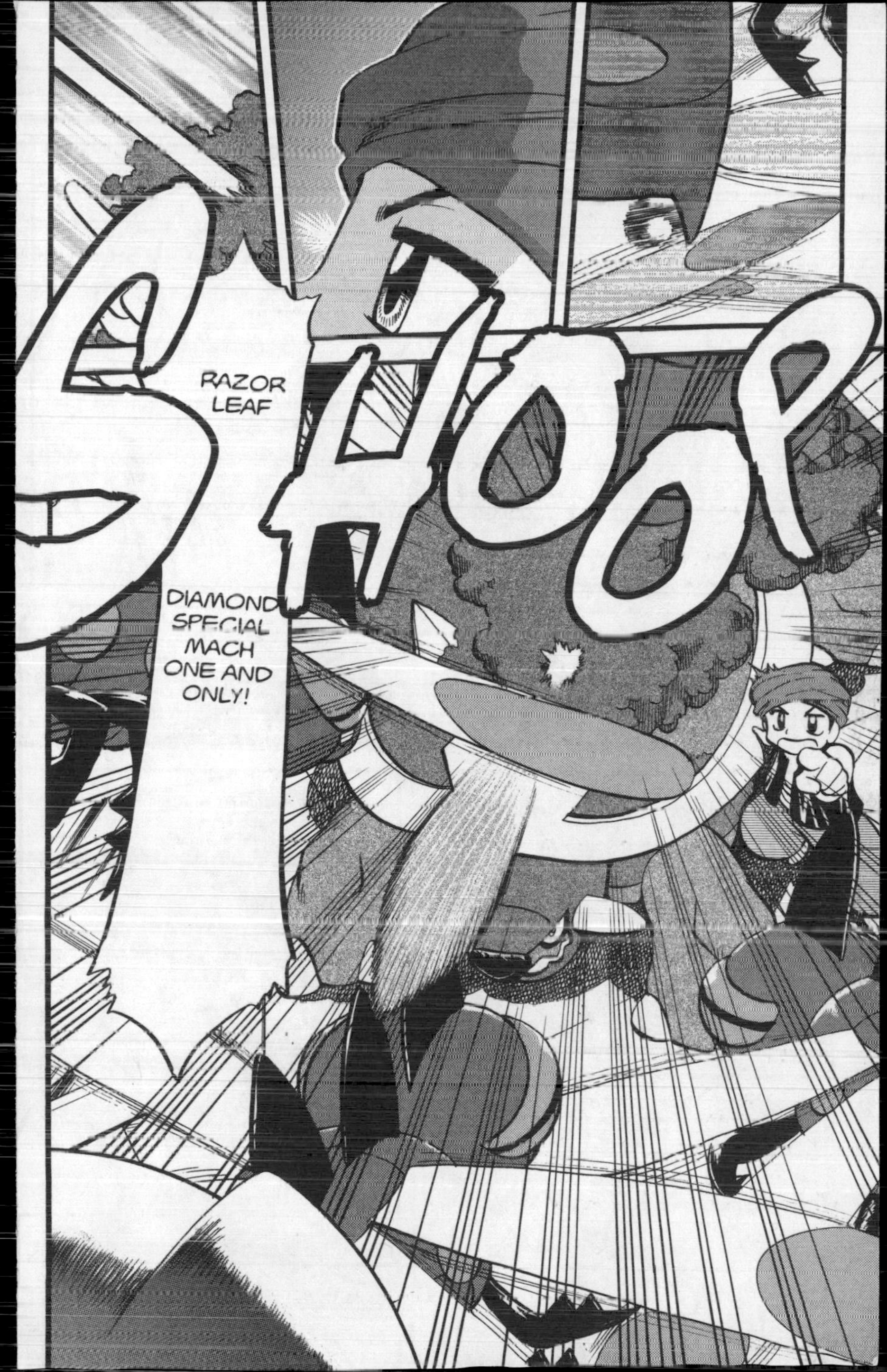
SHOOP
RAZOR LEAF
DIAMOND SPECIAL MACH ONE AND ONLY!

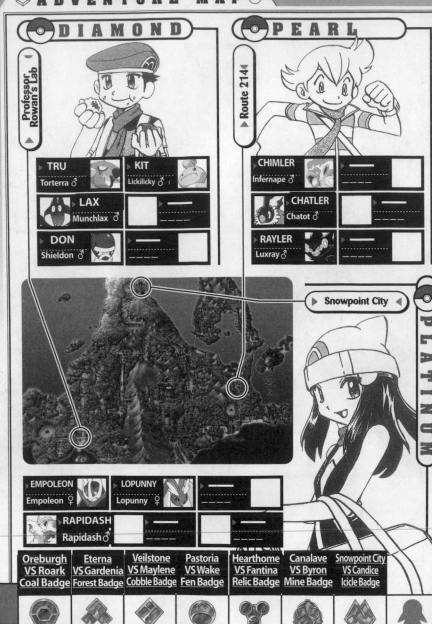

DIAMOND

Professor Rowan's Lab ▲

▶ TRU
Torterra ♂

▶ KIT
Lickilicky ♂ ⌀

▶ LAX
Munchlax ♂

▶ DON
Shieldon ♂

PEARL

▲ Route 214◀

▶ CHIMLER
Infernape ♂

▶ CHATLER
Chatot ♂

▶ RAYLER
Luxray ♂

▶ Snowpoint City ◀

PLATINUM

▶ EMPOLEON
Empoleon ♀

▶ LOPUNNY
Lopunny ♀

▶ RAPIDASH
Rapidash ♂

Oreburgh	Eterna	Veilstone	Pastoria	Hearthome	Canalave	Snowpoint City
VS Roark	VS Gardenia	VS Maylene	VS Wake	VS Fantina	VS Byron	VS Candice
Coal Badge	Forest Badge	Cobble Badge	Fen Badge	Relic Badge	Mine Badge	Icicle Badge

57

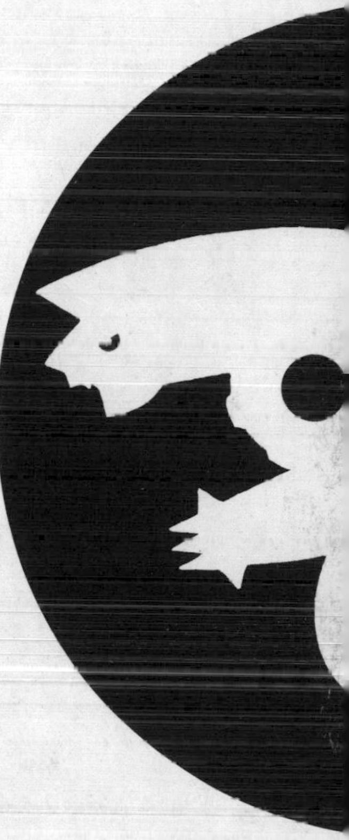

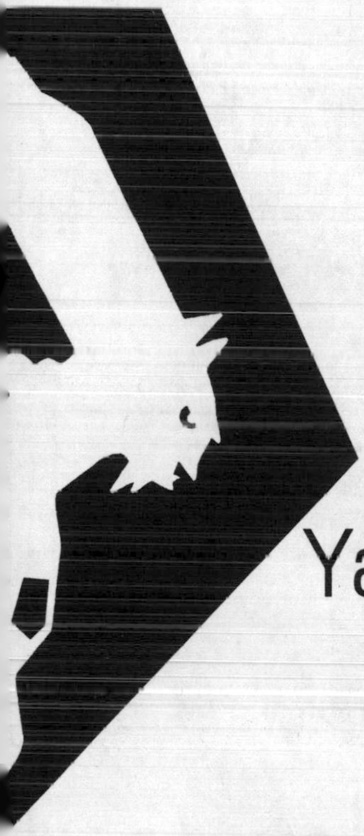

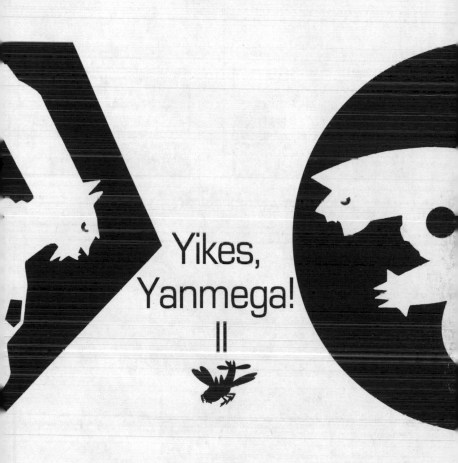

Yikes, Yanmega! II

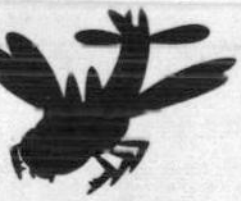

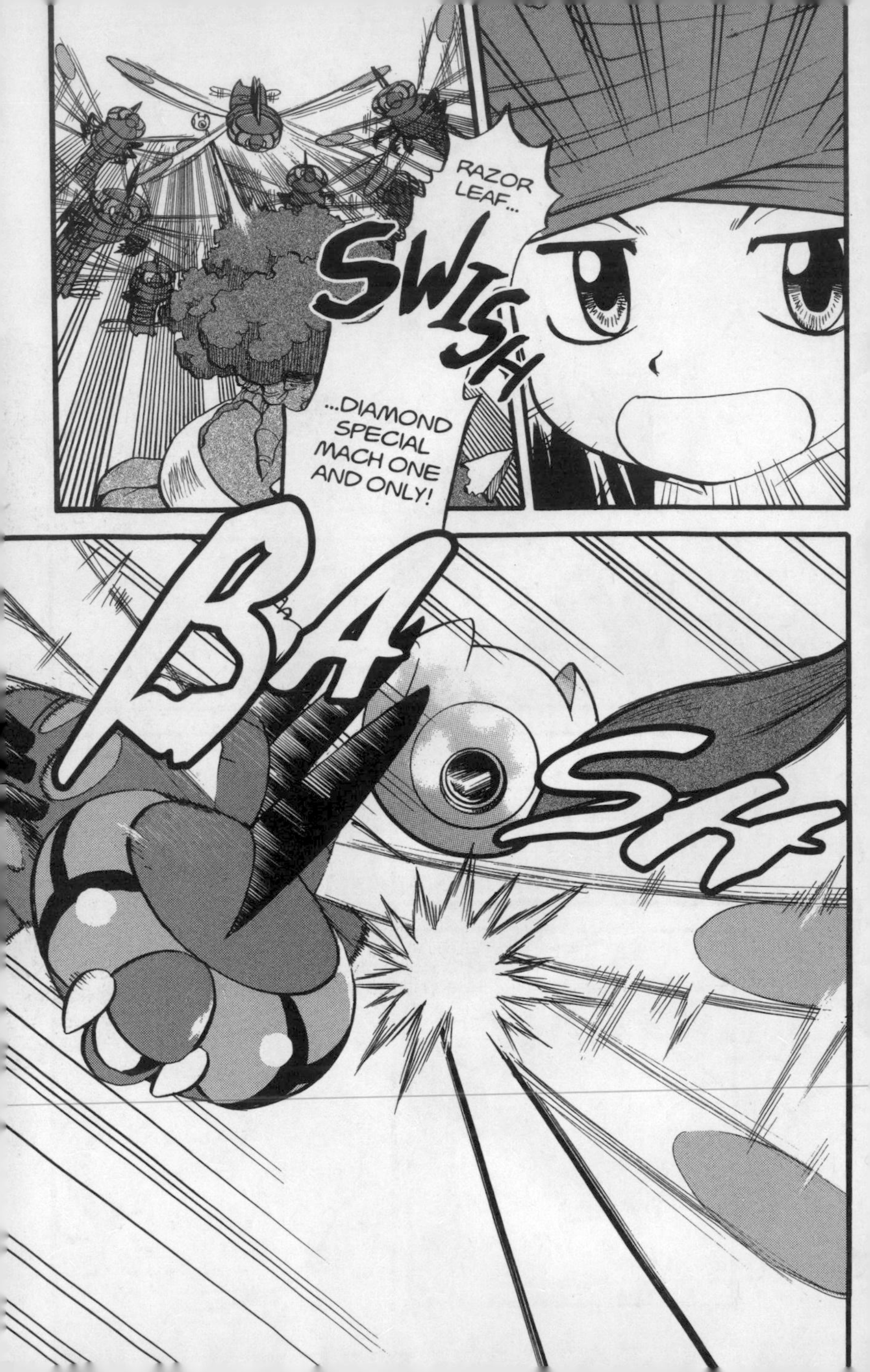
RAZOR LEAF...
SWISH
...DIAMOND SPECIAL MACH ONE AND ONLY!
BASH

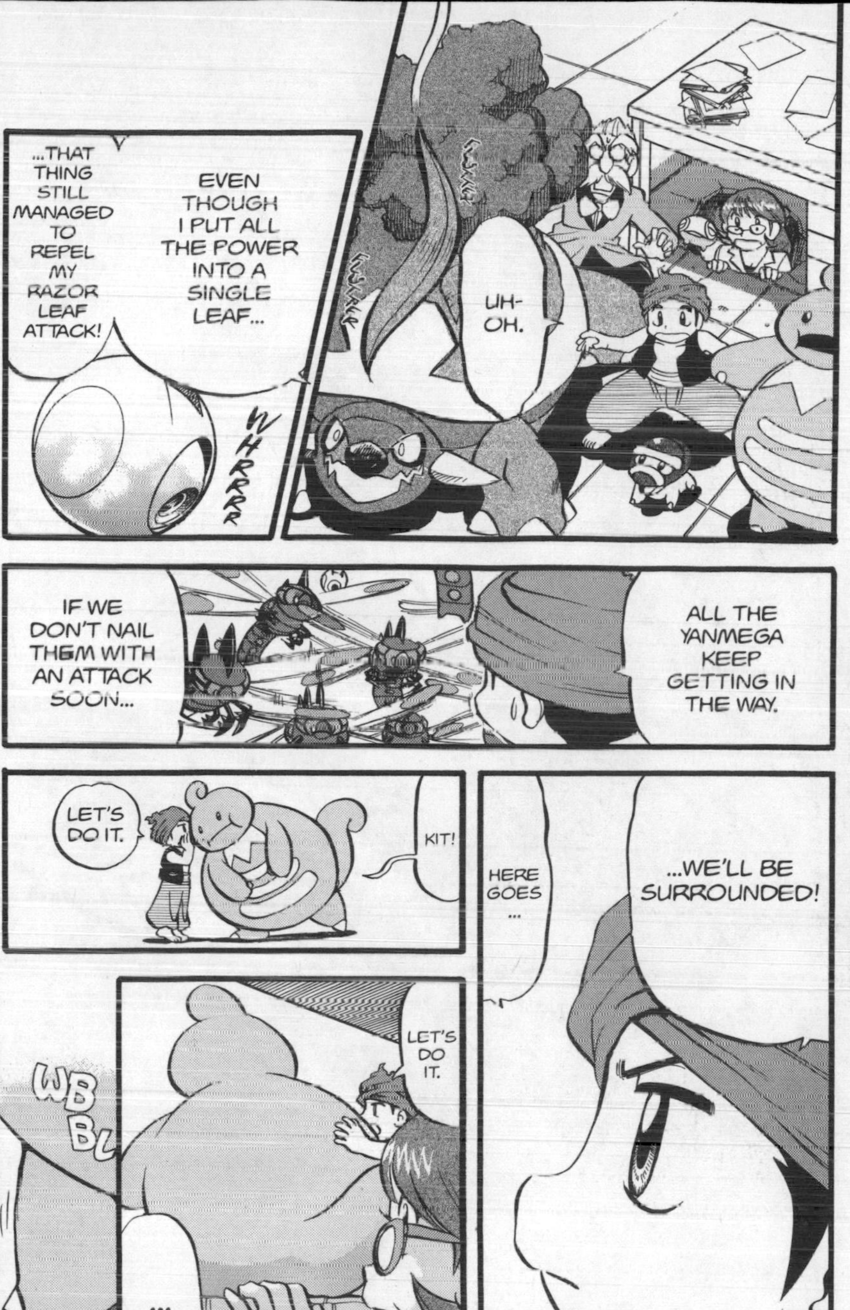
UH-OH.
EVEN THOUGH I PUT ALL THE POWER INTO A SINGLE LEAF...
...THAT THING STILL MANAGED TO REPEL MY RAZOR LEAF ATTACK!
WHRRRR
ALL THE YANMEGA KEEP GETTING IN THE WAY.
IF WE DON'T NAIL THEM WITH AN ATTACK SOON...
...WE'LL BE SURROUNDED!
HERE GOES...
KIT!
LET'S DO IT.
LET'S DO IT.
WBBL
...

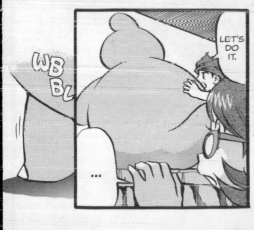

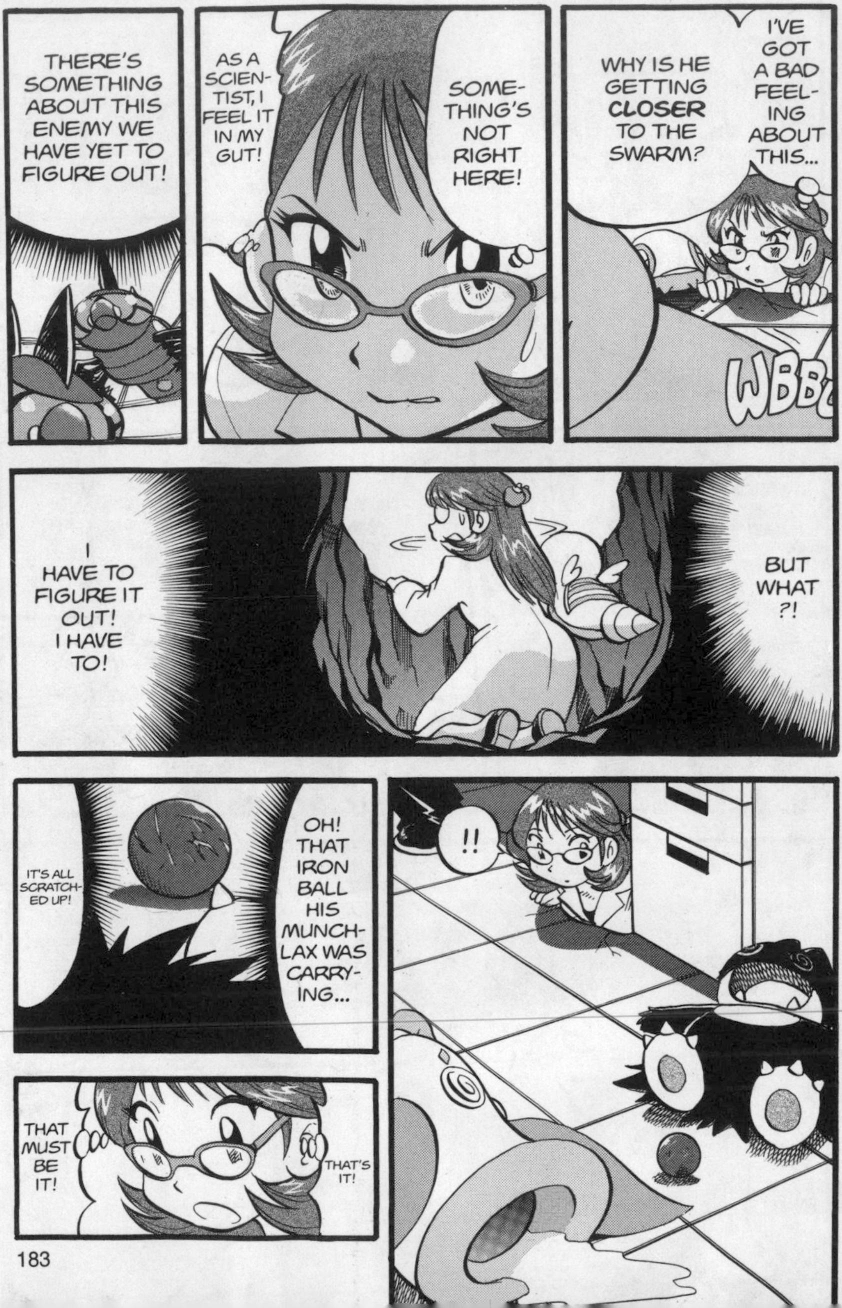
I'VE GOT A BAD FEEL-ING ABOUT THIS...
WHY IS HE GETTING **CLOSER** TO THE SWARM?
WBBL
SOME-THING'S NOT RIGHT HERE!
AS A SCIEN-TIST, I FEEL IT IN MY GUT!
THERE'S SOMETHING ABOUT THIS ENEMY WE HAVE YET TO FIGURE OUT!
BUT WHAT ?!
I HAVE TO FIGURE IT OUT! I HAVE TO!
!!
OH! THAT IRON BALL HIS MUNCH-LAX WAS CARRY-ING...
IT'S ALL SCRATCH-ED UP!
THAT'S IT!
THAT MUST BE IT!

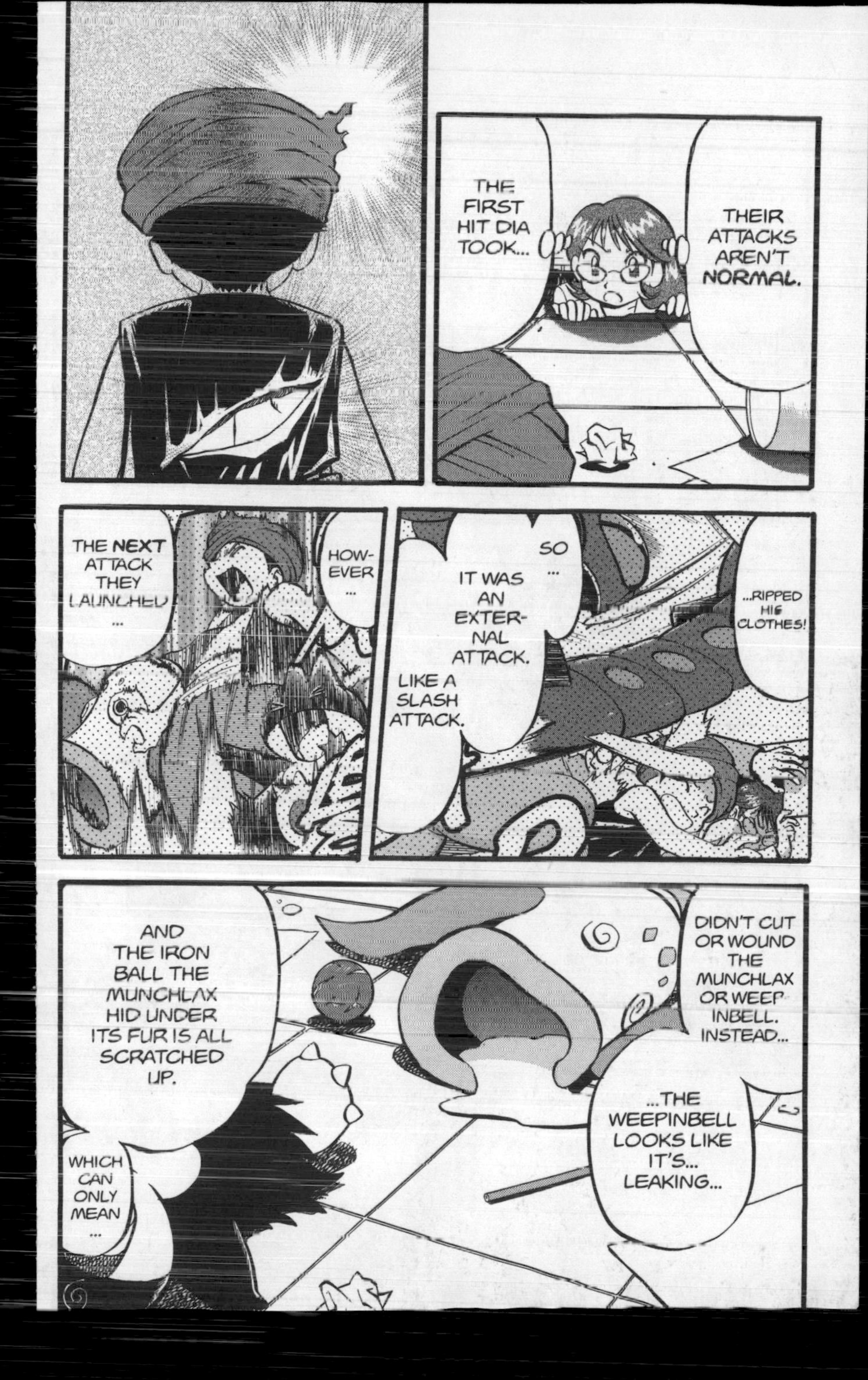
THEIR ATTACKS AREN'T NORMAL.
THE FIRST HIT DIA TOOK...
...RIPPED HIS CLOTHES!
SO...
IT WAS AN EXTERNAL ATTACK.
LIKE A SLASH ATTACK.
HOWEVER...
THE NEXT ATTACK THEY LAUNCHED...
DIDN'T CUT OR WOUND THE MUNCHLAX OR WEEPINBELL. INSTEAD...
...THE WEEPINBELL LOOKS LIKE IT'S... LEAKING...
AND THE IRON BALL THE MUNCHLAX HID UNDER ITS FUR IS ALL SCRATCHED UP.
WHICH CAN ONLY MEAN...

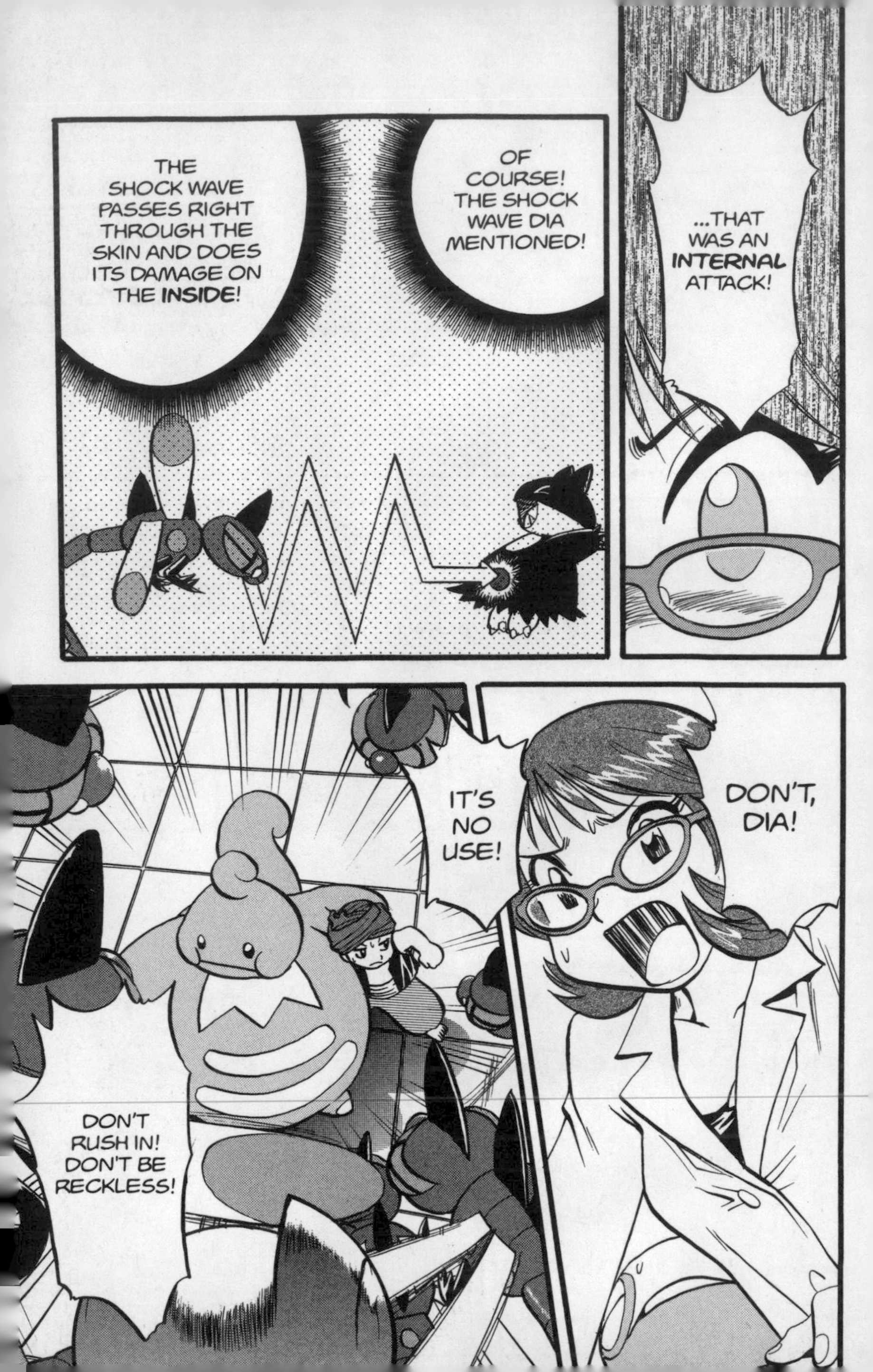
...THAT WAS AN **INTERNAL** ATTACK!
OF COURSE! THE SHOCK WAVE DIA MENTIONED!
THE SHOCK WAVE PASSES RIGHT THROUGH THE SKIN AND DOES ITS DAMAGE ON THE **INSIDE**!
DON'T, DIA!
IT'S NO USE!
DON'T RUSH IN! DON'T BE RECKLESS!

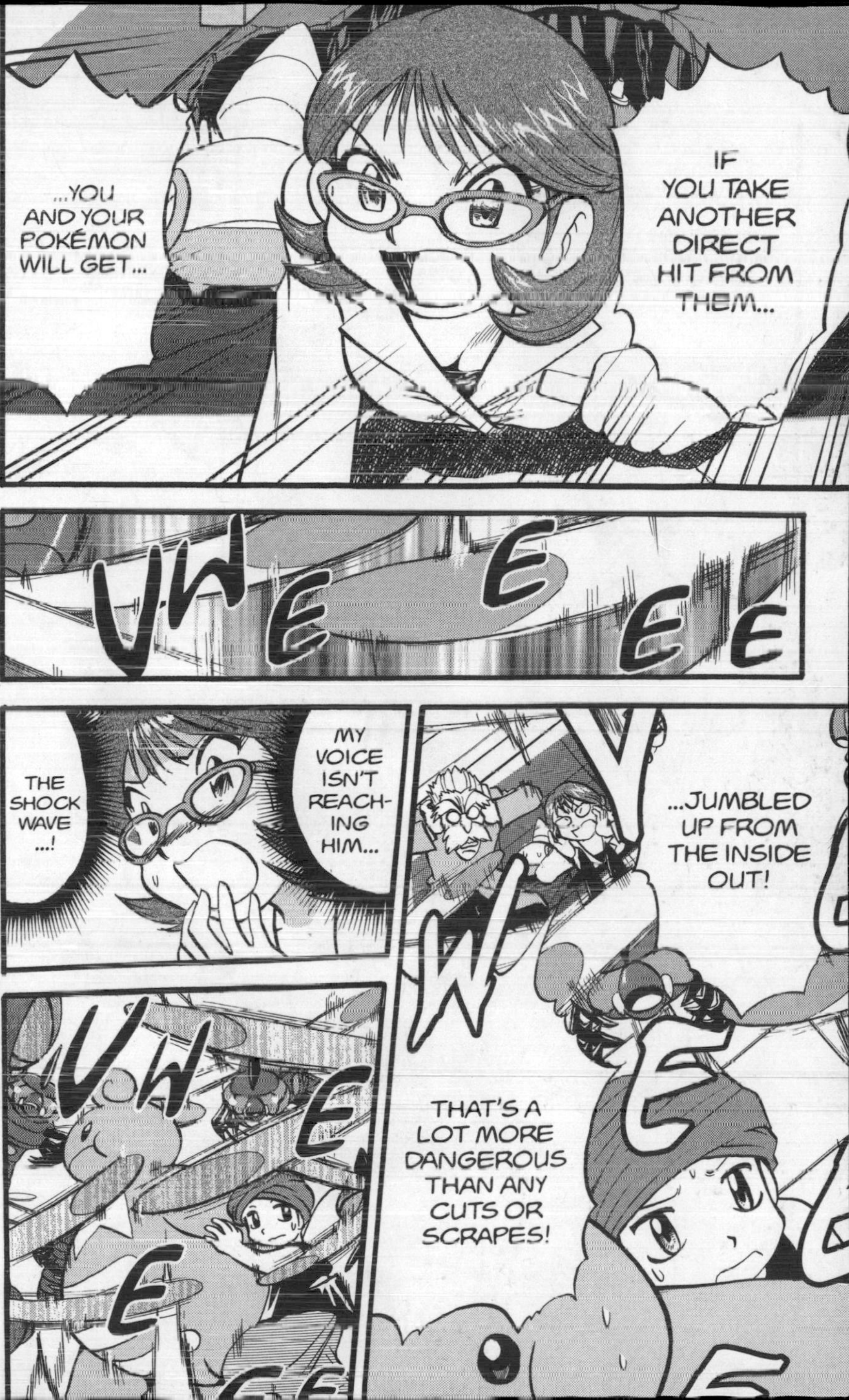
IF YOU TAKE ANOTHER DIRECT HIT FROM THEM...
...YOU AND YOUR POKÉMON WILL GET...
VWEEEEE
...JUMBLED UP FROM THE INSIDE OUT!
MY VOICE ISN'T REACH-ING HIM...
THE SHOCK WAVE ...!
THAT'S A LOT MORE DANGEROUS THAN ANY CUTS OR SCRAPES!
VWEE

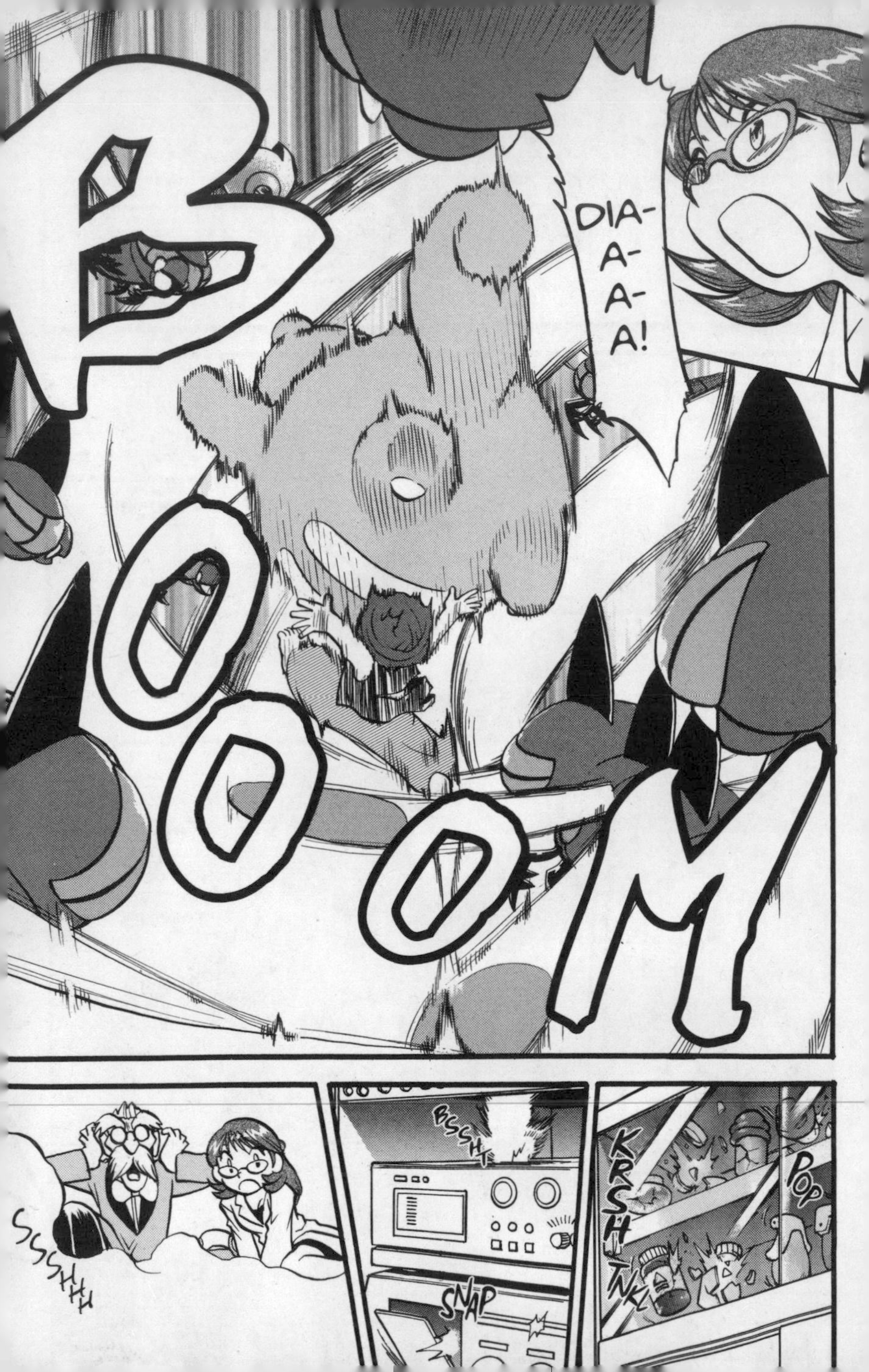
DIA-A-A-A!
BOOOM
POP
KRSHTNK
BSSHT
SNAP
SSSHHH

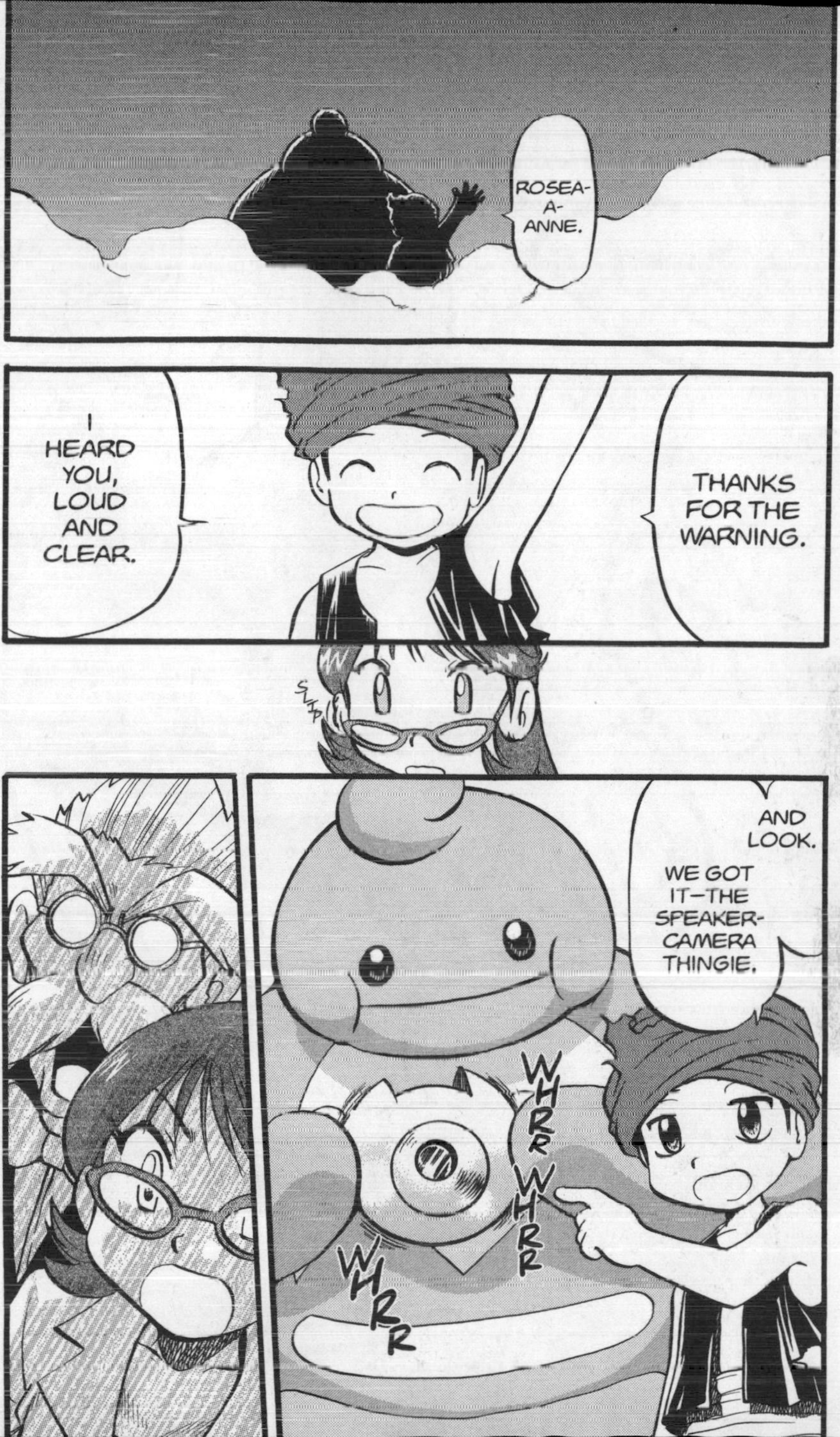
ROSEA-A-ANNE.
THANKS FOR THE WARNING.
I HEARD YOU, LOUD AND CLEAR.
SLIP
AND LOOK.
WE GOT IT—THE SPEAKER-CAMERA THINGIE.
WHRR WHRR WHRR
WHRR

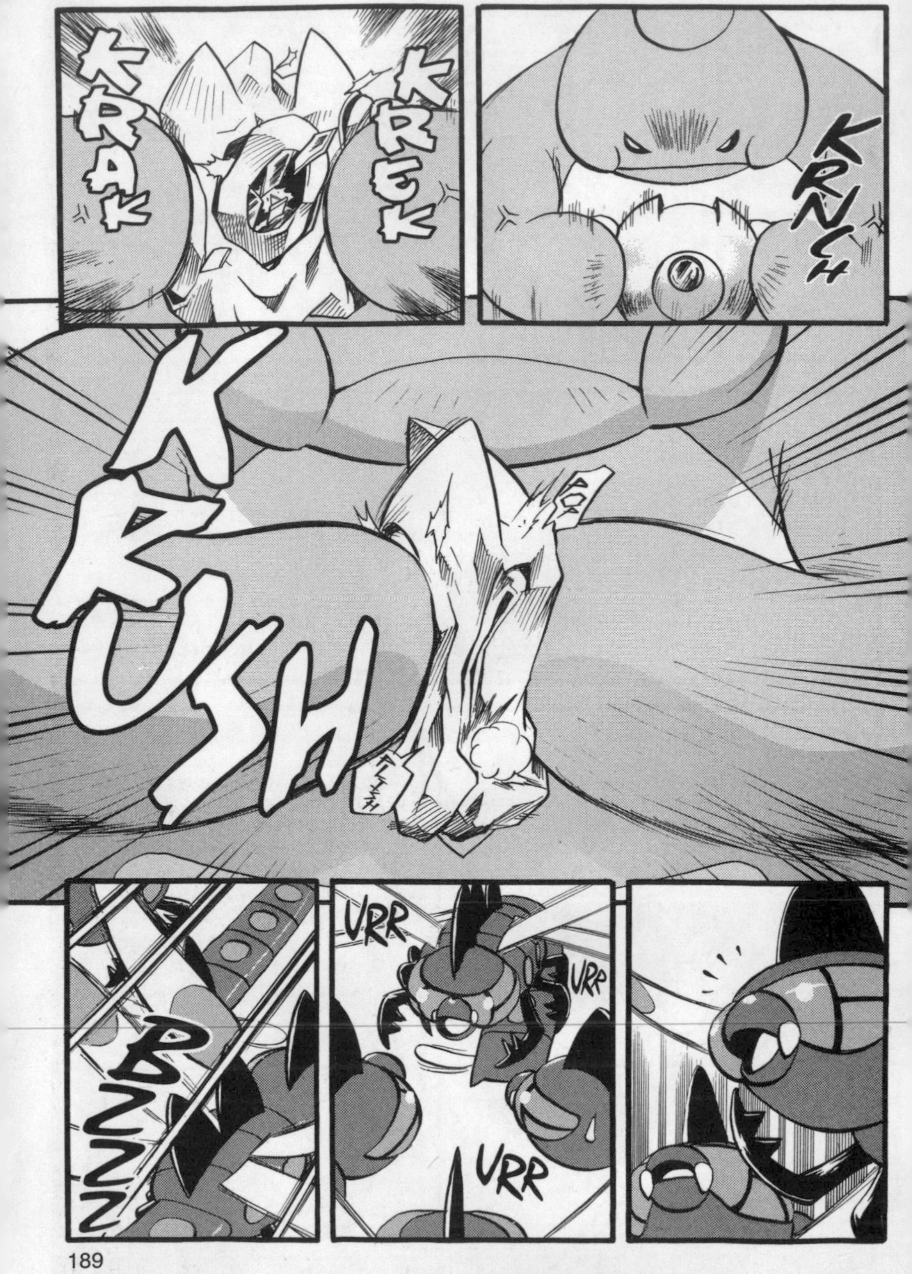
KRNCH
KREK
KRAK
KRUSH
POP
FLISH
URR
URR
URR
BZZZZ

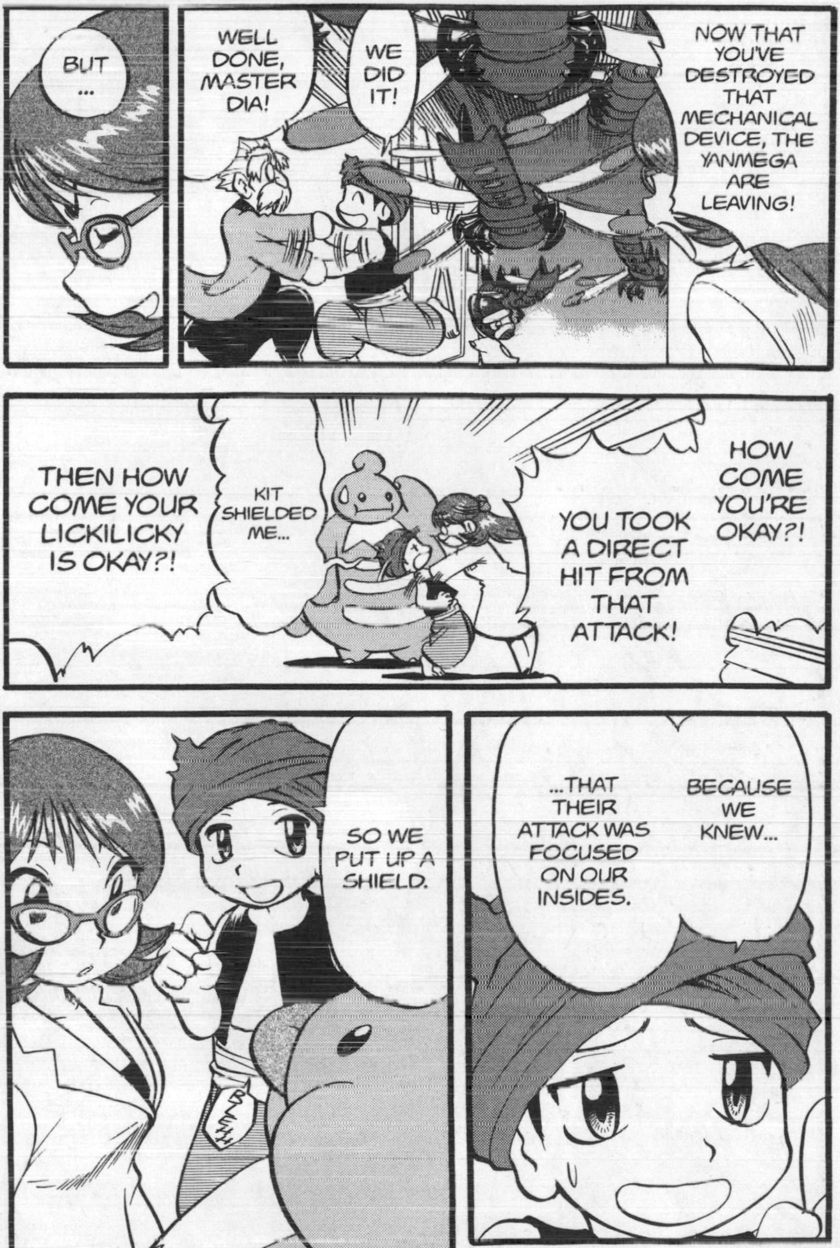
NOW THAT YOU'VE DESTROYED THAT MECHANICAL DEVICE, THE YANMEGA ARE LEAVING!
WE DID IT!
WELL DONE, MASTER DIA!
BUT ...
HOW COME YOU'RE OKAY?!
YOU TOOK A DIRECT HIT FROM THAT ATTACK!
KIT SHIELDED ME...
THEN HOW COME YOUR LICKILICKY IS OKAY?!
BECAUSE WE KNEW...
...THAT THEIR ATTACK WAS FOCUSED ON OUR INSIDES.
SO WE PUT UP A SHIELD.

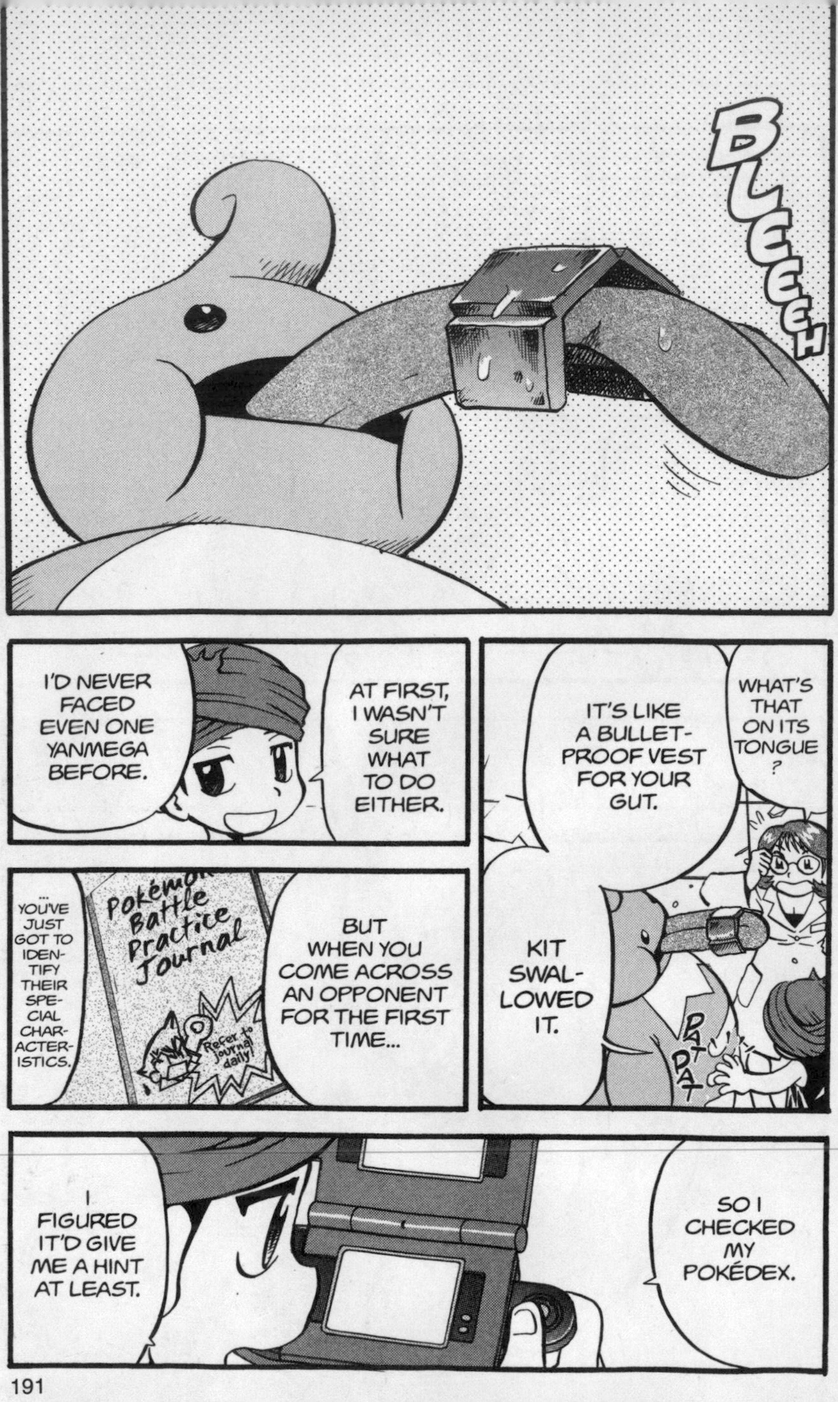
BLEEEH
WHAT'S THAT ON ITS TONGUE?
IT'S LIKE A BULLET-PROOF VEST FOR YOUR GUT.
KIT SWAL-LOWED IT.
PAT PAT
AT FIRST, I WASN'T SURE WHAT TO DO EITHER.
I'D NEVER FACED EVEN ONE YANMEGA BEFORE.
BUT WHEN YOU COME ACROSS AN OPPONENT FOR THE FIRST TIME...
Pokémon Battle Practice Journal
Refer to journal daily!
...YOU'VE JUST GOT TO IDEN-TIFY THEIR SPE-CIAL CHAR-ACTER-ISTICS.
SO I CHECKED MY POKÉDEX.
I FIGURED IT'D GIVE ME A HINT AT LEAST.

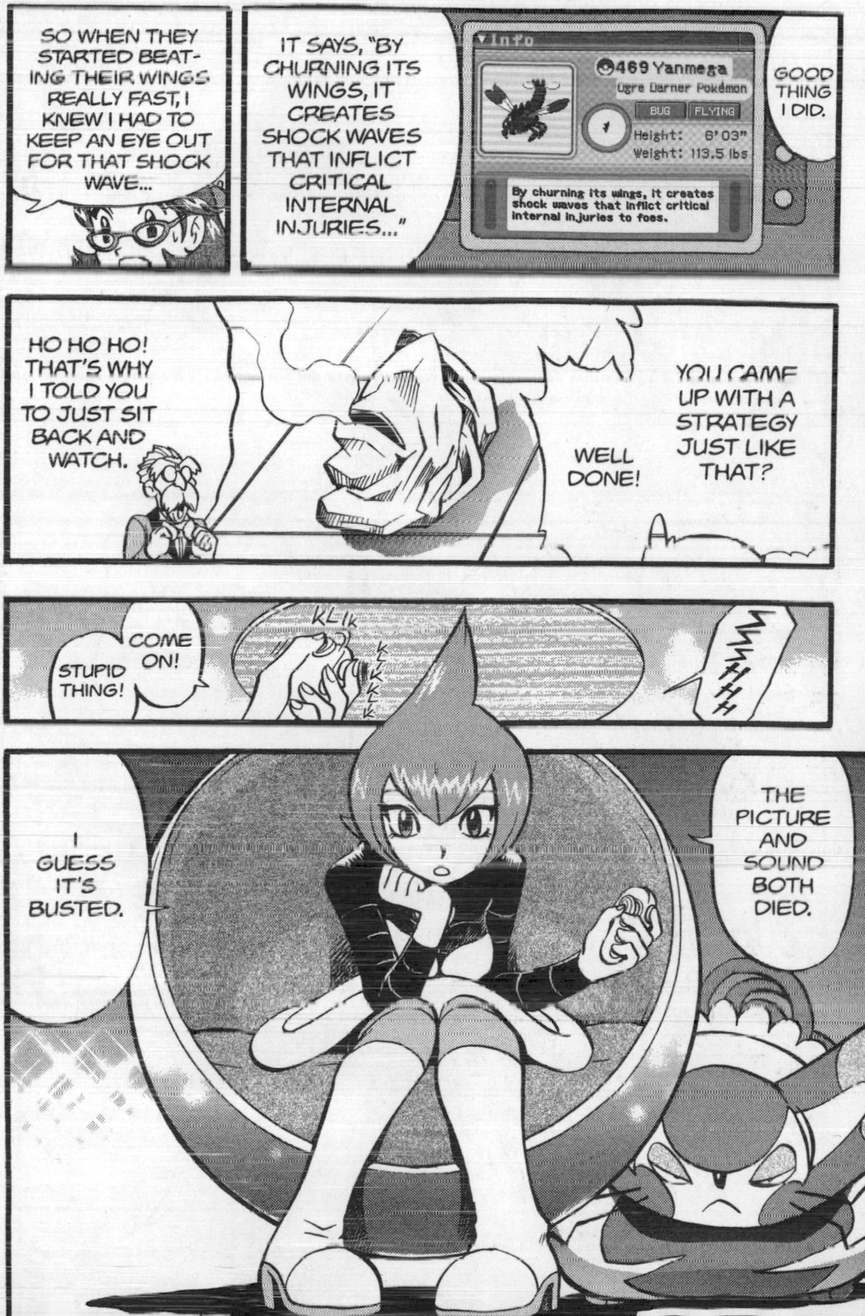
GOOD THING I DID.
▼Info
469 Yanmega
Ogre Darner Pokémon
BUG
FLYING
Height: 6'03"
Weight: 113.5 lbs
By churning its wings, it creates shock waves that inflict critical internal injuries to foes.
IT SAYS, "BY CHURNING ITS WINGS, IT CREATES SHOCK WAVES THAT INFLICT CRITICAL INTERNAL INJURIES..."
SO WHEN THEY STARTED BEAT-ING THEIR WINGS REALLY FAST, I KNEW I HAD TO KEEP AN EYE OUT FOR THAT SHOCK WAVE...
YOU CAME UP WITH A STRATEGY JUST LIKE THAT?
WELL DONE!
HO HO HO! THAT'S WHY I TOLD YOU TO JUST SIT BACK AND WATCH.
KLIK
COME ON!
STUPID THING!
THE PICTURE AND SOUND BOTH DIED.
I GUESS IT'S BUSTED.

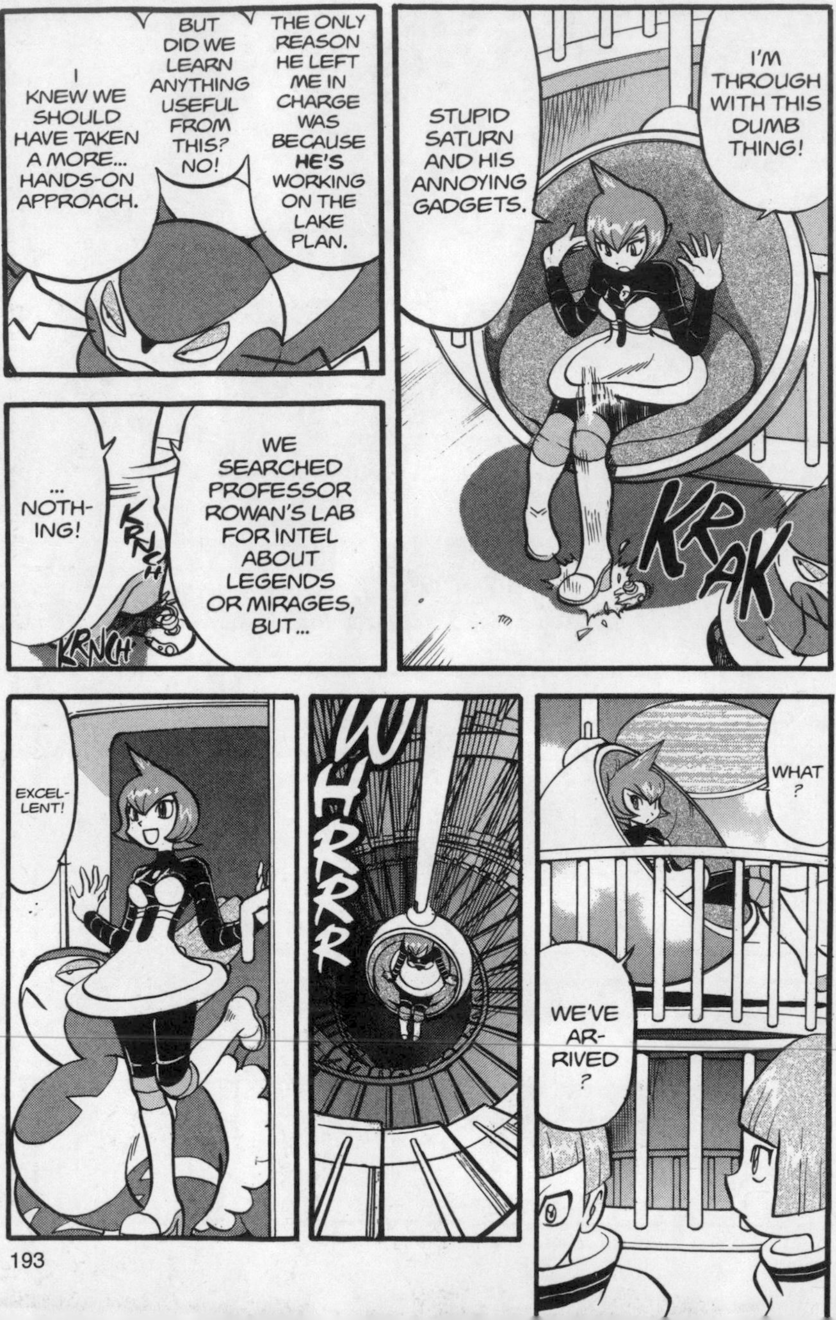
I'M THROUGH WITH THIS DUMB THING!
STUPID SATURN AND HIS ANNOYING GADGETS.
KRAK
THE ONLY REASON HE LEFT ME IN CHARGE WAS BECAUSE **HE'S** WORKING ON THE LAKE PLAN.
BUT DID WE LEARN ANYTHING USEFUL FROM THIS? NO!
I KNEW WE SHOULD HAVE TAKEN A MORE... HANDS-ON APPROACH.
WE SEARCHED PROFESSOR ROWAN'S LAB FOR INTEL ABOUT LEGENDS OR MIRAGES, BUT...
KRNCH
... NOTHING!
KRNCH
WHAT?
WE'VE ARRIVED?
WHRRRR
EXCELLENT!

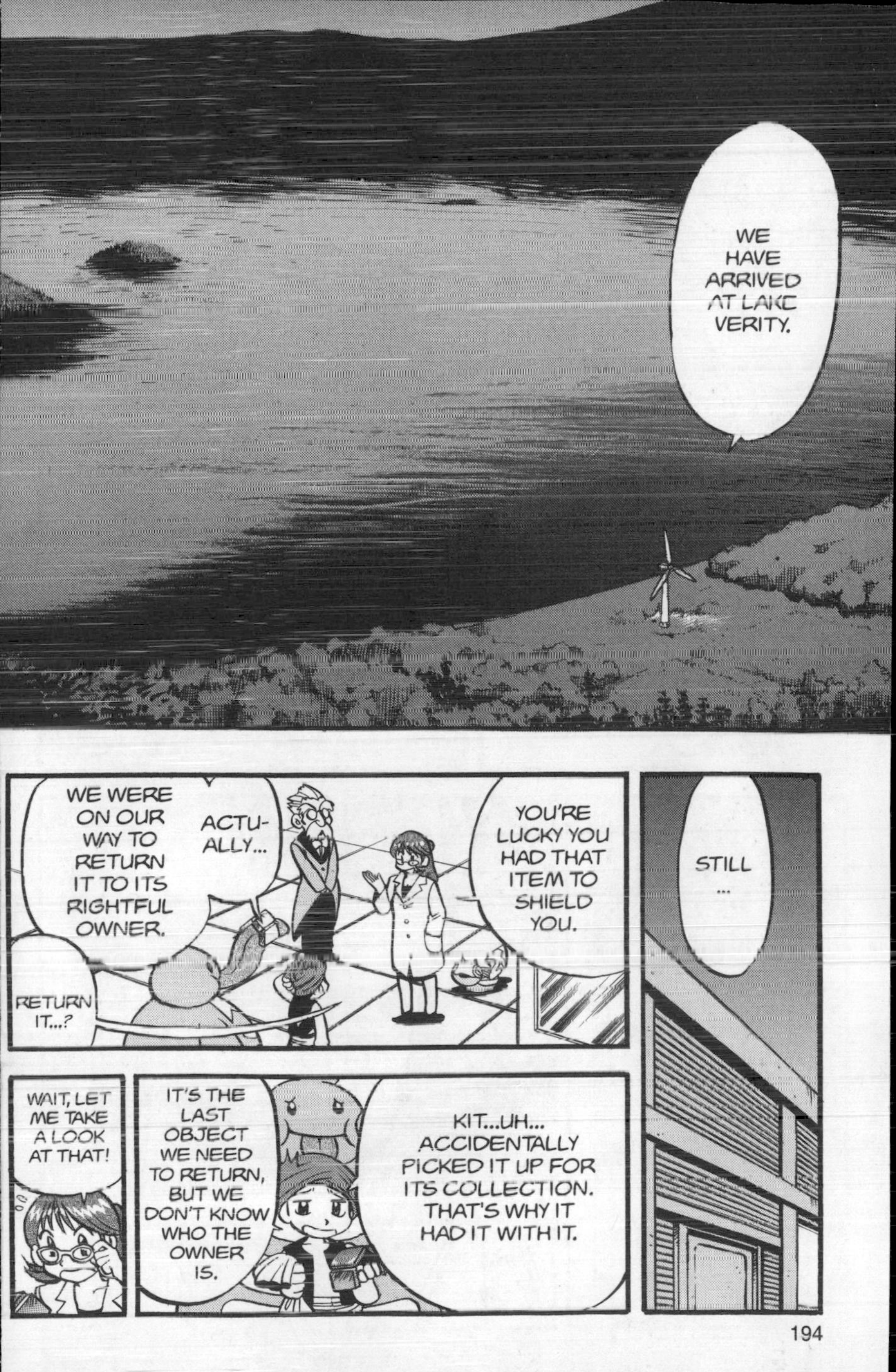
WE HAVE ARRIVED AT LAKE VERITY.
STILL ...
YOU'RE LUCKY YOU HAD THAT ITEM TO SHIELD YOU.
ACTU-ALLY...
WE WERE ON OUR WAY TO RETURN IT TO ITS RIGHTFUL OWNER.
RETURN IT...?
KIT...UH... ACCIDENTALLY PICKED IT UP FOR ITS COLLECTION. THAT'S WHY IT HAD IT WITH IT.
IT'S THE LAST OBJECT WE NEED TO RETURN, BUT WE DON'T KNOW WHO THE OWNER IS.
WAIT, LET ME TAKE A LOOK AT THAT!

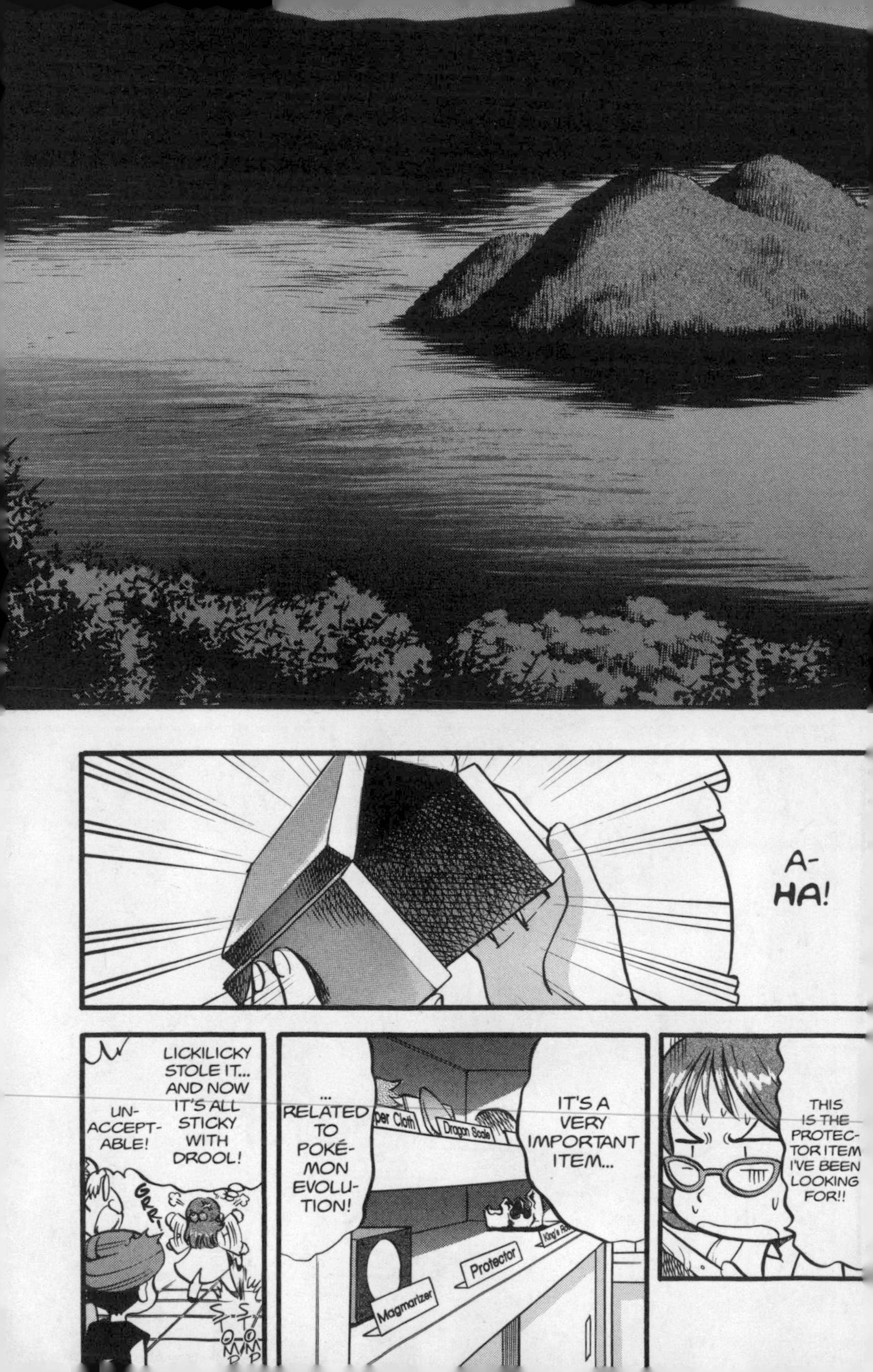
A-HA!
THIS IS THE PROTECTOR ITEM I'VE BEEN LOOKING FOR!!
IT'S A VERY IMPORTANT ITEM...
...RELATED TO POKÉMON EVOLUTION!
Dragon Scale
Protector
Magmarizer
LICKILICKY STOLE IT... AND NOW IT'S ALL STICKY WITH DROOL!
UN-ACCEPT-ABLE!
GRR!

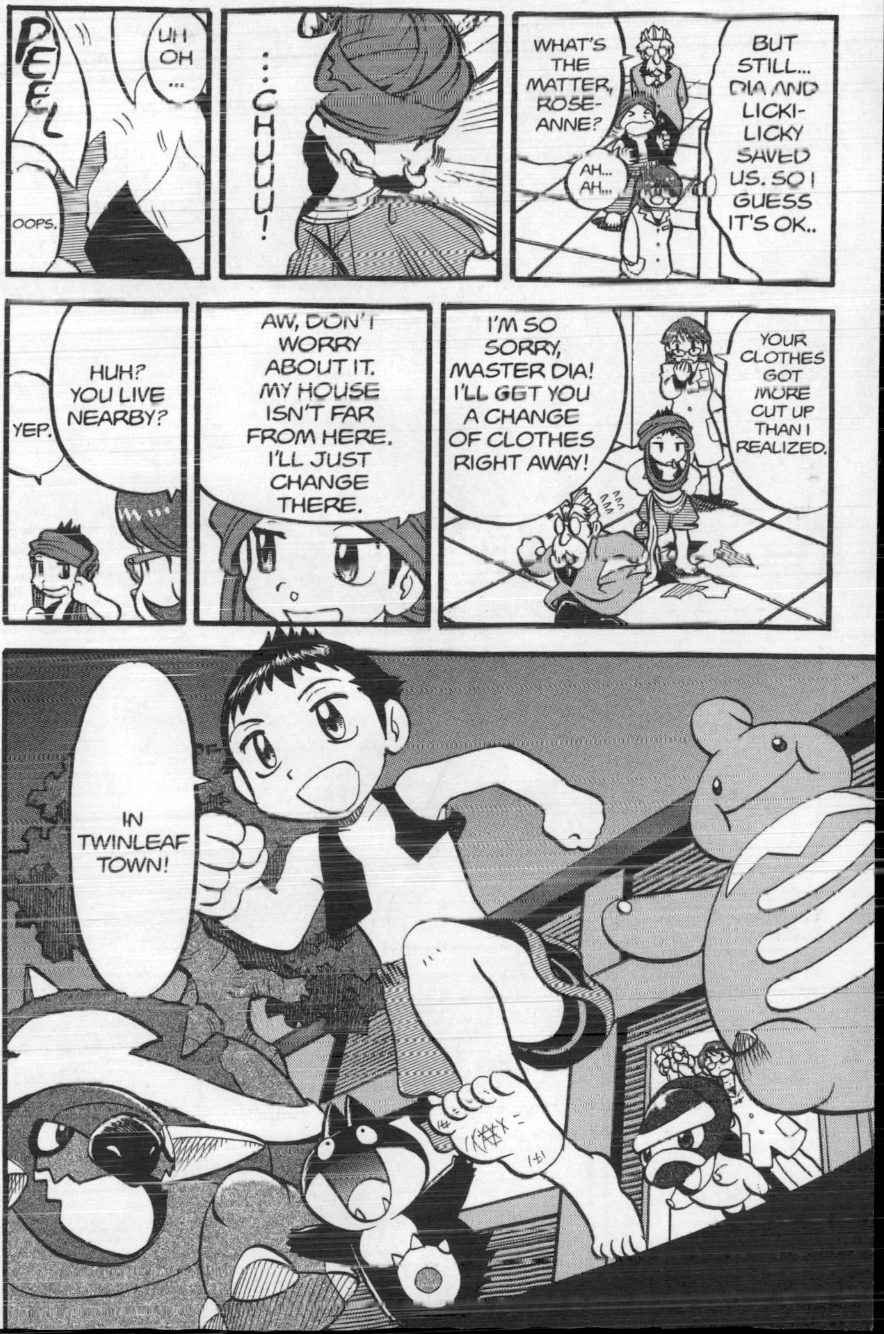
BUT STILL... DIA AND LICKI-LICKY SAVED US. SO I GUESS IT'S OK..
WHAT'S THE MATTER, ROSE-ANNE?
AH... AH...
...CHUUU!
UH OH ...
PEEL
OOPS.
YOUR CLOTHES GOT MORE CUT UP THAN I REALIZED.
I'M SO SORRY, MASTER DIA! I'LL GET YOU A CHANGE OF CLOTHES RIGHT AWAY!
AW, DON'T WORRY ABOUT IT. MY HOUSE ISN'T FAR FROM HERE. I'LL JUST CHANGE THERE.
HUH? YOU LIVE NEARBY?
YEP.
IN TWINLEAF TOWN!

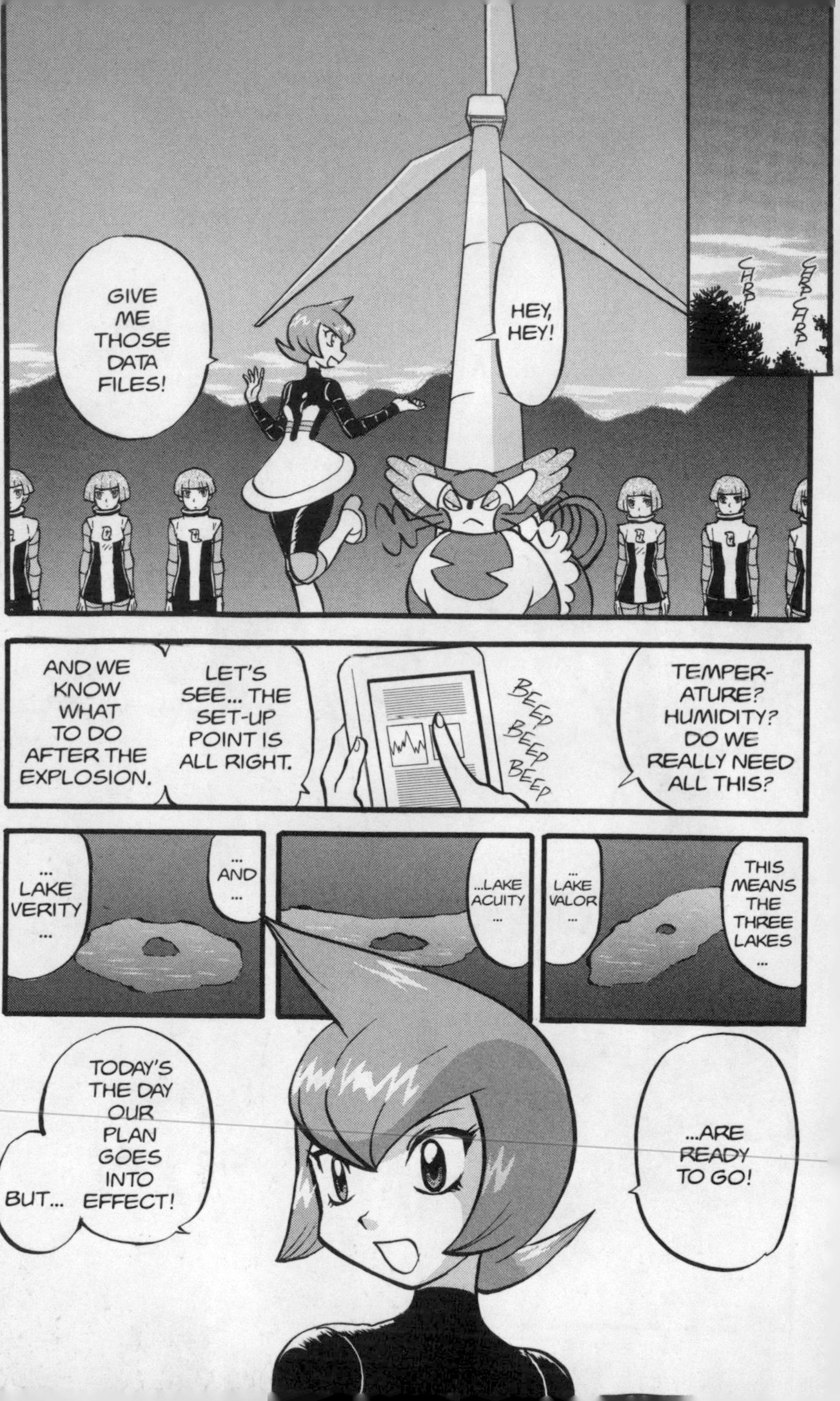
CHRP CHRP
CHRP
HEY, HEY!
GIVE ME THOSE DATA FILES!
TEMPER-ATURE? HUMIDITY? DO WE REALLY NEED ALL THIS?
BEEP BEEP BEEP
LET'S SEE... THE SET-UP POINT IS ALL RIGHT.
AND WE KNOW WHAT TO DO AFTER THE EXPLOSION.
THIS MEANS THE THREE LAKES ...
... LAKE VALOR ...
...LAKE ACUITY ...
... AND ...
... LAKE VERITY ...
...ARE READY TO GO!
TODAY'S THE DAY OUR PLAN GOES INTO EFFECT!
BUT...

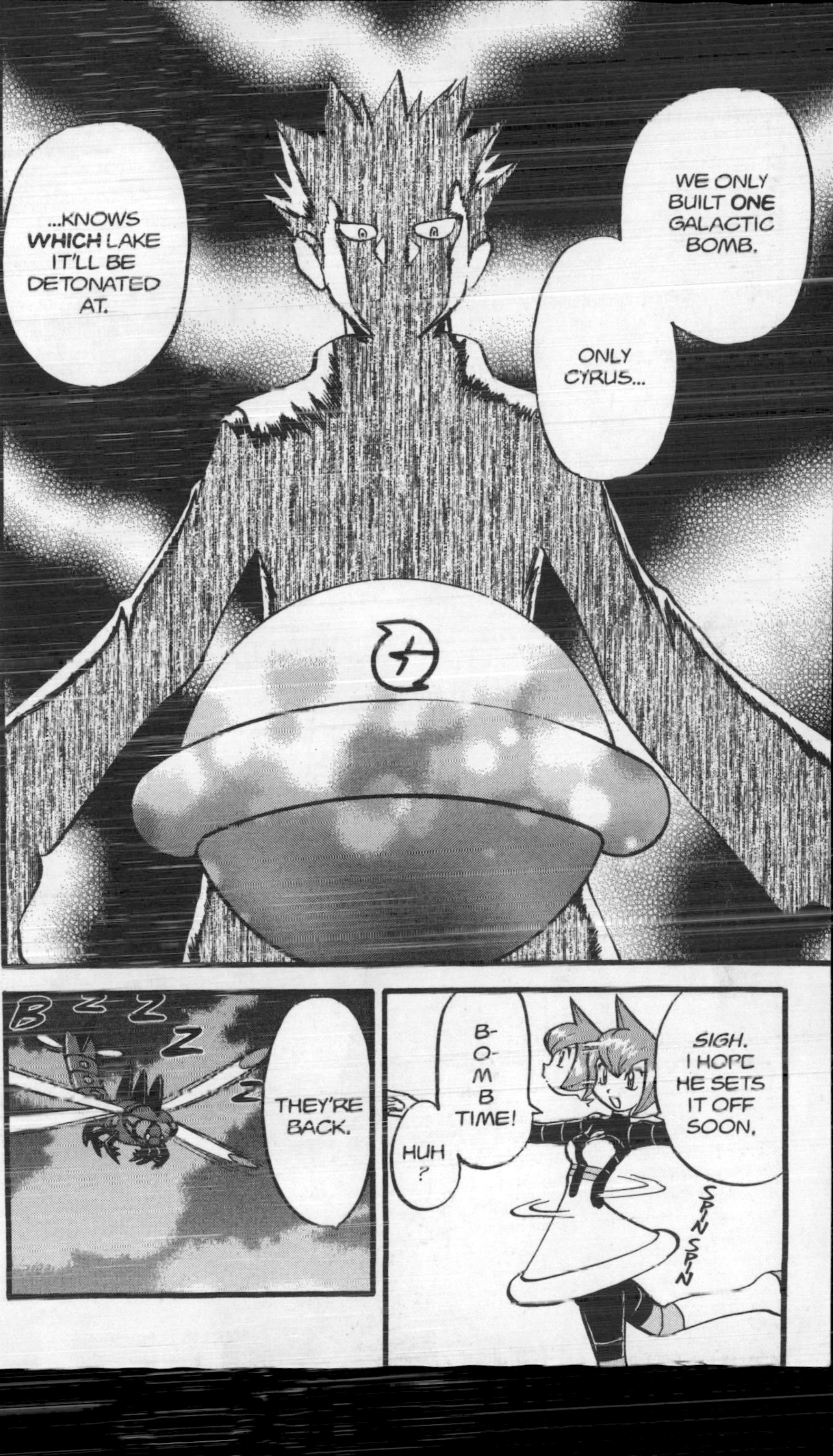
WE ONLY BUILT ONE GALACTIC BOMB.
ONLY CYRUS...
...KNOWS WHICH LAKE IT'LL BE DETONATED AT.
SIGH. I HOPE HE SETS IT OFF SOON.
B-O-M-B TIME!
SPIN SPIN
HUH?
BZZZ
THEY'RE BACK.

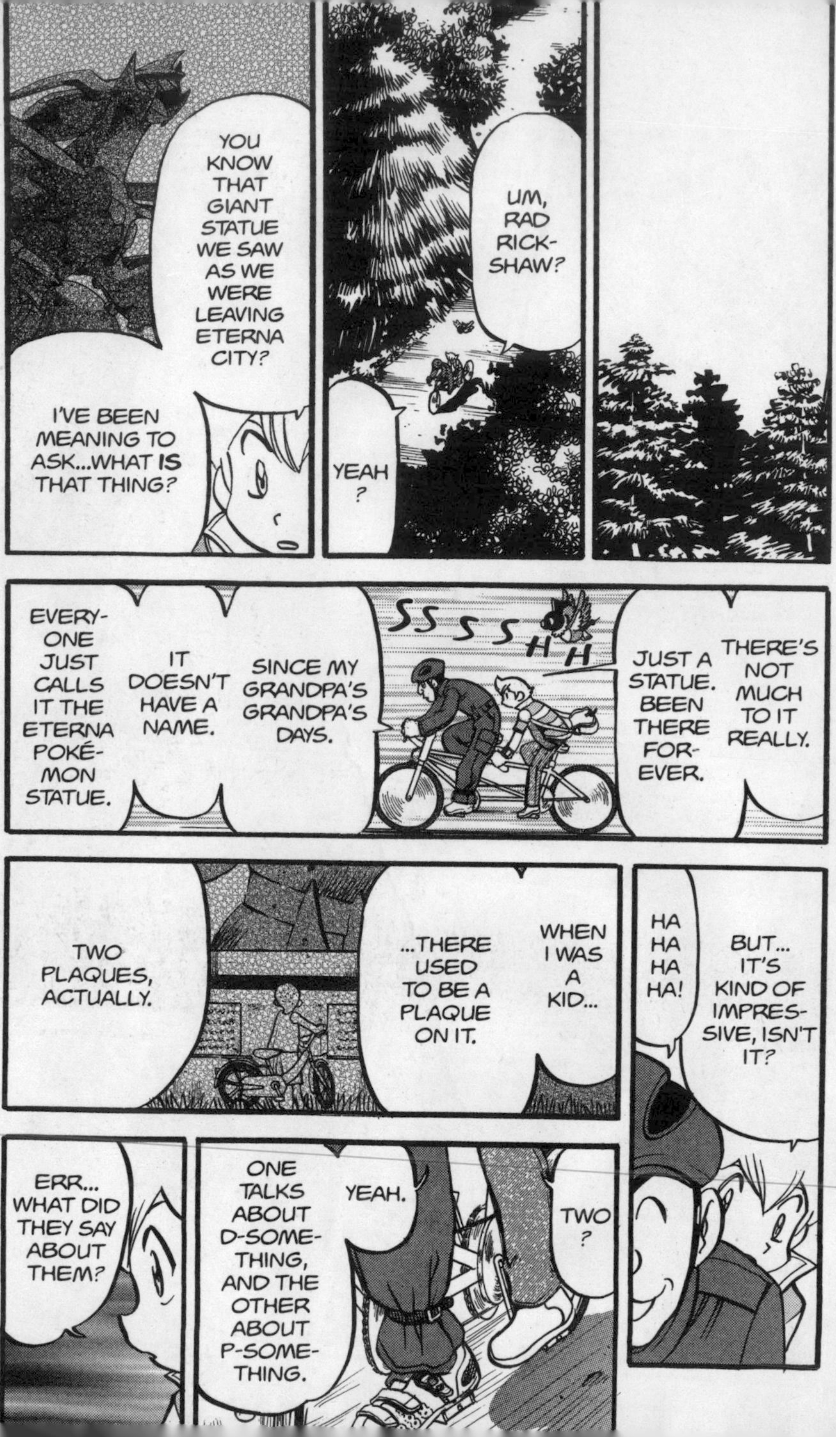
UM, RAD RICK-SHAW?
YEAH?
YOU KNOW THAT GIANT STATUE WE SAW AS WE WERE LEAVING ETERNA CITY?
I'VE BEEN MEANING TO ASK...WHAT IS THAT THING?
THERE'S NOT MUCH TO IT REALLY.
JUST A STATUE. BEEN THERE FOR-EVER.
SSSSHH
SINCE MY GRANDPA'S GRANDPA'S DAYS.
IT DOESN'T HAVE A NAME.
EVERY-ONE JUST CALLS IT THE ETERNA POKÉ-MON STATUE.
BUT... IT'S KIND OF IMPRES-SIVE, ISN'T IT?
HA HA HA HA!
WHEN I WAS A KID...
...THERE USED TO BE A PLAQUE ON IT.
TWO PLAQUES, ACTUALLY.
TWO?
YEAH.
ONE TALKS ABOUT D-SOME-THING, AND THE OTHER ABOUT P-SOME-THING.
ERR... WHAT DID THEY SAY ABOUT THEM?

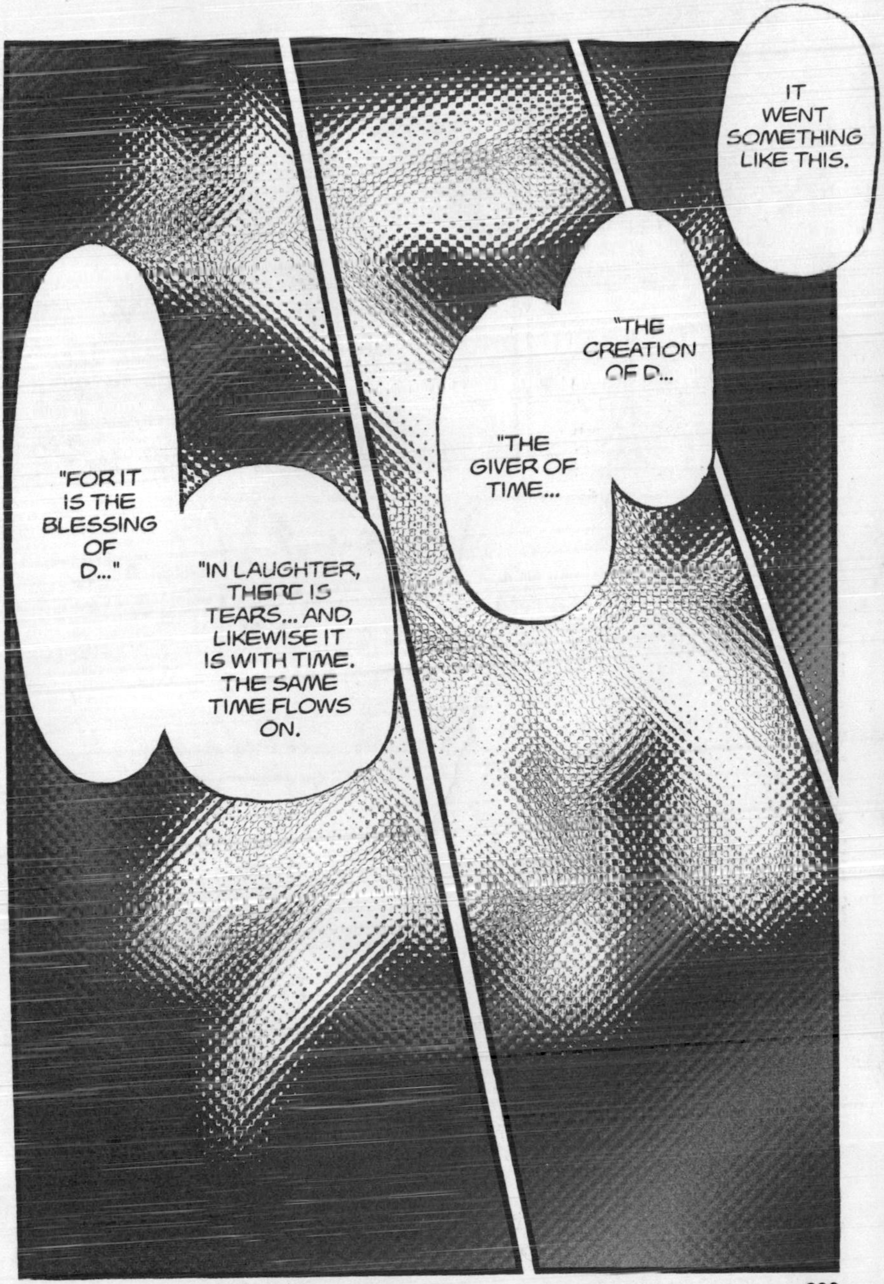
IT WENT SOMETHING LIKE THIS.
"THE CREATION OF D...
"THE GIVER OF TIME...
"IN LAUGHTER, THERE IS TEARS... AND, LIKEWISE IT IS WITH TIME. THE SAME TIME FLOWS ON.
"FOR IT IS THE BLESSING OF D..."

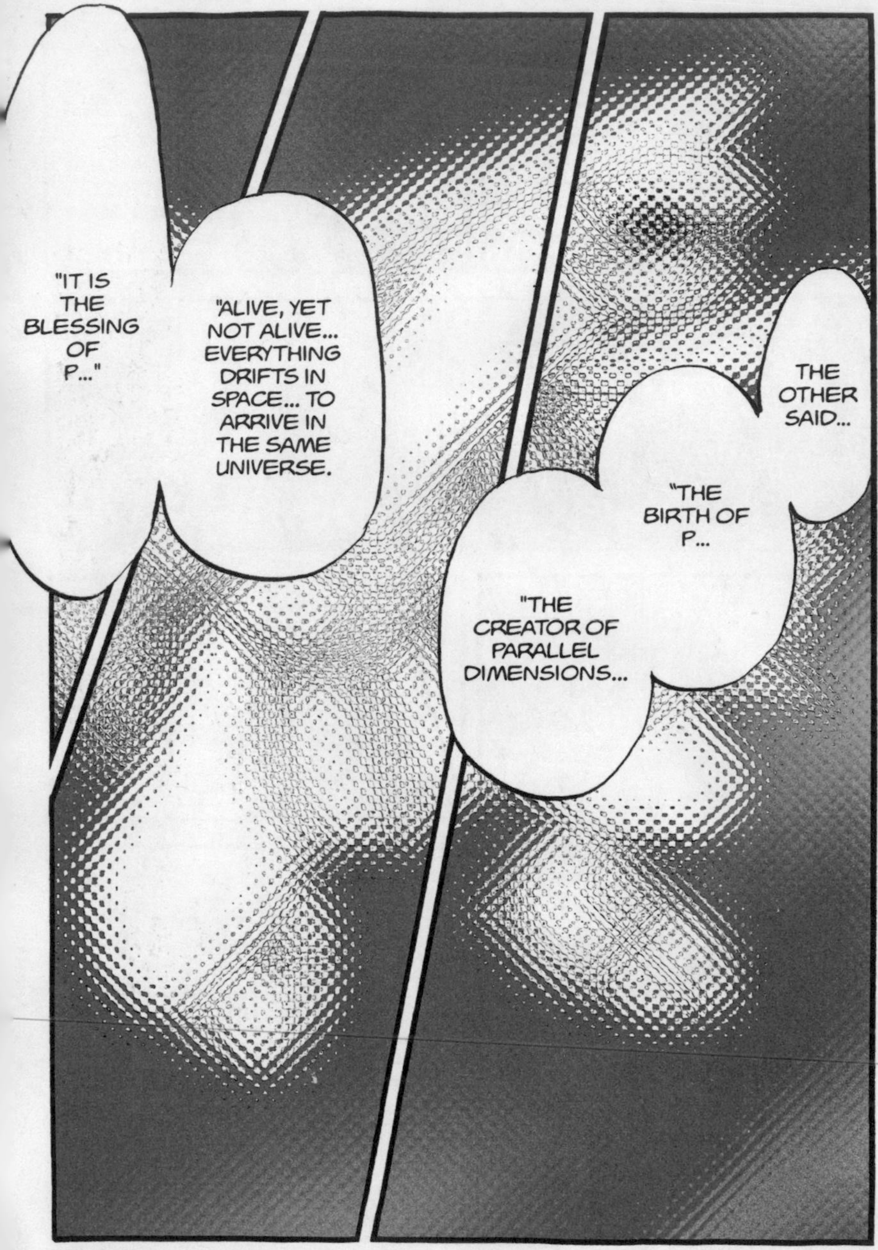
THE OTHER SAID...
"THE BIRTH OF P...
"THE CREATOR OF PARALLEL DIMENSIONS...
"ALIVE, YET NOT ALIVE... EVERYTHING DRIFTS IN SPACE... TO ARRIVE IN THE SAME UNIVERSE.
"IT IS THE BLESSING OF P..."

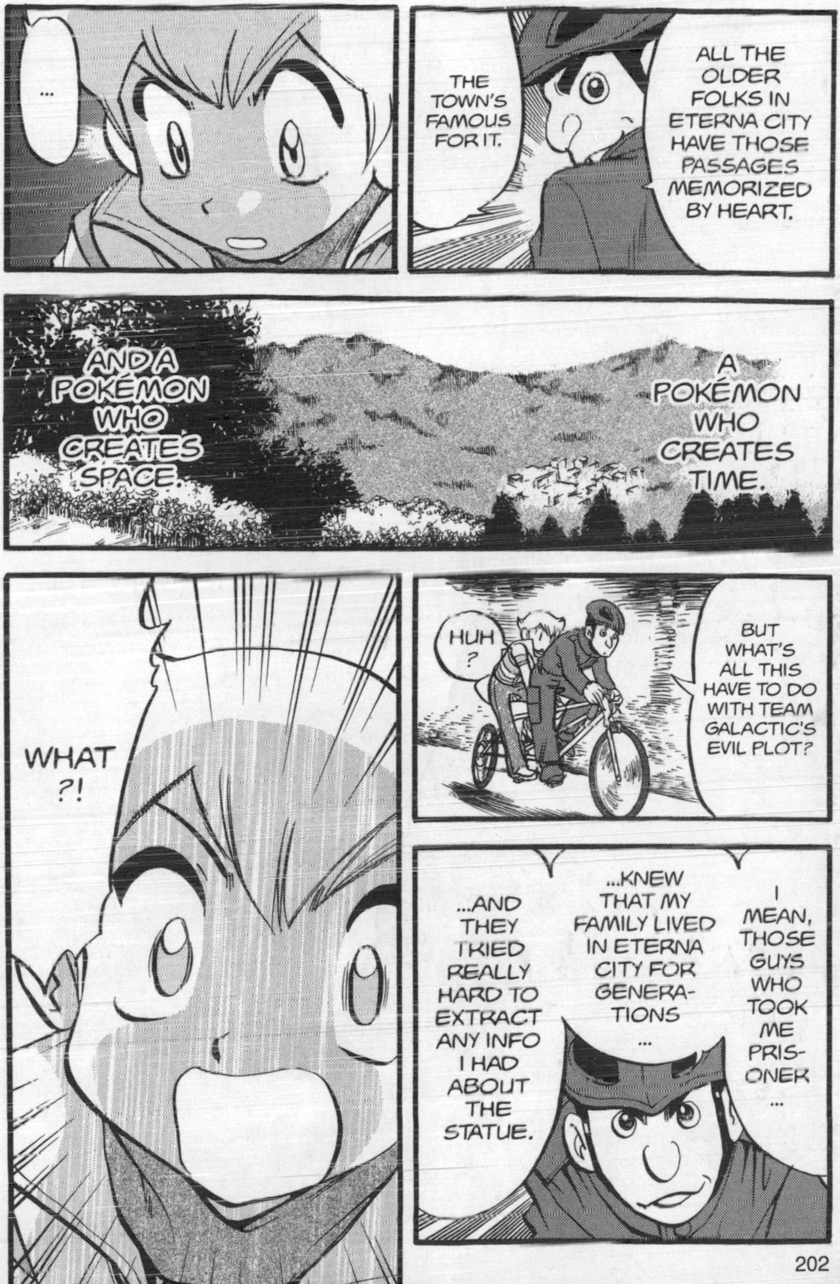
ALL THE OLDER FOLKS IN ETERNA CITY HAVE THOSE PASSAGES MEMORIZED BY HEART.
THE TOWN'S FAMOUS FOR IT.
...
A POKÉMON WHO CREATES TIME.
AND A POKÉMON WHO CREATES SPACE.
BUT WHAT'S ALL THIS HAVE TO DO WITH TEAM GALACTIC'S EVIL PLOT?
HUH?
I MEAN, THOSE GUYS WHO TOOK ME PRISONER...
...KNEW THAT MY FAMILY LIVED IN ETERNA CITY FOR GENERATIONS...
...AND THEY TRIED REALLY HARD TO EXTRACT ANY INFO I HAD ABOUT THE STATUE.
WHAT?!

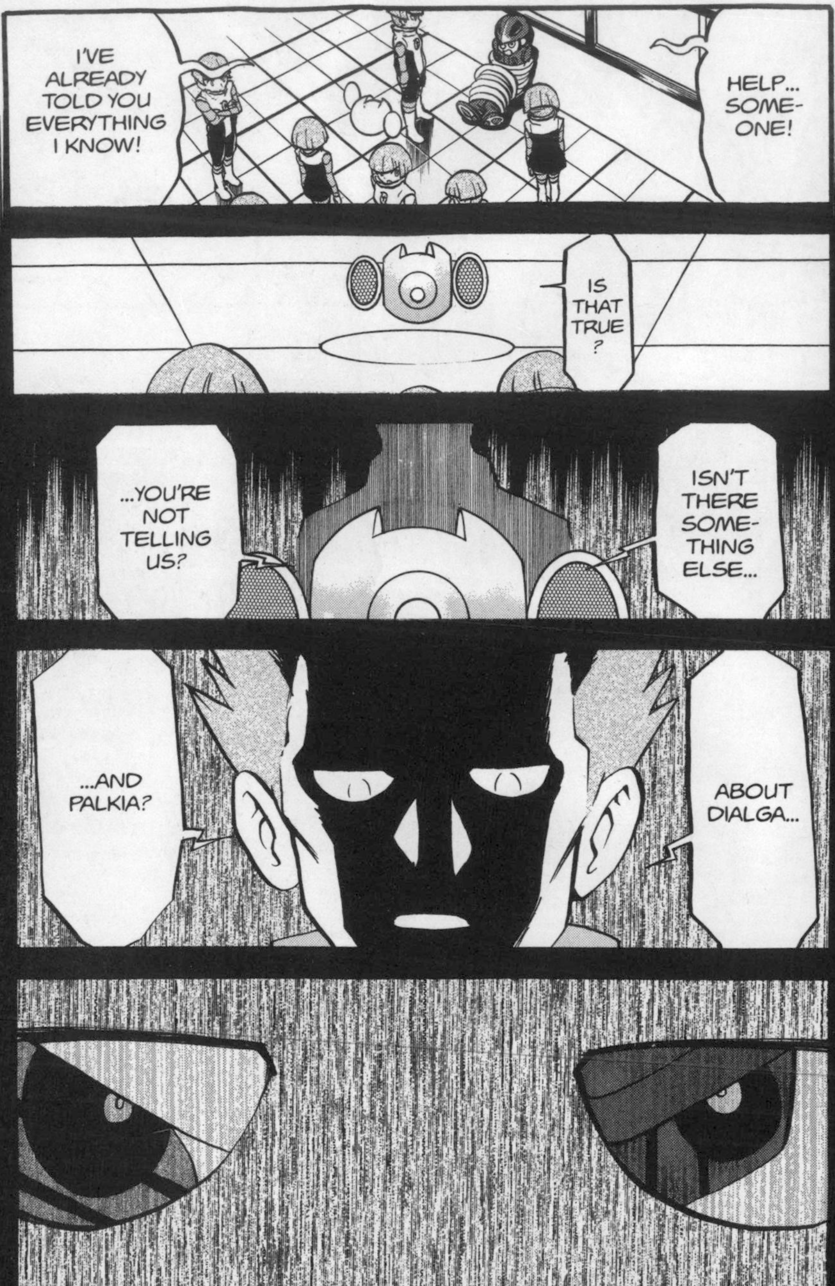
HELP... SOME-ONE!
I'VE ALREADY TOLD YOU EVERYTHING I KNOW!
IS THAT TRUE?
ISN'T THERE SOME-THING ELSE...
...YOU'RE NOT TELLING US?
ABOUT DIALGA...
...AND PALKIA?

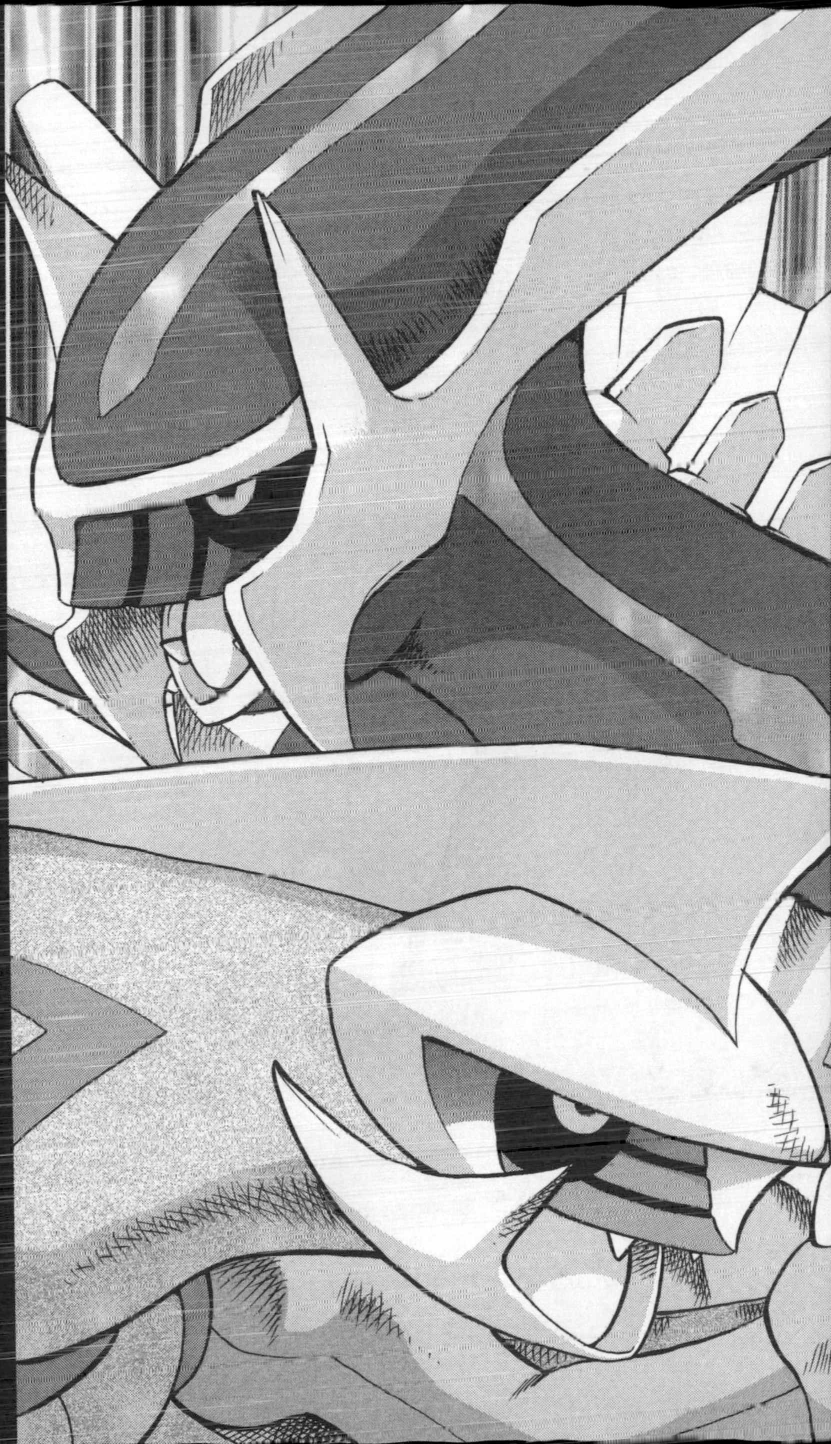

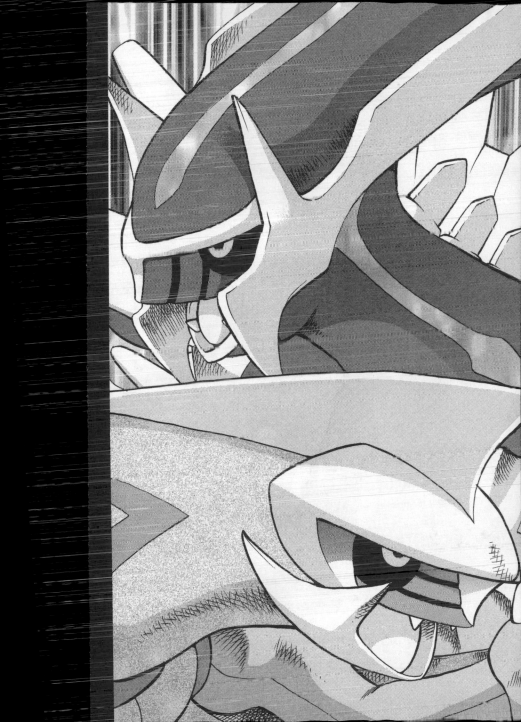

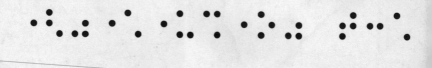

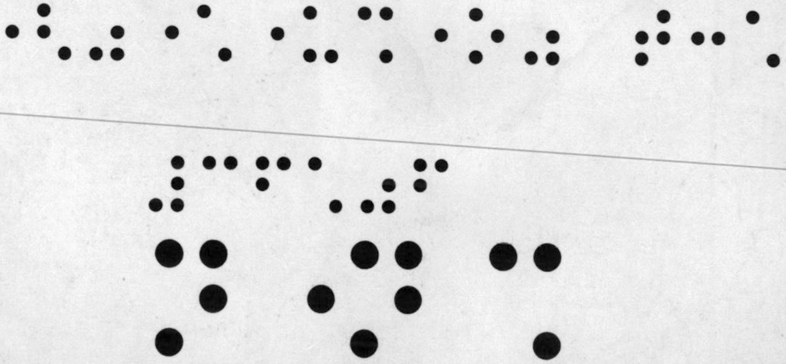

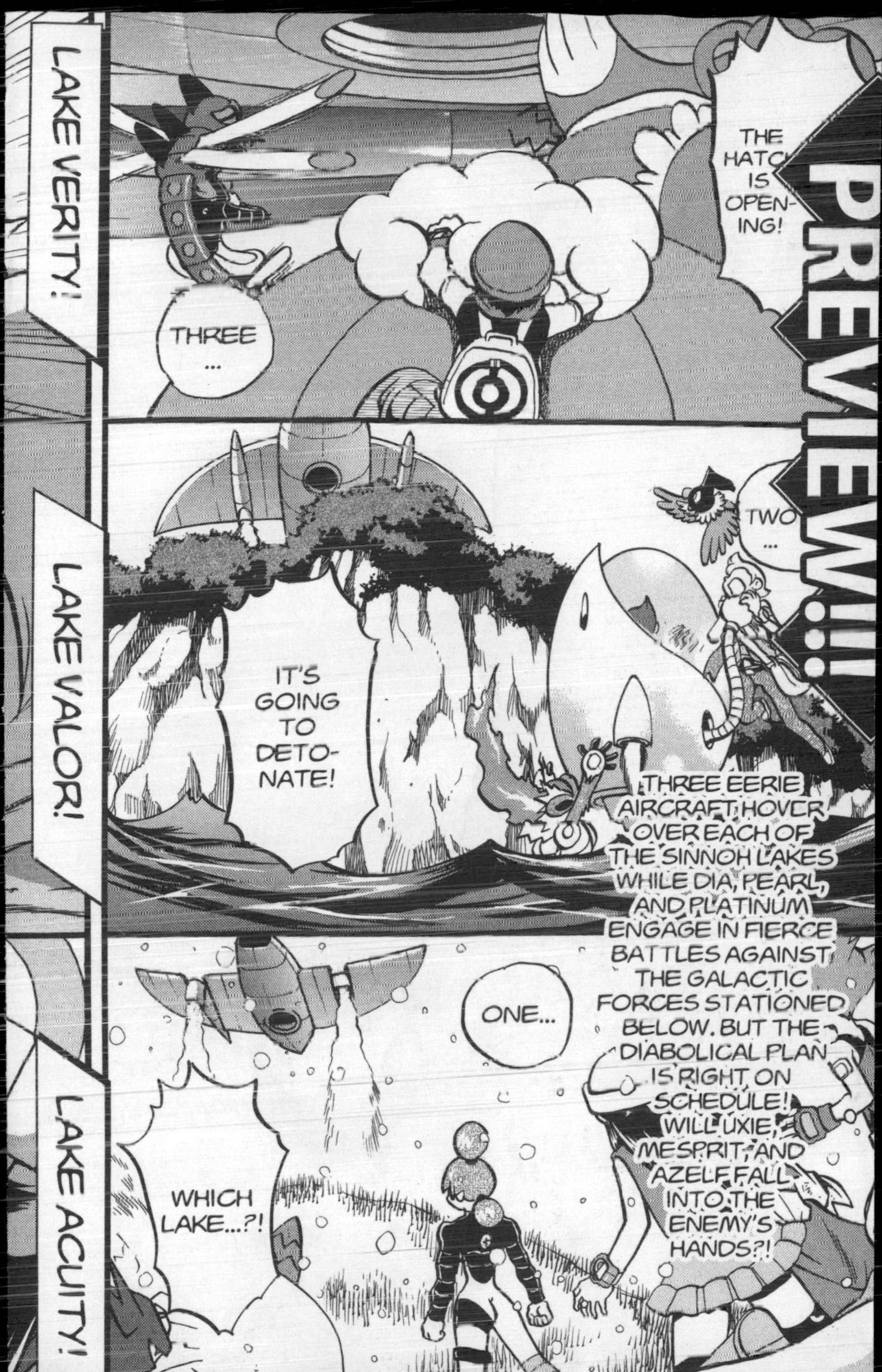
PREVIEW...!!!
THE HATCH IS OPEN-ING!
THREE ...
LAKE VERITY!
TWO ...
IT'S GOING TO DETO-NATE!
LAKE VALOR!
THREE EERIE AIRCRAFT HOVER OVER EACH OF THE SINNOH LAKES WHILE DIA, PEARL, AND PLATINUM ENGAGE IN FIERCE BATTLES AGAINST THE GALACTIC FORCES STATIONED BELOW. BUT THE DIABOLICAL PLAN IS RIGHT ON SCHEDULE! WILL UXIE, MESPRIT, AND AZELF FALL INTO THE ENEMY'S HANDS?!
ONE...
WHICH LAKE...?!
LAKE ACUITY!

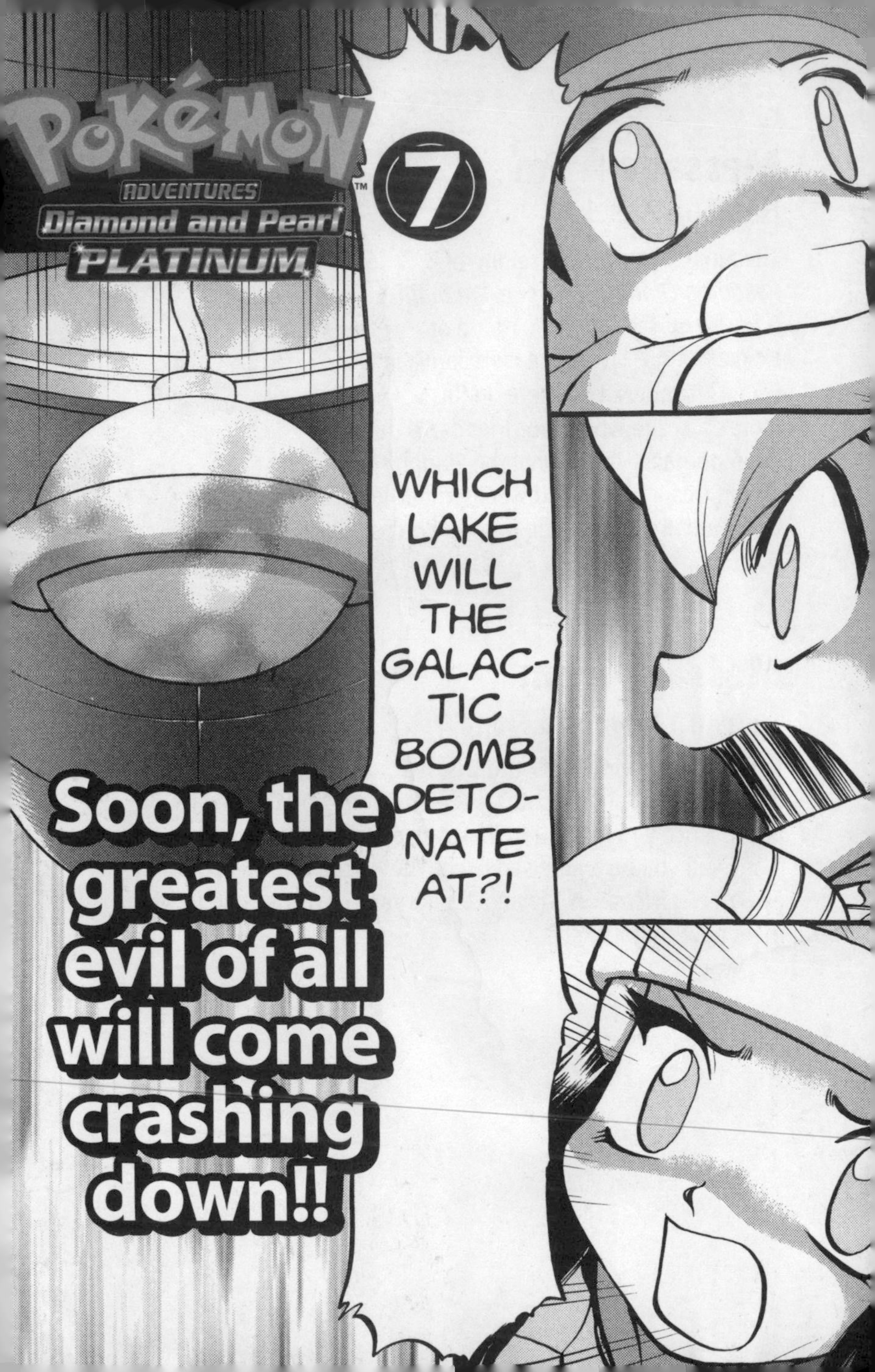
POKÉMON ADVENTURES Diamond and Pearl PLATINUM 7
WHICH LAKE WILL THE GALAC-TIC BOMB DETO-NATE AT?!
Soon, the greatest evil of all will come crashing down!!

Message from
Hidenori Kusaka

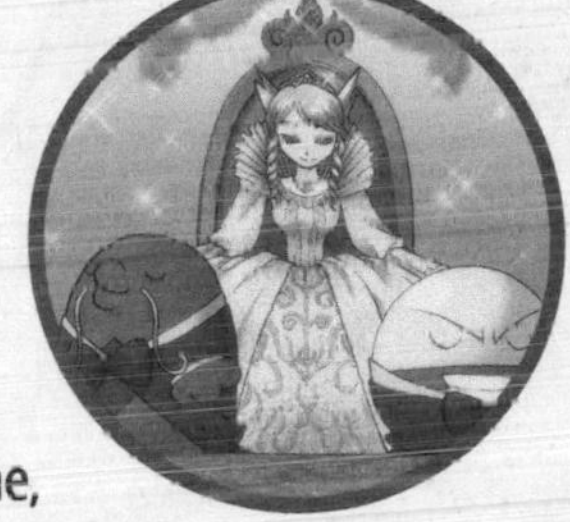

The Sinnoh region, the setting of *Pokémon Diamond & Pearl/Platinum*, is based on the Japanese island of Hokkaido. Are English readers familiar with it? It snows a lot there. In this volume, there's a scene where our friends ski down the mountain—that's what the Sinnoh region is all about! Despite the frigid weather, our heroes and Pokémon are all working hard to do their best!

Message from
Satoshi Yamamoto

The leisurely journey of our three heroes has come to an end... Now Dia and the others are embarking on their own paths. Since you're used to them adventuring together as a team, will you be a little sad to see them separate? Keep an eye on our friends as they encounter new challenges and meet new characters!

More Adventures Coming Soon...

Team Galactic commanders Jupiter, Mars and Saturn are determined to bomb Lake Verity, Lake Valor and Lake Acuity to awaken the Legendary Lake Pokémon that dwell in their depths! Dia, Pearl and Platinum divide forces to stop them—but can they conquer?

Then, when things go awry, it's...*Dia* to the rescue?!

Plus, meet Abomasnow, Tangrowth, Buizel, Gastrodon, Purugly and Staravia!

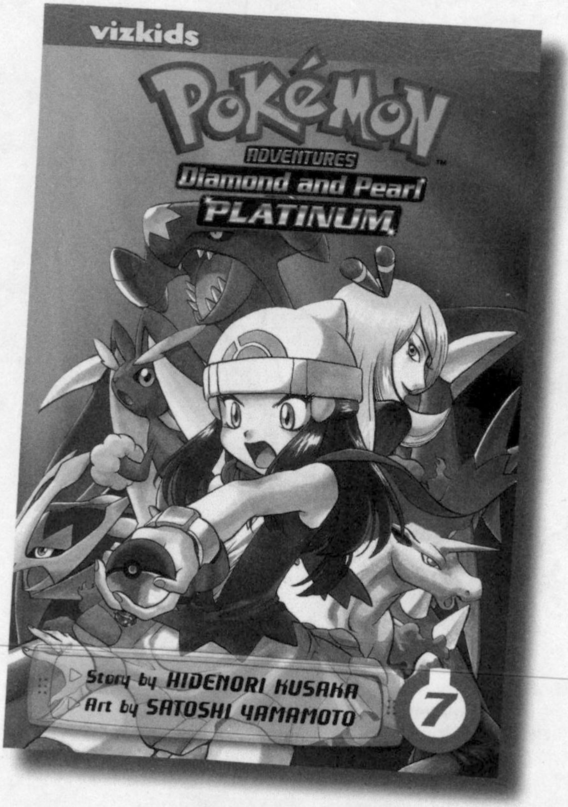
vizkids
POKéMON
ADVENTURES
Diamond and Pearl
PLATINUM
Story by HIDENORI KUSAKA
Art by SATOSHI YAMAMOTO
7

AVAILABLE NOW!

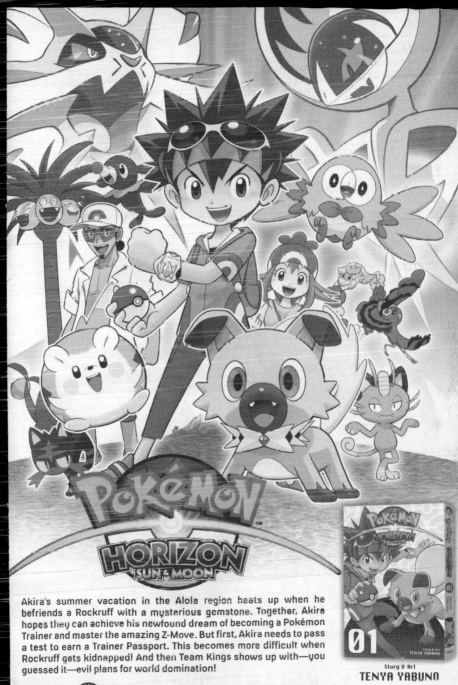

Akira's summer vacation in the Alola region heats up when he befriends a Rockruff with a mysterious gemstone. Together, Akira hopes they can achieve his newfound dream of becoming a Pokémon Trainer and master the amazing Z-Move. But first, Akira needs to pass a test to earn a Trainer Passport. This becomes more difficult when Rockruff gets kidnapped! And then Team Kings shows up with—you guessed it—evil plans for world domination!

Story & Art
TENYA YABUNO

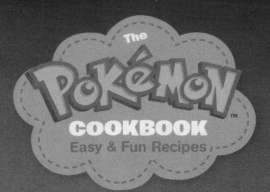

The

POKÉMON™ COOKBOOK

Easy & Fun Recipes

by Maki Kudo

The
POKÉMON
COOKBOOK
Easy & Fun Recipes
MAKI KUDO

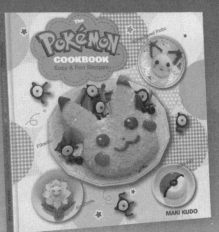

Create delicious dishes that look like your favorite Pokémon characters with more than 35 fun, easy recipes. Make a Poké Ball sushi roll, Pikachu ramen or mashed Meowth potatoes for your next party, weekend activity or powered-up lunch box.

Pikachu
Creamed Corn
Shaymin Green
Salad

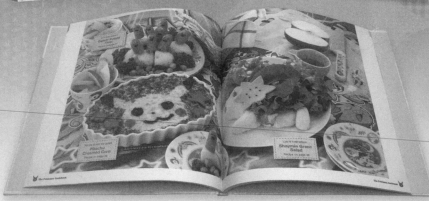

VIZ

viz.com

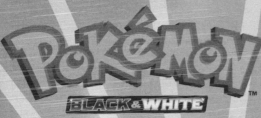
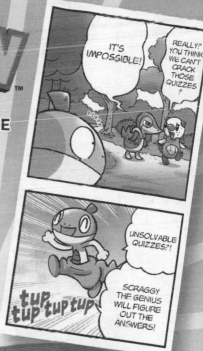
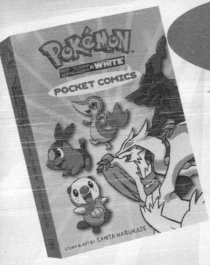

POKÉMON™

POCKET COMICS
Legendary Pokémon

STORY & ART BY SANTA HARUKAZE

grumph
MY FRIEND PIKACHU HASN'T BEEN SMILING RECENTLY...

FOUR-PANEL GAGS, POKÉMON TRIVIA, AND FUN PUZZLES BASED ON THE CHARACTERS FROM THE BEST-SELLING POKÉMON BLACK AND WHITE VIDEO GAMES!

THE LEGENDARY JOKE... IT'S UP TO ME TO FIND IT!
THERE MUST BE A JOKE SOMEWHERE IN THIS WORLD THAT CAN BRING BACK PIKACHU'S SMILE!

Available now!

POKéMON
POCKET COMICS
Legendary Pokémon
STORY & ART BY SANTA HARUKAZE

To the forest! To the sea! To Legendary Island!

Join our Pokémon pals on their quest through Unova—while testing your knowledge and laughing all the way!

Ask for it at your local comic book shop or bookstore!

ISBN: 978-1-4215-8128-6

PERFECT SQUARE www.PerfectSquare.com

VIZ media www.viz.com

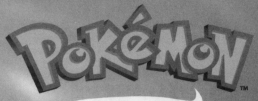

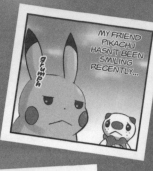

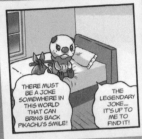

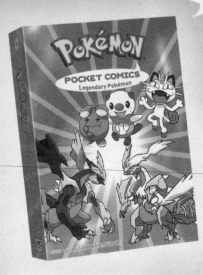

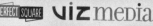

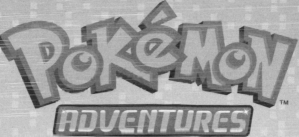
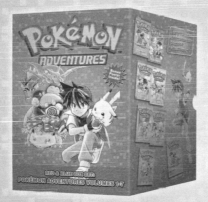
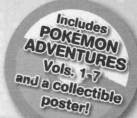

The adventure continues in the Johto region!

POKéMON™ ADVENTURES

GOLD & SILVER BOX SET

Includes POKÉMON ADVENTURES Vols. 8-14 and a collectible poster!

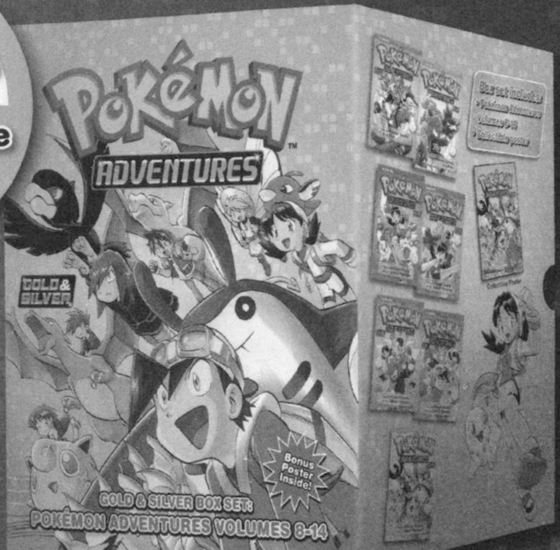
POKéMON ADVENTURES
GOLD & SILVER
Bonus Poster Inside!
GOLD & SILVER BOX SET: POKÉMON ADVENTURES VOLUMES 8-14

Story by
HIDENORI KUSAKA

Art by
MATO, SATOSHI YAMAMOTO

More exciting Pokémon adventures starring Gold and his rival Silver! First someone steals Gold's backpack full of Poké Balls (and Pokémon!). Then someone steals Prof. Elm's Totodile. Can Gold catch the thief—or thieves?!

Keep an eye on Team Rocket, Gold... Could they be behind this crime wave?

viz media www.viz.com

PERFECT SQUARE

RATED A FOR ALL AGES ratings.viz.com

FOLLOW PIPLUP AND READ THIS MANGA FROM RIGHT TO LEFT!

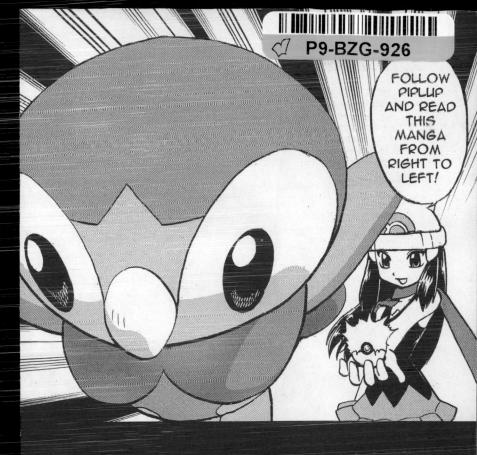

THIS IS THE END OF THIS GRAPHIC NOVEL!

To properly enjoy this VIZ Media graphic novel, please turn it around and begin reading from right to left.

This book has been printed in the original Japanese format in order to preserve the orientation of the original artwork. Have fun with it!

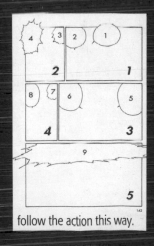

follow the action this way.